D1433957

SOAS
18 0185864 8

A
TIME
FAR
PAST

A Time Far Past

Le Luu

Translated from the Vietnamese by Ngo Vinh Hai, Nguyen Ba Chung, Kevin Bowen, and David Hunt

University of Massachusetts Press
Amherst

Originally published in
Viet Nam in 1986 under the
title *Thời Xa Vắng*.
Translated with the cooperation
and permission of the author and
the Writers Union of the Socialist
Republic of Viet Nam.

Printed in the United States
of America
LC 96-47787
ISBN 1-55849-085-X
Designed by Richard Hendel
Set in Electra type with
Spontan display by
Keystone Typesetting, Inc.
Printed and bound by
Braun-Brumfield, Inc.

This book is published with the support and cooperation of the University of Massachusetts Boston, the William Joiner Center for the Study of War and Social Consequences, and the National Endowment for the Arts, an independent federal agency.

Library of Congress Cataloging-in-Publication Data
Lê, Lựu.
[Thời xa vắng. English]
A time far past / Le Luu ; translated from the
Vietnamese by Ngo Vinh Hai . . . [et al.].
p. cm.
ISBN 1-55849-085-X (cloth : alk. paper)
I. Title.
PL4378.9.L356T4713 1997
895.9′22334—dc21 96-47787
CIP

British Library Cataloguing in Publication data are
available.

CONTENTS

INTRODUCTION

DAVID HUNT

Publication of this translation of Le Luu's *Thoi Xa Vang* is a signal event for Americans hoping to make sense of the Vietnam War. In the thousands of pages written by historians of the war, the people of North Vietnam hardly figure. In survey texts, there are only occasional vignettes, and these invariably of a military character: truck drivers navigating the Ho Chi Minh Trail, bicyclists carrying supplies, peasants digging tunnels between homes and rice fields, repair crews fixing roads and bridges, village militias preparing to resist foreign invasion. Throughout the literature, the former enemy remains a stock figure or is left out of consideration altogether.[1]

Translations of Vietnamese fiction are now beginning to address this deficit. In *A Time Far Past*, war is portrayed through its effects on parents and children, brothers and sisters, husbands and wives. Service in the army lies at the center of the text, where it functions as a pivot rather than as a primary locus within the narrative. The hero is a soldier, but the story is first of all about how he was set on a road to the battlefield and then, years later, about how he tried to make a new life after the fighting stopped. Like the best veteran writers in the United States, Le Luu eschews sentimentality, and in this instance the pain he wishes the reader to confront derives less from combat than from contradictions in Vietnamese society.

The resulting treatment tells us nothing about the DMZ or the Tet Offensive. Rather than dwelling on tactics and firepower, Le Luu's text offers descriptions of daily routines in village huts and urban apartment buildings, of marriage preparations and the politics of grieving at a funeral, of maternity wards and divorce courts. It shows people trying to get promoted, manipulations in the sexual marketplace, parents loving and hurting their children, spouses quarreling over dirty dishes. In short, this is a novel about how the Vietnamese lived and not about how they fought in the era of the American War.

Given the formative role of "Vietnam" in the lives of nearly every person in the United States, we cannot know who we are unless we know who they are. Le Luu's work is a contribution to this joint self-exploration.

CHRONOLOGY OF EVENTS

In the twentieth century, the Vietnamese people have endured a sequence of crises, first at the hands of French colonialism, then under foreign occupation during World War II, a phase that ended in 1944–45, the "Year of the Rooster," when famine claimed the lives of up to two million people. Indeed, hunger or, more broadly speaking, acute poverty and underdevelopment, register throughout Le Luu's novel, in the 1950s and even in the 1980s.

A turning point in modern Vietnamese history was marked by the "August Revolution" that brought Ho Chi Minh and the Viet Minh to power in 1945. The First Indochina War followed, from 1946 to 1954, between France and the Vietnamese resistance. In that struggle, culminating in the expulsion of France, the anti-French forces were led by the Viet Minh and the Communist Party, while on the other side were Vietnamese who sided with the foreigners.

These choices are echoed in *A Time Far Past*, as the protagonist Sai's family, and especially his uncle Ha and brother Tinh, line up with the rebels, while his father-in-law, Cu, serves as Deputy Canton Chief under the French. The novel begins in 1954, when Sai is ten, just after the French had been defeated and after his arranged marriage to the thirteen-year-old Tuyet. Vehemently resisted by Sai, the union follows from an earlier moment when Cu intervened to secure the release of Tinh from a French prison. Ignoring the political incongruity, the groom's family uses the marriage to forge an alliance with an influential neighbor, while on the other side, after the disappearance of the French, Cu rebuilds his position through a connection to the anti-French guerrillas.

Land reform (1953–56) constitutes an early and controversial chapter in the history of North Vietnam, but is not featured in the novel. The implication is that this event, intended to liberate the poor and the landless, changed little in the countryside. More significant is the cooperative movement, begun in 1958, which pooled land previously held by individual households, sponsored the formation of hamlet labor teams, and instituted an income distribution system based on work points. This innovation asked villagers to adopt a collective approach in the rice fields, while leaving individual households with control of domestic plots. The distinction comes into play in the novel when Ha and a villager debate whether a truck garden in the paddy fields is to be classified as "rice land" and therefore cooperatively worked or as a "garden" under continued household control.

Sai's teenage years unfold against the backdrop of oncoming war. After 1954, the Americans and their Vietnamese allies established a separate state in South Vietnam, and the southern revolutionary movement resumed armed struggle against that regime in 1959–60. In 1964, policymakers in both Washington and Hanoi planned escalation, the former to reinforce their allies in Saigon, the latter to assist the guerrillas. During this phase, Sai excels in his studies and gains admission to a district middle school, where he meets and falls in love with a classmate, Huong. Various obstacles keep the two apart, and in 1962 Sai enlists (chapters 3 and 4), then in 1964 volunteers to take part in the first march to the South. Still burdened by the unwanted marriage to Tuyet, he is assigned to duty on the Ho Chi Minh Trail.

Sai's experience in the ten years of war between the People's Army of Vietnam (the North Vietnamese Army) and the American and Saigon ("puppet") forces, is treated in chapter 6. After victory in 1975, Sai remains for a time in the army, secures a divorce from Tuyet, then, around 1979, settles in Hanoi, where he meets and courts Chau. These events take place in the worst phase of the country's postwar history, marked by new wars against China and Cambodia and deteriorating economic conditions. The first of these developments does not figure in the text, but the second, in the form of a subsistence crisis in the countryside, marks Sai's dealings with his home village.

With Chau's pregnancy and the birth of a son, Thuy, there is growing estrangement between Chau and Sai. A painful divorce follows and the novel ends three years later, after Sai's return to his native village. The postdate reads "19 September 1984," two years before the Sixth Party Congress of 1986, when reforms tentatively broached earlier in the decade, and mentioned in the novel, were now sponsored with more emphasis. The attendant chord of "renovation" constitutes the backdrop as Sai attempts to put his life on a new course.

PHYSICAL AND ADMINISTRATIVE SETTING

The topography of northern Vietnam embodies the collective vocation of country people. Open stretches of rice land periodically cede to domains of human habitation, with the boundaries starkly delineated, the flat, empty fields on the one side, the crowded villages, with ponds, lanes, trees, and hundreds of dwellings, on the other. Images of American rural life, with single houses widely dispersed across the terrain, do not apply here.

Villages are divided into hamlets, each including scores of households, and all together grouping as many as 10,000 inhabitants. Driving through the Red River Delta, the visitor is impressed first by the solitude of the terrain, in which not a single soul will be visible as far as the eye can see, and then by the bustling agglomerations, following one upon the other with regularity every three or four miles. In size of population, these are small towns rather than villages.

Supra-village communities, honoring the same tutelary spirit and frequenting the same market, bring together residents who will be familiar with each other's names, faces and personal lives. Before 1945, such entities were grouped administratively in cantons, a designation between the village below and the district above. To a traveler passing through the countryside, a district capital, with its village-like ambiance, is not easily distinguished from any other village. Nonetheless, a district official is no longer a local personage, dealing face-to-face with those under his jurisdiction, but presides over tens of thousands of people. Although the multidistrict middle school that Sai attends in the late 1950s is within walking distance of his home, enrollment there in the 1950s is remembered as the equivalent of studying "abroad." The province capitals of the North also retain a rural flavor, but the bureaucracies they house function at a still more remote level.

By any definition, Hanoi is a city, indeed the only city in northern Vietnam. The uniqueness of this metropolis, an agglomeration without suburbs, ringed by villages, is even more emphasized by its status as an island in a sea of peasants. For the Vietnamese, it represents the summit of the state apparatus, towering far above rural dwellers. Even more potent is its role as arbiter of civility and hothouse of the new, the fashionable, the exciting. For the Vietnamese, it is the embodiment of civilization.

Sai grows up in one of the four hamlets that form Ha Vi village.

Huong is from the adjoining Bai Ninh village, which Ha Vi residents frequent in order to shop in the Bai market and to search for work as day laborers. Sai's family is one of the most firmly established in Ha Vi. "They had never considered themselves second in prestige and dignity to any family in the village – not since the time long ago when one of their ancestors became the District Chief." Considerable status comes with the designation of "scholar," attached to Sai's father, Khang. The village scholar served as a teacher, scribe, convener on festive occasions, and moderator within the local folklore. Exemplars of learning and Confucian rectitude (for years, Khang remembers with shame the occasion when he lost his temper and shouted at his son), scholars were leaders within village culture. Indeed, as evidenced by the huge crowd at his funeral, Khang's standing surpassed that of "Canton Chief Loi" in "bygone days." The appointment of Tinh as a district official and the service of Ha as Village Party Secretary in 1954 and later as District Party Secretary further testify to the eminence of Sai's family (the title "Secretary" designates the presiding officer at many echelons).

A POLITICAL BALANCE SHEET

The Viet Minh revolution impinges on the people of Ha Vi in various, contradictory ways. It brings benefits (see the cheerful description of the village in 1964) but does not empower. The cooperative movement is presented to the population as a diktat outlawing the selling of labor power. Agricultural reform is imposed from the top down – "As the people had been told, Mr. Ha will settle everything"—and Ha's authoritarianism in politics parallels his bullying of Sai and other family members. The scene where he instructs local cadres to cover up transgressions within their ranks must have carried a particular resonance for corruption-weary Vietnamese readers of the 1980s.

Communist Party jargon ("reactionary, petit bourgeois, exploitative, feudalistic") does violence to the troubled state of mind of Sai as a military recruit, while Do Manh, the "morale officer" in his unit, offers a more empathic response. According to Le Luu's account, the Party was an ally of patriarchal values, reinforcing parental authority without heeding the wishes of the young. In the logic of the novel, the "faint-hearted" Sai is blamed for not rebelling against this alliance of

Party and elders in pursuit of his own happiness, a view that Do Manh appears to second.

The war is for Le Luu a backdrop. Sai's patriotism is both affirmed (his enlistment application is "written in blood") and deconstructed, as the narrative shows him hastening to the battlefield to escape from a personal impasse. "He left as if sneaking away, as if fleeing from yesterday, today, and tomorrow, as if he were smugly satisfied with his 'courageous' decision." Le Luu also takes his distance from journalistic accounts of Sai as a war hero, full of "hatred of the imperialists and feudalists" (Le Luu himself was a journalist during the war).

Toward the end of the novel, a less troubled note is sounded, as Sai reorders his life and, under the banner of "socialism," sets out to improve conditions in Ha Vi. But this happy ending is equivocal on both personal and political levels. Sai appears more calm, but is living alone in a shack, having lost his children and his dream of happiness. And the route forward that he engineers for his village is ambiguous (see below).

As these remarks suggest, measuring the degree of "dissidence" in *A Time Far Past* is a sterile exercise, leading away from the strengths of the novel. The author's concern is to explore the disjunctures between a public discourse and the people living within the ambit it helps to construct. The resulting treatment goes beyond any currently available historical or ethnographic treatment in its attention to social textures and the routines of everyday life in the countryside and the city. The outcome is a uniquely substantial portrait of contemporary Vietnamese society.[2]

A STUDY OF ALIENATION

Given this orientation, what larger meanings are suggested by the book? In the 1960s, some defenders of U.S. intervention celebrated the "urban revolution" that American war-making was bringing about in the South. As bombing, shelling, and troop sweeps made the countryside uninhabitable and as thousands and then millions of refugees fled toward the cities, apologists argued that the basis for a "modernization" of Vietnamese society was being established, a process that, among other benefits, was destroying the agrarian social order on which the guerrillas depended. For their part, antiwar critics decried the cynicism of this analysis without being able to call into question its accuracy as a commentary on South Vietnam's present and future.[3]

While the debate raged, there was some talk in the United States of revolutionary changes in the North derived from land reform, but overall almost no attention was paid to connections between war and society in North Vietnam. In retrospect, this neglect is striking. Here was a mass of peasants, living within a regime based on the agrarian cycle. The triumph of the Viet Minh and the coming to power of the Communist Party brought land transfers, universal education, and promotion of people from the "basic social class" into positions of authority.

At the same time, powerful lines of continuity bound the Revolution to the old order. The villages of pre-1945 Vietnam had to deal with a centralized state too, and many villagers, Sai included, retained the mentality of a "hired hand." There was more than a passing resemblance between the local notables of traditional Vietnam on the one hand and the cadres of the new regime on the other, a continuity noted by scholars and evoked by Le Luu as well.[4]

The experience of war eroded custom in a far more fundamental fashion. Millions of young people were mobilized into the armed forces, a bureaucratic structure unlike anything they had experienced in the villages. They marched to the battlefield and stayed away for years, in many cases passing their entire adult lives as soldiers and administrators. When peace came, they would not or could not go home again. The civilization of the countryside was being undermined not by firepower, but by the social consequences of war.

Le Luu's novel underscores this transformation. In the first chapter, Scholar Khang broods over the gap between his worldview and the more modern opinions of Ha and Tinh, both members of the Communist Party. Uncle Ha had refused to attend the wedding of Sai and Tuyet ("He'd said he was opposed to children getting married"), while Tinh disliked "his father's patriarchal, Confucian attitudes." But such differences prove negotiable, as Tinh and Khang arrange Sai's future in line with the traditional code, according to which women and children do what they are told (end of chapter 1).

The rapprochement is part of a larger family adaptation to new circumstances, represented by Tinh's installation as an official, a veritable "king of his district." This eminence is reaffirmed by his new house, like that of "any well-to-do, urbane family residing in a provincial town," and by material goods, obtained through office and Party membership and stored in a trunk. At least in the North, the novel suggests, where more than one village notable found a niche within the new regime, the Vietnamese Revolution was not that revolutionary.

War had a more corrosive effect, pervading the lives of the individuals who lived through it and reflected in their everyday speech, according to which people are "ambushed" by coincidences and "stand guard" on street corners, waiting for a rendezvous with friends. With an advanced education and having excelled as an engineer and combatant on the Ho Chi Minh Trail, Sai is confident he will succeed in the rarified atmosphere of the capital city. New skills come into play when he convenes an "organizing committee" and devises a quasi-military strategy enabling it to complete arrangements for his marriage to Chau.

This attempt at social mobility provides the novel with its central theme. Banking on the power of food as a social currency, Tinh takes pride in the array of spices found in his kitchen and imagines that the gulf between Sai and his second wife can be negotiated through a welcoming banquet for the bride ("Even a Hanoi feast would not have been better"). For his part, Sai at first does not miss the intrusive presence of family and neighbors in the village, where privacy is unknown. How different Hanoi seems, with its lover's lane by the West Lake (Thanh Nien Road), its bicycle riders pedaling through neighborhoods with the freedom of complete strangers, its apartment complexes at mid-day, "as deserted as graveyards," where any assignation is possible, its time-driven residents "too busy" to gossip about their neighbors.

But this anonymity comes to take on a frightening aspect. "Grandmas" in his apartment building lend a hand when Sai's son is sick, but for the most part, as disasters multiply, no one is there to help. The close-packed world of the villagers, "willing to act like members of his own family" even when Sai cannot remember their names, is held together by a mutuality dense enough to function independent of personal preferences and political loyalties, as when Cu got Tinh out of jail and when Cu and Khang arranged the marriage of their children. Once outside that milieu, Sai can no longer count on its sustenance, and the less articulated system of reciprocity in the city, where favors are carefully counted, is soon overtaxed by his demands. Too frequently drawing on urban friends, he runs out his account and finds himself stranded.

A Time Far Past provides a vivid description of household labor, conveying what it is like to shop and cook and change diapers in the Hanoi of the 1980s. But in the world of the novel, nondomestic work is inconsequential. As Sai explains to his son, "Work is . . . is so people can get paid." Le Luu's indifference to the jobs held by his characters is striking, and even in Sai's case no sense emerges of what he does "at the office." Once or twice, readers finding him straining to meet a deadline, but for the most part he and others come and go during the workday with a freedom that suggests the irrelevance of labor to their lives and to the society at large.

Still more telling is the estrangement between men and women. With its arranged marriages and rigid conventions, feudalism is denounced by Le Luu as an enemy of happiness. He shows no nostalgia for an era when wives functioned as domestic servants and takes his distance from Sai's fantasies about the wife of a neighbor, dutifully waiting on her husband and his guests, who eat and drink until 2:00 in the morning. ("Some even threw up on the floor, but she didn't complain.") The men at the beginning of the novel imagine themselves in control. "Perhaps there was something to the old saying that women were like children," one of them reflects, "never wanting to concede while a discussion was on, but all too ready to accept severe and even cruel decisions." A primary objective of the novel is to demonstrate the vanity of this smugness.

On the other hand, Hanoi cannot provide an alternative to the traditional vision of domesticity. The novel's portrait of Sai's wife Chau, a woman straight from hell, is so venomous that when efforts were made to organize a movie version of the book, no Vietnamese actress could be induced to accept the role. Le Luu lashes out at patriarchal values, but he fails to depict this form of oppression through the eyes of Vietnamese women.

In this respect, the novel strikes a chord of wider resonance, at a moment when visitors to Vietnam often hear observers declare that women gained too much power during the war while men were away on the battlefield and that wives exercise a dictatorship within the household. The country's most acclaimed postwar short story features a woman who works in an abortion clinic and who salvages fetuses so that they can be used as dog food. In a recent prize-winning novel, the mother of the protagonist tells her son, before abandoning him: "I'm a New Intellectual dear. I'm a Party member. I'm not an idiot, nor am I dull. You must remember that, please." Whatever its accomplishments on other fronts, the Hanoi Renaissance of the last few years has not achieved much balance in depicting the gender wars. Its most prominent authors come close to blaming the emancipated women of the capital city – who seem more powerful sexually, intellectually, and socially than the men around them – for what is wrong in the new Vietnam.[5]

Cut off from others, from work, from love, Sai is estranged from himself as well. Humble rural origins (even the inhabitants of neighboring Bai Ninh look down on Ha Vi as a "swamp village") cannot be overcome by the status of his family, by success in school, or by battlefield heroics. Sai's disdain for Tuyet is heightened when new friends in the army make fun of her rustic manners, but this class-based scorn falls on Sai himself when Chau, the second wife, ridicules his peasant ways. In Hanoi, he no longer knows how to greet old friends or offer cigarettes to a guest or sit in a chair. Trying to master an unaccustomed comportment, "he seemed to be living someone else's life."

In all these respects, alienation is a fundamental theme of the novel. As revolution and war destabilize the old society, fraternity, industry and love are drained of substance, and people lose a sense of who they are. A revolutionary process puts individual fulfillment on the agenda, but in circumstances where this aspiration cannot be realized. Taught to expect, to demand happiness, Le Luu's characters end in a spiritual impasse.

VIETNAM IN TRANSITION

This Vietnam bears a certain resemblance to France in the era of Balzac and Flaubert, a time of postrevolutionary disappointment as the nation moved from the countryside toward the city, from orally transmitted custom toward written law, from face-to-face reciprocities toward bureaucratic anonymity, from feudal rent toward wage labor and the free market. In France, it was left to the novelists to explore the attendant costs.

Le Luu addresses a similar problematic. Sai longs for "change, for some sort of transformation," for a modernity that will satisfy both individual and social needs. In the end, having returned to Ha Vi, he appears to find an answer, at least in the public domain. "Why don't we specialize in the growing of some particular crop," he asks, "one that goes well with our soil and has a high market value?"

At this moment, Le Luu's sense of irony fails him. "For sure! For sure!" exclaims Sai's companion, the Province Vice Director of the Bureau of Agriculture. The experiment yields a bounty for Ha Vi, where, at the end of the novel, "the sound of earth being scooped into barrels and of wood being hammered" is heard around the clock. "All twenty-three kilns were glowing – red hot from top to bottom – and at the edge of the village the lights of the tofu-making teams were still on." These enterprises are portrayed as emblems of hope rather than as "satanic mills," and when Sai stops to "exchange pleasantries" with the night shift, readers do not see the workers he employs.

The Vietnam wars of 1945–75 set the world economic system, with its requirement that poor societies occupy the periphery, against the desire of the Vietnamese people for a better life, based on full control over their own labor and resources. The seemingly successful campaign on behalf of such objectives was carried forward by a peasantry of uncommon discipline. At the same time, victory required that the agrarian system framing the lives of these country people had to be enlarged, perhaps beyond recognition. By the time the fighting came to an end, Vietnam's rural civilization had been weakened. Its capacity to resist remains in question as the country embarks on a peacetime project more mysterious and potentially destructive than the war. Government officials continue to speak of "renovation," but as the pace of change accelerates, unleashing forces that no one can anticipate or control, official slogans seem increasingly forlorn and irrelevant.

Consideration of this issue can be focused at the top, with praise or blame for Vietnamese leaders who have abandoned revolutionary dreams since 1975.[6] As a novelist, Le Luu looks more deeply, at social transformations beyond the imaginations of the participants to predict and beyond their powers to master. *A Time Far Past* can be seen as a war novel, a veteran's novel, but it is less about war sorrows than about postwar dilemmas. The future remains uncertain, but perhaps it helps us anticipate a time when historians will look back on the "American War" as Vietnam's peculiar route from feudalism to capitalism.

NOTES

1. For more on the Vietnamese in survey texts, see David Hunt, "Images of the Viet Cong," in Robert Slabey, ed., *The United States and Viet Nam:*

From War to Peace (New York: McFarland, 1996, pp. 51–63); and "'North' and 'South' in Surveys of the Vietnam War" (unpublished).

2. Recent work suggests a similar shift of focus away from the war among scholars. See especially the work of Hy Van Luong, including *Revolution in the Village: Tradition and Transformation in North Vietnam, 1925–1988* (Honolulu: University of Hawaii Press, 1992).

3. The "forced-draft urbanization and modernization" of South Vietnam is celebrated in Samuel Huntington, "The Bases of Accommodation," *Foreign Affairs* 46 (1968): 652.

4. Hy Van Luong, *Revolution in the Village*, offers a sensitive analysis of these disjunctures and continuities.

5. Bao Ninh, *The Sorrow of War: A Novel of North Vietnam*, trans. Phan Thanh Hao (New York: Pantheon, 1993; original Vietnamese edition, 1991), p. 123; Nguyen Huy Thieu, "The General Retires," in *The General Retires and Other Stories*, trans. Greg Lockhart (New York: Oxford University Press, 1993; original Vietnamese publication, 1987), pp. 114–36. A different perspective on what is happening to Vietnamese women is presented in Ngo Vinh Long, "Prostitution in Vietnam," in Nanette Davis, *Prostitution: An International Handbook on Trends, Problems, and Politics* (Westport, Conn: Greenwood Press, 1993), pp. 327–50.

6. See the stinging criticism of the Socialist Republic of Vietnam government in the "Postscript" of Gabriel Kolko, *Anatomy of a War: Vietnam, the United States, and the Modern Historical Experience* (New York: Pantheon, 1995; first edition 1985).

NOTES ON THE AUTHOR AND THE TRANSLATION

KEVIN BOWEN

THE AUTHOR

Le Luu was born in 1942 in the village of Phu Khoai in Hai Hung Province on the floodplains of Red River Delta in the north of Viet Nam, an area long known throughout Viet Nam for its poverty. One of eight children, five of whom died in the famine of 1945, Le Luu's early life was marked by extreme hardship. Like Ha Vi village in the novel *A Time Far Past,* Phu Khoai sat under the shadow of the great Red River dikes, subject to heavy flooding each year. To survive, villagers, like the villagers in the novel, sold their labor, working in the fields of more fortunate neighboring villages. Like Sai, *A Time Far Past*'s protagonist, however, Le Luu was born into a scholarly family, his father a fifth-generation Confucian scholar, and so Le Luu was sent to study at the district school at Khoai Chau. He was married at the age of ten. From first to seventh grades, he rose at three each morning to cook rice soup before leaving to walk the ten miles to the district school where he passed the day without lunch, returning the same route at dusk each evening to a dinner of corn soup and a night of study.

In 1959, Le Luu left the village of Phu Khoai to join the army. In the army he was able to continue his studies and complete a high school degree. It was in the army that he first began writing. His first published work, a short story, "The Tet Holiday of Mo Village," was written in 1963, when he was twenty-one, and published in *Van Nghe Quan Doi* (The Army Journal of Arts and Literature) in 1964. Like Ha Vi village in *A Time Far Past,* Mo village was a thinly disguised version of Phu Khoai. "The Tet Holiday of Mo Village" was selected as the best short story of 1964. With this success, in 1965 and 1966 Le Luu was able to attend the Vietnamese Writers Association's School for Writers. But with the war with the United States escalating in 1965 and 1966, Le Luu started out on the first of numerous trips down the

Ho Chi Minh Trail. During the course of the war, Le Luu would complete two collections of short stories and one novel while traveling the battlefields of Quang Binh, Quang Tri, Tay Ninh, and elsewhere. He spent the entire two years of fierce fighting in 1972 and 1973 in the forest, whereas in other years he returned home at least once.

During the war, Le Luu's work enjoyed immense popularity. *Opening the Forest*, his first novel, written in 1973 was read over the radio to troops on the Ho Chi Minh Trail. Like most of the author's work, the subject of the novel is the fate of village life and the concerns of soldiers fighting through the Troung Son Range for families still living in the bombed villages back at home. This theme continued as a preoccupation throughout Le Luu's postwar writing. While other authors continued to write about the fighting, Le Luu focused on the effects of the war at home. *A Time Far Past* would be the culmination of this theme.

As life slowly began to stabilize after 1980, like many writers in Viet Nam, Le Luu began to look back over the past with a fresh eye. Under the enormous pressure of the war, with everyone thinking of going to war, writers had written in the past "of everyone as having the same characteristics." Le Luu wished now to write of the war from the perspective of the individual, from the point of view of people who had their own private thoughts, hopes, and aspirations. He wished as well to write of the lingering effects of the old feudal society and of the war with the French, an event that had never been fully integrated or absorbed. In 1984, he began the plan of the novel that was to become *A Time Far Past*. Le Luu's habit of writing, like many other writers of the war, had been to write intensely and quickly. During the war he had found other soldiers only too ready to take up his work details, to cook for him, leave meals beside him so he could concentrate on the business of writing. For three months in 1984, living alone at the small house on the beach at Do Don near Hai Phong, which the Writers Association provided him, he wrote day and night.

Le Luu delivered the manuscript to the Writers Association Publishing House in 1985. *A Time Far Past* was then published to great popular acclaim in 1986, the novel passing through four editions and eighty thousand copies in the first few months. Le Luu, however, faced official questioning in 1986, forced to answer publicly the questions of critics who accused him of harboring a "dark aim" within this novel, which was the first to question official policy during the war. Le Luu faced hostility and criticism from his colleagues and some of his veteran and writer peers. But he was fortunate on two accounts. The timing of the novel's publication coincided exactly with the Sixth Party Congress and the announcement of the new policy of *Doi Moi,* or Renovation; and, perhaps just as important, readers in the North openly embraced both the book and its author. The village, the characters, the history were familiar ground; as were the sentiments and travails of the characters. Wherever Le Luu went, he was greeted with questions about the characters, about his village, and about himself: Was he Sai?

A Time Far Past occupies an important place in contemporary Vietnamese literature. The story it tells is the story of one village, one family, and one man, giving an insight into village life and life in postwar Ha Noi never before provided. That alone should assure its place in history. In addition it broke with the heroic tradition of Vietnamese literature about the war and courageously opened new ground for other writers to follow. The form of the novel itself reflects Le Luu's own literary experiments. For the first time, a Vietnamese novel attempted to bridge the various strata of life in Viet Nam, to tell a story with so many, and so many varying and shifting, points of view. With Le Luu, the point is in the telling and in "telling all things from the heart."

Le Luu remains an editor at *Van Nghe Quan Doi.* He has visited the United States twice, publishing two books about his visits: *Once There Was a Mistake,* and *Going Back Again.* His novels continue to draw fire and popularity. His most recent works are *The Colonel without a Sense of Humor* and *The Tale of Cuoi Village.* A new novel, *Waves from the Bottom of the River,* awaits publication. Remarried in 1976 after the war, he lives in Ha Noi with his wife and two children.

THE TRANSLATION

Even for many native Vietnamese speakers, the text of *A Time Far Past,* when first encountered, is daunting. With a language, idiom, and vocabulary firmly embedded in the peasant life of the northern countryside, the novel presents the translator with a complex set of difficulties. These are compounded by the narrative style of the novel, a style wherein, much like the case with the European novel of the eighteenth and nineteenth centuries, the narrator may intrude with his or her own comments and fancies at any given time. In *A Time Far Past,* these narrative digressions – often long and labyrinthine – along with the descriptive framework of the novel, are often presented in a language full of allusions, puns, and double entendres impossible to carry over into English. The translators have done their best with these sections. Where possible we have tried to keep the tone of the original narrative; but where that has been impossible and a literal rendering would make little sense in the overall development of the novel, we have sometimes chosen to cut. We believe that the great power of the novel does not suffer overall for this loss.

Our method of proceeding was to divide the novel in half, with a native Vietnamese speaker working in team with one of the U.S. translator/editors on each half. Initial drafts were then exchanged, differences in translation compared and discussed, and a revised draft written by all four working together. This version was then passed on to Debra Spark, a novelist and editor with no background in the text or history, for more general editing and comment. From her annotated draft a final version of the manuscript was prepared. We realize that this method is fraught with hazards, but given the lack of truly experienced literary translators in either Viet Nam or this country – one often unnoted consequence of the postwar embargo – this seemed the best way to proceed if the novel was to see the light of day.

With these shortcomings fully acknowledged, we hope the author will forgive us the slights we have done his text, and the English-speaking reader will understand the limits of a translation which we hope does some justice to the novel, but can never convey its full complexity or richness. Still, we trust the great power of Le Luu's story shines through.

A
TIME
FAR
PAST

CHAPTER 1

The village seemed to float in the frigid night. Betel palms stretched their feathered tips skyward as if ready to take off for the cold and silent heaven. For the last five nights, frost had darkened the leaves of the sweet potato patches and cracked open the bamboo poles set out to age on the frozen ponds. But it was only tonight that the cold had penetrated deeply into the joints of Khang, the village Confucian scholar. Since noon of the previous day, he had eaten nothing, instead he tightened the hemp rope around his narrow waist till it looked as if his stomach were glued to his spine. Now that he had poured his anger on the head of his youngest son, Sai, he felt a chilling emptiness in his stomach. He trembled as he stood up and groped his way down the alley to the village entrance.

A whiff of self-pity shook his thin frame and forced him to reach out a bony hand to hold on to the guava tree by the gate. Convention and honor clung to him as tightly as the hemp rope around his waist. Soon he turned to walk back and sit in the same place he had been sitting all day. The divan was as cold as if someone had poured freezing water on it. Only an hour ago, the old scholar had grumbled, "Where the hell can he be in this cold weather!" Now he thought, "Let him die, the rotten fish! O my God, how can I face people now?"

Sai had done the unspeakable; he had driven out his wife. And now, the old man thought, Sai must understand his actions were not simply his own affair. But who knew if Sai was capable of understanding such a thing? For a long time now, Sai had been only interested in two things: his games of make-believe battles and studies. He could not absorb the fact of his own marriage. He still blushed when someone asked where his wife was, even though the young girl had come to the house over a year ago. Since then, the only thing that had pleased Sai was how the yard and long alleyway were neatly swept every afternoon when he sat down to do his homework. But he was still angry about the young girl: about her arrival and about the way she followed him everywhere and informed on him, telling his parents that he put pitch on his face and pretended he was an African soldier; that he waded and dived into Uncle Ha's muddy pond; that he didn't want to take off his clothes so she could do the washing. She'd even told them that he said her father looked like an undertaker. Sai's resentment had reached its peak that afternoon. Sai, the youngest of the family, was nearly ten. Though his sisters-in-law had once taken care of all the household chores, now that he was married many of these tasks fell to his wife, Tuyet. She was only three years older than Sai, but already Tuyet was capable of doing the heavier work of adults. Sai, when crushing corn, was barely able to lift the large wooden pestle above the brim of the mortar. "That little girl," his wife, however, was able to raise the pestle, high and quickly. She could pound the middle of the mortar with such force that she could create a vortex sucking all the kernels to the center, preventing them from spilling out. What's more, "the little girl" could do all this with the same easy rhythm as an adult.

Every day, when the shadow of the house reached the row of bricks on the threshold, Sai, whether he was studying or playing, ran in to dry the corn that had been soaking in hot water all night. Then he waited until his wife asked him to scrape the corn fragments on the mortar brim while she pounded. If he had a book with him, Sai stuck it in the waistband of his pants, and then sat down on the pile of hay in front of the mortar and gazed at the brim. He did not have to look into the mortar, since he knew by the sound when the kernels had been split once, twice, and three times. He knew the certain "thud" that meant it was time for him to trace his hands around the brim to scrape the corn bits back into the mortar. He helped until the corn was finely ground. Then, "that girl" put down the pestle and sifted the corn flour while Sai walked to the threshold to read his book. When he heard a knock-knock on the mortar – a sound like the one blacksmiths make when testing their hammers on anvils – he knew he had to come back for the second and then the third round until only a few specks of corn were left in the mortar. Then, he would stand up and walk to the door. Once through it, he would dash off like a chicken freed from its coop.

≣ On the afternoon of Scholar Khang's great disgrace, the little girl had accidentally hit one of Sai's hands with the pestle. Sai had yelled as he pulled the hurt hand to his belly and then, with all the energy of his pent-up anger, let his other hand form a fist which flew into his wife's face. The girl stood still, neither stepping back from the blow nor blocking it with her hands. She simply stood there and stoically absorbed the punishment and scolding Sai meted out.

At once, Sai felt exhausted by his own fury. Well aware of the dangers of pressing his attack further, he withdrew with a few tough words to hide his embarrassment. "I don't give a damn about what I've done. Even if your father were here, I wouldn't care. If he came around, I'd send the dogs after him. Let them gouge his eyes out."

Little did Sai know how this kind of talk angered and hurt the old scholar, his father. In the late afternoon, after selling all his bamboos, Scholar Khang came home from the Tao marketplace. Most days, upon returning, he'd watch his daughter-in-law Tuyet strain lime juice into a boiling pot of cornmeal and stir it into a thick yellow consistency. He'd watch as she put out the fire, scraped the cornmeal off the brim of the pot, covered the food and laid out chopsticks, bowls and serving tray. But today when Scholar Khang returned home, there was only complete silence. The old man lit his tobacco water pipe and, after a draw, decided to ask Sai to remind his daughter-in-law to serve the meal since he was about starved. The New Year was fast approaching, and it had been extremely difficult to subsist, as he had been, on only one meal of cornmeal pudding a day like this. What's more, yesterday he had to give his one meal to a visitor. And today he had needed to do extra work, to take his wife's place and carry the bamboo poles to market. On the walk home, his legs had almost buckled under him. Now, as he exhaled tobacco smoke, he looked up through the doorway. He saw his daughter-in-law in tears, carrying a bundle of clothes.

"I'm sorry, Father," sniffed the little girl. "I'm going home to my own family." She then told him the details of what had happened.

"Please don't leave," said the old man, his face darkening.

But the little girl walked out in spite of the old man's half-beseeching, half-threatening words.

Someone told Sai that his father was looking for him and that the old man had summoned all his sons and daughters-in-law to help with the search. Even Tinh, a cadre in the District Agricultural Taxation Office, who had been attending a three-month course at the district capital had been summoned.

"Search him out!" ordered the old man. "I don't need a son like him. If this fellow lives, he'll get us all into trouble."

Somehow Sai heard of those words and he took them to be even more severe than his father's anger, so, under the cover of night, he snuck out into the paddy fields. Through the thick fog nothing could be seen from about fifty yards beyond the bamboo hedge, but the censure of imagined voices pursued him. He ran over the newly plowed field and over the broken clay, hard and glistening. Now and again, he tripped and fell, his face hitting the hard edges of clay that seemed as solid as stones. Once, his fall hurt so much that he swore he would not get up again. He let his tears pour out on a lump of sod, melting it and gluing it to his face. But he clambered up and ran again, clenching his teeth against further falls. When he couldn't run anymore and thought he was quite a distance from home, he lay down in a pile of hay left over from a recently extinguished fire. He spread the ashes out, still warm, and made a bed for himself. He imagined he must be some distance from home, but still he didn't forget to put some hay over himself for camouflage. But even before he could lie down long enough to warm his bed, he heard his brother Tinh and Uncle Ha calling for him. So he was still close to home! But he was too exhausted to get up. A sense of relief mixed with the self-pity had produced enough tears and sweat to drench his short-sleeved cotton shirt. Then a chill came over him and shook his entire body. He quickly raked more hay, ash and earth over his body. Then, curled up like a worm and overcome with fear, exhaustion and hunger, he tried to sleep.

If Uncle Ha was part of the search party, Sai knew he might be forgiven for his crimes. Last year, Uncle Ha had been the only one who had not attended Sai's wedding. He'd said he was opposed to children getting married. Now Sai hoped that Uncle Ha's voice in the night meant that he would be protected. Surely, when they saw that Uncle Ha was displeased, the entire family and even the entire neighborhood would scatter about the fields searching for him. And, when they located him, people would not yell. Instead, they would cry out in joy. They would carry him home with great love and care, would urge each other to wash him up and tenderly change his clothes. Then, Sai imagined, he would keep his eyes lightly closed and his mouth partially open – even after he was fully recovered. He'd let his limbs lie limp as people massaged them. He would groan in answer to all questions about whether he was feeling better or not.

Sai's own thoughts moved him to tears. Just as his eyes were brimming over, he heard Ha's voice ring out in the cold night.

"That you, Tinh?"

"What? Who's asking for me?"

"It's me."

"Oh, you, Uncle. I thought it was someone else. I just got home."

"Idiot!" Ha muttered in anger as Tinh drew near him and stood as still as a bamboo pole stuck in the ground.

"Whatever you say . . . "

"Sai drove his wife out. That's a child's behavior. Your father scolded him and spanked him. That's the behavior of an outdated and feudalistic old man. But you're a cadre and yours is a family with a revolutionary background. What will it be like tomorrow when the entire village – or maybe the entire canton – is talking about how the family of Mr. Tinh, a district cadre who is the nephew of Mr. Ha, the Village Party Secretary, yelled at each other all night. We'll all lose face. I sent you up to the district so that you would have opportunities for education and rectification, so that you'd be enlightened. But you're still . . . "

"I only found out about the matter when I got home."

"Whatever. You must teach your little brother a lesson. He's still too young to lose solidarity with his wife. He's still a child and yet he dares to play husband by roughing her up. If the girl's family sues, we lose everything. You and I will have to cover our faces with areca sheaths in shame. Faced with this situation, what do you, a revolutionary cadre, propose to do? You must clearly explain the Party position and the government policies to your parents. And Sai, you must box Sai's ears."

"Right."

"But if you beat him up you should do it quietly so that people can't accuse you of not behaving like an exemplary cadre."

"Right."

"Actually," said Ha, whose anger was fading as he spoke, "you should only threaten him and then tell his teacher and his adviser to make him perform self-criticism in his classroom or in his Young Pioneer Team."

Due to his feelings for his younger brother and his dislike of his father's old-fashioned, Confucian attitudes, Tinh had panicked earlier when he'd heard about his father's reaction to Sai's behavior. Right away, Tinh had rushed out to search for Sai. Seeing Tinh in a panic, his wife had also become hysterical. His usually phlegmatic aunts had also urged their children to go out searching for Sai. An entire corner of the village had been upset, because Tinh had acted hastily. This little incident had disclosed Tinh's inexperience and allowed Uncle Ha to chastise him. After Ha's reprimand, Tinh trudged home. Once there, he quietly slipped inside and sat down on the divan. After a long while, he looked up.

"Where is everybody?" he yelled in the direction of the kitchen. "I just can't believe it. I just can't believe that you'd let the house look like this – as cold and as dark as a graveyard!" He yelled to his wife, but when he finished speaking, a spark of light flared up on the other side of the divan. His father had been sitting there all along. Khang's hand quavered as he lifted the oil lamp's glass bulb, scraped the creosote off the tip of the wick, readjusted it, applied the fire at the end of a bamboo splinter to the wick, put the bulb back and then rubbed out the fire at the end of the bamboo stick. He did all this in a deft but deliberate manner, as a substitute for thinking of something to say to his son.

The scholar and his wife had given birth to eight children, but only three were left now. Three sons. The oldest was not around much anymore. The youngest was Sai, and in between was Tinh – or Brother Tinh as the old man called him in a respectful but cold manner. Tinh still lived in the same house with Scholar Khang, but he and his wife prepared their meals separately.

Tinh and Scholar Khang had never had an easy time talking; each treated the other as if he were a house guest. Still, they were proud of one another and comfortable with their respective positions as father and son. In certain ways, Scholar Khang and Tinh complemented each other; this proved to be a virtue whenever there was a crisis of some kind. It had certainly proved invaluable when Tinh had been arrested for contacting Ha about underground revolutionary activities. Then, it was the community's respect for Scholar Khang as the area's most – or second most – famous Confucian scholar that made them intervene to help save Tinh. Since that incident, the person Tinh owed the most to was Cu, the Deputy Canton Chief . . . and now Sai's father-in-law. It had been half a year now since peace had been restored. No matter what people might say about despising the old feudal anachronisms, they still respected the old scholar. He and his son had their difficult periods, but at other times each was secretly proud to have a son or father who was attuned to the times.

Through a long and careful process of thought the old scholar had concluded that his son was like countless others who felt very much at ease when they enjoyed the benefits of the work of others, but when it came to sharing difficulties, even with their own flesh and blood, felt apprehensive and anxious, even feeling they had a right to mistreat the unfortunate. Since his son believed this was the way things were, he believed he could drill his father in the style of what he called criticism. But the old man had his own logic, his own tradition, his own habits, the hereditary customs passed down for generations to call upon, and they told him that children could do nothing without the consent of their parents. As he thought more and more of this, he became more and more sure he was right. Feeling himself more in the right, he became more self-assured and more irritated because his son's silence was becoming more oppressive and was now descending heavily on the three rooms of the house.

Finally, Tinh spoke up. "Father, I feel that you've been too lenient with Sai. That's why we're in this mess."

What kind of talk was this? the scholar thought. *Never mind. No matter. In any case, it was an opening to start a conversation.*

"Are you saying that I have been happy with everything he's done?"

"If you'd been stricter with him this would not have happened." Tinh said this, but he didn't believe his own words. In truth, he felt a kind of pity for his studious younger brother, who often tearfully complained about having to share everything with his "wife." What's more, Tinh still bore a grudge toward Cu, for although Cu had managed to get Tinh released from the French fort where he had been imprisoned, he had still continued to collaborate with the French. Tinh knew that what he had said to his father was not true to his heart. Still, he had spoken the words, surprising and relieving the old scholar, who hadn't expected his middle son to agree with him in this matter.

≣ Later that night, Scholar Khang's wife's shrieking stirred the neighborhood once again. She had come home earlier in the day from a trip to Da Hoa village, where she'd gone to pawn a pair of antique vases for a basket of rice to keep the family from going hungry. Exhausted, she'd fallen asleep. The old scholar ordered his daughter-in-law to cook a pot of gruel large enough for everyone to eat. When the gruel was cooked, they woke the old woman up. The scholar's wife had almost finished emptying her bowl before she realized that Sai and his wife were not there. When she found out why, she dashed out into the yard and lit a torch of dried hemp stalks, then rushed through the village, calling out for her son and invoking the names of the gods. She paid no attention to what this behavior meant for the family order her husband prized or for the reputation her cadre son had to maintain. After she ran out, Tinh's wife ran out after her. Nephews, nieces and neighbors followed suit, ignoring their hunger and the cold to follow the old woman and noisy children out to the spot where Sai lay hiding.

≣ Gone is that night when the entire neighborhood huddled together in Khang's front yard and the three rooms of his house to watch the ancient rite of Recalling the Departing Souls.

"Come back you three souls and seven spirits of Sai. Come back from wherever you are."

"Sai's seven spirits and three souls," yelled Madame Khang, "Come back to Father and Mother."

As they called out in fear, they massaged Sai's temples frantically. They passed bowls of chicken feathers and burning soapberries under his nose. Flames from a dish of burning alcohol singed Sai's rumpled hair. A bag of finely minced ginger was used to rub his back, his face, his chest and his hands. Finally someone pried apart his teeth with a set of kitchen chopsticks and poured gruel into his mouth.

Gone are the days when Sai was treated with such pity and indulgence, when he was discovered hidden in his bed of ash and hay, and was allowed to rush out into the yard only seven or eight days later. To be precise, on the afternoon of the seventh day.

It was at this moment that Scholar Khang's wife lost some of her power over "weighty matters" in the family. That night, under the advice of Tinh, a family conference convened which included the scholar and his wife, the oldest son and his wife, Tinh and his wife, and Sai. Of the seven "conferees" only four actively participated. The oldest son deferred everything to his father. His wife deferred everything to him. And Tinh's wife deferred to everyone. As at every family gathering, she was busy serving tea, lighting pipes, only listening to the deliberations from the dark corners of the house. Sai had been the butt of laughter and insults for a week now. Although the whole family looked at him tenderly and talked about things unconnected with him, it was obvious that this meeting was to be about him, so when Madame Tinh fetched Sai from the kitchen, he burst into a wail, plunged into his mother's lap, and started trembling uncontrollably.

"Get it over with!" demanded the scholar's wife sternly as she hugged her son and wiped his tears with tip of her shirt tail. "Can't you see how this child is suffering?"

"Come, come," said the scholar tenderly. "Nobody is touching him."

"There is nothing to be afraid of, Sai darling," the oldest daughter-in-law offered sympathetically. "We are only talking things out. We're not yelling at you or mistreating you or anything like that."

"You shut up, Sai!" said Tinh sternly. "Come, Father, say what is on your mind so that each of us can share the burden. There is always some problem whenever I come home, and I'm tired of everybody thinking their own thing, acting their own way, taking care of their own business, and as for the rest, living or dead, I don't care."

By his manner and his language, Tinh was saying that he was in charge here. Not that he truly wanted to be. But the fact was that anything bad that happened in the family would reflect on him. How many people in this village or district knew of his older brother? How many people outside of the village knew of his father's reputation? But everyone knew him – Comrade Tinh, the district cadre – and if anything happened he was the person who would shoulder the blame. Who knew what this current episode might bring to pass?

For his part, Scholar Khang thought that his middle son could not genuinely understand how he suffered for having lost family honor. As a Confucian scholar, he had tried to maintain the family's dignity through the years. And he had been successful. None of the children had ever been disobedient. No one could look at his family and laugh. They were not a family of shrimp. He himself had never done anything or said anything improper. But now that his son had driven the little girl out, who would understand that this was just something between children? Tinh didn't know Scholar Khang was feeling all this. Tinh couldn't see that his father didn't truly mind Sai's undisciplined behavior or that what most concerned him was his middle son. Still, Khang could not shout at or threaten Tinh. Instead, he had to anticipate his likely feelings and responses. It was for this reason that Scholar Khang was now hesitant as he spoke.

"Nobody wanted this to happen. But it has. Now you all must see how we can apologize and bring Tuyet back. As the saying goes, "Parents must bear the burdens of their children's ignorance."

"No apology to nobody!" yelled Scholar Khang's wife. "My son was close to the grave, but they didn't come around to see how he was. Let me ask you, why is a wife not around to take care of her sick husband?"

"But it was our son who drove her out."

"But he's only a child and on top of that he has no authority to do this. She can only leave this house if you and I send her home. I know this other family. They're used to treating people roughly and oppressing them. They've been this way ever since the old days. A stuck-up bunch."

"Hush! The neighbors can hear you."

Madame Khang said she saw no reason why she had to hush up. She had nothing to hide. She went through terrible labor pains to give birth to a son like Sai, and yet when he was almost dead, the girl's family did not come to offer a single word of consolation. She felt put down and shamed. It was not that she was opposed to making up. It was just that the girl's family had to come to her first. Otherwise what did it matter what happened. A coconut shell in one piece? Use it as a dipper. Broken? Use it for spoons. The more she spoke, the more she was convinced she was in the right. Her daughters-in-law chimed in with their agreement, quietly muttering that the other family *was* ill-behaved.

Through all this, Sai clung to his mother's waist, occasionally hiccuping as if he were about to burst into tears once more. He asked his parents not to force him to go to the girl's house. Meanwhile, Tinh was staring at the ceiling. His eyebrows were knitted, his lips tight. Scholar Khang seemed to be concentrating his eyes and even his ears on the tasks of preparing his water pipe and rinsing out his teacup. But, in truth, he was considering what everyone was thinking. He knew what everybody was thinking except for Tinh. Since Tinh had become a cadre, what bothered the old scholar the most was that he couldn't guess what his son was thinking. And he needed to know, for the old man had to concede to Tinh's logic and rationale, even when it made him uneasy. Certainly everybody in the family seemed to listen to Tinh more than to him. But this was only right. A person with official responsibility always seemed to say the right things.

And Tinh was now going to say something. What the old scholar feared most might be coming, for Tinh had only to express his views and the matter would be resolved. The old man leaned toward the room's area of dim light and played with a pinch of tobacco between his fingers. If this thing were not resolved satisfactorily, life would lose all meaning for him. He would still walk around, but he would be a corpse. Tinh was even more worried than his father. He understood how this kind of family squabble, if not neatly taken care of, could ruin his career. So he spoke in a deliberate manner as if to emphasize how carefully his words were chosen, how unalterable they were.

"There is no reason to make such a fuss about Sai driving his wife out. You've not acted properly in this case, Father."

How the hell could I control myself in that situation? the scholar pondered as Tinh spoke.

"Mr. Cu and his family were also wrong to remain silent during those days when Sai was ill. Their behavior is despicable. Mother has rightly expressed the anger of our family. This is the proper way to show it to them," Tinh continued.

So he's taking his mother's side, the old scholar thought. *It was we who caused the problem and now we're blaming it on others. No matter what you say, no matter what you and your mother plan to do, as far as I'm concerned it is improper for Sai to chase his wife out like that.*

"But that is another matter. Sooner or latter I'll deal with them. But as far as the matter before us is concerned, we must not be petty. We should not fight over the question of who's right and who's wrong, and we should not wait for them to come to us first."

Scholar Khang smiled, so the fellow has really learned something along the way.

"You're saying that we must go to them first?"

"No matter what, Sai cannot divorce Tuyet. Let me take care of this matter. We must talk with them first to show that we're grown-ups who can't be bothered by children's problems. Tomorrow I'll send my wife over there with Sai. All Sai has to say is 'I'm sorry that I've driven my wife out. Please allow her to come with me now.' This is all he will have to say. After I see how they react, I'll act."

He stopped and drank some tea as if to reward himself for the brilliant decision. He looked up to see his mother and Sai's reactions. Scholar Khang did not look at Tinh, but he was proud that his son was such an educated man. He had thought that his son could not get along with him, but now he saw how much alike they were, his son was only using a more modern language so he could be even more persuasive than the father.

"But what if . . . " Madame Khang hesitated.

"Mother, there are no *buts*, no *ifs*. Do what I say tomorrow. That's all the discussion for the night. It's late. Let's go to bed."

With these stern words, he stood up abruptly and walked to the adjoining room where he and his wife lived. Everybody else sat awhile longer, but nobody said another word. Madame Khang did not protest. Even Sai did not throw a temper tantrum about having to do something he feared. Tinh shook his head as he later prepared to retire: perhaps there was something to the old saying that women were like children – never wanting to concede while a discussion was on, but, in the end, they were ready to accept severe and even cruel decisions.

CHAPTER 2

The problems between Sai and his wife were insignificant compared to the hunger threatening the commune. In the end, those outside the families didn't feel disposed to comment on their story; it was an insignificant matter. Soon enough, the children themselves were too busy with lessons or playing to remember their own troubles. As a rule, this was how things had always been in Ha Vi village: people didn't get upset about trifles, although, in that year 1954, they had been more sanguine, for the children's argument took place only a few months after the village had been liberated. In the days following Liberation, the people of the village had been fortunate. Unlike other villages, they didn't have to clear mine fields, remove barbed wire or clean up bomb craters and unexploded shells. They didn't have to level out trenches as other villages around French outposts had to do. What's more, the village fields were thick and rich, a result of the layers of alluvium deposited each year by the receding flood waters. But the peasants didn't care about the land, since, for as far back as anyone could remember, they had been accustomed to working outside the village as hired laborers. A mouthful of rice from outsiders always seemed more delicious to them than rice grown at home.

As a result of this preference, healthy villagers rambled everywhere. They worked as tinkers, barbers, limestone bakers, bricklayers, diggers and divers. Those who were eloquent but often also lazy might sell fresh areca nuts, medicinal herbs, tasty roots to chew with betel, bamboo brooms, earthenware or stone mortars. No one dared to deal in fragile items, anything that might go bad, turn sour or break in transport. Unwilling to take risks in trade, the villagers were not destined to make fortunes. But they didn't care. Their greatest goal, the apparent source of all their future happiness, was to be able to put something into their mouths during the third and eighth lunar months, during those hardest of times when all the old rice had been consumed and the new rice was not yet ready for harvesting.

And so the cycle went, every single year, even years after Liberation when these difficult days passed, the villagers would cease their rambling and remain home. Then they would hastily begin to plough and harrow their own fields. Later they would hoe the fields and thresh the grain, and then quickly sow and plant the fields. Once finished, many simply packed up their families and left. Every week or two, the wife or children would return home to weed and turn the soil. When it was harvest time, they would return, leaving again when the season was over.

So the cycle went. When they were home, they missed the outsider's rice. When they were away, they were restless, recalling with love every single areca tree and every banana plant at home. They didn't really love their fields, but they hadn't the courage to break with the old, familiar patterns they had learned from their parents since birth in this place that everyone called home through habit.

The villagers who stayed at home were old or unskilled or weak. Although they became the main work force left in the village, they planted no more than one crop of corn a year. In the tenth month, they plowed and harrowed sloppily. In the fourth month, they hastily picked the ears and cut down the stalks. Then, with great enthusiasm, they crossed the river to work as hired laborers in the fields on the other side. Rising early each morning, straw hats in hand, they left for the fields, returning each evening with their hats again under their arms, filling the roads with their laughter and chatter.

The village seemed destined to be strictly a village of hired workers. All along the roads the villagers elbowed and pushed each other as they rushed to find masters. Those who gained the trust of the masters considered themselves blessed and therefore became stuck-up and critical of the other hired laborers, even those people from their own commune or village. This attitude showed up even in their work habits, whether when thinning out the cornfields or planting beans. On their own fields, some places might be too thick or too thin. But on the master's fields, every row was straight and even.

Everyone – young, old, pigs – relieved themselves in the fields. Even those who had pigsties would still let the pigs wander about freely. For their masters, however, these same people would pick up the pig manure, clean the pigsties, and carry the dung to the fields.

And yet when the owner's fields yielded abundant plump fruit and full grain and theirs did not, these laborers turned around and blamed their fellow villagers for being stupid and not knowing how to do things.

This habit of seeking the confidence and praise of the masters, of enjoying being ordered and scolded started in a time of need and hunger, in a time when it was difficult to ask for a loan, and virtually impossible to repay one. Working on their own fields, the villagers found their purses too thin for investment. They couldn't wait for harvest to reap profit, for who knew what the harvest might bring? As the saying went, "Three months spent taking care of the plants is not worth one day when the crop is ripe." Just as the fruit was ripe for harvest, a gust of wind, a squall or a drought could wipe everything out. The villagers were better off grabbing their hats early each morning and going out to work for others. And then, sometimes by swindling, sometimes by begging or pleading, they might manage to return from work with a handful of sticky rice, a banana, a fistful of peanuts, a sweet potato or some such poor delicacy for their father or their mother, or for their wife, husband or children. The gift would make the whole family light up in the hope that the next day, and every day after, would bring the same joy. Over time, even this hope became a habit.

In the end, people could leave their fields, but they could not leave positions as hired hands, despite the fact that they were treated with disdain during harvest and belittled even after the season was over.

Every single day, hundreds of people went out and waited to be hired. Sometimes only a few dozen of them were deemed "marketable"; the rest were deemed "unmarketable" and sent home. Still, without exception, they returned the next day, leaving their village long before sunrise. This happened even in Scholar Khang's household, though Khang himself was bound by his reputation as a scholar to eschew the common work of a hired hand. Instead, he looked after the house and stayed up at night to wake his family each morning. The others – Madame Khang, his eldest son and wife, Tinh's wife, Tuyet and even little Sai – all went off to work. Every night, the scholar woke at midnight. He boiled water to soak his poor Eugenia buds for tea, smoked his water pipe and waited until he heard people calling to each other in the village. Sometimes he heard a splashing voice that sounded like someone walking in water – that voice belonged to the neighboring Mongs. When the voices began, the scholar said softly to his wife, "Madame Scholar, are you awake? Get up. Take a sip of water to warm your stomach."

This was enough to rouse Madame Khang. Sai's wife rose quickly as well. Madame Khang wrapped a scarf around her long braids and wound them around her head, and then put on a straw raincoat and fastened it tightly before tying the jute waist-cord. Finally, she took her sandals, which were made of thick areca sheaths, and slipped them on her feet. After all these preparations, she sat down on the bed of dried banana leaves that the scholar and Sai shared. The part of the bed where the scholar and Sai slept became, in the morning, a place of great activity. On it, everyone sat and drank water or smoked, while Sai remained on the other side of the bed, tossing in his sleep.

Every time, after Madame Khang had finished rinsing with her bowl of water, she would turn around, and call, "Sai, Sai, wake up. It is already morning." The young Sai, eyes half-open, got up to receive his bowl of water, then stepped out the door, raising his face and gurgling water to rinse his mouth. Finished, he went back inside, rounded a pellet of tobacco and filled the bowl of the water pipe with movements as deft as those of any grown-up. As Sai inhaled the smoke deeply, his eyes grew glassy, and his mouth opened, panting slightly. His mother tossed him a square cloak to wrap around his head and then put a jute cloak around his shoulders.

As she tied him snugly in his cloak, she said in reminder, "Bring your sandals with you. Your feet are all swollen. Bring them and your feet will be warmer while you sit out there waiting! They're not that heavy."

Meanwhile, Sai's wife, still not warm enough in a sleeveless shirt, went to the side of the water tank to spit out the tooth-blackening resin she had made from the dregs of the water pipe of the night before. She then washed her face, combed her hair, rolled her scarf through her hair and around her head and sat in readiness at the kitchen corner where the flails, sickles and weeding tools stood waiting. By the time her mother-in-law and Sai had stepped out the door, Sai's wife had already walked to the end of the alley with sickles in her hands and the threshers on her shoulder. When she stepped out of the door, the scholar's wife asked, as she did every morning, "Tinh's wife, are you up?" She left only when she heard a voice say, "I am ready." Then they set off, with the scholar's wife walking slowly and deliberately, upbraiding her daughter-in-law as they walked, "It is still early. How come Sai's wife is in such a hurry?" She slowed down then, and Sai's wife slowed down. But Sai ran ahead or lurked behind always, relaxing only when he could no longer hear or see any sign of that young girl who was his wife.

As always, the whole village was out. At the beginning of their walk, they called out, inquiring after each other. But as they drew nearer to their destination they grew more and more quiet, until at last it was as if they were shadows walking to work. Perhaps they were all busy thinking of some secret approach to keep them from being turned away by their prospective masters. The long, growing line of people stretched out for three kilometers. When they arrived at the dike, they rushed ahead, stampeding fiercely to get seats at the top of the dike. When these most tempting seats had been filled, the remaining villagers gathered in small groups and stood in the dark like silent, shadowy mounds of earth. A stranger, passing by this place for the first time on a moonlit night as cold and clear as this night, might have thought he was lost in a cemetery, thick with graves. The mounds remained silent for several hours before a complaint came. First somebody yawned, "Oh God! I wish I had a batch of popcorn to sink my teeth into."

Then came a few vague jokes, fragmented and lost in the hard frost. Flakes of fire followed as straw torches were lit. Water pipe smoke mixed with the warmth from the fire and served as a signal to call people to attention. It was time to "make a living."

In another hour, they would be able to see each other's faces clearly. And only then would their cursed, beloved bosses appear. As the hour neared, the dike grew into a busy marketplace. Men talked, told the latest dirty jokes, discussed the countless forms of happiness they'd seen with their own eyes in the homes of wealthy figures in prosperous villages. The women silently chewed root bark, asked each other for slaked lime, shared bits of plain betel and worried about the coming rain. Some urged others to come along to glean rice or pick greens if they were turned away. But as passionately as they talked, their eyes were still turned through the haze to the pathway that led from the center of the Bai market up to the dike.

After craning their necks in wait, the villagers began to experience alternating moments of anxiety and disappointment, of rejoicing and anger. Someone would see somebody, and hundreds of people would suddenly stand in rising waves. They jostled, pushed, scolded and shouted at each other in one great effort to spring forward toward the pathway that led up the hill and toward the market. But even before the shouts of the men, the curses of the women and the cries of the trampled children had died out; the whole crowd suddenly turned around, dragging their poles behind them, silent and embarrassed.

This morning, the first person who fooled them was a very pretty girl who had walked out onto the dike to relieve herself. Partly in anger at being mistaken and partly in anger at this dim beauty's contrariness, one villager raised his voice, swearing loudly, "Fuck her mother. It is our misfortune to find her out here this early in the morning, teasing hundreds of people into false rejoicing."

A boy's voice intervened. "Hey, mister! Follow her if you like. Your labor would be worth less than one and a half to two dongs today."

"Who are your parents, you bastard?" the man called back, looking around in anger for the source of this challenge.

If there had not been new waves rising up in that instant, perhaps the laborers from Ha Vi and Trung Thanh would have come to blows, using their poles on each other. But the masters were real this time. Dozens of them, men and women, were walking leisurely toward the crowd. In response to the great activity their presence provoked among the villagers, the bosses ran their eyes disdainfully over the heads of the crowd.

If only the villagers had bothered to consult each other, if they had developed a strategy to restrain their desire, if only they could have been indifferent to the pay and the bowls of rice, they would have been more respected, would have been treated with fewer slights and less contempt. As it was, the bosses walked from one end of the line to the other, questioning no one, answering no one. Meanwhile, the people shouted their useless questions at them.

"What do you need?"

"You want to hire men or women?"

Only after they had reviewed the whole crowd did the bosses raise their voices to bark, "Seven threshers." "Two dung mixers," or "Four men to bail a fish pond." "One woman to cut weeds." "Hey, who can deliver a baby buffalo?"

There were all kinds of jobs to do, all kinds of work – constructing fences, whitewashing, building bridges over ponds, draining or digging furrows, clearing weeds, plastering walls, embanking rice fields, hoeing the corners of embanked rice fields and more. As soon as someone called out what was needed, people swarmed toward them, pushing and shoving each other.

Sai was quick for his age. He waited, leaning anxiously on the handle of his carrying pole, which was almost as tall as he was. Whenever he heard that someone needed an earth breaker, he immediately forced his way through to that person, passing under the arms of the others to get up front. With one of his feet he stepped on his club, with the other he leaned forward on tiptoe right in front of the boss's face.

On this day, however, many adults were turned away. It was not surprising, then, that nobody was willing to hire a child. Still, Sai had hopes, for once he had been hired and left alone to work a whole furrow. Not just anyone could have done that, he boasted to himself. But what he didn't know was he had only been placed in the crop furrows because earth breakers were desperately needed that day. What's more, his mother had asked her nephews to accompany Sai on his job. The nephews had worked furrows on both sides of Sai, extending themselves half a pole's reach to cover for Madame Khang's son.

For five days Sai had been turned away. On some of these days his mother had been turned away also because of him. But as long as Sai bore the pride of having been hired for that one day, he remained confident. This day Madame Khang had asked for someone to accompany her daughter-in-law as she went to sweep up after the harrowers. Then, she waited until daylight before she found a job for herself. Looking for her son, Madame Khang rattled, "Where is Sai? Sai, where are you? Hurry up. You always fasten your eyes upon nowhere!"

Sai picked up his pole and ran to his mother's side.

The woman who had offered to hire Madame Khang turned away, "He wants to be hired, too? Even though he's still unable to break a grain of rice in his mouth?"

Madame Khang grasped the woman's arm hastily and implored, "Dear Aunt, he is small but solid, he has worked here before."

"Those who hired your son before only wanted to waste their rice," the woman said.

"All right, no wages needed. You just give him two meals. If the adults can hoe, let's say, ten rows, he can accomplish at least eight or nine."

"Two meals! Your son eats no less than two pints for his two meals. That is more than an adult wage."

"You wouldn't want to let the child go without food till afternoon. If you like, deduct from my wage and let him go along with me. Just a pair of chopsticks and a bowl to be added at meal times."

"Only those to be added? He's not going to eat his way right through the emptied pot to the pot holder? So, four meals for two people, that's four pints of rice and the wage of six xu. All right, five xu. Out of my compassion for you and your son I take the risk. Nobody else would welcome this burden."

Madame Khang followed the mistress into the kitchen. There she scraped off the ash and put the rice pot over the fire. The mistress's husband stood on the other side of the room and stared at little Sai who was timidly hiding himself by the water tank. Sai's mother opened the lid of the rice pot. The sweet smell of newly harvested rice wafted out, together with the smell of pickled cabbage cooked with shrimp in fish sauce.

"Where is this child from?" The husband directed his question at no one.

"Son of the old woman. This boy can hoe the plot at the Thop field."

"Hoe your family's grave. You're fucking blind."

"Say whatever you have to say to your father. You tortured me all night. Broad daylight you were still lying there sleeping with your balls hanging out. Then you wake up and insist on this and that."

"Damn your ancestors, you whore."

Punching and swearing, as if neither Sai nor his mother were there, the couple jumped on one another, pulling each other's hair. Neighbors arrived quickly, but stood watching from the gate. They signaled for Madame Khang and her son to get out.

Out in the front yard, the smells of rice and of shrimp cooked with pickled cabbage mingled together. Sai had just been about to sit down and distribute the chopsticks as the hostess had asked him to, but then the fight had broken out so suddenly that Madame Khang had to dump the bowl of rice she had been scooping back into the pot. At that moment, tears started in Sai's eyes as he realized he had been treated with contempt. He understood suddenly what it was like to share the destiny of those who went to work in exchange for a meal.

The next day at midnight Madame Khang and her daughters-in-law rose for work. Sai said that after his humiliation, he didn't care any more about work, but the rest of the village did. They trudged in a long line back to the dike. Some had been turned away for three or four days straight. They had been down to eating only half a bowl of bran-gruel a day. They were starving, they didn't feel like moving. Still they still forced themselves to wake and go to the dike.

Out on the dike, the sky had been calm, but suddenly a violent storm arose. The people who had been standing feebly and waiting for the morning light now rushed to the market stalls, which were open on all four sides. They nestled into each other, until the rain slackened, and the morning light allowed them to see each other's faces. Then, without paying any attention to each other, they flocked back home.

That night, Ha Vi commune held a meeting at the communal house. The communal house was actually only a roof even four years after Liberation. Years earlier, the sides of the building had been knocked down to get bricks to build the Trung Thuy outpost for the French troops. Now an incandescent gas lamp hung in the center of the communal house, and even from a distance people could see its glow. Ever since noon, propaganda cadres had been climbing Terminalia and Ceiba trees and yelling through their tin megaphones: "Hello, hello, all citizens please pay attention. Ladies, gentlemen, comrades, young people, male and female, please gather at the Ha Vi communal house at exactly seven o'clock tonight. The district needs to inform you of some urgent decisions. Hello, hello. All citizens please pay attention, pay attention, tonight the district leaders will return to our commune to inform us of important decisions. Those who do not come will be held fully responsible later on. Hello, helloooo." Children clustered at the feet of the trees and raised their faces, as if to catch every single word dropped down from the top of the trees. And when the propaganda cadre came down, he was swarmed with children competing with each other to touch the tin megaphone. Those who were successful ran back delighted, as if they might enjoy this happiness for an entire life.

Children of Sai's age did not run along with the crowd, but stood at the end of the alley and memorized the message, so that through them, everyone from the most aged and sick to the most recent mothers with newborns would know. All shared a common feeling that the meeting that night was extremely important.

The sense of urgency wasn't misguided. That night, the general meeting was to publicize binding decisions made by the Administrative Branch of the Resistance Committee of Ha Vi commune. Starting the very next day, all citizens in the commune would be prohibited from hiring out their labor. They were not to engage in trading or side jobs as had been allowed in the past. All permits and passes were now invalid. For those who were away from home, their families had to find ways to notify them so that they could return within the week. All men and women, old and young, were to concentrate on the life and death struggle against hunger. The Revolution had arrived, Liberation had arrived, and the people of Ha Vi commune would not be left alone to die from famine and cold as they had in the Year of the Rooster. Those who resisted this order would be considered reactionaries and would be punished.

The tone of the announcement was both stern and plaintive. The commune's military chief read these words with a cold, serious face. His voice was so solemn that listeners knew they should not defy it. And yet, the decision of the committee was a blow, overturning a way of life that nobody had dared change since the old days. It was a decision that essentially would destroy the source of people's daily bowl of rice. People wondered what they would do. The sweet potatoes had withered with the frost and not yet recovered; the corn and the beans had not pushed up above the earth's surface! Should people shovel the soil and eat it, instead of rice? No one felt good about this decision, and yet the crowd of close to a thousand remained silent.

Everyone expected someone else to speak on behalf of their dissatisfaction, but no one did. Instead people dreamed of a speaker, someone slightly eccentric who would get angry, stir things up. When he was through, everyone would applaud him heartily. Even in their imaginations, the people of Ha Vi dared only to offer support; they didn't consider objecting themselves.

After he had finished reading the decision, the commune's military chief continued on to explain things, as if to occupy time till someone else arrived or spoke up. The villagers remained in orderly silence as if listening attentively, but they too, were waiting for something. When it was clear there was nothing to wait for, the complaints, the reproaches began. At first there were whispers in the dark areas outside the communal house, then they spread inside and became louder. Just as the whispers were increasing, Ha and a few strangers arrived. Ha was dressed in an ebony shirt and trousers. Under his American field jacket, he'd wrapped a brown check scarf around his neck. He stood in the brightest place of the communal house and smiled broadly at the crowd. The old people always said that given his mouth and fine set of teeth, Ha should have had hundreds of lovesick girls begging for his favors if he was not a revolutionary activist.

People quieted down at Ha's arrival. They knew that it was he who was responsible for this decision. And that only he could repeal it. Aside from him, anyone who questioned the feasibility of the project would be damned with misfortune. Mr. Ha spoke for fifteen minutes, then asked everyone if there was anything they didn't approve of or found difficult to understand. If so, they should go ahead and speak. The tasks of the commune could only be carried out when the people spoke all their thoughts to the authorities.

Ha was greeted with silence. He repeated his exhortations three times. The silence remained absolute. "So," he finally said, "it is considered that nobody has rejected the decision of the committee. Therefore he who breaks this decision is against the will of the whole people and will be strictly punished."

At this moment, someone finally spoke up, it was "Tuy Fresh Areca" who traveled all year round – to Thanh, to Thai, to Tuyen—trading fresh areca nuts. Tuy was known for his quick mouth, but when he stood up, he spoke haltingly, protecting himself with words so ornate and polite that Mr. Ha screwed up his face and asked him to say what he had to say directly.

"Yes sir, by your leave, Mr. Chairman, I wanted to ask whether or not this would violate the freedom and democracy that our government has brought back for the entire working people?"

"I say right here that there is no violation. You have the right to make a living, to trade, and the authorities also have the right to compel every citizen not to abandon the rice fields."

"Sir, my rice field and my land have been fully cultivated, in free time, especially during the miserable third and eighth lunar month."

"You have not done it fully. Two and a half sao of the land you use for your vegetable garden is left untended."

"I want to report to you, Mr. Chairman, that that is land for our family gardens and that it is the right of every family to do whatever they want on that land. It has been like that since the old days."

"Don't be mistaken. We not only take into account the main rice fields where work points are earned, but from now on, private land is also not allowed to be left uncultivated."

Seeming to be in a disadvantageous position, Tuy shifted to an adulatory tone, "Permit me, Mr. Chairman, I just raise some general issues, but I don't wish to imply anything by them. May I ask some more questions?"

"You just go ahead and speak. Speak freely. We debate without ceremony."

"If our wives and children stay home and work the field, and we are left free to go out and make a living, may that not also be interpreted as taking safeguards against hunger?"

"First of all, the entire manpower of the commune must be mobilized to plant and harvest rice. And you have to remember what has already been stated, that no able-bodied person will be allowed to avoid this collective work obligation."

Not knowing what else to say, Tuy sat down. Then an old man with a brown patched-up turban rolled around his head and a jute-fiber bag over his shoulder stood up abruptly. "I have never seen anyone who forbade the people to go out to make a living as the present authorities are doing. I thought that after the Liberation there would be no more repression, who would ever have expected . . ."

"In fact who would ever have expected that nobody would hire you for an entire week and that your family would have to eat bran-gruel and that you still would desire the life of an unwanted laborer?"

"Even if I was not hired for another month, nobody can force me to quit that kind of work."

"The authorities will force you to stay home."

"Then these are fascist authorities."

"No. We are not fascists. We just do not give anyone the right to die from hunger and cold, to die without others coming to know of it."

"I am still in good health. I must rent out my labor to make a living. Nobody can prevent me from doing that."

"Are you really still of good health?"

"Why shouldn't I be?"

"That's good. Then you must stay home and work."

"Then who will be responsible if my family starves to death?"

"The authority of this commune will be fully responsible for that. Starting tomorrow you will walk to a distribution center fifteen kilometers from here and carry back on your shoulders a picul of rice seeds. This picul of rice seeds which you are going to shoulder back tomorrow is in fact a picul of relief for your family. Perhaps you've withdrawn your objection now. But even if these were the rice seeds of the commune and the commune insisted you carry them back for it and not for your house, you are still not allowed to resist.

"Let me ask, why during the years of French control, under the authority of Canton Chief Loi, were you so obedient? You did those corvees heartily and attended him faithfully. You're accustomed to servitude, of making your living by begging, by gleaning or by being hired by others. When the time comes for you to be your own boss, the owner of your own rice field, and the master of your own life, you seem unwilling. I want to say right away that from now on, you may not resist any decision made by the authority, except when those decisions have been erroneously carried out. With that picul of relief paddy, the authority could order you and your family how much to eat and how to eat at each meal. This is not charity. You will not be left alone just to consume it wastefully so that three days later your whole family will have to eat bran again."

Having answered the old man, Mr. Ha described what people would have to begin doing. Starting tomorrow, each household would have to plant a prescribed number of patches of sweet potato, of plants of bottle-gourd, of plots of greens. Starting tomorrow people would have to dig privies and buy earthenware pots to store urine, pig and buffalo droppings, ash and bamboo leaves – all in order to produce green fertilizer. The people would be instructed and organized so that they would perform these tasks simultaneously. Starting tomorrow, the people would be told what would have to be done by each organization, each branch and each sector. They would be told who would go and receive potato, paddy and corn relief supplies from the state, who would be in the teams appointed to receive the state's paddy and bring it home to mill and pound and be paid by percentage, and on and on. The numerous tasks of thousands were so organized in neat order. Most important, every brigade and every hamlet must be strictly organized.

The meeting which started with discontent concluded happily. As the people had been told, Mr. Ha would settle everything. That's why he was respected by the province and the district. Ha Vi had been given special priority because of him.

On an ordinary day, the people of Ha Vi would give a basketful of praises in return for a handful of rice. If everybody would receive ten kilograms of paddy tomorrow, they would stay up all night to praise Chairman Ha. For Sai's part, he looked at his uncle with pride and respect. But it was not because of his uncle that three days later, when the Young Pioneers teams were organized, he was elected as head of the joint team of the three hamlets of Ha Vi village. Sai was chosen for other reasons. The adults and the children of this village liked Sai. He greeted everybody he met with courtesy and respect. He was handsome, gentle and affectionate, energetic, quick and hard-working. But most important, he was studious. Indeed, having gone through the fourth grade, he was the most educated boy in the village. He spoke and wrote clearly. He memorized every single formula and table from the first to the last page of the fourth-grade exercise book. In the tutorial sessions for the Young Pioneers, he was more effective than the elder brothers in charge of the class. But even so, he obeyed their instructions, and they liked him. Whenever anyone said something like, "Our friend, Sai, neglected his wife. That makes him unsuitable to be the head of the Young Pioneers Joint Team," those in charge of the Young Pioneers got angry. They'd say, "Those who say things like that of Sai are undisciplined."

Every night, without exception, Sai's team gathered to go around the village and shout out slogans. Afterward they went to Mr. Can's front yard to learn to sing and dance. Sai took time to teach his friends how to do arithmetic calculations and helped them with their writing. Sai's joint team always received compliments and first-place awards. Eventually Sai and five others were appointed Young Pioneers of the August Revolution. Before a meeting of the whole commune, Sai led the group of Young Pioneers of the August Revolution as they walked to the center of the grandstand to receive their congratulatory certificates. Uncle Ha represented the district and the commune in conferring red handkerchiefs round the necks of the Young Pioneers. When his uncle came close to him, Sai felt proud and happy. His uncle bent down, placed the kerchief around his neck and whispered, "Remember not to abandon your wife."

Sai was so shaken, he forgot what he was supposed to say. When his friends pushed him forward to make his pledge he could manage only a few words: "We promise always to follow the advice you gave us tonight." His friends were confused; they had not heard anybody giving out advice that night.

CHAPTER 3

Today and perhaps far into the days to come no one will ever build houses like Scholar Khang's house back then. The five-room brick house was built so low that its roof of elephant grass and sugarcane blades forced anyone worthy to be called a "grown-up" to bend down when stepping in. The two rooms in the middle of the house were built so snug and tight that no matter whether it was day or night, people entering those rooms had to carry lanterns or tapers for light in order to avoid knocking things over. The room to the right was piled high with jars, vases, and containers of food. Hanging along the wall was a bamboo pole sagging under the weight of all manner of torn sleeping mats, jute fiber bags, and articles of clothing thrown on it. The room to the left was "the bedroom of the Sais." But for the past six months, since the time the scholar's wife had claimed that she was suffocating in that room and had turned it over to the young couple, Sai had never turned his face to even look into the room, not even once.

Sai no longer publicly rejected his wife. This shift in position was not the result of any pressure from his father, or threats from his uncle and brother, but because Sai had become concerned about his role as the head of the Young Pioneers. This had been especially true since he had become a member of the August team. Sai was now afraid of whispering and rumors, whether among strangers or acquaintances. Still, his love for his wife was purely a matter of public show. In front of others, Sai would not allow himself to say or do anything that would make people see there were differences between him and his wife. When the festivals of the Lunar New Year arrived, he observed the traditional customs. He went to the house of his in-laws with a dish of sticky rice, a container of meat and a bowl of pumpkin soup. He gave the speech he had memorized: "Dear respectable father and mother, on the occasion of the day when all crimes of the dead are forgiven, my wife and I bring to you with our sincere hearts . . ."

All of Sai's in-laws and all the relatives on his wife's paternal and maternal sides seemed satisfied that the Sais loved each other. Only Tuyet knew the truth. She was now seventeen, past the age of puberty when girls watched their bodies grow and change. Tuyet had discovered desire. She noticed the way her skin heated up under the gaze of boys. She would have liked to wait every night for the footsteps of a husband on his way home. But it was not to be. During the time when all was supposedly well and they made regular visits to Tuyet's parents, Sai was, in fact, always walking ahead of her or lagging far behind. Only when they arrived at the gate of his in-laws' house, did Sai speed up and walk with his wife. And then, after he had closed his eyes and made all the formal speeches his parents had forced him to memorize, he would excuse himself, saying he had to go to a meeting, had to go report something or collect monthly fees from the other Pioneers.

At home, Sai tried to eat before or after Tuyet. When he had no alternative but to sit down with her, Sai sat so as not to have to face her across the rice pot; so as not to have to ask her to scoop rice for him. And if there was a bowl of salted soya bean that Tuyet had touched, Sai would look for another bowl to use.

The scholar and his wife knew all about Sai's behavior. They had been trying to change their son, but Sai still found ways to act according to his own will. When they couldn't correct him, the scholar and his wife turned their backs, pretending these were merely boyish things, not worth mentioning. . . . But the scholar and his wife felt troubled about the sleeping arrangements of the two children. Sai was still afraid of the dark. Every night when he returned home from meetings, he would grab his friends by their shirts, begging them to stay, releasing them only when his mother opened the door for him. If chased out from sleeping with his mother in the kitchen, he ran up to the front of the house and wormed his way to his father's side; pushed out from there, he would lie about on the divan. Unable to sleep there, he went out to stand in the front yard where he would find some object on which to lean his head and sleep.

One morning the scholar's wife woke to see her son sitting on the ground, leaning his head on the step. Tears started to her eyes. She took him to her bed, and that night when he came back from the meeting, she allowed him to sleep in her place. But after a couple of nights, she again had to eject him. There were times when Sai arrived in his wife's room, hid himself behind the door, waited until his parents had gone to bed, then walked out on tiptoe.

The tension finally reached a crisis. One night, the scholar and his wife had waited for Sai to return from his meeting, then forced him into his room and locked the door from outside. Five nights passed this way. Things seemed quiet. Perhaps the couple had worked things out, but then, on the sixth night, when the scholar's wife locked the door, she heard her daughter-in-law softly calling for her to open the door. When she did, Tuyet ran to the kitchen, crying. She asked to be allowed to sleep with her mother-in-law, so that Sai could sleep on the bed, for over the last five nights he had slept on the ground.

None of these stories leaked out of the house. For Tuyet's part, she was still a young girl and a virgin, not as anxious with frustration or desire as an older woman in her position might have been. As far as the villagers were concerned, she had a husband and was happy with him. It took only a slight compliment, a veiled hint about their relationship, a sentence that related Sai's name to hers, to bring her happiness that could linger for weeks, even months.

Scholar Khang remained insistent when it came to controlling Sai, but he could do nothing more. There were several reasons why. In the first place, the scholar was a virtuous man by nature. People in the village, and even in the canton, who had sent their children to study with him found that whether they paid him or not, the scholar treated all of the children equally. Scholar Khang respected the smart students and he loved the dull ones. From the old days right on up to the present, those who built new houses, or who were having a funeral ceremony, would invite him to come to present *cau doi* couplets for their scrolls. Or sometimes they would ask him to prepare *theu truong*, the laudatory writing to be embroidered onto wall hangings. When asked to come, Khang went, even if he had to travel dozens of kilometers.

But it wasn't his virtue alone that prevented him from being sterner with Sai. He was also ashamed. From the time he had threatened to chase and beat Sai, he had felt embarrassed before the villagers. He hadn't had the courage to go out in public until two or three months after the incident. Finally, the scholar didn't do anything, because he firmly believed that his brother Mr. Ha, and his son Tinh, and the mass organizations would never allow Sai to leave his wife.

Sai remained silently bitter. People outside the family praised Tuyet, saying the more she grew, the prettier she became, that her face was as round as a full moon. To Sai, her face was bare and flat as a winnowing basket. People said Tuyet was healthy and solid, that she could handle all her work most properly. Sai thought to himself: *she looks exactly like a jar of bean seeds.* Every time she ran, it seemed like her body was rolling. Outsiders said that one rarely found a girl as virtuous as Tuyet; Sai thought her stupid, incapable of opening her mouth to say anything – intelligent or otherwise.

The young girl was not as bad as Sai thought she was. If she had had a choice, and been allowed to look for a partner, she could have married countless other men. But since her parents had now married her off – sold her – to the scholar's family, she would not do anything to wreck the marriage. As long as she didn't play the game of "boy above, girl below" with other men, nobody had the right to drive her out of that house. And Sai, now that he was head of the joint team, would *not* drive her out, for he was frightened of jeopardizing his position in the Young Pioneers. As Tuyet came to understand more clearly the strength of her position, she felt some sympathy for Sai, especially when she saw him sleeping on the ground, on the veranda or propped up against the hedges. But then she'd think again. She was determined that no matter what, even if he drew a knife across her throat, she wouldn't leave this house. Why didn't he just love her, so she could take care of everything while he studied, so the couple could enjoy a quiet life together, instead of such misery?

In the end, Sai had to endure his situation but nobody – not even Sai himself – could force the young boy inside him to talk, smile, work, eat, drink or sleep with his wife. As a result, he lived as two persons: one true and one counterfeit. He tried to gather his strength, to build his stamina so that the work he did during the day would be praised and admired. Only at night when alone did he live as the true Sai. More and more he found he could not get along with the young girl who had been made his wife. Night after night he returned from classes and meetings, feeling that no one, even if they had threatened to draw a knife and kill him, could force him to go into that room on the left side of the house. Even if they had sneaked inside the room, they still had no right to try to control that last freedom, his freedom to love as a human being.

Four years later, when Sai was eighteen, although he had graduated from the seventh grade of the district school and passed the admissions test to enter the eighth grade of the province school, he dropped out to work as head of the board in charge of the commune's Young Pioneers. That year, the main dike collapsed, and Ha Vi village suffered losses greater than people had ever seen before. But the stories about Sai that circulated then drew even more attention than did the waters which had ruptured the main dike and swept away seventeen houses of Can Boi hamlet.

As a rule, starting in the middle of the sixth lunar month, a time when the sun was so hot that it baked moss, making it cake then float on the surface of the water of wells, tanks and vases, the villagers began their preparations for the flood season. They cut bamboo and bought the larger bamboo called *nua*. They went to the Dau and Chay markets to buy lacquer resin. Every household then tried to build a *thung cau*, a small basket-shaped boat made with bamboo and covered with lacquer. Households that made their living by fishing went to the Cong and Hoi markets for tools. Children bought creels and eelpots and made their own fishing hooks. Old people cut bamboo strips and strings to make hanging shelves to place under the roofs of their kitchens. Women took piles of corn plants from the fields. They unearthed all the bean plants and carried them home with their shoulder poles and piled them at one end of the house.

The preparations were anxious ones, but there was, at the same time, a sense of eager expectation. Both joy and sorrow succumbed to confusion, however, when the waters of the river rose to devour the vast green fields of rice and sesame. Monsoon rain poured relentlessly. The continuous thunder and lightning at night seemed to beckon the water to rise and flow into the village. Finally, the village was flooded. Drums were beaten in rolls of five beats to signal the emergency. Day and night, voices from megaphones commanded the adults to hasten and guard the branch dikes, and urged the children and the elderly to run to the main dike. Pots, pans, blankets and sleeping mats were placed on poles under the roofs. Every family had to husk enough corn for ten days. Then, the villagers somberly resigned themselves to their fates and at the last moment, in spite of all their preparations, they panicked.

Madame Khang had not slept for the last several nights. Sai was not home, he was out hastening people along with his megaphone. He ran back and forth across the village. He shouted, he helped people carry their belongings, but he never took a single glance toward his own home. Tuyet went out to guard the dike. Scholar Khang walked up and down with some newly sprouted areca trees; he did not know where to hang them. All the other tasks – piling up the corn plants again; pouring the salted soya bean into smaller jars to be moved to safer houses; building a raft for the dog and her puppies; making higher shelves for the chicken nest; digging a hole to bury the ash fertilizer; placing dried corn and beans in baskets and putting them away in safer places; packing up clothes, blankets, sleeping mats, pots, pans, bowls, chopsticks, big jars and small jars, big bottles and small bottles – all these chores were left to Madame Khang. It was as if she were a servant in her own home, as if she were the only person who had to eat, to use these things. Had Sai returned, she would not have left him in peace.

But Sai did not come home. Past midnight, the branch dike broke at a place several kilometers up from the far end of the village. There, water roared and shook as if there had been bombs dropping. The horrible cries of people were carried down river; the cries of one village became entangled with the cries of the next; so it all came to sound like an alarmed beehive. The sound continued coming down river for hours, but the water still had not yet reached Ha Vi village.

Finally, Sai returned to his own home. He asked, "Is everything evacuated?" His mother was choked with anger. But before she could yell at Sai, he disappeared once more. Unable to release her anger at her son, Madame Khang yelled at her daughter-in-law and husband. The whole household was engaged in taking their possessions to the branch dike. They took things in any way they could – on shoulder poles, on their heads, in their arms or on shoulders. Elsewhere, Sai carried the children, corn and clothes of other households. Water was pouring on as quickly as the wind that blew at it. In no time at all, the entire uneven surrounding was covered by water as flat as a sheet of ice. The shrieks and shouts from the inner hamlets became urgent. Sai ran up to the surface of the dike and shouted over the megaphone. He told the young people to cut down banana trees and make rafts, so they could swim out to the fields and rescue those trapped by the water. After circling the entire field, Sai crossed the river to ask a passing convoy of barges to come and save the people and their property.

That night, Sai and the workers on the barges rescued all of the people trapped in the hamlets. Then they transported all the others – the pigs, the chickens, the buffalos and the people – who had been on the branch dike to the main dike. On the last trip, they searched from one end of the village to the other till they saw that no one and nothing was left behind.

Sai took off his shirt and pants, tied them around his head, and jumped into the water. He had to swim only a few dozen meters before he arrived at his planned destination – the gate of Canton Chief Loi. Above the entrance, another floor had been built. That floor and the rooftop terrace had once been used as a watchtower for the village soldiers. When Canton Chief Loi had fled to the South, the revolutionary government had confiscated the house and transformed it into a school The outbuilding was now the temporary office of the Commune Committee. The gate was closed. Behind it, the yard was filled with trash, bat and rat droppings and the dried and blackened bodies of dead frogs. Many times before, on beautiful afternoons when school was out, and moonlit nights, Sai had climbed up here to study or just to be away from home. Now he pulled himself over the outer wall and climbed quickly to the terrace. It was almost dawn, but the moonlight was clear and bright. Year after year, the time when water flooded the fields also marked the time when the monsoons were about to end, the time when the sky became clear and blue. Sai had been working hard. Now he felt so tired that as soon as he lay down, he was asleep. He slept facing the clear and bright moon.

He woke only when the sun was going down toward the west. He was lying on his side and the sun was directly on his face, so that the moment he opened his eyes, he was struck back into the dark again. The cement floor and the clothes covering his body were burning hot; he could no longer lie here. Still, it took some time before he could fully wake. When he did, he saw the water licking the thatched roofs of the village's tall houses and submerging the better part of the lower ones. The orchards of aromatic bananas had completely disappeared under the water surface as well. The bamboo trees hung in mid-air, and toads and ants clustered together to form long red borders on their tops. An unclaimed hen took off quickly from the roof of the committee office. She overflew her target just a bit and fluttered before clutching with difficulty to the base of an areca palm frond. She nestled there for a long while, raised her tail and then flapped down. An egg fell freely into the water.

After sitting on the terrace for some time, Sai realized soon he would have to find something to eat. He could be there for a few days before a boat came around. He rolled his shirt and pants and stuffed them into an opening in the wall, then jumped down to soak himself in the water, thick with soil. He had a feeling that he was in a tank of soupy ice cream. Feelings of calm ran through his body. He imagined he could swim the three kilometers to the main dike.

Sai made his way first to his own house. He jumped up to the gable, roaming around, looking without success for a way to get in. He had intended to remove a part of the roof and slip in through the space between the rafters, but he quickly remembered that there was nothing left under the roof. Everything had been brought to the homes of his eldest brother and his neighbors. At his eldest brother's house, water submerged the house only half way, but the doors were locked and tied tightly, making it impossible for him to get inside. Sai lifted the thatched roof and slipped into the kitchen. It was completely empty, except for a sieve of boiled sweet potatoes left on the hanging shelf. Someone must have boiled the potatoes last night, emptied them from the pot and put them up there to cool. But when they had to run from the growing flood, they forgot to bring the potatoes with them.

Sai swung himself up to the hanging shelf and sat there. He began to eat, but his throat caught before he could finish a single potato. There was no way he could avoid the hiccups, having gobbled the soft potato so fast. He smiled at his own greed, then reached his hand out for the earthen kettle hanging on the wall. He tried stuffing the kettle with potatoes, but there was room for less than half of those in the sieve. So Sai removed his shorts, putting the leftover potatoes inside. Struggling to return to his former place above the gate of the Canton chief's house, he packed the potatoes in one corner, scooped up some water with the kettle and leaned it against the wall for the sediment to settle. He then squeezed the water out of his shorts to cool down the cement floor. Finished, he placed the shorts on his head – "killing two birds with one stone," for the shorts would shield his head from the sun and dry faster this way. Alone in his own kingdom, Sai felt no need for clothes. Suddenly, there were rustling sounds. Sai looked over to the water-covered field. Among the sticks of rafters, bead-trees, banana plants, masses of duckweed and garbage floating over the water's surface, Sai saw a shuttle boat heading toward him. He put his clothes back on quickly. He slipped down the pill box, now full of garbage and debris, and approached the boat.

Huong, the only girl on the boat, called out with what seemed like relief, "O Heavens! Brother Sai. Let's go to the other side of the river."

"Have you something to do there, Huong?"

"Visit my brother and then return tomorrow morning."

"Maybe you should just go ahead. I'll wait for a boat to go straight over there. Or you can come up here and stay for a while. When the boat arrives, we'll go together."

"Will that be long?"

"I don't know yet. I don't think so."

While Huong was still hesitating, one of the boatmen pressed her to make her decision quickly, for they had to pick up more passengers from the other side.

Huong asked Sai, "But will there really be boats?"

"If there aren't any, would you dare stay here?"

Having been so forward, Sai blushed and bent his head slightly down. Huong ran her large eyes over Sai's reddened cheeks and smiled. One of the two boatmen said, "Feel free to hang around. In a moment, there will be lots of boats coming by."

Huong was unsure, but then she paid and thanked the boatmen. With one hand she grasped her haversack, with the other she reached over for Sai to pull her up. Both kept looking intently at the departing boat, as if they worried for its fate as it traveled to the middle of the angry river.

Sai knew it was absurd to be silent, but his throat was completely parched. He didn't know what to ask, what to say to Huong now that she was here.

≣ Huong was a young girl who lived inside the main dike. People usually referred to this area as the inner field. It was the place where, for generations, people from the villages along the shore had gone to be hired. It was the place where people ate white rice and wore smooth clothes, where the girls were always pretty. Girls there were rumored to be as white, slim, and gentle as people from provincial cities. There was even a saying: "Boys of Thai canton, girls of Ninh canton." The inner field was Bai Ninh, the center of Bai Ninh village and home to the Bai market, which was even busier than the district capital.

Sai had met Huong years ago in his first year at the district secondary school. In those days, there was only one school for every four districts, and people who went to the fifth grade felt as remarkable as those going abroad to study for advanced degrees. Sai was the great pride of the Ha Vi commune because he had been admitted to the fifth grade. But when Sai arrived at the school in his brown clothes, conical hat, bare feet and haversack patched in two places, he felt awkward. The others all had clogs and shoes. Their trousers were pressed, and they wore white shirts, wool sweaters and all kinds of hats. The girls too had worn neat shirts. They wore their hair pinned up, and their teeth were white – not dyed black. Sai had looked at them as if he were looking at the glittering sun; they were so dazzling he had to turn away.

On the first day of school, Sai took a place at the end of the school line; in front of him was the little girl named Huong. The headmaster called her name, the whole school turned around and watched her walk modestly but self-confidently forward. She was even shorter than Sai, but she wore high-heeled clogs. Sai was barefoot, so when they were standing to salute the colors, Sai faced the back of her white, soft neck. He let his eyes linger on the place where her hair was parted and pinned tidily into two black and smooth rivers which ran down her shoulders. From the first day of the new school year, Sai had tried to stay away from her. Sai had never seen a girl as pretty as she was, and he was a married peasant boy who couldn't entertain such thoughts. For three years, they had studied in the same class. Sai sat at the first table on the left; she sat at the last table on the right. Sai never looked back to her side. He didn't even look at her when she went to the blackboard.

Huong was fully conscious of her beauty. There was an arrogance in her but also genuine charm. She was a strong-willed girl, even more beautiful when angry, a girl of few words, but when any boy attempted to "say something," she just smiled, her eyes smiled too, as if to tell him, "Dear friend, we can't keep sitting together unless you say something other than that." She only had affection for Sai, but like him, she tried to hide her feelings.

Before she even met him, Huong had heard of Sai. In fact, through hired laborers, Huong's entire family had learned of the situation of a good student named Sai, a boy who was forced to live against his will because of a promise made by his parents. Who would have expected that this Sai would become her classmate? Once she knew him, Huong saw how intelligent and industrious he was. Huong liked Sai's truthful manner and bashful disposition. She noticed how he studied even while walking, so those who wanted to walk with him had to study too. Huong regretted wasting time on her way to and from school, but she couldn't be as tenacious as he and study at every moment. She knew that Sai had to wake at three o'clock every morning to study and to cook up rice gruel with corn or sweet potato. After he'd eaten, she knew he'd put a couple of potatoes into his haversack and run out of his house. On his way to school and on his way home – a round trip of about ten kilometers – he studied. At night, Sai reminded himself of what he'd learned by silently repeating lessons. When there was daylight, he opened his books and learned the new lessons. Back from school in the afternoon, he ate only a bit of corn pudding. Then he went about his work with the Young Pioneers till late at night. Those times when he was supposed to be sleeping soundly, he was actually dodging his wife, lying on the ground or sidewalk, in order to stay away from her.

Everything that had happened to Sai was reported fully to Bai Ninh village by the women from Ha Vi village who still managed to go to Bai Ninh to be hired. Sometimes they exaggerated their story to make it more interesting. Everybody said that had the boy been well-fed and free from repression and abuse, he would have been an even better student than he was.

Huong had two girlfriends from another district who came to stay in her house to go to school with her. Every day, when they arrived at the banyan tree of Phu Hoa, they sat down to rest and eat sugarcane or watermelon seeds. This sitting and eating had become a custom. Sai was the only pupil who passed the place on his way home. Huong wanted very much for Sai to sit down and eat with them, but she never invited him. Sometimes, she told her friends to invite him. But Sai never sat down with them, not once in those three school years.

"Too cowardly to be a man," Huong thought. She certainly never guessed that he was embarrassed and accustomed to being alone.

An hour passed uncomfortably between Sai and Huong. Three times Sai offered Huong sweet potatoes and water. The first time Huong refused. The next two times she kept silent and sighed as if she regretted something. Sai stood up twice to look at the field covered with water as if it were the only thing in the world, as if he were bewitched by its strangeness. At last, Huong felt the need to break the silence.

"It's almost dark. Do you think there will be any boats?"

Noticing her impatience, Sai was worried. He idled sadly for a while before he could think of a solution. "Just let me swim to the branch dike. There must be fishing baskets over there. As I remember, last night, when everybody had already gotten on the barge, there were still some baskets tied to the banyan tree at the Quan market."

"Is that far?"

"Only about half a kilometer."

"Forget it. I won't stay here alone."

Sai was stuck. He couldn't figure out how to take Huong home, and she seemed increasingly worried about being left here.

"Please try to wait, Huong. If there still aren't any boats when it gets dark, I'll find a way to make a raft of banana trees to take you to the branch dike, and from there we'll take a bamboo-lathed boat home. There will be moonlight, don't worry."

Huong didn't reply, but a little while later she said, "It seems you don't like me being here?"

"Why do you say that?"

"Since I arrived, you seem unhappy."

It was Sai's turn to sigh. When he spoke, he couldn't keep the sadness out of his voice. "There have been nights sitting here, looking at the moon until very late, that I wished that you had been here too."

Huong burst out laughing, "So Sai is dreamy too?"

"I only wished it. I never dared think it would happen."

"You wished a lot?"

"I knew that you would mock me for being impractical."

"But you're already married."

Sai frowned. He had been unrealistic, he had expected that she would understand his situation or that she wouldn't know about

Tuyet. How could he expect this? Had this sly girl been joking while he foolishly revealed his thoughts? He tried to speak as if to help her understand that what he had just said was of no importance. He spoke as if making a decision that needed no discussion, "All right, it's almost dark. You sit here."

"Where are you going?"

"To find a banana tree around here to make a raft and take you home."

"No, sit down here."

The firmness of his decision disappeared with her order. He lowered himself, falteringly, to the ground.

"You know, since early morning, I walked along the dike, to the place where the people who fled last night stayed, but I couldn't find you. I was frightened. I thought perhaps you had made a dangerous decision, something had happened to you. No one I asked knew where you went since after you'd brought everybody up to the dike . . ."

The more she spoke, the more Sai felt there was no gap between them. She told him how she had filled her haversack up with cake, grapefruit and candies and then taken the shuttle boat to the other side of the river, to where her brother from the Ministry of Irrigation was in charge of the repair of the broken stone wharf. She told him how she had asked to borrow a motor boat to go and look for him. After she told him the reasons for her concern, she spoke of why she loved him and cared for his safety. She told him of how she had been thinking about him for a long time but had hated him because he had always seemed afraid, always shying away from the girls. But since the day she had returned to Bai Ninh, she had never stopped thinking about him: a respectable and, at the same time, unfortunate person. Her feelings had changed to pure respect, however, when, on the day of her return, she had met with Master Choi, their teacher and headmaster at the secondary school. Now the chief of the province's Education Department, the teacher asked Huong, "Have you heard anything?"

"Not yet, sir"

"You have been admitted to the school. Wait until afternoon, I'll get the official announcement for you." *O God!* Huong had remembered thinking. *This is impossible.* She knew she couldn't have passed the admissions exam for the eighth grade. There was only one high school for every two or three provinces. Admission to eighth grade was the dream of tens of thousands of students. Huong knew she had a chance to receive that honor, but, for some reason, when it had come time to take the admissions examination, she had copied down the physics questions incorrectly. Huong knew that she had failed, and she said as much to Master Choi.

He had nodded, then said, "Are you a close friend of Sai?"

"Not really, sir."

"Sai is an extremely good-hearted person. After having seen his scores, he looked for me and asked about your scores. I said that Huong was half a point short; what a pity for the little girl. He sadly asked me if there would be any way for you to be admitted. I said that only three could be chosen from our district, and you lacked half a point. You could only be admitted if one of the three chosen students of our district dropped out.

" 'Respectable Master, I want to drop out,' Sai said.

" 'You want to test me?'

" 'No, master. My household is short of money. We can't afford the costs of room and board in the capital.'

" 'I understand your circumstances. I'll show you how to apply for scholarships. I believe that your case will be approved.'

" 'But, master . . . '

" 'What else?'

" 'Please accept Huong to the school.'

" 'Are you joking?'

" 'I would not dare to joke. It is only that I think that Huong is a very good student. If she hadn't made a mistake in copying down one of the questions in the physics exam, she would have passed. If she fails this year, next year will be more difficult for her, because she is a girl. For my part, I promise you that I will pass next year.' "

Huong coughed as she told the story to Sai. She stopped for a moment, then she continued on, remembering what Master Choi had said to her after he had told her about Sai's offer. "From my heart, I highly esteem you, Huong. But what a waste if Sai, the second-place winner in the exam, dropped out. I told him I felt very uneasy about his offer. But no matter what kind of advice I gave, he didn't listen. I could hardly understand him. Only when we had talked with each other until almost dawn could I grasp his situation. I had heard about it before, but I forgot that the more something is suppressed from the outside, the more it is likely to explode on the inside. Sai is determined to enlist. He feels that the farther, the more dangerous the place he goes, the better. By going like that, he will avoid seeing his wife, and members of the family can not chase after him and force him to obey their wills. What a pity for the boy. But we have to keep this story secret. If it leaks out, they will know how improper his motivation is and maybe the army won't accept him. What a pity for Sai."

It had grown dark as Huong repeated what she knew. When Sai and she finally looked up, the flooded field was covered with moonlight. Behind them, water submerged the roofs, the orchards, the trees; swirling undercurrents lapped against the walls of houses, the roots of trees. When the water subsided, everything would be ruined, rotten, withered and perished.

"Perhaps in this whole country," Sai said, "no place is as miserable as my own village."

"So you consider me an outsider?"

After speaking, Huong felt she had been too forward and she bent her head in shame.

"Huong?"

"Yes?"

"Do you really love me?"

Huong looked at Sai, and she nodded her head slightly. Sai was like a person who had slipped his feet into too deep a hole. He sank his face down into his arms folded around his knees, much in the way people once sat on the dike surface, waiting to be hired. But there was nothing for him to wait for. Huong only felt pity for him, he thought. The pity of a mistress for a servant. She was only pretending to feel more in order not to hurt his feelings. Sai sat in silence.

Suddenly Huong stretched forward and clasped her arms around his neck. She rubbed her face, cooled with tears, into the dryness of the skin of his neck and face. Sai moved closer and wrapped his arms tightly around her. It was the first time he had ever touched a woman's body; he couldn't help shaking. His whole body swelled with happiness. But Sai didn't really even know how to kiss. From the days of their ancestors to the days of Sai's generation, people only expressed their love by fondling and soft caresses. Guided by that long-standing desire, Sai slipped his hand down to unbutton Huong's blouse. Huong bent over and rejected his advance. "I am afraid. Don't, don't do that, Sai!" Her two hands held her blouse tightly shut, but eventually she dropped her hands, and Sai leaned forward to fumble with her bra. Huong pushed his hands to her back, as if to tell him that the key to the problem was over on that side. In the moon's light, her breasts swelled. Huong quickly folded her arms in front of her chest. But she let Sai push her arms away. "O God," Sai said, "as beautiful as a Buddha's statue!"

Huong turned back, looked at him and smiled. "You've to kowtow to the Buddha before you're allowed to look."

"I kowtow to you, my Buddha."

Huong happily clasped her arms around Sai's neck and pressed his face to her breasts. Looking up to the sky, she smiled. All this was a first for her as well; she trembled a bit when his hands touched her. But then her resistance passed.

Sai was like a man struck with an abundant crop in a time of hunger, a man who had no way of knowing how to act in the face of such good fortune; all he could do was stand on his unharvested plot in satisfaction. Even as desire burnt his whole body, he didn't dare reach out for more. Sai and Huong remained clasped together till it was almost dawn, and they tired of their playing. Having been up all night, they lay down side by side and slipped into sleep.

They couldn't know that when the sun rose, a man had climbed up to the terrace and spied on the boy and the half-naked girl. The man took only a quick glance, then silently slid down. Huong heard the sound of a paddle knocking against a basket, and a voice saying, "That exceeds all bounds between heaven and earth." She buttoned her blouse then gently shook her lover, "Dear, dear, there is somebody around." Reflexively, Sai sprang up. He stood straight up and looked down. He saw a fishing basket. In it was an aged man, paddling away like an escaping thief.

For almost a month, stories about the love affair – the moon and wind story of Sai, the son of Scholar Khang, a Confucian scholar – were popular with every citizen. From the youngest prattling child to the oldest toothless men and women, everyone murmored as if expecting a coming invasion, as if expecting Ha Vi village to fall into decay, as if expecting turbulent river waters were to rise again and every family to die of starvation and cold, all because of that infamous affair.

For almost a month, Scholar Khang's household was as quiet as if someone in the family had died. The family members rarely left home, and when they did, they hid their faces under hats and looked down when others walked past them. Tinh didn't dare come home. He stayed in his office to receive numerous representatives from departments throughout the district. They all came to ask for information about the affair or to offer their condolences, criticism and advice. Still, Tinh's unit had not yet asked him to perform self-criticism, to publicly atone for his spoiled and venturesome brother.

Mr. Ha was no longer in Ha Vi to handle the matter. Two years earlier, he had been transferred to another post in the province. Now Tinh wrote to tell him what had transpired. Ha, taking advantage of a Sunday off, dropped by the district and invited Tinh back to the province capital with him. Right away, Mr. Ha blamed Tinh for not knowing how to "set a thief to catch a thief," for not putting down the rumors before they spread. Settling Tinh into his home, Ha sent his nephews to instruct the commune cadres to come for tea that night. The old man who had "discovered" Sai's affair was also told to come. Almost all of the cadres from the various branches and sections in the commune did as they were told. They sat crammed in the front yard, as if for a meeting.

Immediately, the cadres began expressing their regret at the situation. They had all been worried, they insisted, and they had been doing everything to put the rumors down, but the problem was too big and couldn't be easily solved. Ha listened indifferently to everybody. When the one who had witnessed the "affair" began to speak, Mr. Ha stood up abruptly and pointed at his face. "Comrades, why didn't you put this man under arrest?"

Those gathered were shocked into silence. Ha turned to the old man and said, "Do you remember how many cases I have overlooked for you?"

"I do, sir," said the old man.

"But, once again, you took advantage. When people had to run away from the flood, you came to carry off their things. If Sai had not been there to chase you away, you would have stolen two hens and a swan from the villagers."

"Sir, it was not like that, in fact –"

"Comrades, have any of you met Sai directly to ask about this issue?"

None of them had met Sai, and now they said that yes, this fellow must have been stealing and that to save himself when he was caught, he must have made up this terrible story and that . . .

Frightened, the old man said, "It's true I was stupid enough to pluck a bunch of small bananas from the school that was about to be flooded. Other than that – "

"By not sincerely repenting your crime, you are committing another crime. But, then, I know how to force you to admit everything."

The Communal Detachment Chief interrupted Ha, "I'll order the partisans to search your house tomorrow. Who can be sure that they are not going to find a few other things, too?"

The Deputy Chairman of the commune quickly added, "At fifteen hundred hours tomorrow, you must report yourself to the Committee's office."

The Head of the Communal Women's Association said, "O heavens, what a scheme for causing misfortune to others!"

The head of the communal Peasants' Association called out: "I'll summon the members of the Quan hamlet branch to criticize and to demand that you sincerely correct yourself, otherwise we will be obligated to expel you to save the reputation of our Association."

Then, the head of the Communal Information Section told the old man, "Tomorrow night I'll order your crimes broadcasted to all the hamlets, so that the whole population will know to be vigilant about robbery and sabotage activities. We must not let the false rumors of our enemies fool us. Brother Ha, I want to report to you – but maybe you've already learned this in the province – that we've just been informed that the United States and Diem have been sending spies and rangers to sabotage us with just this sort of cunning plot. This man fabricated information to hurt the prestige of comrade Sai, head of the Young Pioneers team in our commune. He may be part of the enemies' plots."

The thief had never imagined that his malicious nature would bring him such problems. He didn't know who to argue with, what he could say to convince others to believe him. He suddenly burst into tears, sobbing and pleading for forgiveness. Mr. Ha told him to go home and think about what he had done; the commune would come to a conclusion later.

When only the cadres remained, Ha made fresh pots of lotus-flavored tea and placed a packet of tobacco wrapped in a piece of dried banana leaf in the middle of the sleeping mat. For those women who preferred to chew betel, even though their black teeth might have been scraped, there were plates of areca nuts and betel leaves. The atmosphere relaxed. Mr. Ha said, "Comrades, I want you to draw a lesson from what has happened. No matter what, things have to be scrutinized carefully; things have to be resolved under strict leadership. It is not just because Sai is my nephew that I say so. Let's assume that sometime in the future, one of our brothers or sisters here was unjustly hurt by the broad circulation of a bad rumor. Would you comrades let the rumor flourish? On one hand, we must quiet public opinion; on the other hand, we must examine the problem to find out the truth.

"I say, suppose this were not a thief's fabricated story but true? You comrades must still find ways to stop the rumor. If Sai had committed a wrong deed, we would punish him within our inner circle. We would take stern measures against him, but we would do it publicly and, ostensibly for another reason, at another time. There would be no lack of reasons to fire him, or to expel him from the Young Pioneers. We could expel him three or four months from now, because he refused to go to clear wasteland for cultivation. That is just one example. That way, we could be strict, but safeguard the prestige of our cadres! It's true you have not yet disciplined Sai. You did this out of respect for me and Brother Tinh. But you let rumors continue, so Sai had no chance to save face."

As Ha spoke, heads nodded. Everybody wanted to express their regret at having relaxed revolutionary vigilance. Now they suggested strong measures to punish the villain in order to restore Sai's prestige.

Mr. Ha poured another round of tea and said, "Despite all of these suggestions, I recommend that the problem be solved like this: Tomorrow, our comrades at the People's Committee should summon the thief to your office to warn him about his crimes. After that, force him to perform self-criticism and admit his crimes before the assembly of the Peasants' Association. You will have him say, 'I was stealing during the recent flood and I spread nonsense rumors, made up stories about others. I want to apologize and I promise to correct myself.' That's it. Don't press any further, for he is only a destitute person. As far as Sai is concerned, you comrades don't have to inquire after or console him, for the people should not think the cadres are inappropriately sympathetic to one another. At the joint branches meeting tomorrow, the Chairman of the People's Committee will say a few words to explain the situation. When all these things have been done, everything will be set right. We have to concentrate on providing guidance so people can prepare the potato and rice crop and repair the damage from the flood. We mustn't waste too much time on nonessential issues."

Everything was settled. When Tinh was alone with his uncle, he praised him, wondering aloud about how he had seen everything so clearly. Ha laughed coldly and replied, "I don't know a damn thing. I was inspired only by an old Han saying that your father taught me a long time ago: 'An adulterer, the evidence; a thief, the trace.' In Sai's case, only the old man knew, but he had no evidence, so he knew nothing."

"But how did you know he had stolen something that day?"

"I didn't, but he's a habitual thief. If I invent one more case, it doesn't change his reputation."

"But what if they arrested him based on your accusation?"

"You think that I would sit here and let them do that? And how could they arrest him without evidence? The surprise was that he stole the bananas and confessed his crime in panic. That he admitted one thing means that he might have done many other things, but you stay home now and remind people not to do anything excessive to the old man, for the story about your brother *is* true. We've tried to 'wash out the insult' for our family, but we mustn't harm other people.

"What we need to do now is find a way for Sai to leave. If he was enlisted and trained by the military, we would be in a better position. We'll wait until there is a recruitment drive. In the meantime, you should pay close attention to the relationship between Sai and his wife in order to prevent more trouble."

"Certainly Sai must have come to his senses after this," Tinh said. "I'm happy with what's happened here tonight."

Ha nodded, but said nothing to confirm this praise from his nephew. Public opinion had stained the reputation of his brothers, his nephews, but public opinion would also wash them clean. The person who spread the story had confessed that he had fabricated it. The confession was made in front of public organizations, and minutes had been taken. The authority had announced that indeed the bunch of bananas the thief had been caught with exactly fit the broken stem at the scene. As the saying goes, "When the house burns, the rats show their faces." What a pity for brother Sai. It had of course been impossible. How could she have arrived there when there was not a boat to be found in those waters and the floods were rising for miles around? How could people believe such an irrational story?

Because the rumors spread all the way to the province, even Huong's teachers came to console her for having been unjustly accused. She was glad for their sympathy, but when they left she sat in her room – the one where she was boarding now that she was in school and cried.

She wrote Sai a letter.

I wonder whether you have heard about this at home? I can't imagine that there could be someone so virtuous and generous as to have saved us! Master Choi said that your commune has filed official documents, certifying that we were subjects of rumored nonsense by the henchmen of the enemy. I am no longer at risk of being expelled from school. For almost a month now, I have been pursued by malicious rumors. But I don't care. I shun whomever shuns me. I only need your love for me.

At first, I could barely help myself from crying every night, and once in my dream, I saw you being besieged by hundreds, even thousands of people holding knives and guns, assaulting you wave after wave. I yelled out, flung myself at you and embraced you. While I was covering your face with my breast and turning my back toward the people to shield you from the attacks, the landlady shook me awake.

Dear love, have your father and mother, your brother Tinh, your relatives and your fellow villagers reproached and scolded you much? I only want to run right back to your house and tell everybody that it was my fault, my fault alone. It was I who came to you. My dear, there have been times that I have wanted to quit school. I would like to go home and do everything for you so that you will continue your studies. When the problem is over, you must take another admissions test. I believe that you will become a mathematician, a chemist, a biologist as you long to. But Uncle Ha has told me that he has asked people in the military to accept you. I will honor your decision, whatever it is.

A few days ago, Uncle Ha came to me of his own will. It turned out that he and my brother have been close friends since they engaged in secret revolutionary activities together. He said that he understood and loved us very much. "But, my niece, this case is very difficult," he said. "I don't agree with Sai's parents about this myself and feel pity for his plight. If he were not caught in this problem, I would have much hope for him."

"Respectable uncle," I said, "this is the first time I'm meeting you, but I heard about you a long time ago. Sai has also spoken of you. Would you please allow me to express all my feelings and thoughts?"

"Go ahead. As I said, I love Sai, the same as I love my own children. I want also to tell you everything, not just things limited to this problem."

"I think if you take responsibility to solve this problem, Sai will be saved."

"I've been thinking a lot about that. If we ventured, there might be a chance to succeed, but we also might lose everything. I tell you the truth: even Sai's parents and brothers don't really like Tuyet, and we know the families don't get along. But no matter how much they hate their daughter-in-law and are hostile to her parents, they would never allow Sai to abandon his wife. They are afraid of public opinion. For their whole lives, these people have been trying to improve themselves, to cultivate virtue and morals."

"But don't they want their own children to be liberated?"

"They don't see things like that. Dear niece, in this life, people are prepared to die of hunger, die of cold, die of bombs and bullets to protect their children, but none are ready to bear bad reputations and insults."

"I thought that public opinion condemned only acts that are contrary to our conscience and the law. . . . Dear uncle, would you allow me to ask one more question?"

"I told you that I would spare nothing, if that thing will help you understand the complexity of men and society."

"What is public opinion?"

"I'm not sure about this. Maybe it's me, maybe it's you, maybe it's countless other people discussing, criticizing, judging, praising and blaming. Maybe there isn't anybody or anything that it is, but public opinion still exists and people cling to it. But, it's time for me to go. I only want to say to you today that your problem is very difficult, extremely difficult, and unchangeable. Both of you have to be courageous."

Sai, love, have you read all of my conversation with Uncle Ha?

Uncle Ha is, regrettably, a man of profound knowledge. But do I have to accept his words and courageously forget you? I cried right after he stepped out of my door, and I am still crying. I know that nobody understands me better than you do. I have faith in your ability to endure, and I believe in your "courageous" decision. Still, come to my place or let me know how I can come to you before you leave for the military. I kiss you a thousand times.

Before he closed his eyes on his deathbed, Sai would still be saying, "Let there be nobody else as foolish and as cowardly as I. Let there be nobody else who destroys his first love at the age of eighteen!" But shortly after he received Huong's letter, Sai stood on the familiar, small muddy road that led from Ha Vi village to the Bai market. He stood there and then, in front of his father and mother, his brothers, sisters and relatives, his friends and his fellow villagers, he left to join the army. He maintained his silence to everyone. He maintained his silence to all those nights sitting out on the terrace, those nights in the midst of the boundless fields of water, waiting for the moon to rise. He left as if sneaking away, as if fleeing from yesterday, today and tomorrow, as if he were smugly satisfied with his "courageous" decision to endure in silence!

CHAPTER 4

Major Do Manh, head of the Party Committee of the 25th Regiment and responsible for the defense of the coastline, was a tall man with a fair complexion. From his appearance people might think he was from the city, but, in fact, he was from the countryside area of Nam Dinh. To his superiors, he was of the "main" class background. His subordinates spoke of his being "mild, not so bad for an officer." He and Ha had been close friends in the Maquis together. At that time, Do Manh had been the Secretary of the District Party Committee, and Ha had been the platoon leader of the District Detachment. After Ha had written him a letter about wanting to find a spot in the military for his nephew, the Political Officer had written back to tell Ha to "toss" Sai over to his place. It was difficult, he said, to be an officer, but to be a soldier, even an exemplary soldier, was not difficult at all. Do Manh did all the paperwork necessary to bring Sai to his command, but he didn't meet Sai for several months. Meanwhile Ha never told his nephew of his friend in the Coastal Guard Regiment, so Sai had no reason to seek the Political Officer out.

It was only after three months had passed that Do Manh began to wonder about Ha's nephew. One Saturday evening, he strolled over to the 12th Company and waited outside for a while before finding a soldier who told him Sai was studying in the club located in a wing of the main house. Inside the club were three dining tables on top of which were picture magazines, books and stacks of *Nhan Dan*, *Quan Doi* and *Tien Phong*. All were placed under small pieces of rubber and nailed to the table. About a dozen soldiers were reading the materials attentively. Sai was sitting way inside to the left, facing inward. The Political Officer stood at the door and stared into the quiet room for a long time before finally stepping in, holding out a cigarette to ask for a match. Do Manh had guessed the one sitting inside with his back to the door was Sai. He appeared to be busy solving math problems. Do Manh bent down and stood at the door and observed Sai for a while before he decided to enter with a cigarette and ask him, "Do you have a light?"

"No," said Sai.

"Why don't you take a break and smoke a cigarette with me?" Do Manh asked.

Sai looked up. "I apologize, sir," he said, then he stood and left to look for a light. Do Manh turned his book over, looked at its cover and recognized it as ninth-grade trigonometry. Sai returned and handed him a book of matches.

"Where are you from, sir?"

"I am the warehouse keeper for the infantry regiment," the Officer said. For the moment the falsehood served his purpose. "Is it difficult for you to teach yourself like this?"

"Nothing is easy. But when we get used to it, maybe we begin to like it better"

"What grade have you been through?"

"I have gone up to the fourth grade."

"Have you been in the army long?"

"Three months."

"Have you gotten used to it yet?"

"I have to get used to it, but I still miss –"

"Where is your home?"

"Ha Nam."

"Oh, so we are from the same province. Let's go outside for a while."

"Why?"

"In order not to disturb the others. We'll talk about our home!"

Sai hesitated a bit before he closed his books. Then the two men went out to sit on a cold park bench near the beach. It was the winter season, it seemed ridiculous for two men to chat by the noisy and restless sea, still they sat for about half an hour. Sai asked Do Manh if he knew anybody in Bai Ninh village, but Do Manh said he hadn't been there for decades. This answer left Sai with nothing else to ask. For his part, the Officer knew that Sai had no recent news from his village, for since arriving here, Sai had received no letters from his family. (Of course, Sai didn't disclose that he hadn't given anyone his address.) Sai confessed that he had met no old acquaintances here and felt very sad. When he was sad and had free time, he studied.

Do Manh changed the subject, asking Sai how he felt about doing night guard. Sai confessed that it was the job that made him most uneasy in the army. He was not afraid of the enemy, not afraid of ghosts, but he was afraid that in the darkness of the night, somebody might suddenly strike him and then run away.

The Officer laughed and said, "So volunteer to do it more often and you'll get used to it." He gave Sai a pack of *bong lua* cigarettes and then headed home.

A pack of cigarettes meant nothing to a warehouse keeper, but for Sai it meant a half-month's supply. Since the days in the village, Sai had been a serious addict of the water pipe. But there was no pipe here, so he shifted to cigarettes. Sai's monthly salary was five dong. He deposited two dong in a savings account, and, with what was left, he could afford to smoke only half a cigarette each day. With each cigarette, Sai inhaled just a few times, holding all the smoke in his lungs, then extinguished the cigarette, saving the remainder for before bed.

The Political Officer was well aware of the conditions the soldiers lived in with their monthly wages of five dong, their shirts torn and wrinkled so much they looked like maps of the thirty-six old streets of Hanoi. Even had Sai not said anything, Do Manh could have guessed that his lot was hard, for he saw how Sai saved his cigarette and noted his sorrowful expression. The next day, Do Manh went to the administrative office to take a look at the records of the recruits. Here, he found a partial explanation for Sai's sorrow: Sai was married, a star student. He had been awarded a diploma of merit by the Province Educational Department. Apparently, he had passed the admission tests for the eighth grade with honors, but because his family needed his labor, he had to drop out of school. Back home, he served as head of the Young Pioneers. Then, he joined the military. Last night, he had said that he hadn't received any mail from his family during the last three months. If that was true, the key to his sadness must be with his wife and *her* family.

All this information was helpful, but it only raised new questions. If Sai had dropped out of school because his family needed him, why did he leave for the military? Perhaps he had not been allowed to study because of his wife's family record? It certainly couldn't be because of his own family. After all, his brother and all his uncles were cadres for the revolution. His family was part of a secret grassroots effort of the Viet Minh. He clearly was still eager to learn. So why did he quit school?

In his initial letter, Ha had told the Political Officer, "My family wants to send Sai over to your place so that you can help us mold him." Even though Ha's words had moved him, the Political Officer felt he should leave Sai alone and not interfere too much for he didn't want to create difficulties. There were some soldiers at the regiment who relied upon the fact that their uncles or their fathers were cadres to undermine discipline. These soldiers gave their leaders trouble and were transferred from one company to another. The unit leaders didn't dare discharge these soldiers, but they felt that in keeping them, they only kept misfortune and misery. A unit leader might be criticized for disciplining one of these soldiers or for being too lax with another. Having observed this pattern, Do Manh had decided to remain uninvolved in the training of Sai, and eventually the young man drifted out of his thoughts.

Two months later, at a Joint Section meeting, Do Manh was listening to the report of the political section. As always, the report was boring. But today, after the recitation of "the situation in general," the Political Officer was enjoined to pay "particular" attention to a new matter. Apparently, ideas that could lead to inertia and evasion of duty had appeared among the new soldiers in the 12th Company of the 9th Battalion.

The problem was soldier Giang Minh Sai, a married man, who maintained an illicit relationship with another woman, and had the intention of deserting the company. The soldier Sai had kept an indecent, boasting diary. Some part of the journal even revealed a rather reactionary ideology. The company had confiscated the diary. The Youth Unit had organized a forum about the case. Most of the Youth League members had made statements attacking the soldier's petit bourgeois, exploitative, feudalistic ideology. At that forum, the soldier Sai recognized his mistakes and promised to correct himself, but for the last week, he had eaten only gruel and had not done any labor. His unit affirmed that he was suffering from an "ideological" sickness. The 9th Battalion responded by instructing the company to keep watch over the development of the soldier's ideology. Sai was to be blocked from regular contact with other new soldiers, so he wouldn't be a bad influence on their desire for progress.

The Political Officer sat and listened to the report as if listening to an indictment of himself. He had promised to help his friend's nephew. Even though he was not clear about what kind of help was needed, he assumed he was to help Sai become a good person. Do Manh had always considered himself a shrewd judge of character. Two months ago he'd noticed something about Sai; he couldn't quite say what that something was, but he had definitely thought the boy was worthy of respect. Now, it turned out he might have been wrong.

Later, at lunch time, Do Manh pedaled his bicycle down to the 12th Company. He asked the cook where Sai was. Again, the club. The Officer walked straight over. Inside, a table had been pushed aside to make room for a bed. The bed was separated from the rest of the room by a sheet of corrugated iron leaning against mosquito-netting poles. Do Manh thought to himself, *So, they're not allowing Sai to go inside the house and communicate with others.* Do Manh moved the piece of corrugated iron aside and raised the mosquito netting. *God!* he thought. The boy was paler and skinnier than he would have ever expected. He lay facing away from Do Manh and breathing faintly. When Do Manh reached to take hold of his wrist, he found it feverish. Sai was too enervated to turn around and see who was holding him. The Political Officer lowered the mosquito netting, leaned the piece of corrugated iron back against the mosquito-netting poles, and went straight to the house of the Board of Command.

All four of the highest leaders of the company – including the Commander and the Deputy Commander, the Secretary and the Deputy Secretary of the Party Cell—were inside the house where they were busily picking their teeth over tea, smoking and listening to the radio. Seeing Do Manh, the assembled men all stood up and stepped back, as if they'd been suddenly driven to the wall. Do Manh tried his best to be calm. "Keep sitting, comrades. I come down here suddenly for two things. First, you comrades must send somebody immediately with a stretcher for one of our comrades is sick and lying in the club. Second, let me borrow the diary of soldier Giang Minh Sai."

Do Manh ignored their noisy, obsequious replies, their invitation for him to have some tea, a cigarette. Once he had the diary in his hand, he smiled, "All right, comrades, relax. I have to go." He rode his bicycle back to the regiment dispensary, met with the doctor, Lieutenant and Commander of the Medical Company and offered some instructions. He arrived home only after the tureen of rice, which his aide had wrapped up carefully to keep hot, had turned cold and curdled. He ate and rushed off to check on a construction project of the 8th Battalion.

That night, he would read from the beginning to the end of Sai's diary. A shame to read another's diary, he thought, but in this case he had no choice.

Strangely enough, the diary was almost only about the soldier Sai's nighttime thoughts. It was as if the daytime hours didn't exist.

Night. . . . This is the first time I have ever done this. If I had started keeping a diary when I was in school, as friends of mine did, or if I were as good as Huong with letters, then I would not have this much difficulty. In those days, I had friends to complain to. If there was somebody that I loved, hated, or was angry with, I could run to my friends. I didn't need to waste my time with a diary. But during the last two weeks, I have become "a soldier." I have had nobody to share my feelings with. My tertiary team arranges daily "intimate talks," but these talks are really to enable the team leader to grasp our thoughts and report them to the authorities. How can I tell them how wretched I feel? I am not allowed to approach the ones I love; I am not allowed to avoid the ones I hate. This diary can help me remember these days. In fact, these nights. For I have nothing to write about the days. In the daytime, I learn ballistics and build national defense projects. Those are secret things, and I am not allowed to talk about them, not even allowed to write about them. And anyway, I don't think anything in the daytime. I don't have time, and I am encouraged to avoid "spontaneous thinking."

≣ *Night. . . . A letter from Huong:*

Sai, my love and mine alone. It has been six months and five days since you left. You didn't tell me anything about your departure. I had to track you down myself! How ruthless you are! Do you know that I kept crying for the whole month? I only dared to cry at night, while doing my homework. The more I miss and love you, the harder I have to study. I am the only one in the school who hasn't received any grade lower than eight points. I was selected as the best student and was awarded the Diploma of Merit by the Ministry of Education.

But my love, what now makes me happy is the news that uncle Ha and brother Tinh have brought me. Both our uncle and our brother treat me lovingly as if I were their de facto in-law. "From now on," Tinh told me, "the two of you are completely free. Uncle and I have sent a proposal to the court. It has been investigated carefully, and the authorities agree to let Sai divorce his wife."

Hearing this, I clasped my arms tightly around Brother Tinh's neck and sank my head on his shoulder. I cried and said, "I am very, very grateful to you, Uncle. I am very, very grateful to you, Brother."

Brother Tinh stroked my hair and said, "You should ask your school for a leave to go home this Sunday. Our parents are expecting you. And then, when the summer comes, the three of us will go to visit Sai."

The siren sounded for equipment inspection. Fortunately, I was still wearing my shoes and had not yet hung my mosquito-netting.

"Night . . . Our whole battalion practiced Lesson One of real bullet firing. There were hundreds of junior officers, senior officers, and even the major-general, commander-in-chief of the military zone present to observe this pilot program for the whole zone. Uncle Ha led the party from Province Headquarters. I am having trouble with my eye, so in the report my company anticipated a maximum score of ninety-five percent. I was listed as among the five percent and left to fire the last shots. The guests were just returning to their cars, but suddenly, hearing that the first three shots had all been bulls' eyes, they rushed back. This was the only instance in the whole regiment where a recruit had scored thirty points in three shots. I was allowed to shoot again for the major-general to see with his own eyes. The pennant from the target signaled the same result as before. The entire firing range thunderously applauded. The major-general came to shake hands with me, he then threw his arm around my shoulder in front of the eyes of the praising crowd. Uncle Ha looked at me, smiled and nodded with satisfaction. . . . "

The Political Officer put Sai's diary down and opened his chest to reach for the daily calendar which recorded the accomplishments and events of the last four months. He placed the calendar next to the diary and turned one page at a time, matching the dates to find out what the 12th Company had done during the days that came right before the nights recorded in the diary.

"The day of the 25th, the 12th Company sifted sand and carried water to mix plaster at H1. The quorum reached 100%. The productivity exceeded the norm by 15%."

Night . . . 25th. Huong came. She said that she belonged to a group of honor students visiting the coastal area. My company was assigned to receive these students. After having introduced her friends, Huong told stories about their studies. Then, Huong saw me while I was carrying a big basin of mash to feed the pigs. Huong rushed to me and called, "Sai! O God, is it you?"

When her friends flocked about her, she proudly introduced me, "This is Sai, the one I have been talking about." My clothes and my face were so dirty, I had to turn away. Huong said, "Please stay, my friends esteem you. The more hardship you soldiers have to face, the more we love you." Everyone laughed at this. My fellow soldiers in the company clicked their tongues in admiration; no one could have ever guessed that I had such a wonderful lover. Everybody seemed to like Huong, and they took good care of her. They started to refer to her as the "daughter-in-law of the company."

Do Manh put the diary down and made a call to the dispensary. He asked the doctor whether Sai showed any signs of mental illness. The doctor assured him that the patient only had a case of exhaustion and high fever because of bronchopneumonia.

"29th. . . . The 12th Company studied ballistics Lesson One all morning. Relaxed in the afternoon. West to get water at night."

≣ *Night, 29th . . . Huong graduated from high school just when I completed my tenth-grade self-study program, so we went to take the college admissions test together.*

Huong always cared a lot about my studying, so that when she saw me at the gathering of the candidates, she called, "O Sai! I can't imagine how you could have finished the whole high school program during your three years in the army. But . . . anyway, let's review everything that we've learned tonight."

"Fate surpasses talent in the exams, but if ten percent of the candidates pass, perhaps we'll be among those names. But before we study, let's go eat ice cream at the lake shore. I've never been to the Hoan Kiem Lake."

Huong said, "Can we go have a picture taken together, too? That's a favor you can do for me in return for waiting for you for three years."

On both days of the examination, it took me only half the time provided to do the work. After the exams, we stayed at the house of Huong's brother. She encouraged me to have new clothes tailored, and to learn to ride a bicycle. Then we took turns peddling the bicycle, carrying one another back to Ha Vi village. Only when I returned home did people realize that I had left the army. In my absence, Tuyet had died of throat cancer. I felt sad for her. If she had not brought me such misfortune, I would have treated her as respectfully as I did all others. I told my parents to sell our house and organize a big funeral. Every year, on the anniversary of her death, I said, we will cook a meal and invite her parents, her brothers and sisters over. . . .

Oh, I can't keep on thinking. It is too horrible.

"The day of the 4th of . . . The 12th Company continued to transport stones and soil to the K5 estuary. Except for two sent to the hospital, one on a mission, all the rest were present and accounted for."

The night of the 4th of . . . I fled from my unit. The laboring day stretched from early in the morning until the evening. Some days I was too tired to eat. Nights, we were on alert or practicing shooting. I come from a swampy area and have worked as a hired labor, so I could endure the hardships. What made me suffer was the question of whether Huong completely understood why I had to leave for the army. I intended to go back to town to tell her, but, once I was there, Huong insisted I stay. She wanted to go back with me to my unit on Saturday.

Huong has an uncle who is the Commander-in-Chief of my regiment. On Saturday, the Commander-in-Chief invited both of us to have dinner with him, but I declined in order to get back to my company. Huong ran after me. The Commander-in-Chief had to yield to our intention. The three of us came down to the 12th Company. Since that day, everybody knows that I am the nephew-in-law-to-be of the Commander-in-Chief of the regiment. They all have high regard for me and are trying their best to "nurture" the love between Huong and me.

The Political Officer threw the diary on the table and cried, "A crazy boy." He turned off the light and lay down to sleep, but his eyes remained open, looking fixedly at the darkness of the roof. Truly, Sai was like a mad man. Why did he have to fabricate all these stories? What kind of a person was he?

The next day, both the Political Instructor and the Commander of the 12th Company had to answer questions raised by the Political Officer.

The Political Instructor said, "We found plenty of improper expressions in the diary, so the Board of Command decided unanimously to seize it. Everybody on the Board of Command was shocked by his dangerous and boastful writing."

"Has he done anything that he wrote in the diary?" Do Manh asked.

"Not yet, sir! We told each other that though this fellow imagined some very picturesque scenes, his thinking reeked of quixotic petit-bourgeois thinking."

"Quixotic," the Commander of the Company said, "If we don't stop him in time, his imagination will become a reality. I want to report to you, Officer, that this boy seems close-mouthed and mild-mannered, but clearly he is capable of reckless behavior. At the youth forum recently, our men analyzed its profound dangers. He admitted them himself"

"How is his attitude to labor and study?" asked Do Manh.

"Seems fine, sir."

"But not fine behind the scenes."

"All right now. Comrades, do you think that he is really sick or is he suffering from ideological sickness?" asked Do Manh.

"Some among us think that he is suffering from ideological sickness."

"Sir, at first we thought that he was being stubborn and clinging to lies, but later . . . "

"When?" the Officer cut off the Political Instructor. "When was 'later'?"

No one said anything. The Officer went on, "By later do you mean yesterday, when he had been taken to the hospital! Maybe you still don't know what kind of sickness he has. The Army Medical Company has examined him and discovered that he has bronchopneumonia. He fell sick the day your unit was washing stones. For the whole day, he soaked himself in the water and caught a cold. Back at the unit, he couldn't eat. You responded by insulting him and isolating him so he wouldn't affect other people's thoughts. Really, you have foresight. If he had not been isolated like that, the pneumonia would have spread very rapidly to others."

Do Manh's voice became even more stern. He said, "Tomorrow, I want both of you to give me all your letters from your wives and lovers, and also your letters to them. If I don't receive enough, I'll order a Security Assistant to search every place where these sorts of letters might be hidden. I am sure I will find things that are 'indecent' or deceitful. I know that each of you had a few lovers before you married. When you were in love, you made all sorts of promises: to love each other, to be faithful to each other. . . . " The Officer stopped for a moment, then went on. "You seem surprised, but it is within my authority to demand your letters in the name of purification and rectification. You can't argue. And if you do argue, I may retaliate. You can't then try to go around me. The higher echelons have more sympathy for me than you."

The Officer paused again. The two men seemed stunned into silence. Do Manh continued, "What would you think if I did that? Even if you were discharged from your posts and had to return home to work on the rice field, would the image of that crazy, inhuman Officer ever fade? Yet, toward Sai you were just this sort of madman. I should not have to speak to you of decent behavior between comrades. Our law stipulates a certain freedom for all people, and you have violated this principle. Who instructed you to politicize others' thoughts in this way? I agree the soldier's thinking is troublesome, that it could lead to wrongdoing. It is clear that the boy is complicated. But we should reconsider our conduct. Information received by stealth may be helpful, but it must be reexamined, analyzed and double-checked. Double-checking doesn't mean spying. True, words and deeds that violate the discipline of the military, the virtue of soldiers, the decisive will of combatants or the dignity of humans must be watched closely and treated sternly. But personal affairs must be studied in different ways – with persistence and patience. We must understand a person thoroughly, if we honestly want to help him.

"Are you tired of hearing me speak? I can say that you treated a soldier ruthlessly. You didn't even consider his physical state when you decided he had ideological sickness and was to be 'isolated.' I merely want to criticize you so that you can learn from this experience. I don't want to dismiss you. I can't get rid of four cadres because of one soldier. I can't get rid of more than half of the regiment cadres who believe ideological work should be done the way you've done it. And I can't disregard the 12th Company's labor achievements. That is why I choose a 'quiet' settlement of this matter. You people take this diary and return it to him 'quietly.' That way this matter will be less shameful for you.

"But I want to say I will not forgive those who do not sincerely love their soldiers, those who do not sincerely love their duties, those who work chiefly for the praise of their superiors, those who do not care about the life and death issues of our soldiers. Now, it's already afternoon. You're dismissed."

Having slept in one position for so long, Sai was numb in every joint. His arms and legs seemed as if they'd been detached from his body. Over the course of the last month, daily injections of antibiotics had hardened his skin. Now the nurses couldn't get the needles into him, and Sai's nights were sleepless. This day, he tried to walk to a park bench. The effort exhausted him, but once there, he couldn't bear sitting and doing nothing. He pulled out his trigonometry book from under his shirt and read the formulas, checking the exercises he had done. While he was absorbed in reading, a voice spoke to him.

"Brother Sai, I told you that you're not allowed to read yet. You'll see me seizing that book again."

A girl approached and sat next to Sai. It was Kim, a nurse who had befriended him.

When Sai was first sent to the dispensary, Kim had noticed him, for he seemed trustworthy and she found him somewhat handsome. As she came to know him, she complimented herself on her talent for judging people. He was reticent. Timid as a girl, really. He was always ready to submit to the young nurses' orders. It was rumored that he was very good in mathematics. Kim didn't know about that. She only knew that whenever he was awake, the trigonometry book was in his hands. She had confiscated the books many times. She took it and then returned it, making her decisions at random. Sai silently turned the book in and received it back.

A week after Sai had arrived, Kim went to look for his clinical record. She had been stunned to read: "In case of emergency, notify the patient's spouse, Hoang Thi Tuyet." But she didn't let this news bother her. She would become Sai's friend. She would make friends with anyone she thought kind, even though people—particularly elderly relatives – were always telling her that lasting friendships between people of the opposite sex were not possible. There was no such thing as an adopted brother or an adopted uncle. If there were not some attraction, some love between a man and a woman, then one of them was taking advantage of the other in the name of friendship. "Don't you ever agree to become someone's adopted niece," people advised Kim. "Your 'uncle' will 'eat you raw' someday." Kim couldn't understand how old people could use such unseemly expressions. But Kim didn't bother with what the older people said. As long as her conscience was clear, she was not afraid of anything. She appreciated Sai and addressed him as "elder-brother" even though he was only six or seven months older than she. Sai's own conscience was less clear. His mind was darkened by thoughts of Huong. Still, he was willing to treat Kim with the same sort of affection he'd treat a male friend. He politely answered all her questions.

"Do you often receive letters from Sister Tuyet?"

"I do."

"Can I see them?"

Sai was quiet.

"When your health is restored, go back there and bring them for me to see, will you? Why don't you write and tell her to come here?"

"She's busy studying. It's almost time for mid-term exams."

"My! Got married while still going to school?"

"She's my age. She's very good in letters and she sings very well too."

"Then her letters must be very well-written."

"I learn every single word by heart."

"Oh, how wonderful! Will you read them to me sometime?"

Sai promised he would but, even if he *were* truly receiving letters, he would never have shared them with anyone. He felt the same way about his diary – which he still kept in his backpack, even though he didn't dare write anything more in it. It was true that the Political Instructor had apologized for reading it and had said that he would never again let anybody read it without Sai's permission. But those days were gone, those days when, unable to sleep, he'd let his imagination wander to escape the true reality of his days. He had almost ended up in jail for his scribblings. He still didn't understand why he had ended up that night sitting before the Youth Forum, hearing words like reactionary, destructive, parasitic and bourgeoisie, and the next night he'd been told everything was fine. "No problem." "No problem" a few more times and he'd be dead for sure. Now, whenever he couldn't sleep, he would find something to study. Nobody would denounce a person who spent his free time studying.

≣ A half month later, when Sai was discharged from the hospital, he was assigned to the infantry regiment to take care of miscellaneous projects and to teach general education. The new assignment had come about because Second Lieutenant Hieu, the Cultural Assistant of the regiment, had gone to the dispensary for a toothache. There, Hieu observed Sai's passionate interest in learning. Straight away, he saw Sai as a potential resource for the regiment's professional teaching staff.

Now, every week Sai taught two sessions of fourth-grade mathematics to the officers of the regiment. He was allowed two half-days off to prepare teaching projects. Sai was as if in heaven with this new situation. He had time for studying and nobody cared if he stayed up an extra hour or two at night.

Sai's friends didn't want to be rude; and though they didn't say anything, they thought that the regiment didn't take Sai's classes seriously. They observed that though students had no ground for complaints, they still found reasons to cut Sai's class. For the initial sessions, only a handful of the twenty-three who registered were in attendance. Shy by nature, and because he sensed the disdain of the cadres, Sai always began by addressing his students, "Dear respectable superiors." After sitting through one session, Hieu praised him. "You're all right. You've got a thorough understanding of the subject. But drop the 'dear respectable superiors.' You're the teacher. You don't have to cringe. Teach confidently. You can frankly criticize those who do not listen or who do not want to study."

Almost half a month after the day Sai started teaching, the Political Director summoned Hieu and asked, "What do you think about the dreadful reactions our men are having to the fourth-grade teacher? They've said that we've been treating them without any respect. That we've allowed a deranged man to teach men who have fought till their skulls cracked, till their foreheads peeled off in battle."

Hieu said angrily, "I want to report to you, Sir, that if this represents your opinion of soldier Sai, I, as a brevet second lieutenant, am also not qualified to teach you and Brother Do Manh anymore."

"Wait!" said the Political Director "We only wanted to take a look at the matter in response to the reports."

"I want to report to you about that, Mr. Director. I suggest that you should discipline those who complained, for those are the men who didn't come to class after they saw who the teacher was. They showed no respect. Those who attended the first session have attended all the others quite happily. I suggest, Mr. Director, that you send a message to the units that have cadres registered in the fourth grade, and you request all of them to be present in class this Friday afternoon. I suggest that you, too, sit in and express your opinion about the class."

In the end, those who actually attended Sai's classes loved and trusted him. This was not only true when Sai was teaching the fourth grade, but also when he was substituting in the fifth, the sixth and even the seventh grade. In each one of those classes, the participants had the impression that Sai had studied far past the seventh grade, for he lectured fluently and could answer all questions without needing to do any "further research."

Sai was finally given more classes to teach and put on the staff as a faculty member. The appointment did not mean, however, that he was exempt from the work of the Political Commission. Sai continued to do everything from cleaning wash basins to helping the cook on Saturday morning to carrying rice, picking firewood and watering the vegetable garden.

Sai continued with all these tasks for almost a year. During that time, those of his fellow instructors who had the benefit of higher education taught Sai what they knew. These instructors loved Sai as a younger brother, and they eagerly did what they could for him. Eventually, this meant that they supported the regiment in its decision to send Sai to the Raise-the-Standard-of-Culture School of the Military Zone, so Sai could take his tenth-grade graduation exams. Sai passed with distinction and was selected to be sent to the College of Pedagogy in Hanoi.

The entire 25th Regiment was excited about Sai's talents. They spoke of him as an exemplary figure, and the rumors about his diary had changed so now there were stories about a talented person who had almost been destroyed by unfair abuse. Second Lieutenant Hieu never discussed the story and pretended to have no real knowledge about it. Do Manh also remained silent though he knew everything about Sai, from the story about Kim, the nurse, who cared for "elder brother Sai" to the fact that Sai had still never written a letter during his days in the army. He knew about Miss Huong too, though he didn't know if she were a real person or an imaginary character. But

Do Manh acted as if he knew nothing. In his dealing with Sai, Do Manh had done nothing other than reprimand the two cadres of the 12th Company who had taken his diary. He had intervened in this because he cared for Sai as he cared for all his soldiers. But Do Manh had never written to Ha, and Ha never wrote to ask about Sai. For Sai's part, after having been transferred, he realized who the "warehouse keeper" really was. But Do Manh still acted as if their meeting at the club had never happened, and Sai did the same.

On the day when Sai returned from the Cultural School of the Military Zone to pack up for college, Hieu told Do Manh, "I'll bring Sai over to report to you tonight." But Do Manh turned down the suggestion, saying "Like everyone else, I would like to send him my congratulations. You men help to prepare for his departure. Don't waste his time standing on ceremony concerning me."

Sai's final days at the regiment were busy. Many people had to be bidden farewell; countless things had to be done. In the midst of making all his preparations for departure, Sai heard Hieu yelling joyfully, "Sai, where are you? Come to the guest house, your wife has arrived." Sai wondered how this could be. Who would have leaked the address for Tuyet to discover this place? Hieu came in from the school committee office, smiling. Seeing Sai's pale face, Hieu looked confused, and then said flatly, "All right now, get ready to go out there. We'll come over to see you and your wife after dinner." Sai had wanted to sink down on his bed and burst into tears, but he pushed the word "yes" up out of his throat.

With the help of a soldier traveling on a ferryboat with her, Tuyet had ferreted out Sai's address. She'd dressed up to visit her husband, donning a shirt the color of a young banana leaf, with a pink *dong xuan* undershirt. The flashy pink of the undershirt revealed itself at the collar and stuck out at the bottom of the shirt. Her hair was glossy with brilliantine, combed upward and then pressed tightly down with a new, light brown, cotton kerchief. Her black taffeta pants, overly ample and long for her, were rolled up at the waist, so that the legs of the pants were above her ankles. They revealed her bulky feet, covered with thin black marks as if they had been scratched by thorns. Her feet were swollen, appearing ready to pop from the tight straps of her rubber sandals. After less than two hours at the guest house, she was running to each of the camp's offices to greet whomever she met and do whatever she could to help others.

When he arrived at the gate, Sai saw her leaning over the well. She was raising a water bucket for a young woman with a small baby, who was also visiting her husband. Both Tuyet's inner and outer shirt were pulled up, revealing a portion of her black, fleshy back. The young woman advised Tuyet gently: "Perhaps you should tuck your inner shirt in."

Tuyet laughed freely and said, as if for all passers-by to hear, "In my home village, people just leave it like that. It's cooler that way."

"If you want to be cool," the young mother said, "you need only wear the outer shirt."

"Faugh! Then I would look semi-naked like a fool. I couldn't stand that."

Because Tuyet talked so loudly, the young woman looked away in embarrassment. She saw Sai by the gate and turned around to say softly, "There is a soldier over there, see if it's him."

Tuyet looked over and cheered, "Right, my husband. I got to go now!" She was too busy laughing and chattering to have time to wipe away the crimson betel juice which had dried around her lips and made her mouth look even wider. She walked hastily away; Sai silently following her. When he was about to take a turn to the reading room at the club, she called him and said, "Our house is over here, dear." Sai turned back reluctantly and stepped quicker as if he wanted to slip into the room before anyone could see him.

On the small table beside the bed, she had already set out a few things: a tea set, a tankard, some lemons, some sugar, a bunch of bananas, a parcel of letters, a package of gifts, and a bunch of sugarcane. After having poured the water into the tankard, she walked outside. Her loud voice floated back to Sai in bits:

"Do you have a knife for me to borrow? I want to cut a lemon and make a drink for my husband."

"After dinner, please come over to our place for a drink."

"You have gone to pick up your dinner early in order to have enough time to go to the movie tonight, right?"

"Yes, right! There is a movie at the bus station. When you go, please call us," she said laughing. "There will still be a long night ahead, so it doesn't matter if we spend a while at the movie!"

Then she turned back, talking and laughing and out of breath.

Sai was holding his temples in both hands, burying his face down on the table. He suddenly stood up with a book in his hand and stepped toward the door.

"Have a drink before you go. I'm making it."

But Sai didn't feel like saying a word. He went to the club and sat to read his book. After dinner, the instructors, and people from the 5th Section, together with Kim and a group of nurses from the dispensary came to jam Tuyet's room. They got Tuyet talking on and on. She began, "My village has been collectivized 100%. That's right, 100%. Pigs are no longer allowed to roam about and leave their droppings everywhere on the streets while the village needs fertilizer. Pigs now have their sties. The adults as well as the children now have to go to the privies. Wrong practices are now prohibited. The swamp field has to use the correct kind of rice seeds – all in accordance with policy." Then she shifted the subject. "One cotton-filled blanket for every two families of the war dead or of handicapped veterans, while the general population is allocated one blanket for every ten families. And the last corn harvest was an unprecedented Boi Thu [overeating]." When Tuyet said this, people couldn't restrain themselves any longer; they burst out laughing, then nodded in approval. "Unprecedented BOI THU, a bumper crop. So we don't have to worry anymore, there will be no more famine in our village."

Tuyet had come from a well-to-do family, but her mother was a concubine who had left home to serve her husband's family. Tuyet had attended the mass education program for five years before she learned to read, and even then she read with great difficulty, as if she were a wrestler and the book were her opponent. As for her team activities, she was enlisted in the Young Pioneers team, but she never went to the meetings. When she grew up, she was enrolled in both the Women's Association and the Youth League, but she never went to these meetings either, so no cadres in charge of those organizations could remember that she was one of their members.

Still, she listened to the government's policies and directives. Picking up a few words here and there, she patched them together in her own way. She didn't dare ask anybody for more information, because she was uneasy about her ability to communicate. Since Sai had left for the army more than a year ago, her friends had told her that Sai made fun of her because she was too timid. That's why she'd trained herself to be more bold and talkative. When working in the field, she boldly joined in all kinds of improper and sometimes obscene conversations. She talked about current topics using terminology she often didn't understand. She spoke just because her mouth was in the mood for speaking. She spoke so others would hear her and stop judging her as inferior to other women. The more she spoke, the more she became addicted to it. The more she became addicted, the more she thought that she was talented, and hence, the more she wanted to speak. Until today she had been confident that the way she had been talking was not that bad.

Right after she stepped out of the gate of the guest house, Kim whispered, "But Mr. Sai lied. He said his wife was attending high school and was very good in literature." Others laughed, but they spent the week trying to push Sai toward his wife. They said that this was the time when Sai ought to love his wife more than ever. Otherwise, people would say that after having made some progress improving himself, he was all too ready to disregard his wife from the home village. Some even spoke lewdly, "When necessary, just cover her face with a blanket, and everything will be all set."

But Sai couldn't force himself to approach Tuyet. The three nights of her visit were three nights Sai stayed up all night reading. This did not make Tuyet happy. Each night, she breathed a deep sigh before going to bed. She tossed and turned before eventually rising to walk outside. When she returned, she blew out the kerosene lamp. Silently, Sai relit the lamp. The routine repeated itself again. And again. But Tuyet didn't dare say a word, partly because she was a little afraid of Sai. Still, she knew that Sai couldn't avoid her now as he had been able to at home. He had to sit down and share the rations she carried back from the common kitchen. Although he scooped his own bowl of rice, Sai had to answer when she spoke, even if his responses were brusque.

Tuyet would say, "People said that things are very beautiful over there. Let's go take a look tomorrow." And Sai would say, "Go if you like. I will be busy studying."

"Let's buy some sea crabs tomorrow. I've heard that they are very nutritious, and we have the money from our parents on both sides."

"I don't like crabs," Sai said.

"Oh," Tuyet said, "do you like sea shrimps?"

"I beg you, please leave me alone."

Finally, when the two of them were supposed to go back to their home village, Sai consented to buy tickets with Tuyet. But on the bus, Sai found a seat way back in the rear. That morning, Officer Do Manh dropped by the bus station very early, as if he had been on his way back from somewhere. He greeted Tuyet and then pulled Sai aside. He handed Sai a twenty dong bill and said, "Take this to buy some thing to drink along the road." Sai jerked his hands back, but Do Manh still pressed the money into Sai's hand and said quickly, "Try to contain yourself. Focus on your studies." He bid Tuyet farewell and rode away on his bicycle, leaving Sai no chance to respond.

But Sai didn't go home. Halfway there, he took off and went straight to Hanoi. He arrived at office number 66 in Hanoi to do the final paperwork for his college admission. While waiting for school to start, he went to visit Huong's high school. Sai had heard that the students would be there, even though classes didn't start for another week, because they were taking summer school exams.

As he approached the school, Sai thought surely Master Choi and Huong's other teachers and friends would be shocked to learn that he'd been admitted to college. Huong, he imagined, would be so happy for him. Sai was, in part, right. Huong's teachers and friends surrounded him and praised him when they learned the good news. Only Huong avoided him. When she saw Sai at her boardinghouse, she disappeared and nobody saw her for the rest of the day. At eight o'clock in the evening, she finally returned to the boardinghouse with a fair-skinned young man.

Seeing her, the children in the landlord's family cried joyfully, "Here she is. Sister Huong, everybody has been expecting you. Brother Sai has also been waiting for you since this morning."

Sai ran out to the yard. He tried to restrain his joy. "Huong!" he called.

She asked coldly, "What are you here for, Brother Sai?"

Sai was stunned. The landlord's entire family was also shocked. Before the summer vacation, they had heard her telling a new story about Sai or his flooded village every few days. She had unburdened her heart to the landlord's eldest daughter, whom she considered like a sister; she had spoken of her anxiety about Sai, of wondering why he had left without writing her. Now, perhaps because of this, she was too angry to react.

Sai said, "Have you had fun on your summer vacation?"

"It wasn't bad."

"Have our villages had good yields recently?"

She shrugged.

"How are your parents?"

"Normal."

"Perhaps you were at home for summer vacation when my uncle Ha went for further training?"

"I'm not sure."

"I've heard that Master Choi went to school in Hanoi?"

"I don't know."

The conversation was so ridiculous Sai couldn't continue. He stood and went into the house to say good-bye to the landlord before leaving. Everybody was astonished and tried to comfort him. The eldest daughter of the landlord ran out to the yard, "What are you thinking, Huong?"

"He has no business here. Just let him go."

Huong had seemed sad and quiet since the day she had moved back in, but the landlord's daughter hadn't had a chance to ask her why. Now she thought that it was only her accumulated emotions that drove Huong to act as she did. The landlord's daughter said decisively, "No matter what you say, I'll urge him to stay."

"Urging him to stay means driving me out."

"But it's the middle of the night."

"That's none of my business."

The landlord's daughter finally had to relent. Sai stepped back into the yard as if ready to depart, "Good-bye, Huong."

Huong, acted as if she hadn't heard his words, saying only to the other boy, "Let's go."

For twenty-one years Huong would regret this moment. But, for the time being, she was very satisfied with herself. Usually, she didn't wait when there was any sign that a suitor was no longer faithful to her. But with Sai she had waited. She had waited for news of him even though he'd left with no explanation. Over the summer, when she was at home, Huong had finally heard news of Sai, that Tuyet was about to go visit her husband. People in Sai's village had known for a month that Tuyet had Sai's address.

The day before Huong returned to school, she learned that that very morning Tuyet had shouldered a sugarcane, hung with two bags at either end and set off to visit Sai. Huong had not gone mad at the news, as she thought she might. She had returned to school. Over the week, her friends and teachers had been kind, and she'd finally calmed down. But, on hearing Sai had come to her place, Huong had been unable to contain her anger. She had wandered about the streets all day, before "borrowing" a classmate. The young man followed her back home without noticing what role he had been assigned to play.

After Sai left her landlord's house, Huong told the younger man, "You may go home now." Huong then shadowed Sai throughout the night, so she could relish his suffering. There was no bus to Hanoi until early the next morning, and Sai was in a town where he had no acquaintances. If not for Huong, he would not have come here.

Now Huong wondered if he meant to offer an explanation or to apologize for taking a lover while he still had a wife. Huong was furious again. Perhaps he thought if he managed to hide things well enough, he could have both a family and a lover. He could satisfy his family and preserve his career and . . . and Huong? She would hang in the wind until he lost interest in her. Family and career! *Well, that's life,* she thought. The coward who doesn't dare to lose anything wins everything. The one ready to sacrifice ends up a lonely ghost. So the boy from the swamp village was, in fact, extremely cunning. No wonder he had sneaked away without a word. He planned to wait a year and then, when things were settled, send word for his wife to come and visit him.

Huong wanted to rush forward and attack Sai. But by nature, she was not a violent person – she stopped and stared at the darkness on the road in front of her. She looked, but she saw nothing; she couldn't guess where he was headed. She stood like that for a long while, then suddenly turned around and ran as if she were being chased. When she arrived home, she sank down on her bed and sobbed like a woman who had just returned from burying the dead.

CHAPTER 5

That was it, as far as Sai was concerned. Things with Huong were over, though he still hoped that somebody, someday, could explain to him why Huong had treated him as she had. If she had decided that loving him was foolish, if she had taken another lover, she needed only to be courteous with him. He would have understood. But even if she had treated him politely, the result would have been the same; he would still be just where he was, up wandering alone all night.

Love! Sai thought, with some disgust. He knew that he had some hopeful thoughts, just as his friends did, about love. The difference was he wasn't allowed to have a love. He understood this, but still he had his desires. Huong had come to him as if she'd been sent from heaven. She had given him love and then discarded him. Huong had the right to take her love back, Sai knew this, but, as a man, he could not allow himself to be humiliated in the name of love – or of love departed. They should have been frank with each other. In front of Huong, Sai should have been courageous enough to say, "All right, let's part, and I wish you happiness."

Over Tet, Sai returned home on his two-week leave. It was the first time he'd been home since college. His presence this time was an occasion of pride for his family – for relatives on his father's side as well as on his mother's. It had been a great honor for the community on the outer side of the main dike to have one of their own admitted to college. The honor was augmented by Sai's quick progress through school. Despite the hardships of military life, Sai had managed to pass his exams in little over a year. And he didn't have to take money from his village to go to school. So, on his return, everybody took care of Sai and treated him with respect. Even when he refused to speak to

Tuyet, they didn't criticize. They only sighed and said, "Poor Tuyet! But that's her lot, what can we do?"

Sai's father and mother, his brothers and uncles, his relatives and neighbors, all seemed to realize that he had slipped away from their sphere of influence. The one exception was Madame Khang. When she saw her son going out on his frequent bicycle trips, she reproached him: "Why do you have to exert yourself by going out? Stay home and rest." But Sai still went out every day. He went to the district capital so that his brother Tinh could introduce him to people in all the district offices and organizations. He went to the market and visited friends. For Sai, the destination was immaterial. What was important was the route to his destination – for Sai invariably passed Huong's village as he came and went from his parents' home. Twice Sai saw Huong behind her gate, but both times, on catching sight of her, he sped away. And both times, on his return trip, he gazed at her house, hoping to catch sight of her again, but these times, he saw nothing beyond the ornamental brick wall that circled her home.

The embarrassment he felt, as well as his anger, prevented him from approaching Huong, prevented him from speaking to her, prevented him from asking the question that kept him awake at nights: Why had she treated him so ruthlessly?

Huong had returned from school two days before Sai. On her first day home, her mother asked, "Has that young man from the swamp come to your place lately?"

"Why do you ask?" Huong said.

"Because I'm afraid of being an object of notoriety." Huong's mother's words made Huong even angrier at Sai. Her mother tried to console her. "Poor boy," she said. "The girl's family has urged her to write to his unit and tell them to call him back, not to let him go to college because he is guilty of rejecting his wife."

"That was before," Huong told her mother. "You always keep mixing things up."

"Not only before. The women in that swamp village have come to the conclusion that no one can ever force him to get together with his wife. When she returned from visiting her husband, she dodged all questions with a smile. But when her own aunt, the woman who usually comes to work for our family, asked her about the situation, she said that he had treated her badly. He read for the entire three nights and scolded her every time she asked him for anything. When his unit allowed him to go home with her, he bought tickets so that they had to sit far apart on the bus, and half way home he got off the bus and said that he had to go do something!"

Huong's mother went on to tell her daughter about how Tuyet had found Sai's address. "Apparently he had told his superiors, who are generals or colonels or whatever I'm not sure, that he just couldn't love her. He said, 'If you comrades don't allow me to go to college, that's fine!' But he was too good to be replaced, so his unit reluctantly asked him to go."

This story convinced Huong. Her mother heard it from her hired woman who was Sai's aunt. Even though she believed the story, Huong told her mother, "I'm busy studying and have no spare energy to think about such matters any more. A waste of time."

"Right," Huong's mother said, "there is no shortage of good boys."

Huong knew what her mother was thinking. Like everyone else, her mother didn't understand why Huong had spent her youth rejecting advances from boys and then thrown herself at Sai like a moth heading for fire. But Huong couldn't help herself. Even at times when her grudge against him was at its worst, she couldn't think of anyone else. She didn't worry about this, however, because she considered herself still young, that her "advantages" could attract whomever she wanted, whenever she wanted. She had been in haste once and was still suffering for her haste, so why hurry again? But these sensible thoughts didn't erase her feelings for Sai. She had no idea where her love for him would lead, but still she couldn't rid herself of it.

Huong's mother told her that during the last few nights Sai had induced the young children of Ha Vi to go to Bai market. There, they wandered around, without going to any house in particular. Past midnight, they snuggled into a straw nest at one of the children's houses. They would lay stacked up or tangled together in sleep. People didn't know why all of the young boys wanted to make friends with Brother Sai. Sai seemed to spend time wandering around with them without any specific goal. Maybe he wanted to seek relief from his sorrow.

Huong heard all this and understood that Sai's behavior was the result of her snubbing him at the beginning of the school year. Now she knew why Sai passed by her house every day but didn't dare see her. Had Huong known all this before, she wouldn't have been so upset. Now she wondered if she should take the initiative to see Sai. But she dropped the idea immediately. She had been aggressive once before and her directness brought her trouble. What's more, people held aggressive girls in contempt. Instead, she decided to stand "unintentionally" by her gate a few times each day. Whenever she did, Sai passed by, but didn't stop. For two weeks, including Lunar New Year's Eve and the first day of Tet, while one was passing by "unintentionally," the other was waiting "equally unintentionally." Still they did not meet. The reason was simple and stupid: they both wanted to win. And that forced them apart forever.

≣ It was two and a half years later that Huong, while attending the Polytechnical Institute, registered for a summer vacation camp located at the beach where Sai's unit was billeted. She felt no need to be discreet. She still felt that for him there would be no other girl but her. After she arrived at the beach with her friends, Huong sent word to Sai. She told him to ask for permission to see her at the central beach. That night, a lieutenant came to Huong's place, introducing himself as Hieu, the Cultural Assistant of the regiment, the man directly in charge of Sai. He had a straightforward appearance, a sincere voice and his concern for Huong was evident. "You are unlucky," he said, "Comrade Sai has just gone out on a mission this morning."

"Will he be away long?"

"How long will you be here?"

"Five days."

The Cultural Assistant seemed to be doing mental arithmetic. "Maybe you won't meet him. Sai has to be away for more than a week."

"Is his mission far from here?"

"Somewhat."

"Would you kindly give me directions there?"

"But don't you still have to participate in the activities of the camp?"

"I'll ask permission to leave. There are urgent matters that Sai's family wanted me to tell him about."

Hieu seemed to be calculating again. Then, he offered, sympathetically, "You won't be allowed to go into the military area, Huong. If you allow me to consider myself as your brother, I'll talk to you more about this later. But now, please understand that I can't show you there."

Suddenly Huong realized her error. By seeming too anxious to see Sai, she had pushed Sai's direct superior into an awkward position.

"It doesn't matter," she said. "But when Sai comes back, please tell him that his little sister Huong wanted to see him, or just forget it, I'll see him next time."

"Yes, I'll tell him, but I want to make sure we understand each other completely."

"No problem, I am totally at ease."

Although Huong had claimed to be at ease, during the five days at the beach, she never touched the water. Each morning, she volunteered to stay behind and look after the house. She blamed herself for not taking the initiative to write Sai and inform him that she was coming to the camp. How could he know to wait and meet her if he didn't know she was coming?

On the day she was to return to the Polytechnical Institute, Huong was one of the first to get onto the bus. A soldier came to ask a girl sitting behind Huong to forward a letter to his family in Hanoi. Overhearing that he was from the infantry regiment, Huong turned around through the window of the bus and asked him if Sai had returned.

"Sai hasn't been anywhere. He's right here."

"But I mean the Sai at the Cultural Section,' " she said.

"Right, the 'Sai Huong' who graduated from the Pedagogy College five or six months ago?" The girl behind Huong gave her a wink.

"Why 'Sai Huong'?"

"I don't know when it started, but somebody named Huong or Haunt or something like that has haunted him. Once, while sleeping, he shouted 'Huong, Huong where are you running to?' and he has since been named Sai Huong."

"You soldiers are all such dreamers," said the girl behind Huong.

"Heavens! I've heard that he even kept a diary with imagined scenes in which the two of them took turns as the best and second best students in school. There were passages describing how they loved each other and ate ice cream together at Hoan Kiem Lake.

Seeing that he was too romantic and out of touch, people in the company 'shaved him' so clean that he was rushed to the hospital for emergency treatment."

"Is he still infatuated by this girl now?" Huong asked the gossiping soldier.

"Only heaven knows. He's the silent type. Besides, nobody cares because everybody appreciates him. He not only won the first prize for teachers in our military zone, but he's also been very active in farming. He's increased the food supply for his unit. So nobody thinks him an improper person."

Part of Huong wanted to continue listening to the story, and part of her wanted to sob. The soldier went on and on, as if to prove his extensive knowledge to the girls.

"But I heard Sai was out on a mission," Huong said.

"Am I supposed to rush back to the camp and carry him on my shoulders over here just to prove it to you? We have been eating at the same table for a whole month now. This very morning we were eating popcorn together, so I can't be mistaken. But you clearly know him. Isn't Sai just like I've said?"

Huong nodded slightly.

"What's your relationship to him?"

"I'm his cousin," Huong said.

The soldier looked at Huong and nodded, "Right, cousin. The daughter of an uncle, maybe. You've been here for almost a week, why didn't you look for him? You didn't know that Sai has been here? I'll run back to tell him to borrow a bicycle and ride over here immediately."

But the bus engine had started.

"Thank you for your kindness."

The bus departed. Huong turned back and buried her face in the back of the seat in front of her and tried not to cry. *O, God!* she thought. *Why are things so complicated? For the whole week, I've been hoping some kind of magic would allow me to see you, and you were only one and a half kilometers away. How could Mr. Hieu be so cruel?*

But Huong couldn't think of Hieu as a deceiver, even though he had lied to her. From his look, his smile, his voice – he seemed perfectly honest. At the closing party for summer camp, he had come to sit next to Huong. They had talked as brother and sister. Between Hieu and the glib soldier by the side of the bus, who was more trustworthy? Huong didn't like the boastful manner of that soldier, but everything he said about Sai must have been true, for he really was about to run back and fetch Sai. He could have gained nothing by telling a lie. So why? Why would he lie, if, indeed, he was lying? And why on earth did Huong have to be so unfortunate?

≣ Early in the morning, the political section, which consisted of the faculty staff and the club activities staff, went to harvest taro for the kitchen. The infantry regiment had only one taro field. In those days, taro was important because it was considered a "high-quality starch," as well as a substitute at a one-fourth ratio for greens. Once the taro was collected, the cook would write out a receipt for the political section on the plain side of an emptied pack of Tam Dao cigarettes. The receipt – for six piculs of taro – was a source of happiness and pride for everybody in the section.

≣ For some it was surprising that the political section was able to accomplish anything, because not all of the section's fourteen members were hard workers. Three were "idle" teachers; their long backs only made for a waste of cloth. Another was a librarian who also served as a sound technician, banner maker and warehouse keeper for the club. Still another was a photographer and reporter for the "Our League" public address system. This same member was also a playwright, a popular music composer, a poet and a songwriter. At gatherings he often served as conductor, producer, accordion player, guitarist and drummer. Despite his artistic talents, he, like the librarian and the teachers, usually disappeared when it was time for farm work, showing up only later with all kinds of excuses.

All these men were under Hieu's command. As a result, ever since it was created, the political branch of which Hieu's section was a unit had never reached the "norm" for greens and starch production. No one had any doubt that the problem for the political branch as a whole was Hieu's section. The resolution of the Regiment Party Committee was that every cadre had to help reach the norm by producing ten kilos of starch, twenty kilos of greens and two kilos of meat a year. No one intended to let the branch get away with doing less work, just because Hieu's faction never came near the norm. Until today, the chief cook thought the taro he received was from Hieu and his men because Hieu said that the taro was from the whole political section. This meant that in a mere six months, the political section had achieved up to forty-three kilos of starch equivalent per capita. Now they could lie idle until the end of the year. By "transferring" their taro to the branch ledger at the one-quarter rate for greens, they made it look as if all norms would be met. But the political branch wasn't going to accept this tactic. The greens of the branch had reached more than a hundred kilos; those of Hieu's section had reached just seventeen kilos. If the "old folks" cleared the weeds in their vegetable patches, if they had enough urine to water them regularly, they would harvest at least a hundred kilos by the end of the year. In response to the pressure, Mr. Hieu's men had also piled up the manure necessary for cultivating kohlrabi and cabbage this coming fall.

"Good, good, Hieu's band has done well this year," praised the Political Director.

Hearing this, Hieu smiled to himself and thought, *Why is it in a political organ like this, the criteria for judging whether a person is effective or not is based only on that individual's activity in agricultural works? Sometimes that activity doesn't have any positive results. But it is still better than staying up all night for a month to write a cheo opera. Sometimes people didn't care whether you were really "increasing the production" or not. They didn't care what kind of produce or products you were increasing. They only cared about whether or not you were tying the bamboo splinters into meticulous bundles and bringing them with you to the rehearsal, or whether or not you had poked a hole in the cover of your lighter, threaded it with a parachute string and pinned it to your trousers' pocket with a safety pin, or whether or not every time people asked for toothpicks, you were ready with your bright aluminum aspirin tube filled with round, smooth and even toothpicks. Just like that, people could come to the conclusion that you were industrious in "increasing production," excellent in "increasing the production."*

Not only Hieu, but people in both groups of the political section had recognized that the task of "increasing production" was not impossible. At the beginning of the year, they discussed the matter with each other. They decided that, if necessary, they would reduce their professional working hours, so more time could be spent "increasing production." They agreed that those who did not meet the production norms would be criticized, while those who were not particularly effective at their professional tasks would not be judged too harshly.

As a result, people found countless reasons for not doing their professional jobs. They told Hieu that this year was the year of "increasing production." Hieu had no patience with these excuses. He agreed that the unit had to find ways to fulfill its production norms, but he didn't think this should be done at the expense of the unit's professional tasks. In his mind, those tasks deserved absolute priority.

During a "resolute" discussion about these matters, Sai's peasant background became apparent. As a result, he was elected head of the team for "increasing production" for the club and the faculty staff.

"Brother Sai, with you elected," Hieu said, "we're very much at ease. When you need us to do anything, just yell, and we'll follow your orders immediately. Those who do not follow your orders will be seriously punished. Be self-confident, go ahead and command strictly."

But Hieu offered Sai this job with another intention. Sai was the newcomer to the unit; recently, he had been promoted to corporal, as well as been "noticed" by the Party. When Sai was at college, the Military Student Party Cell had recommended him to the Party cell of Hieu's unit. The Party cell of the political section had also made a favorable recommendation. They saw Sai as one of the masses who had a "main class background," one who strove to better himself, especially in studying. In offering Sai this job, Hieu meant to provide Sai with an opportunity to be "tried out" in a sphere other than teaching. Sai ended up surprising the entire infantry regiment with his industry. Sai's political section was proud of itself – for Sai was an example of how they had been able to educate the masses to a high level of volunteer labor consciousness.

In truth, Sai didn't have to "try" to do what the section wanted him to do. Waking up at three o'clock every morning to carry manure and soak it in water was no more difficult for him than carrying his pole and running out to the Bai market. Clearing weeds, fertilizing potatoes and watering greens were tasks he was accustomed to doing alone. What's more, given his sedentary life of studying, reading and teaching, Sai was afraid of being unable to sleep. Therefore, he'd set up rules for himself. He wouldn't go downtown or to the beach needlessly. If he had not "increased production" in his spare time, what else would he have done? He certainly wasn't going to socialize, not even with Kim, his "younger sister," who had many times chastised him for keeping himself so scarce. In truth, Sai had tried to avoid her in order to curtail potential rumors about his complicated personal relationships. But it was more than just his fear of gossip that kept him away from her and others. He dodged everyone because no one could share his sadness at being "rejected" by Huong. He felt – even now – as if he had just been kicked; at the same time, he hoped Huong's rejection wasn't real. Perhaps it had only been some misunderstanding. If that was the case, he was sure Huong would understand him sooner or later. This had been his secret concern, the source of his persistent pain the last few years, and it was the same concern that pushed him to set himself the goal of "working to forget in order to work." Only work could bring joy. Without work he would again become a mental patient in the dispensary, as people said he had been four years ago.

Sai was truly happy when he learned about the unprecedented productivity of the taro harvest: six piculs per sao. The cadres of his regiment were clearly impressed with Sai. At the political section, after office hours, everyone called him "little brother." They all wanted to invite him to visit them, to share their feelings with him or give him advice. Through their affection, Sai knew that sooner or later he would be admitted to the Party. It seemed all the Party members in the cell were ready to approve him.

One day, Political Officer Do Manh called Sai to see him in his office. He gave Sai a pack of cigarettes and said, "There are things that people do just for public approval. But, as far as I can see, you are not doing things simply for commendation and that is good. Keep striving."

Six days after Huong had left the coastal area, Sai heard about her visit. The soldier who had talked to her by the side of the bus was the repairman of the communication subsection. After his talk with Huong, he had gone off to fix equipment for the regiment. Upon his return, he told Sai the story of a student at the Polytechnical Institute who suffered for being unable to meet her lover. The soldier told Sai how someone had told Huong that Sai had gone on a mission. The repairman swore on his life he was not making this story up.

Fortunately, Sai did not need to ask who had lied to Huong, for that night, after dinner, Hieu asked Sai to go for a walk and revealed that he himself had lied to Huong. He told Sai in great detail what he had heard and seen during Huong's visit. He described the state of Huong's heart. The more Sai heard, the more stunned he was. Hieu knew. There were times when Hieu himself wondered why he had been so cruel. Twice, while unable to sleep, he had risen up, intending to call Sai and tell him the story. But, thinking things over, he recognized that he had acted according to his responsibilities. Before, there had been rumors about Huong, but Sai's success as a student had drowned them out. Now people only considered Sai as having once been "confused" by too much studying. They had stopped talking about his improper relations with the opposite sex. People mustn't start suspecting Sai again.

As he listened to Hieu, Sai felt the pain rise up all over again, but he also felt gratitude. Sai knew everything he had obtained up till now was due to Hieu. Hieu had taken Sai into his unit. He had opposed everybody who judged Sai harshly. He had arranged for Sai to be sent to college, and before Sai left for school, Hieu and the faculty staff had tutored him. Then, during the two years Sai attended the Teachers' College, every time Hieu came to Hanoi, he visited Sai and "supplied" him with gifts from the political section. If Sai were never to see Hieu again after these days, he would never have forgotten him or doubted his good heart.

Hieu was the member of the Cell Committee directly in charge of helping Sai with his admission into the Party. As such, he couldn't be blamed for what he'd done. Still, Sai felt as if something was stuck in his throat. Sai knew he no longer needed to conceal things from Hieu. Indeed, if Hieu had asked to hear the story of how Sai and Huong had first revealed their love to one another, Sai would have told him. The two men walked side by side in silence for a long while. Finally, Sai asked, "If I wanted to write to Huong, would I be allowed to do so?"

"What would you want to write her about?" Hieu asked.

Oh! Sai thought. *How could one tell what would be in a letter to a lover?*

"Sai," Hieu said, "in my opinion, you should keep silent."

"Until when, brother?"

"I don't know how to answer that, but I must ask you whether you're really interested in joining the Party."

"Why? Do you still have doubts about that?"

"Well, I ask, because I'm afraid I'm forcing you to try something that is too difficult for you. Based on what you have told me, this is my suggestion: terminate your relationship with Huong decisively."

"Why?"

"You'll understand later on. In my opinion, this affair is somehow compromising."

That night, Sai started thinking again of things real and imaginary. He wished that someone from heaven would come down and allow him to divorce his wife. Tuyet could have his rice field and orchard land. Then, he hoped she would remarry. He imagined she would find a man who was not very handsome but healthy and wealthy. The couple would give birth to a dozen children, all fair and plump. Wherever they went, they would travel in a flock, laughing and chirping with satisfaction.

Meanwhile, Sai and Huong would go to the front in the South. Huong would be on the civilian side, a reporter for some kind of newspaper. She would meet Sai, a valiant "U.S. annihilating soldier." She would be assigned to interview him. They would pretend that they didn't know each other. Then, when the interview was over, Huong would burst into tears, would hug him tightly and say, "Do you know that I walked until my feet were torn up. I lost my hair from malaria and hunger. And the bombs, and mosquitos, and other insects . . . there have been all kinds of hardships in the year it has taken for me to get to you."

Sai dreamed on . . . as he had once before, only now he didn't dare record his thoughts, not even a word.

Hieu's bed was next to Sai's. He knew what had been making Sai restless for the last several nights. Based on what he knew of the soldier's life, Hieu anticipated that the restlessness would pass. As far as he was concerned, the important thing was that Sai was loved by everybody. He had a teaching position countless friends his age would envy. Sai could not abandon all of this. Or, rather, Hieu knew that Sai would not abandon all of this, because Sai was an essentially timid man.

By the end of the year, Sai was elected as the Single Emulation Fighter, the *chien si thi dua* of the infantry regiment. The Party cell agreed unanimously to admit Sai on two conditions. One, they needed to determine whether Sai really loved his wife, and, two, they needed to verify a few things about his wife's family.

To do all this, the Political Deputy Director met with Sai alone in his room.

"Drink your tea!" demanded the Political Deputy Director, "And tell me: What is your situation with your wife?"

"I report to you, sir, that it is the same as before."

"What docs that mean?"

"I report to you, sir, that I don't reject her, but we still find it difficult to talk with each other."

"It doesn't sound right. Remember that we can't afford to be politically backward in a political organ like ours. Now, the situation is that the Party cell has just met and approved your personal history record and your application to the Party. The only impediment is your relationship with your wife. To tell the truth, I like you, and our men here like you too. Don't let us down. Now, on behalf of a direct superior of yours, I request you to love your wife, can you do that?"

"Yes, sir . . . "

"Can you? I want to hear you say something sensitive!"

"Yes, sir. . . . I can, sir"

"That's what I want! But it has to be real love, all right?"

"Yes, I'll try to comply with your will."

"But we are not inducing you to do something foolishly. Remember, by acting decisively, you allow yourself to have a wife and children. And us? We gain nothing. But I do want to tell you that you are not the only man on bad terms with his wife. In fact, you are the seventh. Six soldiers before you in this political section were on bad terms with their wives, but when they came to me, I settled everything. Now that we've had this talk, everything is in proper order. After all, you are still young and have lots of career prospects. But, I warn you, if this affair with your wife becomes more complicated, you could be stripped of everything. That's all I wanted to tell you. It's good we have had this talk. You still have lots of prospects. We think so. We really think so!"

It is safe to say that in the past decade, Ha Vi village had never experienced happiness as secure as in the last few days of that year. Although the year was coming to a close, every household still had a few drums of corn, a few dozen kilos of rice, a few baskets of paddy, a few chickens, a few pigs and so on. They felt secure and satisfied having all these provisions.

Each morning, when the fog and mist was still on the ground, families poured pots of sweet potatoes mixed with roots out onto their kitchen floors and onto the corners of their yards. While the baskets of potatoes and roots were steaming, children hurriedly folded up flaps of their shirts and blew the roots cool before picking up the biggest ones and putting them into their shirt flaps. Then, they ran to alleyways and corners to hide the food away for lunch. With both hands holding up the ends of the flaps, they ran, crouching as they went, as if afraid that the heat would make their hands let go of the flaps. Pleased with their accomplishments, they would then go about their business: they would go to school, tend the water buffaloes or wander about until dark.

While their parents finished digging ditches, forming walks and clearing roots and weeds, the children hurried home for lunch. At this hour, everyone was busy running back and forth calling out greetings to the children. To judge from the scene, they could have been getting set to butcher buffaloes and cows for a big feast, but in fact the meal was nothing more than corn pudding and skinned potatoes, chopped into sausage-like chunks. When the potatoes were completely cooked, the villagers mashed them with corn flour for the pudding. Now that they had to work in accordance with the time tables of the cooperatives, no one had any time left to pound lime-soaked corn. A pot of corn pudding and a bowl of boiled bindweed or stir-fry spinach to eat with salted soybean was enough to make any family enthusiastic. As soon as the pot was lifted off the stove, they scooped the food out with large flat chopsticks until their dishes and bowls overflowed. They swirled their little chopsticks around the brims of the bowls, as if they were artists and mathematicians drawing circles. After each swirl, they dipped the chopsticks, stuck with pudding, into the bowls of salted soybean, hissing as they put it in their mouths because it was still hot enough to burn their tongues. When they finished eating this, their only meal of the day, each family quickly went out.

Those who worked on the household plots automatically went back to work. Those who worked for points gathered at the bamboo bank before Scholar Khang's house. It was exactly the same, every day; they always had to wait for an hour and a half to two hours. Those who arrived earliest let their mouths run freely from the depths of the earth to the heights of heaven. At times their speech was as gritty as dirt, and at other times it was as clear as the sky. They talked until they almost ran out of things to say. Then they flocked together around the team leader to do whatever chore was required. It was up to the team leader to decide when to come, when to go, when to work hard and when not to, when to keep going and when to stop. The people need not know. They only needed to laugh and to joke.

The field of Ha Vi village rang with laughter and chatter throughout the year. This was the undying music of the countryside, a feature that had returned when the Ha Vi village built cooperatives in each of its four hamlets. Fewer and fewer workers went to the other side of the dike "to help relatives." People had to work for points, to take care of the household plot, to prepare the fertilizer and to tend cattle. Still, in some years, they received only three cents for a day's work . . . and a kilo of rice cost fifty cents. Although the Ha Vi villagers were short of food in between seasons, they still had some potatoes, roots and manioc to eat, so they felt quite confident and happy with their situation.

In reality there were years that the district had to adjust the norms, but in the reports the village never experienced decreases. Amid the pleasant atmosphere of plenty, Khang's family had an unprecedented warm and happy gathering. Plans started when the official in charge of public service for the District Party Committee informed Tinh that a second lieutenant who was the political guard assistant and a cell committee member of Sai's unit was in the office of the District Party Committee, and he was asking for a letter of introduction to the village, so he could verify Sai's record. This was, the man explained, simply part of the process of admitting Sai to the Party. Sai later would return to the district with him.

Tinh phoned to his niece, a salesperson at the state department store, asking her to ride her bicycle home and tell the family to prepare in advance for the coming event. He hung up the phone, wrote a letter to the state restaurant to order lunch for six persons, wrote to the food store for a set of pig organs to be delivered by the next morning, and wrote to the state department store for a carton of silver Dien Bien's and five packs of Ba Dinh cigarettes. Then, he ordered his contact man to deliver the letters and report the results to him immediately. Since Tinh was a permanent member of the People's Committee in charge of Internal Affairs, the other offices were pleased to fulfill his demands, and they even surprised him with their eagerness to help. For example, the restaurant obliged Tinh by preparing lunch for six at the price of only one dong and fifty cents per person, and they placed fifteen bottles of beer on the table. They prepared roasted fish, simmered duck, boiled chicken, spring rolls, grilled meat, fish bladder and stir-fried cauliflower. Everyone had more than enough to eat. For dessert they had oranges, bananas and coffee made with individual coffeepots. The district was thoroughly "rural," from the chairman to the youngest of babies, but the restaurant's feast would have been admired by the most sophisticated of town or city dwellers.

The reason for the restaurant's success was that when Tinh had been transferred to the People's Committee and been placed in charge of Internal Affairs, he had allowed the rural restaurant to hire two sausage makers and two banquet cooks from Hanoi. In showing their gratitude to Tinh, they prepared meals so sumptuous that Tinh and his guests were always left with memories of an unusually delicious meal that would stay with them for months. The restaurant was sufficiently impressive that the Chairman of the province's People's Committee had once said, "If the only thing your entire district can do is cook, fine. Just send us some of those cooks."

Tinh's niece delivered Tinh's message before noon. Instantly, everyone was overjoyed and frantically running back and forth in excitement. The first thing they had to do was to remove the bedding from the room where Scholar Khang's wife slept and carry a Western-style bed that belonged to the Tinhs there. Then, they covered the bed with two layers of straw before spreading a floral sleeping mat over it. In Khang's place on the other side of the room, dried banana leaves were replaced with straw. Sai's eldest brother – a detail-oriented man – deftly smoothed the straw, so it was neat and lovely. Then, the eldest brother hung up a new mosquito net, still stiff with starch, and folded a three-kilo cotton-filled blanket into its outer cover of Chinese floral material. The words "bright future" were embroidered with blue and red thread onto a spotlessly white pillow. Next to the words were stitched two birds with their bills touching each other. The Western-style bed looked as elegant as beds for the district's official guests used to look in the old days. On the table were a Giang Tay porcelain tea set, a two-and-a-half-liter vacuum flask with a marble glaze, an ashtray also made of porcelain, and a brown ceramic jar containing tea. Only the water pipe and the tube holding soaked bamboo splinters were inherited from the past. The rest of the goods had just been pulled by Tinh's wife from the trunk.

The trunk in the middle room was filled with blankets and mosquito nets, pots and cups, trays and bowls, combs and mirrors, fabrics and flower vases – even a glass fish and a water buffalo on a lacquered plate. All of these housewares, toys and souvenirs had been allocated to Tinh by the state's main trading service, or they had been given to him as gifts. Tinh had brought them home and placed them carefully into the trunk. Once in a while, his wife was permitted to open the trunk to see whether anything was missing or broken; otherwise no one was allowed to touch these items without Tinh's consent. These objects were like the objects in the Province's Guest House; they could only be used when there were very special guests – and even then only with the permission of the authorities. After Tinh's wife had dusted, cleaned and displayed these things, everyone in the family looked at them, as if they were looking at items in a stranger's house, in a place far away from their village.

In the early 1960s, it was a great honor to be a second lieutenant in the army. Tinh valued the position for another reason. In his district, there were some who did not know who Tinh was, but all knew Sai by name and had heard about his academic success. Decades later, stories about people who went to college, in spite of the hardship of a soldier's life, would be common, but, at the time, people like Sai were considered so strange and marvelous that everybody wanted to know them. They wanted, too, to know their brothers and sisters, their relatives, their origins and flaws. With a brother like that, Tinh could afford a few sacrifices. In the past weeks, he'd willingly abstained from breakfast and limited his clothing expenses, so he could buy a bicycle for Sai's use. Now, Sai was about to be admitted to the Party. Others had strived unceasingly but were still not even close to being "in the favorable domain" of the Party.

After lunch, Sai and Hien, a second lieutenant comrade, went to Tinh's room for a nap. Tinh told them, "Whenever you two wake up, take my bicycle and ride each other home. I'll borrow another bicycle and ride home now."

Hien was a Political Security Guard Assistant, but he didn't seem as preoccupied, as quiet or as on guard as people might have thought he would be. He laughed and talked openly. On this trip, it seemed as if he were merely visiting Sai's family and not acting in his security capacity. The Chief of the Organization Board of the District Party Committee and the District Police Chief were present at the lunch earlier in the day. Both told Hien just to continue on to Ha Vi village. On the way back, they said he should drop by the district office, and they would provide him with further details about what he was supposed to do. At the village, they said, "Just stay at Sai's house." In the evening, the Secretary of the Party, the Chairman of the People's Committee, the Deputy Chairman of the People's Committee and the Police Chief of the village would come for dinner and bring along their seals.

Hien and Sai arrived home at about four in the afternoon. It was a cold winter's day, and the sky had turned violet as they made their way to the house. Hien had borrowed a radio while back at the club, and he had slung it over his shoulder for the trip. Now, the radio blared louder or softer, depending on the shock the bumpy road gave the bicycle as it moved along the fields. The cooperative members working along the road looked up covetously at the radio. Children on their way back from school ran after the soldiers' bicycle, and children tending buffaloes lashed their animals' flanks so the animals would keep pace with the bicycle and its radio. Everyone wanted to be able to listen. At the gate to Scholar Khang's house, the children all stopped. They lowered their voice to argue about what kind of a radio it was. Could it be an expensive one? And did Mr. Ha, Brother Sai's uncle, have a radio himself?

In the yard, younger relatives from the hamlet had arrived. They were looking up solemnly at every gesture of the strange soldier with the radio. Thirty or forty children arrived, some with their baby brothers or sisters on their backs or in their arms. Some were wearing the cotton smocks of adults; others wore army shirts that reached down below their knees. Some wore their trouser waists tightened high on their chests. Their pants legs were rolled up but still trailed over their feet like sweeping brooms. Their faces were stained with ink. Some had runny noses. Now and then, they sniffed the snot back in quickly, as if they were eating noodle soup.

As Hien and Sai entered the house, young relatives clustered around the bamboo hedge, staring and pointing at the object containing all the secrets that they were competing to discover. The arguments in the yard became tumultuous, the shouting of the children noisy. Tinh went out and yelled at them to scatter. But after a while, they returned to peek in and out from behind the hedge, discussing things, finally, forcing Tinh to tell his eldest brother to climb the areca tree in front of the house and hang the radio on the top branch of the tree. When Tinh's eldest brother did this, the children cheered loudly. Now not only the children, but the whole hamlet, could listen to the radio.

On his arrival, Hien had asked Sai's family to consider him as son of the family. They needn't, he said, be on formal terms. He urged his "mother" to relax. He offered to do the cooking with "Miss Tuyet." While working, he asked Tuyet about the farming, about her parents, about the collectivization of Ha Vi, about whether she had been able to visit Sai, and finally about whether there were still any problems between her and Sai. He asked her to feel free to take him into her confidence.

Only six years older than Sai, Hien seemed far more mature, both in appearance and manner than Sai. Still, Tuyet, despite her feelings, could never open her mouth to say anything harmful to her husband. She spoke to Hien happily, and when the talk turned to her husband, she defended him. "My husband must have been very busy, because he didn't have time to write to me. I don't feel uneasy about that. . . . When I saw him last, we treated each other nicely. . . . Yes, it's true that there have been problems with 'that activity,' but we're still young. It's nothing to worry about. I feel sure that . . . uncles and brothers at the unit would never allow Sai and me to 'lose solidarity.' I've heard rumors about this girl or that, but I don't consider the rumors. As far as I'm concerned, it is as if nothing has happened, until I've caught some woman by the hand, grabbed her by the hair."

Elsewhere in the house, Tinh was upset, busy wondering what his sister-in-law was saying to Hien. He hoped it wasn't anything that could have a negative effect on his brother's struggle with his career. Several times, he came to the kitchen door to interrupt Tuyet and Hien. "Let's have tea, comrade. Let them do the work," he said.

But Hien said, "Don't worry about me."

That left Tinh with no choice but to walk back and forth at the front end of the house with his hands clasped behind him. Still anxious, he went down to the *nha ngang*, the transversal house, to ask his wife, "Mother of the children, go over and help Sister Tuyet for me. Act as if it were not until just now that you could slip away from the baby to see how she was doing with her cooking."

Tinh's wife was close-mouthed and always acted as if she didn't know what was going on. Now, however, she called her husband back and whispered, "Father of the children, he was sent here mainly to investigate our brother. By doing this, it is as if we have done something wrong, but brother Sai has committed no fault. Our whole family has done nothing wrong. If there is a problem, it is a problem relating to Tuyet's father and brother. If she reported that Brother Sai rejected her, treated her badly or indifferently, Sai would miss the chance to be admitted to the Party. Father of our children, you shouldn't have to feel regret for anything, let alone for Sai abandoning her. Our father and mother have realized that they were foolish to cause their own son to suffer. Father and Mother won't force him anymore. Think about it and see what we can do to take care of our brother."

Tinh thought to himself that a whole year could go by and he wouldn't hear his wife say anything that sounded right, but perhaps this was his fault, perhaps he hadn't given her a chance to participate in any important discussion. Now she seemed to know even more about the investigation and Sai's admission to the Party than he. She sounded reasonable, calm, yet vigilant. But he couldn't follow her advice. He felt compelled, instead, to raise his voice in order to drown out her opinions, "I forbid you to say to anybody, especially to brother Sai that anybody would permit him to abandon his wife. His unit is curious about the relationship between him and his wife. They want to see whether or not he is behaving with the morality and the dignity of a revolutionary person."

After dinner and some strong drinks, the guests gathered in Scholar Khang's house for tea and talk until nine-thirty. The permanent staff members of the Village Party Committee and Hien left for Tinh's house then to discuss matters more formally. Tinh told his wife to take the children to go sleep with their grandmother in the kitchen, while he and his father sat in silence drinking tea, smoking, and waiting to talk with the others when the meeting was over. Before going to the meeting, Hien had whispered to Sai, "You don't have to wait for us. Go ahead and go to bed. Go to sleep in your room. She has been working hard. You have to love her. Good night."

Tuyet woke up very early the next morning to steam sticky rice and fry the leftover chicken for breakfast. Soon after, Hien woke. Through the open door, he saw Sai sitting in his room reading a book. Hien washed his face and brushed his teeth with the warm water that Scholar Khang had prepared. Down in the kitchen he took the liberty to ask Tuyet, "How was it, good?"

Tuyet looked up at him, smiled gently and then bent her head. A while later she turned to the wall and wiped her eyes with the flap of her shirt. When she turned back, she stared at the fire of damp brushwood as it crackled and sputtered.

"He must have been reading again!"

"No," Tuyet allowed, "he was sleeping from dark till dawn." Hien kept silent to show his sympathy. After a moment, he comforted her, "All right, be at ease!"

That evening, Hien and Sai went out for a walk. They walked side-by-side, so closely it was as if they were protecting each other from the immense coolness of the field. Although they worked in the same section and ate from the same kitchen, they had had, in the past, different responsibilities and had seldom had the opportunity to talk intimately. Now Hien had come to understand Sai and his family better. He explained that the section worried because they loved him. They were afraid that something would happen that would negatively affect Sai's bright future. "Don't let worthless things ruin your prospects, Sai," Hien advised.

Sai didn't respond.

"In fact, she may not make a good match for you, but she's well-behaved and doesn't mind hardship. While you're away from home, she helps care for your old parents when they are sick."

Sai remained silent.

Hien went on to point out that the local authorities had spoken favorably of Sai. It was true that the records of his wife's family were complicated, but Sai had nothing to do with these records, nor was he affected by them economically or politically. In the end, the local authority concluded, "If Sai has been striving hard enough by himself, we suggest that his unit admit him to the Party. The direct and important influences on Sai have been from his own parents, uncles and brothers. They are all cadres and Party members. His family is part of the strong foundation that makes up the mass base of the revolution. We will ask for further verifications from the district."

"The rest," Hien told Sai now, "depends upon your relationship with your wife. If we could get this settled, basically everything would be all set."

Hien said everything, everything in his heart and mind, but he saw Sai was still silent. In fact, he had been silent since they started walking together. "Now I have something to tell you. Before I left, the Deputy Director told me to do everything I could to help the two of you love each other. Real love, not love 'in general' as before. He told me that you had promised him you would love your wife. I came here to see whether you have kept your promise. I find it hard to talk about this matter. But just imagine, if you were to be admitted to the Party, and later, people in the regiment found out you loved your wife only when it was expedient, then how would the Party cell explain the situation?"

"All right, be at ease. I know that all of the superiors and brothers love me and care for me. I'll try not to betray your kindness." Sai had wanted to add, "If I don't do exactly what you ask, then when I return to the unit, the faculty staff, the youth branch and the political section will have to waste more time on this, and I will have to write self-criticism explaining why I rejected my wife. The superiors will say, 'You reject her because your hearts are unmatched? What have hearts to do with this? There's no such things as unmatched hearts.' "

Sai kept silent. He wiped his eyes with a handkerchief. Hien consoled him, expressing his emotion and love for him even more clearly than before. The next morning, while washing his face by the tank, Hien saw Tuyet coming out to get water, he asked the same question as the day before, "How was it, my sister, good?"

Tuyet blushed scarlet and tried to evade the question. She said things like: "When will you and my husband leave?" and "When you have a mission in this area, please drop by to visit my parents. Brother, it must be very cold at your unit now. . . . When I was there the sea was roaring all day. At night, it was frightening, just wind and more wind"

Madame Khang felt that after all his hardships, happiness had finally come to her son. After seven or eight years of putting pressure on Sai, the fire of affinity between Tuyet and Sai seemed to have flamed up. Madame Khang felt that if her life were to end today, she would be fully satisfied with her fate, because her son was not to be parted from his wife. In the past, Madame Khang had felt for her youngest son's unhappy situation with Tuyet, but it was not good for the family's reputation if Sai "threw away his load half-way." At times, the old woman had to contain her impulses, because she thought Tuyet was like her father, the old Canton Chief, insolent and impolite to others. Madame Khang couldn't say she'd never had an urge to throw Tuyet out herself, but now, things had been settled by Sai's unit. For the old woman, such a method of resolution was ideal.

As Sai and Hien were heading up the road with the bicycle, she ran after them. She took Hien's hand hastily in both of her own hands, and said something that perhaps only Hien could understand, "My nephew, I am grateful to you and to the superiors. Only the superiors could have scared Sai. Through the years, countless people, including his father, have spoken to him, but it did no good. Now happiness has come to our family. Due to the help of the unit, the couple is getting along well with each other. I entrust you, and the other brothers and comrades, to advise and to coach him as your younger brother. A word from the superiors is worth more than tens of thousands of words from parents, brothers and sisters at home."

She turned and spoke loudly to her son standing a few steps from her, "I wish you good health while you're away from home, and don't do anything against the will of your superiors, your brothers in the unit."

Hien laughed loudly, and grasped her hand tightly, "Mother, don't worry, in the army, even wild tigers and bears can be trained into rabbits."

The mother smiled at the man's exuberant confidence. Tears flowed to the wrinkled corners of her eyes and rolled down her cheeks to her mouth. She swallowed them and smiled again, a smile that looked as if it would soon be followed by more tears. She had to turn away quickly in order not weaken her son's resolve before he left to travel to a faraway place from which there would be little news.

Huong wrote a letter to Hieu on the fifteenth of August, or exactly one month after leaving the area where Sai's unit was quartered:

"Because I respect you as my real brother, I don't want to conceal anything from you. I am wondering why you weren't honest with me. If I had known Sai and I were not permitted to see each other, I wouldn't have been expecting so much. I was startled on the bus when I heard that Sai had been in his home unit during my visit. I had wanted to throw myself under the bus then. But it was not possible. A girl like me can't do such things.

"I have written a few letters to Sai to find out the truth, but I always tear them up, for fear that he is having difficulties, and these letters would only aggravate his problems. I know that Sai has always been very faint-hearted.

"Fortunately, it's now summer; otherwise my studies would have suffered. I can't tell you how hard things have been. For almost a month, I fussed, moping about, unable to understand why Sai hadn't come to me when I visited. Had Sai really been sent on mission or was he in his unit? Not until the day before yesterday when I arrived at the hospital to ask for medical advice about my 'breakdown,' did I meet Kim, the nurse at the regiment's dispensary. Kim is a sister of the doctor who was treating me. Kim said that Sai didn't go anywhere during those days I was visiting.

"To tell the truth, when I heard this, I was very angry at you. But I think that a man like you would not be cruel, so please forgive me for these discourteous words. Kim said that you're a man of virtue, that you brought Sai into your unit and that you were responsible for sending him to college. So why did you do what you did? Is Sai still angry with me? If that is the case, will you please tell him that I am willing to spend my whole summer vacation at his place, and am ready to do whatever he wants me to do. Even if he doesn't want anything from me, that will be fine too. He doesn't have to be evasive.

"Only to you, I want to say that I once misunderstood Sai, and now I don't want to make him suffer anymore. You can consider me a sister of yours. Tell me what has happened and what I should do. I know that you're very busy, but please try to find time to write me a few words. I thank you very much. Please remind Sai not to smoke the water pipe too much. If you're not angry at me any more, write me a few words. Please extend my regards for the good health of your wife and children."

One month later Hieu sent Huong a letter. He said that he was just returning from a mission and started writing his reply right after receiving Huong's letter. In truth, it had taken such a long time to write because it was difficult for him to tell lies for an entire letter. What he had wanted to do was write and say that for Sai and Huong, he would do anything. If they had found it necessary, he would have been willing to sell the Thong Nhat bicycle that he had just been allocated. He would be willing to give away his watch, his only possession. But if they asked him to explain everything he had done, he couldn't do that. He also couldn't give her any advice. Would he tell Huong to stop her relationship with Sai? How could he? Their love was so pure, so passionate. Would he tell them to go ahead? He didn't dare.

From the beginning he had tried to advise or protect Sai whenever he could, but he was caught between human feelings and professional obligations. If he had seen things only from the latter point of view, he would be a vicious person. If he acted only to satisfy his heart, he would be a man without goals. Why couldn't these two duties be reconciled? From time to time, Hieu asked himself that question. He asked, but he didn't know how to answer. He only knew that if the affair between Sai and Huong became public, Sai would have nothing. No matter how talented he was, he would not be acceptable. Sensing the danger, Hieu had to interfere – sometimes callously – to prevent Sai from revealing his feelings or acting on his will. When Sai was fired and disdained, would Huong still have the courage to love him? If she did, Hien would respect her bravery, but condemn her foolhardiness.

Hieu thought all these things. But when he finally had to consider what to write to Sai's young friend, he was at a loss. After hesitating, he wrote a letter which avoided all her questions, while still showing, to the greatest extent possible, his sincerity. He wrote that from now on, he would officially consider Huong his sister. He would forever love her frankness and gentleness. About what she asked, he promised that some time in the future, when the situation allowed, he would tell her everything. For the time being, Huong had to be calm and concentrate on her studies. No matter what might happen in her relationship with Sai, he would always be her brother and his brother. He loved them both.

About a half month after he had mailed his letter, he received another letter from Huong. She was, she told him, very happy because from now on she had a brother, one who was trustworthy and a great consolation for her sufferings and loneliness. No matter what happened between her and Sai, she would still earnestly hope to be Hieu's sister, to be taught and advised by him.

But, she confessed, though Hieu's letters made her happy, they did not subdue her anxiety, her longing for news from Sai. *Dear Brother, why does Sai still not write to me? Please tell Sai not to keep silent any longer. Does Sai know that I'm dying every hour, every minute because of him? Why has Sai been so selfish, so cruel? For what reason? I would accept a letter even if it were only just one line. There is no reason for him to keep silent any longer. My respectable brother, would you speak to Sai for me? I thank you very much.*

Hieu couldn't answer Huong, because he didn't know how to. How could he let her know that Sai didn't know about her letters?

In the absence of letters, Sai wondered about Huong all the time. He told Hieu, "Last Tet, I thought that she didn't want to see me. During my time at college, I went to the Polytechnical Institute twice, but both times she was out. I thought she was trying to dodge me, and I developed a grudge which started to obliterate my love for her. But then Huong took the initiative to come here looking for me. Let me write a last letter telling her everything and hoping that she will understand my present situation. I'll advise Huong to love another, so that she will suffer less."

"It won't be the last letter," Hieu said. "She doesn't need your advice telling her to go ahead and love another. The best solution is silence. Try to restrain yourself and you'll be gradually accustomed to it."

Another letter from Huong arrived. Hieu kept silent. The letter was dated on the fifteenth of March, three months after the second letter, for which she had not yet received any reply from Hieu.

In this letter, she wrote, "*Dear respectable Brother Hieu, now I've found out why you didn't explain to me what I asked you to explain. I also understand your silence after my last two letters. I beg your pardon for having disturbed you. If you don't hold me in contempt, let us maintain a brother-sister relationship as you agreed to in your previous letter. Writing you this time, I feel embarrassed and ashamed, because I have loved other people too much, trusted them too much, let my emotions go too freely. I have been deceived. My only regret is that the one who has deceived me, who betrayed me, who pushed me down to the bottom of the pit is the same one whom I pity for not knowing how to hold on to happiness when it is in his hand.*

"*For the last five years, I have been crazy enough to believe that a resolute-minded person like Sai might be planning something, might be preparing to bring in a new era for himself and for me. I had been willing to endure, willing to wait until Sai was 'liberated.' Ten days together in freedom would have been worth the five years I've spent under constraint. But I was totally mistaken.*

"Perhaps, for the last few years, you have purposely kept Sai from seeing me, from playing cat and mouse with his fake love! If you had not done this, what would have become of me as a result of his betrayal?

"Dear Brother Hieu, once again please forgive me for my unrefined words. Because I want to confide in you, I can't find any better words. I have to stop here, because if I keep going on, I will be unable to contain my resentment. Please extend my regards and respect to my sister, your wife, and tell the children to keep well-behaved and studious. If you don't feel it inconvenient, write me a few lines. Your little sister."

She did not explain her resentment. Perhaps she assumed that Hieu knew everything, and she need not speak about something she considered sickening.

Sai's wife had been pregnant now for three months when Sai received the news through Tinh. Neither sad, nor happy, he had been as indifferent as any pedestrian seeing a woman carrying a heaving belly toward him. After scanning the letter once, he put it in the middle of the table as if it were a public document. Anyone who wanted to read it carefully or just take a glance at it could. At the news, friends in the section offered neither congratulations, comments nor jokes. Everybody felt that this information was like a fragile object, resting atop an unstable base.

During the last month, had Sai been sad or happy? People had no need to discuss it. They only knew that Sai still had to go to class and prepare his lectures regularly, had to wake up early to work in the morning and do his agricultural tasks in the afternoon, had to eat and sleep, participate in the Youth League activities on Friday evenings, practice singing on Thursday nights, do socialist labor on Sunday mornings, and go to the Section Five meeting that same night to review the week's achievements. He had to maintain order and discipline, neither languish nor be absent, gradually, as Hieu had said, he would get used to it. Tonight, after a whole day of "representing" the political section in shoveling coal for the cook, Sai had been sleeping soundly since nine. Hieu had just finished reading Huong's angry letter. Hieu stood up to drop the mosquito net for Sai. With his hand still on the mosquito net, Hieu looked at Sai's face, sullen but full of energy, even in sleep. Should he have to bear, however unknowingly, Huong's insults? Hieu drew a long sigh, then he quietly turned to switch off the table lamp beside his bed, drop his own mosquito net and lie down to sleep.

Two hours later, he was still awake, a dull pain on one side of his head. He got up, walked quietly up and down the paved road that in daytime shimmered like a new aluminum handle fitted to the pan of the round hill. He thought about how Sai had "loved" his wife. The result was a baby to be born, and a letter from Huong!

Nearly two months later, Hieu had still said nothing about Huong's letter when he received another note from her. This time the note was a wedding card; Huong was going to get married. A few days before Hieu received the card, the Staff-Political-Logistic Joint Party Committee refused to admit Sai to the Party. Sai's individual record was very good, the Joint Party Committee admitted. His family was of the basic class background, and they had had a good influence on him. Before and after the revolution, the family had not been involved in anything that could be considered politically complicated.

However, his wife's family was a grave problem. Sai's father-in-law had blood debts. His brother-in-law and father-in-law had worked as informers for the former regime, bringing about the arrests of a large number of local cadres, including Sai's uncle and brother. The local authorities had confirmed that Sai had not been influenced – either economically or politically – by his wife's family. But that didn't matter, it was a social problem that remained very complicated and needed time for scrutiny.

Nobody could say how much time would be needed for this scrutiny. It was only said that there must be enough time to judge the influence Tuyet's family had on Sai and then there must be time to evaluate whether Sai was properly motivated, whether his determination and enthusiasm could be shaken and whether his acts would lack courage.

As a Cell Committee member Directly in Charge of the Masses, Hieu could no better answer the question of how long this would take than anyone else. Hieu didn't bother to tell Sai that, even he had no right to ask about Sai's status. He only told Sai to be persistent, to consider this ordeal as a test of his endurance.

Fifteen days later, Sai found out that the matter was decided: he was not to be admitted to the Party. On the same day, Sai learned that Huong had married. It was the worst possible outcome as far as Hieu was concerned. So bad, that Hieu could barely eat his bowl of rice when it came time for meals; and since officers ate in a separate mess hall from enlisted men then, later even soldiers like Sai, men who were clever and paid close attention to every minor gesture of their superiors, couldn't figure out why Hieu had become so suddenly emaciated.

Chief of the Party Committee Do Manh and the Commander of the regiment lived in a flat-roofed house on top of the hill. This was the only house that had a "sky-terrace" so people jokingly referred to Do Manh and the Commander as the "sky-men." The "sky-men" listened and had a thorough understanding about everything, not only at the infantry regiment headquarters, but in every company in the regiment. Nothing could be concealed from Do Manh. But, though he knew a lot, he could not do a lot. He didn't have sufficient power, not because his regulations and orders were not strict enough to make things work in an appropriate manner, the problem was there were still quite a few relationships that he couldn't ignore simply to do things his own way. The result was Do Manh often felt frustrated. There were certainly times when he couldn't act, even when he saw how things could be resolved to satisfy the demands of the people and the Revolution.

Sai's situation was a perfect example. As the Secretary of the Party Committee of the Regiment (which was the superior Party organization of the Staff-Political-Logistic Joint Party Cell's Committee), he could not make use of his individual power as a Political Officer to impose his will on the lower Party committees. Nor could he use the collective power of the regiment Party committee to do things in the domain where lower Party committees had authority to make decisions. What's more, the act of refusing or delaying the admission of a person from the masses to the Party could never be contested. Only a crazy person would try to argue the decision by saying, "I am very good" or "I've contributed a lot and have sacrificed a lot. The higher authority should order the Party cell to admit me to the Party."

Indeed, even if the higher apparatus had received letters questioning the decision, the most they could do was suggest that the local cells study the case more thoroughly. In the case of Sai, not only had the local cells refused to continue the case, they had provided enough reasons for turning Sai down that their superiors could not blame them for making the decision they had. The majority of the members of the joint Party cells had made the decision and had announced the joint resolution, and now the Political Officer had no more options.

Nobody knew when the Political Officer had been given notice, but two days before he left the regiment they learned that he had been mobilized for the front. After his farewell party with the regimental cadres, Do Manh detained Hieu and Hien. The two of them stayed with the Political Officer until late into the night. He talked to them about what he considered decent human behavior, about how to conduct oneself and pay attention to others' interests. Do Manh told them they were criminals in the satisfaction they took concerning their contributions to the masses, and their involvement with Sai and his wife was a case in point.

"Who," Do Manh asked, "did you think you were? You told him to love his wife as a precondition to being admitted to the Party. He 'loved' his wife as you instructed. Then he was not admitted because her family history records were bad. Can you see that you have created a tragedy? I am not supposed to urge him, or urge you to tell him, to abandon his wife. I can't do that. I'm not like you two. It's not that I'm afraid the giving of such advice would mitigate my achievements in the task of educating our men. I worry more about those who already have children, who have had chances to get to know and love their wives, who have sworn oaths as lasting as steel and stone, but at a new billet, especially in a crowded and pleasant town, upon seeing young women, find reason to abandon their wives and their children. As Political Officer, I do not allow myself to let things like this happen in my regiment. That's why whenever there is any threat of this kind in the social environment, I have to give warnings.

"Your way of dealing with the situation with Sai made things easier for you. That was swift and wise. But haven't you killed his purity of heart, genuine faith and true love of the Revolution, the army and our splendid society?

"I talk to you about these things after what has happened, so the experience will prove useful. As a Political Officer I've done a few things for the regiment as a whole, but as for particular individuals, I've had nothing but regret and endless 'useful' experiences.

"When an experience is 'useful,' things have already proceeded too far. We have already in essence terminated a soul, pushed a person from good to bad, from love to hate, sometimes even destroyed his whole life! Don't you think so? It's true we must be resolute, resolute to a merciless and ruthless extent. We must force every soldier to take seriously the principles behind the regulations, orders, rules and laws of the army and of the state. We must make our soldiers cherish human dignity and socialist morality. But we're not allowed to force others to love what we love, hate what we hate. This would be love or hate as commanded by the leaders. When the leader loved somebody, the rest would flock around and love that same one, identifying themselves with that person in order to be honored. When the leader hated someone, all the rest would try to stay away from that person, hate him. They would offer him an 'additional push as he goes down hill.'

"I apologize, I am going to tell you a story about Hieu. A few years ago I noticed and smiled to myself about the 'progressiveness' of Hieu.

"Hien, you came later and didn't see all this.

"Hieu, for perhaps more than a decade, you've known my affection for you. Whenever I needed a capable cadre, one who could do tasks intelligently, meticulously, quickly and accurately, one who could make concessions and take care of his inferiors, one who would live honestly and who would not provoke envy in others, I would come to you, dear Hieu.

"I have felt this way about you for almost a decade. But recently, you have become 'backward,' then 'progressive' again. When the regulations started allowing officers to wear civilian clothes on holidays and after office hours, you, as well as others, purchased 'dress' clothes. You had a spotlessly white 'shrimp tail' shirt, a pair of French khaki trousers and a pair of sandals with tan straps. All this looked very chic and went well with your tall figure and fair complexion. One Sunday morning, I saw you downtown, and you looked terrific. I thought to myself that if I had been young and good-looking, I would have tried to get a suit of clothes like that myself. But I am an old man – clumsy and old. I couldn't put myself in the 'race.' Still, I had no objection to your attire. If the conditions of an individual allowed it, and if it didn't violate any principle or regulation, why should we restrict our men from being well-dressed?

"A few months later, there were rumors in the regiment headquarters. I heard that Hieu had 'degenerated,' that he was 'pinned with a petit-bourgeois tail.' He had 'departed from the masses' and was 'no longer simple and humble.' There were countless other evil charges. The Political Director whispered to me, 'Something's wrong with Hieu's thought.'

"I burst into laughter: 'What misery! He has had only one suit of civilian clothes in his entire life. Let him wear it; it has nothing to do with his thoughts. Of course, given our looks, even if we had ourselves painted, we couldn't improve our appearance much, so we have no choice but to stay in military dress.'

"I quieted those rumors immediately, but Hieu himself didn't want to be responsible for what he was fond of, for his sense of style. He pleased everybody by tucking his 'shrimp tail' shirt into his roomy, patched-up military pants. Dressed so, he went hoeing and carried dung and ash, so that not long after, the shirt turned dirty, wrinkled and stained. Then on Sundays he went downtown with the khaki pants and the army shirt with the collar turned inside out and patched at the shoulder. With the odd match of clothes that betrayed his sense of style, Hieu became a 'simple' person, 'a good mixer,' 'a man with a clear-cut stand,' a cadre of 'pure ethics.' He turned out to be absolutely 'progressive.'

"You see why I am telling you this story? It points to a danger, and that danger is that we don't know in what way this thinking of ours has permeated us to become a part of our very flesh and blood. We don't recognize when it has taken hold of us and affected every area of our social activities.

"I must admit that I feel very depressed about this matter of 'living other people's lives,' about the so-called collective concern.

"Feel free to demand from every individual their utmost contribution to the needs of the society and community. But as a community, our concern must take into account what he needs, what he himself is hungry or thirsty for, not what we want him to be.

"Apropos of Sai, I just want to tell you my thoughts, without suggesting that these thoughts can do anything to help him now. As I said, it is up to the joint Party cell to reconsider and act accordingly in this case. You should also mobilize to comfort him. You have to stand up for what you think is correct. You have to have the courage to be responsible for his personality and record."

But as Do Manh had said, all this knowledgc just amounted to useful information for the future. What had passed, had passed. Sai was not to be admitted to the Party, and Huong had married. Sai could not go crazy at this news. He could not get angry, lie idle or start acting irresponsibly. He still had to get up early and go to work. He still had to work in the field, prepare lectures, go to class regularly, attend Youth League activities on Friday evenings and voice lessons on Thursday nights. His life still had to go on, as before.

CHAPTER 6

Even today, no one could fully explain the idealism of soldiers in those days. These were the last months of 1964. Units sent to reinforce the front had reached the scale of regiments. A phrase such as "going B," which meant go to the South, still had to be whispered. Soldiers wishing to "go B" had to be selected and out of every several hundred volunteers, only ten were picked. Those who were already soldiers put in their applications to go B. Young people in the countryside, in factories or in schools volunteered to join the army. Almost every youth volunteered at least once to fight. They were ready to sacrifice their lives for their country, for victory over the southern regime and for all their compatriots in the South. Applications were written in ink, in pencil, even in blood.

Nobody knew the precise motivation for this fervor. But certainly, there were ample reasons: the Maddox, the 7th Fleet, the Destroyers, the "retaliatory" bombing of the jets. The bombs that were dropped on Lach Truong, Hon Gai on the fifth of August ignited people's anger and stirred their fighting spirit, the spirit that has always been more than ample in every citizen. This spirit rumbled over all the radio broadcasts. It occupied the pages of the daily papers. The energy built like the momentum of a tank; and it wouldn't be stopped for a particle of dust stuck in its tread.

A year after the Political Officer Do Manh left for the front, the infantry regiment was waiting for information about who would be sent next. The soldiers asked their superiors when it would be their turn to fulfill their sacred duty. "Regardless of hardships," they were ready to shed their blood, and they didn't think about the day of their return. Sai was among these most enthusiastic. He had put in three applications and dispatched several letters to the regiment Party committee and to the Party committee of the headquarters of the military zone requesting to be sent. Two of Sai's letters were written in blood pricked from his finger.

Sai's actions were hardly surprising. In the meetings of the Military Zone, his name, together with hundreds of others, had been mentioned, since he was considered a leader in his fighting duties. Cadres and soldiers looked at him with respect and affection. Only Hieu and Hien could read between the lines of Sai's applications. They couldn't deny his great desire to become a valiant soldier at the front like tens of thousands of other young people, but the regiment was in need of teachers, especially good ones. Besides, they were fond of Sai and wanted to do everything for their "youngest brother." Hieu, in particular, felt the love of a father, mother, teacher, friend, lover and even obedient younger brother for Sai.

One night, not long after Sai had submitted his third application to go to the front, he and Hieu were out walking. Hieu turned to Sai, "I've heard that in the near future an entire E or F battalion or regiment might be mobilized for the front. Stay so that we can go together."

"Oh, please!" Sai said, "Push that application for me. The sooner I go, the less suffering I have to bear." Hieu was silent, as if he had committed a crime by speaking. It was almost a year now since Tuyet had given birth to a boy. After the birth, Tuyet started to act as if she had, at last, a hold on happiness in her family. Meanwhile Sai had grown sadder and sadder. He felt for himself, but he was even more worried about his child. He wondered what would happen to him. Only one thing was sure: his son would have only one parent, either father or mother. Since the time he had forced himself to carry out Hien's "instruction," Sai realized he couldn't be that "courageous" again in his life. So, divorce? It was now more impossible than before. Sai could figure only one way out: Go South. Once he crossed the border, nobody could pursue him to bring him back. The war was half-open, half-secret. In such an atmosphere, nobody would force him to write home, to be in "solidarity" with his wife. In combat, there would be countless reasons not to bother about these affairs.

Hieu understood all this. He knew that since his son had been born, Sai had been willing to send home all the sugar from his monthly ration. He was willing to buy fresh prawns to make gruel for his son, but he was afraid to go home himself. Sai often wished Tuyet would go off somewhere. If only she would have an affair! Then, she would have to leave the baby home with his grandparents, and Sai could ask for some days off to go home and play with his son. The dreamed-of situation never occurred, but Sai did have to go home, finally, when he was chosen as one of the fifty-two cadres and soldiers from his regiment to reinforce a unit going B. Hieu took the opportunity to volunteer to spend the entire two-week leave before the deployment with Sai. Hieu was thinking that this might be a last farewell and the friendship between the two had been looking for just such an opportunity to find expression.

They arrived in Ha Vi at dusk. This time, no children followed them and nothing was prepared in advance. Scholar Khang was the first one to see them. From his house, he called toward the alley, "It seems like Sai is coming home. Is that you, my son?"

His wife rushed out from the kitchen and scolded him, "If it is Sai why are you standing dumbfounded like that? Where is he?"

She ran toward the alley just as Sai and Hieu were entering. They greeted her with one voice: "Hello, Mother."

As usual, she touched his arms then the head, then the back of her son. She smiled, and tears trickled down her cheeks. "Is this Hien?"

"Mother, I am Hieu."

"It's brother Hieu this time," Sai said. "Brother Tinh has probably told you and father about him."

"Right, right, Brother Hieu from My Duc in Ha Dong. Oh, we are honored to receive you. Our entire family has been expecting you and Sai."

Tinh's wife acted as if she had just passed by chance, and after saying "Welcome" and "Hello, Brother Sai!" she went straight to the inner hamlet half a kilometer away to call a cousin for whom Tinh had just found a job as a railroad worker. "I have to ask you to help me with something very important. Take your bicycle and go immediately to the district to tell Tinh that Sai and Hieu are home."

On her way back, Tinh's wife dropped in on the eldest brother's house. "Sai has brought a friend home, go over there and see what you can do," she told him.

Her sister-in-law was indifferent to the news. "Our parents and Brother Tinh are there already. My husband is in the middle of something that has to be done."

"Tell him to forget it," Tinh's wife ordered. "Run over to talk with our guest for a while. My husband has not yet arrived. Our father is old, not accustomed to talking in a modern way. We are not supposed to let our guest sit idle there."

"Have you sent anyone for Tinh yet?" asked the eldest brother. Tinh's wife nodded her head. "All right, you just go home first, I'll be there in a moment."

Although the eldest brother had ventured, as he always did, to make the decision without asking his wife's opinion, Tinh's wife smiled on her way home and thought, his "in a moment" might stretch until midnight.

Arriving home, Tinh's wife was scolded by her mother-in-law, "How good Tinh's wife is! She must have intended to leave everything to this old woman!"

Tinh's wife said matter-of-factly, "Every little thing makes you irritable. Didn't you send someone to call your son home?"

Scholar Khang's wife suddenly realized that she had forgotten the most important thing. To disguise her embarrassment, she raised her voice, "So what are we going to do now?"

"What else but tell Tuyet to kill a chicken, cook a pot of rice, stir-fry a plate of turnips and make a bowl of noodle soup?"

"No matter what," Khang's wife said, "hurry or we won't have anything to eat until very late at night."

Familiar with her mother-in-law's irritable nature, Tinh's wife went back into the house and began preparations. She and her husband had been cooking separately from their in-laws for a decade now. They had no "economic relation" with the big family, but every time there were guests, especially guests of brother Sai, the "back house" only had to kill a chicken and cook a pot of rice, and she would take care of the rest.

Tinh and his wife had built a house, large and neat, called the "front house." In between the "back house" and the "front house" there was only a small yard, and guests often didn't realize the households were separate. The "back house" remained ragged and poor as it had been in the days of the flooding of Ha Vi village. Meanwhile the "front house" was fully furnished, and Tinh and his wife lived there like any well-to-do, urbane family residing in a provincial town.

For the last few years, the Ha Vi villagers had been growing potatoes and manioc for the state and had been allocated rice on a monthly basis in exchange. As a result, Ha Vi no longer experienced hunger. No matter how poor a household was, they had a pig, several chickens and dozens of kilos of rice. Still, when they received distinguished guests, the "back house" only had boiled chicken blood mixed with salt for dipping. This (dip) they made, however, had such a distinguishing characteristic that some families that had left the village three generations previously still couldn't use any other sauce for boiled chicken. The "front house," however, always had onion, garlic, galingale, fermented rice, ginger and saffron. They also had black pepper and curry powder; fresh and dried hot pepper; lemon, vinegar, and berry jam; arrow root and herb liquor. In the front house, the bottles were always full of filtered water and the thermos full of hot water.

Whenever distinguished guests of Tinh or friends from Sai's unit visited, Tinh's wife had to know what to serve in keeping with the season and current fashion to satisfy the appetite of the guests. If guests of the "back house" stayed for dinner, her mother-in-law would kill a chicken, and Tinh's wife would "supply" the spices. If they wanted a "special dish," however, they would call a certain cousin, a bit hard of hearing and very clever, who had been trained by Tinh and had been sent on a "visiting tour" of the district restaurants. As a result, those who came for dinner or even just for a glass of arrow root couldn't say that Ha Vi village "chopped big and fried salty." Instead, guests admired Ha Vi as a civilized country village.

Now, Tinh's wife would arrange biscuits and place a pack of peanut candy on a plate. Then, she would call Sai outside and would say, "Ask Father and Brother Hieu to have some of these to hold them over till dinner."

Meanwhile, she would go to the garden to pull up some turnips and a bunch of onions, then she would gather ginger, black pepper, herb liquor, bowls and trays, hot pepper and other spices, then give them with instructions to Tuyet. After that, she would wash her hands and feet, go back to the "front house" to place a blanket, sleeping mat, mosquito net and pillow on the fan-shaped bed in the guest room. Finally, she would call her two children in to wash. "Hurry up, Father is about to arrive," she said.

≣ The next morning she would rise early to boil the water, clean the kettle and wash the cups, so that when the guests awoke hot water would be ready for them to wash their faces and make tea. After doing all this work for others, she would never eat a piece of meat or take a bowl of broth until after the "back house" was through with the meal. Even the children were not allowed to loiter around, though their grandmother sometimes hid something away for them, behind Tinh's wife's back.

At first the grandmother would feel uneasy, causing Tinh to raise his voice, "Did you prepare this meal to serve the guests, or to serve my wife and my kids? If they want, fix something for them separately. There's chicken and everything else here. We lack nothing." The old woman responded by bursting into a diatribe about those who took advantage of the presence of guests to abandon their children.

Tinh arrived home when they were about to bring the tray of food up from the kitchen. Hearing the bicycle's wheels approaching the yard, Hieu ran out and called, "Is that Brother Tinh?" Tinh threw the bicycle on the bamboo screen and hugged Hieu tightly. They had been writing to each other for a year now. Their friendship grew around their love for Sai. They greeted each other warmly, trading stories of the circumstances that had brought them together. Tinh then excused himself to bring the lantern down to the kitchen to examine the tray of food. The pieces of chicken had been arranged in a dish with the insides up, so it could be flipped over onto a second plate. Once flipped, the chicken would take the shape of the dish. The rich golden skin would make the chicken look so smooth that it would seem as if it had no bones. In addition to the chicken, there was a dish of stir-fry turnip, a dish of fried vermicelli and two bowls of soup. Next to all of this was mixed with salt blood pudding, lemon, hot pepper and black pepper. Empty dishes and bowls were also laid with chopsticks on a tray along with a pot filled with liquor. Inside every bowl was a piece of paper. Tinh could see that the meal had been cooked and arranged under the instruction of his wife. He nodded, satisfied: "This is fine. Very good."

After he had given his approval, Tinh handed the lantern to his mother and carried the tray of food himself. When he reached the door, he began to speak without stopping, "All right, Father, Brother Hieu, Sai, let's be seated. Oh, eldest brother is here already. Please have dinner with us. It is not very well-prepared, but let's just eat what is available for the time being. Fortunately, I just returned from one of the villages when our cousin came to inform me of your arrival. I didn't even have time to change my shirt. I want to report to Brother Hieu that this year my district has had the most abundant crop ever, an average of 37.5 kilos of paddy rice per capita per month. The zone on the other side of the main dike has been specializing in planting jute, soy bean and sugarcane. They sell all this to the state and live on rationed rice. Corn, sweet potato and banana root used to be our main food supplies, but now those items are used for livestock. Now, let's start, Father, Brother. Eldest Brother, please draw your legs up properly. This medicinal liquor is made with a pair of jungle gekkos that a logger gave me. I soaked them with three kilograms of wild roots in alcohol. I report to you, Brother, that in my district, some villages have collected tons of *thuc dia* this year. Help yourself! Make yourself at home. This year my district has recruited three times more troops than in the previous decade. The departure of troops has resulted in a better living condition for the people in the rear. A great occasion. Eldest Brother, please hand me a bamboo splinter. Brother Hieu, while staying here, please consider our parents, brothers and sisters as your own family. Sai, help yourself to the food. If you think it necessary, take the bicycle with you when you leave . . ."

Tinh talked ceaselessly throughout the meal, stopping only to serve the guest and his father. When the meal was over, only Tinh and Hieu remained talking. Both Scholar Khang and the eldest brother were nodding off, but they still had to sit on the divan to "keep the guest company." But when Tinh realized that the conversation only needed two people, he urged his father and brother to go to sleep. Both acted like they had just been "liberated," but said, "We apologize, please continue."

It was then that Hieu told Tinh the reasons why Sai had not been admitted to the Party. After more than a year of consideration, the matter had still seemed complicated. "A problem of history," Hieu explained. What could be done? Every responsible person in the Party cell and in the youth joint cell, lamented and regretted the decision. Everyone—from Do Manh, the former Political Officer, all the way down to members of Sai's section – loved Sai with a love that had only increased over time.

All of this information from Hieu left Tinh at ease about the motivations of his brother. Tinh felt confident that, sooner or later,

Sai would be admitted to the Party, and when he was, all sorts of possibilities would open. But then Hieu informed Tinh that Sai was "going B." Tinh was stunned. His whole body flushed and he felt suddenly dizzy. He had always hoped that his loved ones would be on the front lines, and now his brother would be the first from this village to go to "B," to that place which meant separation and sacrifice, but also great honor for those who went!

The next day Tinh wrote a solemn letter and had it carried to Mr. Ha in the province capital. He then went to buy a watch – a Russian Poliot – batteries, vitamins, ginseng roots and pills. . . . Everything Sai might need or want, as well as those things rumored necessary for the battlefield. Tinh bought the best items for his brother. Dozens of his friends ran back and forth to help him do the shopping. If Tinh had had to tear down his own house to buy the necessary things for Sai, he would have done it.

For all of his five nights at home, Sai slept in the same bed as Hieu. Nobody urged him to sleep with Tuyet. This was in part because Khang and his wife knew how little influence they had over Sai now, and also because they were satisfied with their grandson, a healthy boy who looked exactly like his father. No matter where Sai might go now, Khang and his wife felt at ease – though they didn't yet know about his current plans to "go B." They told their grandson, "No matter what happens between your father and mother. You're our grandson. Don't worry about them."

Meanwhile, the happiness that Tuyet had "grasped" had made her feel more self-assured, but she still felt an ardent desire for Sai's attention. She would have settled on being scolded, even punched or slapped . . . for if Sai treated her roughly and rudely she would at least have the reputation of being a married woman who was fought with, cursed at and been rejected by her husband. But as things were, it was as if she had no husband. When the two met each other, it was as if wood were meeting stone. They never opened their mouths to talk – not even for half a sentence. "He sees me as a leper," Tuyet would think. "He has to step aside and turn around to face the other way when he sees me coming."

Sometimes when Sai was alone in the "front house," Tuyet carried her son to the house and told him to call "Da Da." At the sound, Sai hurriedly ran out the door as if being chased, running all the way to his eldest brother's house, telling his nephews to call his son over to play. Sai never received his son directly from Tuyet's hands and there was nothing she could do about it. There was no way she could leverage his love.

Hieu talked with her, but never mentioned anything about her living together with her husband, or what the unit would do to help Sai love his wife. Tinh also said nothing to remind his brother about Tuyet. And when Tuyet saw that Tinh, too, seemed to be avoiding her, she knew something had happened. Every night she wondered what it was. She'd cry and embrace her son. Finally, she was no longer comforted by her father and brother's assurances. They'd always said, "Even if he had five heads and six hands, he wouldn't dare abandon you! You tell Ha, Tinh and Sai that if they really want to go home and tend chickens, they should be brave enough to let Sai divorce you. I dare the whole batch of them."

After five days, it was time for Sai to depart. Everyone came to see Sai off: Uncle Ha from the province, Tinh's friends, and countless acquaintances and relatives. Sai still had ten vacation days before he had to report to the troop's embarkation point, but he didn't want to stay home any longer. Hieu planned for Sai to stay at his house for the rest of his leave. Hieu hoped that with the love and care of his parents and his wife, the stay in Hieu's home village would help appease Sai's sadness. But Sai stayed with Hieu's family for only three days, then asked Hieu to go to Hanoi. "Let's not stay at anyone's house any more," Sai said. "It limits our freedom."

Hieu conceded. They went to the 66th Station. Every day Hieu busied himself buying equipment or textbooks for the club or stayed home and read. Sai, meanwhile, took the streetcar to Cau Giay then strolled slowly toward Mai Dich. He walked without stopping at anyone's house, without buying anything. For four days he walked around seemingly without purpose.

At the end of the fourth day, after dinner, Sai said to Hieu, "Come to Cau Giay with me."

Hieu, as if he knew nothing, said, "Why do you want to go there?"

"Do you know the place where Huong lives?"

"I do."

"Go with me there."

Hieu had not intended to see Huong on this visit. He didn't know what he would say in the presence of Sai, Huong and her husband. And what good would a visit do if Huong's attitude was the same as it had been in the letter she had written before she married? Sai still knew nothing about the letter, and Hieu still couldn't bring himself to say anything about the matter. But Sai insisted, saying that to see Huong just once more before leaving the North would be like seeing his youth: like seeing all the cities and towns, rice fields and villages, the flooding fields, the prosperous Bai Ninh village again. It would be like seeing summer days that were as noisy as storms from the sea, even like seeing the 25th Regiment again with all its strictness. It would be like seeing all these things simultaneously – all with the passion and love and unhappiness that had marked this period of his life.

The two set out at five, but didn't arrive until seven o'clock in the evening. Huong and her husband were living in the first unit of a collective housing project, a group of houses with brick walls and thatched roofs set in the middle of an orchard, thick with banana trees situated next to a village just at the outskirts of the city. The unit seemed low and damp, with branches and moth-eaten leaves scattered all over the yard. Hieu didn't know what to do when someone finally showed him directly to Huong's room.

Sai whispered, "You just stay here, I'll go inside first."

"That's fine."

"Or you go inside with me!"

Sai's voice was off-key. Hieu knew that Sai was nervous, but sensed he wouldn't change his mind. Sai tucked in his shirt and brushed down the hair under his helmet with his fingers.

Through the window he could see Huong leaning against the headboard of a bed. She was bent over and intently reading a thick hardcover book. She looked up, every few moments, murmuring something to herself and writing a few words in the small notebook beside her. Half of her face was masked by short, crimped hair, but Sai could still see her beautiful eyes, her white even teeth. Huong looked thinner than before, but that only made her seem more beautiful. *O Dear*, Sai thought. *Why are you so beautiful tonight? Who is behind the curtain right next to the wall? Is it your husband?* Sai wanted to push the door wide open, go inside and embrace Huong tightly. Then, he imagined, he would tiptoe with her outside. They would close the door quietly behind them and go off together for the whole night. *How I would love to bury my head in your loving arms! Just one night together, we would have everything. All the walking and hunger, all the malaria and bombs, all would be nothing.*

Perhaps Huong sensed that someone was standing at the door, for she turned in that direction every now and then. When she finally stood up, Sai quickly moved away from her room, and went back to where Hieu was standing. Huong brought a mug of water back to where she had been sitting and started reading again.

Hieu almost laughed at Sai's perplexed and pitiful face, he asked, "What is Huong doing?"

"Perhaps studying a foreign language."

"Alone?"

"Perhaps the husband is on the bed, too. I can't see that much of the room."

"Should we go home now?"

"Wait!"

"What for?"

"Perhaps you should go inside for a moment. I'll wait out here for you."

"I don't think we should go in."

Having said this, Hieu realized that Sai's wanted to know if Huong would ask after him when she saw Hieu. He wanted to know if she would make some comment or try to use Hieu to arrange a meeting with him. It would be awkward to visit Huong, late at night like this, but Hieu didn't care about that. He cared about Sai, and he didn't want Sai to have anything to regret later, so while Sai walked toward the main road, Hieu went inside. He knocked softly at the door.

Still holding her book in her hands, Huong called, "Who's that?"

"Excuse me, I want to ask whether this is Miss Huong's house?"

"Huong who, sir?"

"Huong from the Polytechnical Institute who has just been transferred here."

"Excuse me, what can I do for you?"

"I am Hieu, the soldier."

"O God! Kim, come here. It's Brother Hieu, Kim!" Huong threw the book down on the bed and ran to open the door. From behind the curtain, Kim sprang to her feet, pushed the curtain aside and asked, without waiting for his answer, "Did you know that I was here? Did

Hien mention me? I haven't received any mail from him for a month now." Huong told Hieu that since Kim had started medical school, she had come to her place every Sunday. Her husband, however, was not home. He went to the library on Sundays, since he was about to go abroad to study in a doctoral program. They had just moved, Huong explained, everything was still a mess because she and her husband had been busy studying foreign languages.

"He has to study in order to go, and my job requires that I read technical documents and scientific information in foreign languages. So, on Sundays, I cook with Kim. Weekdays we bring food home from the collective kitchen to save time for studying. Where will you sleep tonight? Stay here with us! My husband likes friends more than he likes me, so don't worry."

Hieu made apologies, telling Huong that he had been on his way to the Military Division for the Performing Arts and had suddenly remembered that she was living in this area, so he had dropped in just to say hello. Next time he would stay longer. As they talked Hieu made it a point of recalling the summer days Huong had spent in the coastal area and the hard work of people in his unit including Sai. But Huong avoided any mention of Sai. She remained silent even when Hieu told them, "Sai has already gone B." Kim cried out at this news, but Huong acted as if she didn't know Sai. Finally Hieu said, "I'm still in your debt, perhaps when the condition permits I'll repay you."

"When the condition permits please come and stay with me and my husband longer. And about 'that matter' perhaps we don't need to talk about it anymore."

Clearly, Huong's anger had not yet abated. She seemed to be making an effort to load her conversation with references to "my husband." Fortunately, Sai overheard none of this, but Hieu still could feel his own heart growing cold as the conversation proceeded.

Back outside, he wanted to yell at Sai. He wanted to say, "Why the hell do you have to work yourself up thinking about her? She's not worth your grief and suffering." But when he met Sai, he didn't have the heart to say anything. Sai walked along silently beside him. Hieu knew Sai wanted to know as much as possible. Trying not to convey the coldness he'd previously felt in his heart, Hieu finally smiled cheerfully and said, "Very delighted!"

"Really? Did Huong seem unhappy about her husband?"

"Maybe, but how could she speak in front of an outsider?"

"Was Huong still upset about me?"

"Probably!"

"Could Huong understand my situation entirely?"

"Maybe she couldn't understand it entirely."

Walking quietly beside Hieu, Sai tried to restrain his thoughts, but he couldn't keep himself from asking, "Did Huong know that I was going far away?"

"I told her."

"I wonder whether Huong will complain about my going!"

"She still admires you as a decisive person."

"It seems she's lost weight."

"She has had to study, to work and, at the same time, to learn a foreign language. Her school is all the way in the inner city."

"I don't understand why Huong moved here. She has always been afraid of the dark. Now she has to be at school until late in the night!"

"Well, this is where she works, and she never had her own house before."

"What a pity! I wonder whether the husband has paid any attention to her transportation problem?" Hieu was quiet. "Brother, it can be solved this way: I'll write to my brother Tinh. But . . . I'm afraid that Tinh doesn't like Huong much. . . . All right, I'll tell him to help Huong for me. If he doesn't help Huong, he'll have to abandon me. I'll say, 'Be at ease. Huong won't hurt your brother anymore.' I'll write to Tinh and tell him all that. At home, you can write to Tinh or go to Hanoi. You can try to see him and talk to him further."

"About what?"

"The old couple who were evacuated to our house. In Hanoi, they have a very large house with two unoccupied rooms. They promised my family that if I or my close friends were to go to school or to work in Hanoi they would reserve one room for us so we would always have a place to live. Please tell Tinh to try, actually he doesn't need to try, he needs only to love me."

"He would be willing to split himself open for you. He would spare nothing."

"I know. But you still have to tell him that if he can do this for Huong, he will never need to do anything else for me."

"All right, rest assured that while you're away, I'll discuss the matter with Tinh. But what happens will depend on the circumstances."

"Why does it depend?"
"What if she finds a house that's more convenient for her?"
"Right! That's all right. But certainly we can provide better conditions for her as she attends school. As it is, she could drop out of school, because she is afraid of the dark or scared by the ghosts or deserted streets."

Perhaps for the entire decade ahead, in the midst of bombs, shells and the hardships of a soldier's life, Sai morale and enthusiasm would remain high just because of the happiness he experienced at that moment. Hieu walked silently by Sai. He recognized that he was in the company of a person filled with faith and aspiration. It was just as people said it was in the papers and on the radio; soldiers really did go to the front just as if they were going off to a festival.

Hieu knew this to be true now, true and necessary.

Nobody would be foolish enough to grieve over the past when they enjoyed happiness in the present. At the same time, no one would boast about their prosperity when they were truly prosperous – just as one who has something to eat never flaunts it in front of the hungry. The truth was that Huong was sick of her husband even before their wedding. A senior faculty member at the Polytechnic, Thinh was industrious. Neither talented nor stupid, he was an ordinary sort, in fact, almost insipid in nature. Though thirty-five, he had never dated. Some of the young girls with gossiping tongues called him the "director," but then changed his title to "that sick doctor." This was both a reference to the one-sided obsessions he seemed to have for certain women, and a reference to the joking matchmaking of the girls who had made him the imagined lover of all the school beauties.

Early in her time at the Polytechnical Institute, Huong became the object of Thinh's witless affections, and the others teased him about being her lover. Huong herself would say to her friends, "I have kicked the soldier out, now I only love the Ph.D. It doesn't matter who it is as long as I love. Those who are loyal, fine. Those who aren't . . . well, it's not important."

Thinh was persistent with his "one-way love." In the past, he had been the devoted follower of a pair of students in love. He had trailed after them on his bike, never caring if they knew. He loved, therefore he followed. The couple talked and laughed loudly and passionately.

On a typical day, they walked together, while he pedaled his bicycle slowly behind them. When they arrived at the girl's house, he waited until the girl had disappeared completely behind the door before turning around and heading home. For a year, he had not asked the woman a question, or talked to her, and he didn't mind if she noticed him following her.

When he started "loving" Huong, he eagerly brought her gifts from his home: a canteen for hot boiled water and an old army backpack for her to go camping where Sai's unit was billeted.

Every Sunday, Huong received job training at a factory forty kilometers outside of Hanoi. Regularly, Thinh rode his bicycle to "visit" outside the factory gate. Sometimes he arrived to find Huong "had gone out," or that she was "ill." But once he caught Huong right in front of the gate, and she was obliged to stop and talk to him. Knowing that she could no longer trifle with this affair, but also knowing it was necessary to watch her words, she said, "Professor, I know that you're very enthusiastic, but I've already had a love. I hope you appreciate that."

"No problem, no problem, just go ahead and love your soldier comrade. I'll do nothing to bother you. But you have to give me my own freedom to do whatever I want. If you don't want to see me, no problem."

All right, Huong thought, *let him do whatever he wants.* So she asked the gatekeeper to give him permission to stand there alone in front of the gate before riding his bicycle back to Hanoi. He stood there for hours.

A few days after she made this decision, Huong fell sick. No one knew how Thinh managed to come again and bring Huong half a kilo of sugar and a dozen lemons. Huong refused his gifts, but he said, "Lemon is cheap these days, only seven dimes a dozen. Don't worry."

Huong started laughing, then with a straight face, she said, as if delivering an order, "Professor, I suggest you put all these things back into the bag and take them away from me. Please have sympathy. It's now noon, and all the other girls are tired and need a nap. It would be inconvenient with you sitting here."

Thinh followed Huong's order and carried the bag home silently. The girls blamed Huong for being mean, but for her part, she couldn't allow the old man to continue on this way. The man had no self-respect!

For years, Thinh remained sincere and obedient, never demanding or expecting anything from Huong. As for Huong, since nothing was clear about Sai's situation, others always talked of her "handsome and intelligent soldier." Huong continued to hold that love sacred, moving ahead with the momentum of her memory and the impressions of an honest heart.

Behind Huong's mild and timid appearance, there lay an extraordinary fortitude. She had waited for Sai's sudden breakthrough, for something that would astonish her, as when he had silently yielded her his place in school or joined the army or gone off to college. Huong never expected that the sudden breakthrough would be the news that Sai had returned to Ha Vi to take up with his wife in earnest.

Back at school, when first learning of Tuyet's pregnancy, Huong had sunk into her bed for three days straight. The "doctor" again brought her lemons. Her stares were like arrows aimed at him; they made his feet tremble. She had wanted to shout, "Get out, you bastard!" But she was a person determined to take revenge and she had no weapon. In the past she'd rejected the ones she might have loved, those who might have brought her happiness, even more happiness than Sai, had rejected them all without hesitation. Now she thought that a thorny stick wasn't a powerful weapon, but it could still poke someone's eye out. She looked at Thinh and laughed, a ghost-like laugh that forced the Professor to step back toward the door. The laughter froze on her lips, she asked, "Do you really love me, Professor?"

The Professor suddenly shivered and collapsed to his knees, clasped his hands before him, kowtowing to the girl in front of him as if she were some supernatural spirit.

"Afraid? Speak! Do you really love me?"

The Professor pulled himself together, "Please don't ask me that question! If you were to ask me to die right now under your feet, I would not hesitate at all."

"Stop it, Professor, it sounds too melodramatic. Stand up and go report to the organizations in charge that I love you, and that we are ready to get married!"

Despite his dizziness, the Professor stood up and immediately carried out her orders. Her commands were like blessings to him, the kind of blessings God bestows on his lambs. And half a month later the whole school was in an uproar about the very simple wedding that had taken place, in about ten minutes, at the groom's parents' home.

Now in front of everybody, Huong had to try to become a sweet wife, proud of an attentive, caring husband. The responsibility of motherhood too was now upon her. She was three months pregnant, and this was a fact she could not contradict with gestures and words.

The night after Sai's unit had crossed the Bac River, he had been forced to remain behind. Malaria attacks rolled through his body for three days. He was unable to eat, but still when evening came, he had to roll up his hammock and walk, his body leaning hard into his walking stick. At times he lost consciousness. His eyes became wild, his skin black and blue, his jaw so stiff he couldn't even swallow the bowl of ginseng the nurse prepared for him. Finally, she gave Sai three consecutive shots. Then, with two soldiers from Sai's unit, she carried Sai to the medical station one day's walk away.

After six months in the hospital fighting the fevers and convulsions of malaria, Sai's health improved. Discharged, he was appointed a platoon leader of an engineering company in charge of an underwater bridge along a part of the Ho Chi Minh Trail that went under the shallows of the Thao River, south of Xe Bang Hieng. Sai had always been a restless person, full of projects and longings. Now he was as silent as an old man. In spite of his dream of fighting the enemy and becoming a hero, he was content with this assignment. He was willing to accept any responsibility assigned to him. Nearly a year had passed since he left the North for the front, and since then he had done nothing. Many of his companions-in-arms had been in difficulties and suffered hardships for him. If he could do anything to show his gratitude, to deserve his place among them, he would do it.

When Sai arrived at his new unit, he went straight to the trail. The company commander told him to take another week to rest. The company commander was sure that then Sai would be helpful in lots of ways. He would have him teach the new ethnic minority recruits how to read and he would have him help the company write reports.

After these first days of rest at his unit, Sai was feeling much better, but he had a strong craving for some greens to eat. He didn't care what kind. It was a simple enough want, but as a new member of the unit, he was not allowed to cross into the steep mountains and defoliated jungles alone. To please Sai, the company commander decided to send Them, his contact man, to help Sai to find greens, bamboo shoots, mushrooms and sour fruits. The trip back and forth would take two days, but Sai and Them prepared by bringing shredded dried meat and other provisions sufficient for four days. Carrying their guns and backpacks, the two left early in the morning. By afternoon, they had arrived at a forest of tall, thinly growing trees, mostly ironwood and *bong tau*, trees round and straight with perfect white bark, as hard as nails.

Them walked at a fast clip, talking quickly as he walked, acting as if the jungle were his family orchard. He knew where to find the greens and mushrooms and where the spring water under him was flowing to.

"Do you like honey?" Them asked as they walked. "We can come back here tomorrow, when we have used up our water and use a canteen to store honey."

Sai assumed Them had been to the area before, but he soon learned this was not the case. This was Them's first time in this part of the jungle, yet, wherever he went, he never missed a thing. In only a few hours, the two had filled a backpack with bamboo shoots and a two-kilo bag of cat's ear. The trip would have been a great triumph if it hadn't been for the unexpected rainstorm. The rain had been coming in on the forest since that morning. Them and Sai had walked in the day's stifling air, and both their inner and outer shirts were soaked.

At dusk, the jungle rustled and was filled with a soft yellow light. Devoting all their attention to searching for greens and bamboo shoots, the men scarcely said a word and paid little attention to the sun or wind. When darkness came, they sat down to chew their dry provisions and drink their water. Climbing into their hammocks, they immediately fell asleep.

The water level rose steadily all night. It was almost dawn when Sai felt cold at his back. He searched with his hand and found that his hammock was flooded with water. He turned around to wake Them. They flashed their lights and saw the area around them all silver with water. Only a few dozen meters away a swift current was sweeping everything downstream. The sound of raindrops on their tents had drowned out the sound of running water. The two soldiers jumped down from their hammocks into the water. They slung their guns and backpacks over their shoulders, took down the tents to cover themselves and furled their mosquito-net hammocks. After a long struggle, they reached higher ground and built a fire, never bothering to take precautions to hide the smoke. In the midst of the deserted jungle on a rainy night they were not worried, and even had they worried they would have reassured themselves that night that enemy planes couldn't smell smoke.

Before daybreak, a group of jets flew over their position and began bombing all around their fire. Volleys of bombs exploded fifteen meters from Sai and Them. Sai's eyes were struck dark. He had been lying between the ribs of a huge tree. Perhaps that saved him, for all the shrapnel stuck in the tree. But Them, who was sitting a bit farther from the tree, was struck by the first series of explosions. After the attack, Sai raised himself up and saw that Them was not moving. He jumped over the fire quickly and held his friend. A bomb fragment had sliced off a piece of flesh as big as a hand from Them's left buttock. His left thigh had also been struck by three bomb fragments. Blood flowed into a pool under him. Sai wiped his hands off on his shorts and the mosquito net, then started to dress Them's wounds. He used both his own and Them's supply of bandages, but was still only able to cover three wounds. He took a pack of water pipe tobacco, already soaked with water, from his shirt pocket and applied it to the last wound, then took off his T-shirt, tore it up and tied it around the wound.

It was only after having dressed Them's wounds and feeling his chest to make sure he was still breathing, that Sai realized what had happened. He wondered what to do next. Water was surrounding his feet, which way should he go? How could he bring Them home? With all the bleeding, he might not be able to survive the trip back to the hospital. Sai didn't dare to keep on thinking. He took the shirt and the mosquito net to wipe the tent clean, then he spread the tent over the two mosquito nets in the hollow of the tree and carried Them over and placed him on it. He then wiped the other tent clean and stretched it above Them to protect him from the rain. Them was groaning softly; he mumbled, "Water, please give your little brother a sip of water!" How pitiful the word "little brother" sounded. Sai felt limp. He turned around to take the canteen full of water and carefully pour a small amount into the empty canteen. He hid the one with more water in a tree and took the canteen with only a bowl full of water and poured it into his friend's mouth. Them suddenly grabbed the canteen. He held the canteen tightly to his mouth as if he were afraid Sai would snatch it away. In two gulps, the water was finished. Them sucked then licked all around the canteen's mouth. Tears started to Sai's eyes, but he couldn't let Them quench his thirst. Dipping the canteen over his friend's mouth, Sai whispered words, pleading with Them. Them also knew the danger of drinking too much water in times like this. Them licked the canteen's mouth until his tongue and lips dried up, then he fainted into sleep, moaning softly.

Sai took his rifle and ran down the hillside through waves of thorn bushes. Layers of rotten leaves formed a soft bed under his feet. Every step seemed to make him shorter. Around him, the water still swirled swiftly by, striking the cliffs, splashing all over before running noisily down toward the mountain.

Sai ran until he was out of breath. He couldn't find the militia path. The later it got, the more he worried about Them's wounds, so the more he pressed on. Finally, Sai collapsed flat on a rock, pressed his face down on the hard, cold stone ready to pass out. A few minutes later, he in desperation decided to fire a few shots to draw aid. Perhaps there were units billeted nearby, or perhaps someone else was out looking for greens. Sai had barely enough feeling left to lift his gun, he just rested it against the rock and clicked the bolt, pointed the gun slightly upward and fired two shots, the whole jungle stirred for a short moment. Sai again sank his head down to the gun's butt. He held the gun so he couldn't drop off to sleep as he wished, then he stood up and stretched his arm, still holding the gun. Looking down to the bottom of the mountain, he saw two men splashing across the stream. From their camouflage uniforms, he knew that they were two soldiers from the puppet army. The two must have slept on the same hill with Sai and Them last night. They must have been the ones who called the jets to bomb this morning. Sai stood up, leaned his gun against a branch of a tree and fired two more rounds. The two men had reached the other side of the stream and were running along the side of the mountain to the left. Sai didn't see them, but still he pointed his gun in their direction and fired five more shots. He knew he didn't have enough energy to pursue them. He fired hoping only to chase them off and to give himself the opportunity to run as well. Their path had shown him the way to the other side of the swirling stream. Crossing the stream where they had crossed and going in the direction where they had run was inviting death, but only by going along the stream could he hope to find the militia path. Calculating the odds of success, Sai ran back to wake Them. The thirst was still raging in Them, Sai took the canteen to pour out two more sips of water. Them licked the corners of his lips, but this time he didn't try to seize the canteen. Sai took the hammock from the backpack, tied its two ends together and hung it across his shoulder. Them placed one hand on Sai's shoulder, the other on a walking stick. He put the wounded leg in the hammock-sling, immobilizing it. The set-up would slow them down, but there was no other way to get out of the jungle. The two men limped down the mountain, then started to grope their way across the stream.

Suddenly Them, puffing and panting, pushed Sai over and tumbled down on top of him, his mouth wide open. "Water, water . . . O God . . . waaater," he cried. Sai pushed Them up, then opened the canteen and poured more water into Them's mouth. Them held the canteen tightly. This time he was stronger than Sai. The water gurgled into his mouth, oozed out at the corners, and ran down to soak the collar of his shirt. Sai kept still for almost ten seconds before he used force to snatch the canteen away from Them's hands. He felt like the ground under his feet was dissolving; Them cursed and stared at Sai with vengeful eyes. Sai didn't dare look at the pain and misery in Them's face. He turned away and twisted the canteen cap tightly closed. He took off the bandage to squeeze out the water and redress Them's wounds. Sai was in panic when he saw that blood was still trickling down Them's thigh. Sai didn't know what kinds of herbs to look for to treat the wound, and there was nothing but his sweaty T-shirt to use to as a dressing. Sai felt the only thing he could do, at this point, was find a way back to the unit as quickly as possible.

The sun was directly overhead. It was quiet except for the sound of the stream. Too quiet. At every step, Sai had a feeling that the two enemy soldiers were ready to jump out like tigers on them. Sai tried to concentrate only on finding a way out. He leaned forward. As he moved, he clung to whatever he could get his hands on for support. He didn't care that he was scratched by thorns or that his head banged up against trees and rocks. He didn't care that hunger attacked and sweat drenched him like a shower. Sai half-carried his friend on his back and half-dragged him.

The jungle closed in on them. Them rested his head quietly on Sai's shoulder. Maybe he had dropped off to sleep. They came across a block of rock as wide as a house. Although it was only as high as his knee, Sai didn't have enough energy to climb over it. He lay down to wait for his strength to return. But strength from where? All the elements a living body needed had been used up. Sai fell into a deep, sound sleep, oblivious to everything around him.

Eventually, the silence called back both the pain and the burning thirst that had forced Them to cry out. He called out again and again but Sai didn't move. He pushed himself up and away from Sai's back and crawled with his hands, dragging his wounded leg. He could see nothing in the dark night. The gurgling noise of flowing water from a brook seemed to beckon him to it. His thirst had peaked. He would quench it whatever the consequences, he would rather die tonight than drink for a hundred more years. Propping himself with his hand against a rock, he put his mouth to the water and drank without stopping, without taking a breath. He kept drinking until his stomach was swollen, but the thirst was not quenched. He touched his face on the surface of the cool water, which splashed up as if playing with him. He leaned against the rock and stretched out his arms, so he could set his face against the water that was so generous and indifferent about bringing him the happiness and satisfaction he had never found in his life. The happiness was great enough to end pain and hope forever. It had been twenty years, two months and six days since the night Them had first touched the warm water in the stoneware basin of the midwife. Now, all his ideals and capacity for love were going to end with this last touch of cool water.

≣ Sai didn't know whether it was midnight or near dawn. He didn't know whether he was on the beach or in an airtight room. He felt a little cold on his back. He wanted to raise his hands but he could not. He had to make an effort just to open his eyes. Sai touched his back. Them was not there. He stretched his arm to feel around, and Them was not there either. Dripping with sweat, he jumped up. His legs almost collapsed beneath him. He swept his flashlight swiftly from side to side. Everywhere the night seemed thick and dark, and it felt like the enemy was watching. Sai decided to call Them, but his tongue was tied, his throat stuck and dry, and he was unable to say a single word.

Sai walked down to the spring, sweeping his flashlight, looking for his friend. He walked backward until the water came up to his knees; then he saw Them stretching his arms, lying face down at the edge of the spring. Out of joy, Sai rushed over to his friend. But on touching Them, a shiver ran through him. Looking at Them, his face buried in the water, Sai knew what had led to this horrible end. He wanted to yell, but he didn't have the energy. He wanted to cry, but the tears wouldn't come. His anger at himself rushed over him. Ignoring his fear, Sai lifted Them, carried him on his shoulder and walked along the stream.

Numb, Sai wanted to believe his friend was still alive. He knew only that with Them over his shoulder, he felt more confident. Later, nobody could understand or explain how Sai could carry his sacrificed companion, up and down hills, for fifteen hours. Finally, reaching the militia path, Sai fell flat down. He lay with Them on his side. The two faced each other like two close friends talking. Sai held his friend's waist. Them's wounded leg lay wrapped over Sai's body. Even from a short distance, the two young soldiers seemed to be sound asleep.

Huong was determined to return home and pay her final respects to Scholar Khang, Sai's father. News of his death had come to Huong from a former classmate now working in Hanoi.

Huong told her husband, "I'll take our child to visit her grandmother today, we'll be back next week. Everything is ready here: shrimp and salty fried meat for two days, eggs and dried sausage for another two days. For Sunday, I've asked Aunt An to buy fish. She'll clean and fry it for you. When it's ready, she'll call you to bring it home. Take pains to cook and eat hot rice twice a day, also boil some greens to avoid heartburn."

"Why don't you go later, you don't have to be in such a hurry," her husband said.

"For me it's no 'hurry,'" she answered.

"I'd like us to visit grandma together."

"Forget it, there's no need for all of us to go together. Maybe next time." Aware she was being abrupt, Huong walked up to her husband, buttoned his collar button and smoothed the wrinkles on his shirt with her hands. "How many times have I told you, you have to dress tidily. You are too slovenly!" Thinh silently drank in the attention she bestowed on him, and kept his mouth shut.

Huong told the cyclo driver to stop at the Cua Nam market so she could buy a dozen lilies and a few bunches of incense. As she got off the bus at the Vang market, two former classmates were waiting to give her and her child a ride on their bicycles. It was about three kilometers to the wharf, and one kilometer further to Sai's house. Along that road of nearly five kilometers, people were in motion carrying incense and candles, lilies and wreaths from Hanoi to Ha Vi. Hearing people on the street talking, "No sooner than four or five o'clock. The procession can't take place yet. It's peak time for air-defense," Huong and her friends knew that they were still in time.

Scholar Khang's funeral was an event. In bygone days, at the funeral of Canton Chief Loi's father, people had killed hundreds of pigs, buffaloes and cows. They'd beaten pork to make meat loaf and had managed to keep busily eating for ten long days. But the crowds for Canton Chief Loi were not as great as at the scholar's funeral. The scholar had had students everywhere, and they wanted to prove their gratitude to their loving, gentle teacher. In these days, it was still considered a virtue to "Respect your teacher and honor the Way." Further, Scholar Khang had also been the father of a valiant soldier who was fighting in the South, who single-handedly had downed an American airplane and who also had countless other merits. The paper had run articles about the soldier of the Liberation Army from the V. village, on the H. river; everybody knew that this man was Sai, the son of Scholar Khang. What's more, Scholar Khang had many relatives, and in the village everybody admired him as one of the "virtuous poor," for whom, as the saying went, "although the paper is torn, the binding must be maintained." He had taught his children that even in times of hunger, they should not steal or take from others. When they had grown up and joined in revolutionary activities, he had cared for them and had run back and forth entreating for their release from prison. He reminded his brother and children of only one thing, "You must work toward virtuous goals. There must come a time of old age and retirement. Remember this, so that in your old age, people will still receive you warmly and respectfully."

In Scholar Khang's whole life, there had been only one regret and that had been the time when he chased Sai out to the field and almost caused him to die from hunger and cold. He recalled the incident right before his own death, saying, "Sai, my dear son, please forgive your father. I was so cruel to you and the consequence is that I am unable to see you before closing my eyes. Sai, my dear!" The villagers burst out sobbing for the old man and for the youngest son. They wondered in what faraway place he was at this moment when he was to be forever separated from his respected father.

For all these reasons, people had come together to express their sympathy and pay their respects, while they paid tribute to the sacredness of life and death.

But there were also others at the funeral. These were relative, if not complete, strangers who came because they admired the revolutionary family or because they had affection for Ha or one of the scholar's sons.

There were still others who went to the funeral because it was to their advantage to be seen there. Just as it had been to their advantage, months earlier, to attend the procession that brought Mr. Ha to the District Party Committee and celebrated his appointment as Party Committee Secretary or the procession that took Brother Tinh to the district where he was placed in charge of Internal Affairs for the Administrative Committee.

Some had come as early as the afternoon of the day before yesterday, when the family had started wearing mourning clothes. Out on the street people had joked noisily, but entering the house, they became solemnly silent. On the street they were still observing the customs and habits of the village, but in the house they tried to master all the ceremonies and did everything as if they had been in their own homes. From the corner of their eye, they watched to see when to light the incense and when to say the prayers and pay obeisance to Ha or Tinh.

"I am Tran Van Dat," said one man. "I am the Deputy Director of the collective in charge of animal husbandry of the Thuong hamlet, Hong Thuy village. With my respect to the spirit of our old scholar – intelligent in life and holy in death – I have this small token to offer." The man raised a carton of Tam Thanh cigarettes and a dozen bundles of incense in front of his face and then dropped on his knees and kowtowed three times. Standing up, his eyes were red and his hands shaking. He placed the offerings on the altar already piled with incense and flowers. Tinh, after bowing in return, had to thank him and to accept his sincere sentiments. On his way out, Dat was bowing down painfully still, well satisfied with himself, for he was sure the request for two thousand pieces of roofing tiles on Tinh's desk would not be refused now. And if necessary, Tran Van Dat would say prayers again to make sure Tinh did not forget his name. There were others who had been around since early morning, but they would not come in to light the incense until it was Ha's turn to approach the coffin.

As for the nephews and nieces, brothers and sisters, near and far, those who cried the loudest were those who had not paid the scholar a visit in years, if ever. They were the ones who had never shared half a potato with him in times of hunger. Among the family, the most touching and painful cry was that which came from the eldest daughter-in-law. She threw herself on the ground, sometimes fainting away. Although her voice went hoarse, she continued to lament. "O Father," she cried, "you have passed away, leaving behind your children, young and old, with nobody to rely upon, O Father, ooh."

Tuyet was also one of the "permanent" mourners, along with the eldest sister. Tinh's wife was more circumspect. She cried at the moment the old man stopped breathing and then again when he was shrouded. Other than that, she was too busy for tears. She had to take care of the countless tasks that needed to be done: getting betel and areca, tea and tobacco, food for the horn players and drummers . . .

When Tinh's friends arrived and they didn't see his wife, Tinh was so ashamed his face turned violet. He looked for her, calling, "Mrs. Tinh, where are you?"

She called back, "Do you want me to drop everything? Don't you see that nobody helps me with anything!" Then Tinh reminded himself that nobody could accuse his wife of filial impiety; the whole village had spoken for months of how well his wife had served her sick father-in-law.

≣ Huong and her daughter and two friends arrived as the others started carrying the coffin out to the yard to rest it on the poles already set in place there. Cries rose up in waves and moved along with the coffin. Huong walked with her daughter to the altar to offer incense and flowers. She looked up at the old man's portrait. In the silence of the deserted house, she recognized Sai in the portrait of the scholar in his youth. Huong grew uncomfortable with the silence in the empty house. Her daughter pulled at her shirt, and Huong wiped away her tears and moved to go outside. Her two friends were waiting for her at the door. Together, the group moved silently with the crowd as it pushed forward. On the way to the burial site, Huong couldn't hold back her tears. She tried to hide in the midst of the noisy throng. She cried because of the suffering she heard in the cries around her and because of the music. The sounds of the woodwinds were as distressing as the sounds of the people. The drums, cymbals and bamboo kept rhythm . . . all of sounding a farewell. She cried out of sympathy for the old man. She cried for the absence of Sai. She cried for her own suffering, for not knowing why she had linked herself with this family. In those few sacred moments, Huong also cried as a daughter-in-law, someone who had to cry on behalf of a person far away.

Dear Sai, she thought, *do you know how pained I've been, thinking about our love?* She tried to conceal her tears from others, especially from her daughter who clung to her dress.

Near the grave, Huong saw Uncle Ha. As he passed by Huong, he stopped to say, "I knew you had come when we were still in the house, but the situation was awkward. Please understand." After the burial, Huong and her friends said good-bye to Tinh, then turned to the road leading to the Bai market. Tinh thanked Sai's friends, then asked Huong, "How long will you be staying home? I'll come to see you on Sunday then I'll take you to visit my office."

Why didn't all this care and affection come to me several years ago? Huong thought to herself. *Only now they care, now that they know I can no longer destroy the career and the happiness of their loved one.* Or maybe, she thought, they spoke to her because they felt badly for Sai.

That night, back at her mother's home, Huong sat quietly with a lamp and a rumbled copy of *The Liberation Army* newspaper that her Hanoi friend had given her. The two middle pages of the paper were filled with pictures of Sai and articles about his feats. Huong had memorized every period and comma, but still she kept reading. She looked at the photographs. The more she looked, the more the pictures seemed to fade. She couldn't make out any particular detail, but by holding them at a distance, she had a general impression of the sadness in Sai's eyes. She could still see his thick lips pressing together. He seemed to be silently urging others to look at him, to discover his inner virtues.

Huong remembered that it was always said that people with a deep groove in their upper lip were benevolent. Wasn't that true? She sighed. Why had she learned everything too late? Why hadn't Kim, her dear friend, told her the truth sooner?

The articles about Sai let Huong know what his life had been like over the past years. She read about how for hundreds of nights, Sai had cut through mountain rock and built roads under the water's surface. He had destroyed unexploded bombs and leveled bomb craters in the midst of fierce attacks. Under his command, an engineering platoon had arranged for trucks to cross the river without waiting, without losing a single kilo of supplies heading for the front. Before Sai's command, trucks had rolled over regularly on the dangerous, steep grade of the river road.

Standing guard over that area for almost a year now, he had faced the enemy's bombs and shells every night. Some nights, the area was bombed up to five times, but, each time, his unit cleared the road within half an hour, and the convoy was again on its way. They had fortified a part of the road under the water's surface, rebuilt both sides of the river banks, making them the smoothest parts of the strategic trail. The slippery slope was also replaced with an easier pathway through the Khoc forest. Sai's platoon had even built three alternate crossriver roads. The enemy would not have expected this spot to be the important junction of the K and H roads, controlled easily now thanks to its perilous terrain. Now the enemy had no way to stop the traffic flow. One of the enemy captains had said, during an interrogation, "We estimated that there were any where from two companies to one battalion guarding the two crossriver areas and those parts of the road curving along the mountain side. So we organized an operation with one regiment. We saturated the area with bombers. Together with the units already on the spot, we wanted to cut that important link on your trail."

In the articles about him, Platoon Leader Giang Minh Sai was reported as saying that there were two unusual things about the enemy's response to his platoon's completion of work on the trail. First, they started bombing at five o'clock in the morning. This was a total change in strategy from their practice of bombing from noon of one day until two or three o'clock the next morning. Of course, when there was something suspicious, they would bomb whenever they wanted. Second, out of hundreds of bombs dropped, only five were aimed at the crossriver road and the slope. The rest were concentrated on the part of the forest around the bald hill, behind where we were camped. This behavior by the enemy suggested something was about to happen.

"I sounded the alarm for our platoon to fall in. One squad was to remain in place as a reserve force and to provide guard for the crossriver section of the road and to guarantee safety for the trucks traveling during the night. The rest were to be ready to fight. Two squads were in mobile positions, ready to cope with any new situations. About half an hour later, I heard the helicopters. I felt sure that they would land. I cried out for my men to run toward the bald hill. I started running right after that, carrying the machine gun. I ordered each squad to occupy one sector of the forest that circled the bald hill but remained separated from it by a spring.

"The squad under my command was occupying the sector in the southern of part of the hill. It was the same place where our unit had been quartered. The forest was on fire. The bitter smell of bomb smoke was still swirling in our noses. I ordered our men to quickly choose advantageous positions, to use rifles if the enemy lowered rope ladders. Machine guns were to be aimed at the landing helicopters.

"I had just found a flat boulder and adjusted the machine gun when three helicopters started swirling down toward us. After lowering, the first one turned around and followed the creek. I followed it. Through the cockpit windshield, I could clearly see the enemy. This was my best chance. A moment later, I would be able to see the helicopter, but not the pilot. I clenched my teeth and squeezed the trigger. At the first burst of fire, the helicopter started swinging in toward the mountainside then it turned end over end upside down in the creek. Our men jumped up and down, yelling and cheering, while I was dripping with sweat. I didn't dare believe what had happened. The two remaining helicopters quickly took off. I fired over half a belt more. Firing like I did was my way of trying to chase them away and also to calm myself. 'Follow through' shots like that, even if they hit the helicopter, would rarely bring it down.

"Out of thirty-three in that helicopter, the captain was one of the three who survived. Right after having been pulled out, his face was ashen, but he acted indifferent to his position. I whispered to my two soldiers just loud enough for him to hear, 'I'd guess this one's from the city, or at least he went to school there.' His face paled.

"He approached me and stammered, Mr. . . . Commander . . ."

"'You will be allowed to live only if you clearly spell out your plans.'

"'May I talk to you privately?' he asked, his voice a whisper. He and I walked a little farther away from our soldiers and the two soldiers of the puppet army. Within five minutes, he had told me everything about the planning of the operation, and I had a guarantee for the accuracy of his words. I knew also that he had a wife and a child in Saigon. His wife had asked for him to be transferred back to the special-zone of the capital next month. A fighting plan had been sketched, and a platoon was waiting to fight a full regiment on the other side."

As Huong read all this, she could not help but wonder why Sai was not as daring and adventurous in the days when he was still at home. She wondered if it was true that Sai had wandered with Hieu for a whole week near her place in Hanoi. *If only you had been more courageous,* she thought now, *everything would have been different.*

Huong turned back to the paper and read the story of the end of the battle.

After three hours of fighting a force twentyfold greater in numbers, Sai's platoon had downed seven planes and killed hundreds of the enemy. His platoon stood firm on the battlefield till they were reinforced by troops from the transit station, the junction station and the drivers force. The enemy had no choice but to withdraw. They left behind twelve helicopters and 273 dead bodies. On the night of the victory, Sai, as leader of the heroic platoon, was promoted as an Emulation Soldier, and he received the honor of becoming a member of the People's Revolutionary Party.

At the military station, every cadre or soldier now knew about Giang Minh Sai. They knew that for him hardship and sacrifice meant nothing. His revolutionary enthusiasm was that strong; his will was that determined. And Sai's comrades knew that, in the case of the battle by the bald hill, part of Sai's determination had to do with the location of the battle. The whole fight had taken place among the very forest trees and by the very creek that had witnessed the death of Sai's comrade, Them, three years earlier.

As a result of that loss, Sai's grief had turned into infinite hatred at those who had betrayed his country. Even more deep rooted was his hatred of the imperialists and feudalists who had exploited the peasants. He'd felt that hatred when he saw the way people from Ha Vi village used to work as hired laborers. And he felt that hatred until at age eighteen, he volunteered for the army and found a way to be sent to the battlefield, to kill the enemy and to perform a feat of valor. Or, at least, this is what Sai told the writer of the articles in the *Liberation* newspaper.

But Huong remembered another reason. She remembered the moonlit night when Sai told her, "I'll enlist. The farther away I go the better. The more dangerous the task the better. Even if I have to plunge into fire and be killed, it will be better than living with 'her.' " Hadn't Sai said all that?

But forget it, Huong thought. *Leave things as the journalists have written them. I am only wondering what you have been truly thinking all these years. Don't be foolhardy, as you were when you spoke those words to me on that moonlit night. I'm always by your side, even though I am a married woman expecting a second child. I cannot abandon my husband and come back to you, but I'm still your love, just as you're mine. Don't cry when you come back and see me with my husband and children. But also don't keep silent. Don't stay away from me. How can I make you understand my heart? How can your pain and grief be healed?*

CHAPTER 7

Sai had never imagined the harsh life of a soldier could come to seem so precious to him. Of his seventeen years in the army, he spent eleven years on the front line. Eleven years without a leave, eleven years contending with death. And yet for eleven years, the thought of going home never crossed his mind. If not blocked by the family record on his wife's side, he would have been made a Hero of the Liberation Army. However, in the face of his fallen friends, that honor would have been meaningless. Some had laid down their lives for him. Many others had risked their lives to save him when sick with malaria, encircled by enemy fire, or caught in bombardments. To those who had come to his rescue, he was forever grateful.

On Liberation Day, people from all over the country went searching for one another. They returned to their villages and birthplaces trying to make up for the periods of long separation and loss. Each of Sai's colleagues arranged a leave or an off-site assignment in order to go home – to go home not merely to satisfy their longings, but also to have the opportunity to present themselves, alive and well, to their families, friends and neighbors.

But the thought of home merely saddened Sai. It was true that he craved the salty fried prawns and the corn pudding dipped in thick soybean sauce of his village. And it was true that he had some good memories. He thought of the time his mother paddled three or four miles in a small bamboo basket to take him to the Nam Mau area for first grade. In that immense span of water, he used to squirm furiously when his brother Tinh took some of his popcorn. He remembered the evenings his father balanced him on his shoulder and let the river water rise up over his own groin, then his chest. His father once carried him this way for two miles, because he wanted to see the folk song contest at Ha Chau temple.

Eleven years I have been away, Sai thought now. Mother and

Father are gone. Who can I go home to? My brother and sister still love me as parents do, but I am over thirty years old. I can no longer live off them as if I were a child.

Besides, there was still that woman – it never failed to jar him when others spoke of her as his wife. He would never again consent to share food or live in the same house with her.

Sai had asked Tinh to apply for "Parent on the Southern Front" status for him, so he could get a stipend for the support of his son. His brother's family, he knew, would provide for his son above and beyond the state allowance.

The days were full of uncertainty. After the Liberation, North and South were one again. The whole country united to deal with the consequences of war. Sai had recovered without any aftereffects from the malarial fevers, but he still didn't know where to go. That he had to accept. He had spent half of his youth in service to others; now it was time to make a decision to live for himself. "No one can force me, no matter what they do, to come back and live with a woman to whom I have never wanted to utter the word 'love.' "

Sai accepted an assignment at the Military and Technical Institute. There he would receive further training to become an Institute instructor. That would give him an occupation, a means of subsistence, for the remainder of his life. But it offered no variety, no challenges. Could he put up with that kind of stability?

Sai's sadness at all these thoughts enveloped him. It was with him in his fitful sleep, and he could taste it in every grain of rice, in every sip of water. Then out of nowhere, Do Manh, the Political Officer, came to help ease his sadness. Since they had last seen each other, Do Manh had survived many battles. He had picked up various assignments – as Political Chairman, as Vice Political Officer and as Political Officer of the Division. He was currently Political Chairman of an army corps that the General Staff favored. This was the gossip Sai had picked up. Now with Do Manh finally standing before him, Sai could not believe that his former superior still remembered him. Feeling awkward, he didn't know what to say. He was almost in tears. Do Manh looked him over from head to toe. His lips, always in a half smile, and his eyes, a bit drier now, had their quizzical glint. His head of soft hair, cut close, but still long enough to curl slightly, was dotted with white, as if sprinkled with powder. His once hardy face had paled into an ashen gray, and the lines of his eyes had begun to droop.

"Thin, too pale," he mumbled as if talking to himself. Then to break the oppressive atmosphere of this reunion, he said, "When did you go, and where did you go? I didn't have a clue. In the first few years, I couldn't make any contact with that region. Only by reading the newspaper in the last five or six years did I learn that you had joined the Southern Front. Great, really great!" He nodded as if to allow his high regard for Sai to sink in.

Still surprised by the sudden visit and moved by his unexpected interest, Sai's face turned crimson. He abruptly stood up, excused himself to make some tea.

"No! Stay here and talk. I have to leave soon. I just got back from Hanoi where I ran into Ha. He's already transferred to the Department of Operations. He showed me all your letters. Good heavens! Why so much groaning and moaning?" His eyes had that mischievous look again, and he broke out in mocking laughter.

His face reddening, his head lowered, Sai laughed along. Do Manh spoke with an authoritative voice, as if everything had already been taken care of and there was nothing to worry about: "I've talked with Ha about how to find a way to set you free. Actually, she isn't too happy either. Ha will discuss this with the family and get her ready for it. Let's get it over with by whatever means. No point in dragging on this mutual bondage." Sai wondered if this could really be true. "I've also just talked with Quang Van. My dear Sai, make an official request for a legal separation. The Bureau of Political Affairs will send a letter of support to the court. If necessary, we will send a representative to the local district to explain the corps' position on this matter."

After all these years, Sai could barely believe Do Manh was saying what he was saying. The more Sai heard, the happier he felt. It was like the story his mother once told him. There was a great famine. People dropped dead as if they were no more than banana trees uprooted by a hurricane. An order came to enter Cu Hien hamlet to attack the granary. Everyone in the village, in the canton and in the district ran out howling and yelling. And when they returned, each with a basketful of grain, they were still jumping up and down, yelling and screaming.

No one could have anticipated that life could be so strange! For this was a revolution – an August Uprising in his personal life – and it was coming to Sai with such ease! His heart was tied in knots, words stuck in his throat.

"The main thing for you now is to find a way to support your little boy. Even if he lives with his mother, it's still your responsibility to take good care of him, a little better than others perhaps, so that he won't pity himself."

Yes, Sai thought, anything for my son, even if I have to cut myself up into little pieces.

He sat in silence, weeping.

The Commissar could not suppress his own emotion. He stood up and said angrily, "Only that innocent child will suffer."

"Had my family and my superiors not coerced me years ago, it wouldn't have come to this."

"Right, you are absolutely right! But you know why?" Sensing that Sai would not reply, he continued, "Your own life is nothing but the well-worn life of a hired hand. Eat whatever food is given, do whatever job is assigned, always anxiously waiting for the boss's orders, never having the nerve to decide anything on your own. That's okay for a little child. But after your graduation, you became a citizen, a combatant, why couldn't you take responsibility for your own life? Why couldn't you openly say, 'This is a coercive situation. My feelings will not allow me to live with that woman. If you insist on browbeating me into it, I stand ready to give up everything I have. Even if I have to return home as a plowman, I will do it to be able to live the kind of life I want.' But you didn't say this. Instead, like a man tied with ropes, you dared not move, you only waited anxiously, hoping against hope. When I was the Political Officer, how could I have urged you to abandon your wife?"

"Sir, I was scared then."

"True, that says it well. I myself dared not intervene in the affairs of the joint branch and the work of the Political Committee. Afraid of whom? Afraid of what? Hard to say. It was the norm at the time, and there is no one to blame. The most important thing is to settle the matter at hand. Now that you can decide for yourself, you won't make that mistake again. But I expect more from you in the future. Ha and I agree that we will 'liberate' you to create a situation where you can go farther."

≡ It was as if all the misfortunes of childhood and the hard and heroic years on the battlefields led up to this – a return to Hanoi and a period of life when happiness came and held him in its arms. Sai excelled in many different fields and became the object of envy and desire of others. A member of the political committee at school. President of the postgraduate class. A brave fighter whose name was well known far and wide. A captain at the young age of thirty, a rare case.

At first, Sai went to live with Hieu. Five years earlier, Hieu had changed jobs to become Head of the Bureau of Organization for a hospital. He had a private apartment in the hospital's collective housing project. It was a small room at the corner on the first floor – one of the most convenient units in the building. The men shared the place during the week, then on weekends Hieu went back to his village, and Sai was left in charge of the apartment until Monday morning.

But, on his return from his village, Hieu often found his apartment unoccupied and in the same condition it had been when he'd departed. Looking at the pair of sandals that hadn't moved all weekend, Hieu knew that Sai had stayed overnight with friends. If he had gone out to dinner three times a week, it still would have taken him a year to exhaust all the possibilities. He had so many friends – friends from the village, from school, from college, from the battlefield, from recent days. There were friends of his friends, of Uncle Ha, of Brother Tinh, of other relatives and residents of Ha Vi village. Counting themselves among the chosen few, everyone wanted to have Sai over for dinner, to hear about his rise from humble beginnings.

When Sai returned from his overnight stays with friends, there were, almost without fail, five or six notes pinned to the door. "Sai dear, come to my place at once," one would read. Another would say, "As we have planned, I will wait for you here tomorrow morning." Still another: "Why did you miss our appointment? Everything down the drain. Let's try to meet again: Sunday night at my house."

Without glancing at the signatures, Sai could tell who wrote these notes and why. They were an enthusiastic group with one mission: to hook Sai up with a girl who would make a "perfect match" or who would prove "eminently befitting" of Sai's station or "most dutiful and capable" or "professionally established and of sound mind and body." The notes read: "Well-domiciled, mother fit as a fiddle, could baby-sit all day" or "Daughter of the deputy minister, a bit homely in looks" or "A doctor, Hanoi resident, children will be in very good hands." There were dozens of girls for Sai to get to know, and to grow tired of. He got so bored that eventually he refused all entreaties from those who claimed to have found him "the right girl." Uncle Ha and Brother Tinh both urged him to marry someone from his village. Brother Tinh already has his eye on a department store salesgirl and another who was a member of the District Party Committee, and still two others with third-grade educations.

Sai was a bit offended by his brother and uncle. He considered himself fully capable of finding a wife in Hanoi. Why should he have to run back to the village? What he really needed was love, a kind of love that would make up for his years of bondage. Other than that, he needed nothing. His relatives, once responsible for causing havoc with Sai's marriage, no longer made demands on him.

A friend of Uncle Ha ran into Sai on the street. He stopped his bike and spoke warmly. "I have set my eyes on a girl for you, come to see me sometime."

"Yes, sir."

"When then?"

"Please let me hold off for a while. I am just a bit tied up right now."

"How about next week?"

"I am afraid not."

"You want me to take her to your place?"

"No sir, I'm seldom at home these days!"

"Let's do it this way: give me a call whenever you have time. I can then ask her to go to either my house or yours. Either way is fine. She has heard your name. She said she heard stories of your military exploits while still in high school. They touched her deeply. Don't worry. Ha told me that you wanted someone with decent looks, so I have found you a winner."

Sai laughed. "I've met quite a few 'beauties.' If this one does not have tiny tiny eyes, she should be pretty good. Isn't that so, my dear uncle?"

"Nonsense! You'll fall head over heels in love when you see her."

"Please forgive me. I'm just so tired of this. Listen. Noon time next Saturday, you ask her to come to your house. I will also be there. If all goes well, I'll invite you both to my house. If I don't say a word, we will just say good-bye there and save time. Do you agree?"

Unfortunately, when all three met briefly at noon on Saturday to schedule a visit for later in the afternoon, Chau – that was her name – could not take up Sai's invitation. Later that day, she had to go to a meeting at work. "Could you come by tomorrow?" Sai asked her in a low voice.

"I'm sorry I can't. I have a little errand to take care of."

"Could I come by to see you some other time then?"

"All right. If I am not tied up, I'll come by to see you next Sunday."

Sai was surprised but intrigued by her answer. For the whole week he waited anxiously. Having Saturday off, he ironed his winter military outfit and his white poplin shirt. His black shoes got a complete shine. Then he shaved and boiled water for a warm bath. He cleaned, dusted, and rearranged the room, which was in a state of disorder because Hieu had gone away for the entire week. Finally, he tried on his clothes and shoes. The clothes belonged to him; the white shirt and the blue sweater belonged to him; the pair of black shoes belonged to him. And yet these things felt stiff, as if the clothes were borrowed. He stayed up late, then got up early the next morning, full of energy and delight. He boiled water for the thermos, drew on the water pipe in the kitchen. Slightly glassy-eyed from the tobacco, he buttoned his uniform. It felt softer than the night before, and he admired himself in the anchor-shaped mirror.

Sai walked back and forth, arms swinging to make the outfit more comfortable. It was still only 7:30 A.M. – time to monitor every little movement, every little sound from the gate. For the next four hours, Sai paced, looking at every object in the room and keeping his ears cocked for any movement of the gate. He did not sit down although he was tired and did not smoke any tobacco from the water pipe, although he craved it intensely.

"Brother Sai, your guest is here!" someone finally bellowed. Startled, Sai sprung to the door, only to find Brother Tinh, clasping his briefcase and a bundle of plastic bags. Sai felt embarrassed, but not unhappy because his brother was bringing him new "supplies" and offering him an opportunity to arrive at a unified view with his brother.

Sai told Tinh what was going on, but it was after 12 noon and no one had appeared. Was she too busy, or had she lost the address, or had something else happened? Uncle's Ha friend, the matchmaker, was also Tinh's friend. "I asked some leading questions," Tinh confessed, "and it appeared that she liked you. Beyond that, I couldn't tell a thing. But he did tell me that dozens have pursued her, some very handsome, university types, sons of ministers, but she didn't fall for any of them." If that was the case, Sai thought, how could she love me?

At noon the two brothers went out for *pho* at a stall near the project, so Sai could continue to "stand guard." Still, there was no sign. Sai blamed himself for not being specific. Even though she hadn't been able to commit to an hour, he would have saved a lot of time if he knew she was coming in the morning or evening. At Sai's urging, Tinh agreed to stay. For the entire noon hour, they drank tea and waited. Finally, Tinh got impatient, "What should we do now?"

"Well, we've just been introduced. If she doesn't show up, there shouldn't be any problem." At 3:30 P.M., Tinh wanted to ride his bike home. Sai was about to respond when Chau suddenly appeared with another woman on the doorstep. "Nghia, my friend," she said.

Nervous, Sai eagerly invited them in, although they already had taken the liberty of leaving their sandals at the door entry. Chau handed Sai a bouquet of roses and said matter-of-factly, "Please find a vase for the flowers. Passing by the market, I saw these beautiful roses and couldn't resist." When he went to get some water for the vase at the water pump, Nghia followed him.

"On the occasion of the New Year, Chau bought the flowers for you," Nghia said.

Sai remembered that today was the Solar New Year, and emotion rushed through him. With that revelation, Nghia had already gained his confidence. "What do you do?" he asked.

"School of Commerce, second year."

"Do you live far from here?"

"Right above Chau's apartment. Please drop by when you come to see Chau."

"How do I know if Chau will ask me to come?"

"I am sure she will."

"Although I was a soldier," Sai confessed. "I don't like dueling."

"You are the star right now. There is no opponent."

"But I am very clumsy."

"You have your strong points."

"What are they?"

"I don't know, but you must know what they are."

That evening, Sai went out with Chau and her friend. About halfway home, Nghia excused herself to see a friend on some business. Sai and Chau continued to ride their bikes. They went past

Chau's house toward Thanh Nien Road. When the road was in sight, they turned around and pedaled away. Chau appeared to be scared of the "unsavory" street. They rode about for four hours, from one street to another, back and forth, without stopping, without anything to eat. Many times Sai had wanted to stop and eat, because both were hungry, but Chau refused.

"On the battlefield you could go without eating for days!" she said. "Well now, bear it a little longer." Or, "If you insist on eating, I'd rather go home." Or, "An army comrade must set an example by enduring all kinds of hardship."

Whatever Sai asked about stopping to eat, he would get a gentle protest of this sort. Still, he was happy. He felt as if he were a field of dry, cracked earth, and she were a rainstorm, a storm signaling the coming coolness. But then it would be over and the drought would increase tenfold.

"I probably won't get married," she told him. "Frankly, I am sick of everything. There is no decent man left on this earth. Forgive me, I do not know people in the army very well, but city men, they are all degenerate and can't be trusted. I'm afraid whenever I have to go out at night." Nghia had said that she had never seen Chau go out without the company of some girlfriend. Perhaps tonight was the first exception? When Nghia left for her friend's house, Chau thought things over for a long time before allowing Sai to take her back home. Still, during the ride she was so engrossed in conversation that she stayed on the bike all the way to her home.

Sai turned to her and suggested that the reason she was talking so directly with him was because she had, for the evening, not stuck to her very strict habits.

"No, not really. I am not really that austere, but you have to sympathize with us young women. We can't afford to be free the way you men can."

"Men like myself? Can we all be so profligate, so depraved that you cannot even find one worthy of your hand?"

"Not so far."

"Why not?"

"Many young men have tried. Some just loved my twenty-square-meter house or the fact that my mother was still in good health. Some loved the kind of job I had – unpressured and conveniently located. Some loved the fact that my brother was the head of the Bureau of

Organization. They thought he could help them on their way. Some loved the fact that my elder sister was the Vice-Director of a meat cooperative, that two of my very close friends worked for the rice cooperative. Surely, that would mean a steady source of supplies. Some fell madly in love with me when they realized I had no contagious diseases, that I wouldn't be a burden later on. Nobody disregarded these matters and simply loved me. If I didn't have a home, a job, close ones to turn to, if I had been diseased, who would care for me?"

The more he listened, the angrier he felt at those contemptible realists. As a soldier, whose whole life revolved around nothing but love and death, he felt respect for her noble spirit. How rare this was in a woman barely twenty-five years of age!

His appreciation kept him silent, and he pedaled on. Finally, he asked, "Have you ever heard of how a soldier on the battlefield thinks and lives?

"Sure. When I heard the story about your friend – he was killed while searching for a handful of greens for you – I cried. I long for the pure life you led."

"You believe that still exists?"

She turned her head to look at him and nodded: "Yes, I do." But, after a few more blocks, she said, as if to protect herself, "But no one can really tell. . . . "

"Why?"

"I have to confess, I once loved a man, though not very deeply. But I have lost my faith because of him."

"Am I like him?"

"You are different. But don't make me accept anything on faith instantly."

That was the end of the exhausting, winter night bike ride. Sai was worn out, yet excited. It was a night of love that was not quite there, not quite yet. Later, as he reflected back on the evening, he thought there was a moment when things were almost realized. Just a tilt of the face would have brought him into contact with her soft, pleasing skin. It excited him to think of it, to recall every little detail, looking for a sign that might indicate the gathering scent of love.

Knowing that his brother liked soup, Tinh took out a portion of the cabbage he'd just fried and added water to make a broth. Except for the rice pot, which was being warmed, everything was cold – the omelette, the turnip, the clear broth with its fat coagulated into rings around the bowl. He had cooked the rice at 5 P.M., as soon as his brother had left with his guest. It was now ten and there was still no sign of him. He sat smoking his water pipe. Then, tired of sitting, he lay down on the bed. Tired of that, he started to clean. He took the teapot, cups, and water pipe to the pump. Then, out from under the bed, he retrieved a pair of cloth shoes filled with roach droppings; a pair of socks, stiff enough to be broken in half like rice cakes; an army uniform rolled into a bundle; and a white shirt with a blackened ring around the collar. He took all of this to the pump, soaped up profusely and rinsed everything three times, but the water in the pan was still black. He did the laundry, the cleaning, the dusting, but still there was no sign of his brother.

Tinh grew impatient, but not angry. He was the king of his district, always ready to explode at office workers or Party secretaries who crossed him. Here, with his brother, he was the servant. Here he had to smile cheerfully, speak softly, and acquiesce agreeably. When strangers or friends came by to ask for his brother, Tinh would rush to the door and thrust out both hands to seize theirs. Hanoians had to be well mannered like this. But men like Sai could be messy and dirty. This was such an alteration in the way things used to be that even the Party Secretary and the Chairwoman of the District Party Committee could not yet understand it.

Not surprisingly, Tinh felt constrained every time he visited his brother. But to make up for all the loss and pain his brother had suffered, Tinh had to make these special efforts. In the end, it was worth it, for Tinh's steady, unflinching support of his brother had helped make Sai the respected and admired figure he was – not only in the hamlet and the district, but in Hanoi itself. People of stature and reputation loved and treasured him. They associated him with his brother and Tinh quietly enjoyed the way people would say, "Sai of Mr. Tinh's family," or "One has to admit this; no one takes care of a younger brother better than Mr. and Mrs. Tinh." Even those who did not know Tinh's name would say, "Sai has a brother."

For this respect, Tinh could suffer the mumbling about Sai's divorce. Some people had said, "It was because Tinh and his wife didn't take to the sister-in-law that the whole thing started." Or they had told each other, "Their family was living in perfect harmony. But Tinh has a grudge against her father. He abused his power." Because of these rumors, Tinh had had to answer to dozens of investigative teams concerning the petitions of Tuyet's family and other detractors in the hamlets. Different bureaus in the district had also made inquiries. People had been organized, coached, supplied with documents so that Tuyet could file dozens of complaints to all the Party organizations and judicial organs of the province. Without the help of the Secretary of the District Party Committee, the Party organs and Mr. Ha's friends, Tinh could not have escaped unscathed from such public scrutiny. Still, he had been ready to face the challenge even if he risked losing everything – as long as Sai could avoid being sullied by Tuyet's wrath.

Still, Tinh was almost fifty years old. He could fight on, but not forever. In a few years, it would be time to retire. All his energies, even all his wealth, were devoted to the future of his brother, a young man in his mid-thirties whom everyone saw as so full of promise. But, after dinner, with his brother still out, Tinh felt uneasy about his brother's affairs. When Sai returned home, Tinh hoped to have a chat with his brother. He felt confident that when he knew the full story, he would have some peace of mind for his journey home.

Sai spoke even before Tinh had a chance to ask his questions. "What do you think of her?"

"Well, she looks all right."

Sai didn't like the sound of that "well." Considering all the women whom Tinh knew, he'd hoped for a decisive, "Very good." Sensing his brother's displeasure, Tinh spoke carefully, "Her appearance is very good – strong and healthy, salary at grade 63 at such a young age is really rare. Good family, nice house . . . "

Sai thought to himself, *If that great, why the hesitation?* But aloud, he said, "Who cares about the house? If we mention it, she'll think that's the only thing we're interested in."

"True, we don't really need the house." Tinh had already saved about 5,000 dong in the thrift account for Sai's future home, and Tinh knew he could arrange an honorarium somewhere for a lot of about thirty square meters. Or else, he could look for a piece of new land. He already had the *xoan* lumber soaked. Bricks, roof tiles, cement, plaster – he would ask the District Supply Bureau to provide enough for a unit with two or three rooms. That should not be too hard.

"Then why worry too much about those things. The main issue is how do you like her personality?"

"In general, she's quite gentle, well behaved and articulate, it seems."

There was nothing Tinh could complain about, for she would be a sister-in-law to be proud of. But Tinh was not quite at ease. It bothered him that Sai was so taken. Now, he would have to share Sai with another. True, he did not have any right to take exclusive care of his brother. Still, he wanted a sister-in-law who would listen and wholeheartedly welcome the support of Sai's family. But, even after a brief meeting, it was clear that Chau would end up the stronger half of the couple. Clearly, she'd have a controlling power over Sai's emotions. Where would Tinh and his wife fit in?

"I am only concerned that she is an intellectual, born and bred in the city, while our family is uncouth, from the country, from a muddy village. Your elder sister-in-law is kind-hearted, but uncultured and clumsy, your nieces and nephews, dirty. Our gatherings wouldn't be too comfortable."

"I will have to stay up here anyhow, two or three trips home every year at the most. I don't think it should be a problem. Besides, I am not even sure she will fall in love with me."

"I just want to put the issues on the table. In this period of mutual exploration, you should clearly explain to her the situation in our family." Tinh stopped and looked at his brother. "But how did things go today?"

"Nothing definitive yet."

"There must be something. Otherwise, why would she give you the roses? And the way you two talk."

"You just can't tell with a Hanoi girl."

"True. Take time to know each other well. Why be in a hurry? You've stumbled once already. It's a pity. Fate, as our ancestors would say. If we had cleared up that mess years ago, we would have avoided all the heartache and the broken vows with Miss Huong. More and more, I come to realize what a great woman she is."

The conversation ended with those words. Tinh's carelessness in mentioning the name of that woman who had nothing to do with the matter at hand drove both men into silence. Once, twenty years before, they had also sat in silence and complete disagreement. Now, their feelings for the woman in question, in this silent space, were also different, very different.

Sai did not come to see the school principal until after 7 P.M. They were to meet after the afternoon class, around 4:30 P.M., but Sai didn't get out until seven. Sai's days had begun to take on a predictable pattern. He rode to school at seven in the morning and came home at seven in the evening. After classes, he tutored the weaker students. At home, he studied and read until midnight or later. In addition, Sai was meeting his friends, doing the work of the Party cell and the school Youth League. As always, he was fully dedicated to every task.

Although always busy and with little time to rest, he was strong in mind and body. For the first time in his life, he felt the desire to live and work. He was taking revenge for the years that had been lost, for the time when he had to live for other people. And he was in love, able to fall in love and for the first time in his life openly express it. After six months of these efforts, the school principal called him in for a meeting. He asked him to prepare for an exam that would allow him to study abroad. The test was to take place after the Lunar New Year. In those days, going abroad was not an uncommon event, but it was an important event to Sai. He felt that had his whole life been as pleasant as it was in these first few months in Hanoi, he would have been able to accomplish much more.

Sai was getting ready to go out with Chau. After that first day when Chau had brought him flowers, they had met on two more occasions. Once Chau and Nghia came to visit him on Sunday morning; and on another occasion he had visited Chau and been introduced to her mother. The first time, while seeing her to the gate, he had said to her quietly, "If you are not too busy, let's go out tonight."

She gently shook her head, "I can't go out yet." The second time, hearing his request again, she smiled, "My dear army comrade, let's take it slow. What about next Saturday night?"

"What time?"

"Seven."

"Where?"

"Wait for me at the head of the street."

Sai worked through the following days without any feelings of fatigue, then on Saturday he touched up the army uniform that he had had on when Chau first came to see him. Just in case his bike broke down, he left an hour early. Pedaling slowly, he still arrived forty-five minutes early.

With plenty of time to wait, Sai entered a stall for a cup of tea and to smoke his water pipe to his heart's delight. He left to walk down the street, then returned to the stall again, drank more tea and smoked more tobacco. Three times he took the bike back and forth. Still it was only a quarter to seven. He walked back to the intersection appointed for their meeting. He looked at the house across the street with its balcony protruding over the street like a water tank in the country. He smoked a cigarette and gazed at his watch. Finally, it was seven. It reminded him of the long waits on the trail when vehicles with supplies were passing through. He rearranged his hair and clothes, expecting any minute to see her face. Ten minutes passed. Another five minutes went by. Where was she? 7:20. Perhaps an unexpected event? 7:25. Sai was suspicious and angry. For the first time . . . good heavens, how many first times in one month? For the first time, he had been stood up by a girl ten years his junior.

At 7:30, he decided to go home, but he lingered a few more minutes just in case there was a reason for her tardiness. Her watch might be running slow, or it might have taken her an hour to walk the two minutes from her house. At 7:35, Sai made up his mind to go. After all, he thought, I have my dignity. Why should I let her take me for granted? He walked away slowly but didn't mount his bike. Occasionally, he turned his head back to the intersection. But anger had led him too far away, and he could no longer distinguish the riders on the bikes. He quickly turned around and pedaled back as if he had left something valuable at the intersection.

Looking forward and back, intent on the people around him, he felt relieved. Enough is enough, he thought, still before really leaving, he lit a cigarette. When he looked up, he saw a smiling face walking toward him. His anger rose. I'll say something. I'll make some gesture to let her know that I can not accept such grave tardiness. But her voice, sweet as water for the thirsty, gave him no cause for anger.

"Did you wait long for me?"

He smiled, "Quite awhile."

Only years later did he find out that girls with experience in the city never showed up on time for a date unless they were already in love. But for the moment, though he could not understand why he had to expose himself to the bone-chilling winds from the northeast, he still could not take offense.

"Could I ride with you?"

"I plan to ride with you for the rest of my life."

"No, my dear soldier, don't take advantage of me."

"Is saying 'I love you' now a crime?"

"You are very clever. And yet Tinh said his brother was as gentle as a Buddha."

"Even the Buddha might have to wander about and get his eyes pecked by the roosters."

"Every bit a soldier. They all know how to court a girl."

Such moments of "enchantment" came from his old habits as a soldier, bantering to get over dissatisfaction. In truth, Sai didn't know how to court a girl. He was basically shy and too ready to display his sincerity like some unwrapped cake.

For a long time, Sai and Chau sat together on the stone dais beneath Ly Tu Trong sculpture on Thanh Niem Road. He trembled; it was getting chilly and late, and he hadn't yet found a way to express his feelings. He bent his head, letting his hands cover his face. She smiled as if she had already uncovered his secrets.

"Can I ask you something?" she said.

He looked up, awaiting her next words.

"Do you really love me?"

He wanted to cry out for joy, for all his grievances could now be shared. "How can you doubt it?"

"Why do you love me?" Her voice was chilly, her face sober. He had to clear his throat several times; yet the sentences still tumbled out. "I don't know what to tell you. Soldiers can't do anything unless their hearts are in it." His words sounded pitiful to him, as if he were lying.

She looked at him steadily, her eyes lit with a fire that beckoned him to unburden himself of his most inmost thoughts.

"Through Tinh and my uncle's friends, you must have heard of what has happened to me. Since I was nine years old, the only thing I wanted was to run away to some distant place, put an end to my life in the village, never to see the day I'd have to return. I had to give up everything in order to have a moment like this. . . . After all that, do you think I'd trifle with you?"

She still looked at him. Tears flowed down her cheeks, her whole body shaking uncontrollably.

"Is it my past that weighs so heavily, making you put up with gossip and resistance from your family?"

With a determined gesture, she wiped away the tears with a handkerchief, tidied up her hair, and said, as if it were a command, "Let's go."

He could only follow her order in silence. That was it, he thought. What foolishness drove him to speak words that stirred up so much fear, that created an abyss over which she could not cross? They returned home in complete silence. It was, he knew, the end of a love that had just barely begun, but then, at the intersection, she said, "Wait for me here tomorrow night."

≣ And that next night, the couple went to West Lake, and Chau finally told him her story:

I fell in love when I was almost eighteen. I had just passed the university entrance exam. My school was evacuated to a village in the highlands. In the first month we dug trenches, filled up the foundation, cut wild grass and built houses for the school.

We girls were contracted to make twenty straw screens for the school. We cut and dried the grass ourselves, and split the bamboo to make the screens. Up the mountain we went, gathering grass in the morning, and down to the streams we went, picking pebbles and tiny fish in the afternoon. We caught those tiny, film-like fish, the ones with round bodies and tails spreading out like fans. They clung to the pebbles, and we would just lift the pebbles to catch them. We brought them home for "general improvement." Some took out their brand new handkerchiefs to collect them. Without those diversions and the trip to the mountain to gather flowers, the boredom would have been unbearable.

A pharmaceutical company had also evacuated to the highland village with us, but they had arrived a few years before we did. We lived in the houses that they either hadn't used or had vacated to make room for us. My friend and I lived behind the quarters of an electrical worker. We girls of sixteen or seventeen called the men a few years older than us "uncle," to increase the distance between us.

But if they patronized us by calling themselves "uncle," we would immediately put them in their place. "Uncle" electrical worker was nine years older than I, about your age. But – please don't be offended – he had a fairer complexion and looked very young, about twenty-two or twenty-three. Still, he was a man of considerable maturity and experience, and he carried himself beautifully. I don't know what he wore to work, but at home he dressed neatly. Simply but well. Even when it was hot, he wore blue trousers and a white shirt. When it got cold, he wore a dark red, short-sleeved sweater, occasionally covered by a jacket with print woven with blue flowers. We passed through the yard day in and day out, running into each other, but never offering each other a word of greeting.

One day a girl's sandal strap broke and we could not find any nails. Everyone pushed me to go get the nails. "All right," I said. "I'll go. Surely those men will have some." At the door I hesitated, not knowing what form of address to use because I knew that he called himself "uncle" to many of my classmates. Still unsure, I heard a sweet voice. "What do you need, my little girl?"

I was angered by his tone, but I could not say anything. "Sir," I asked, "are there any nails here?"

"To fix the sandal? Yes, 'Uncle' has some." Even if the nails cost one piaster each, I'd rather have bought them than listen to his form of address. Well, I thought, I'll play along. "Uncle, sir, do you also have a hammer or a pair of pliers?"

"Yes."

"Uncle, do you have leather or a piece of rubber that can be made into a strap?"

"No, but let Uncle cut a piece of the bike's rubber tire, won't that do?"

"Oh, I think so. Thank you very much, Uncle." Both of us were smooth talking each other, almost ready to laugh. I nodded my head and left.

In general, I had to admit "Uncle" handled himself well. He helped us when we needed help, but he never overdid things. For instance, he played the guitar and sang well. But we never saw him show off. Every night a group of workers, some even older than our "uncle," came to visit us. "Uncle" showed no interest. He stayed home to read. This continued for a couple of months. During that time, I felt unhappy because the engineers, the pharmacists from the company, the teachers and the students in the higher grades at school were always harassing me. When I couldn't stand it anymore, I went over to his quarters to hide and borrow books to read. He did not have many, but what he did have was good – Aimatop, Pushkin, Dostoyevski, Pautopxki and titles like *What Is To Be Done, Jane Eyre, The Path of Suffering* and *Anna Karenina*. He even lent me the unpublished copy of *Letter of a Woman Stranger*, the work of Stefan Zweig, an Austrian or Dutch author translated by his friend from the university.

I had loved reading since childhood, from fifth grade, but especially from ninth grade. But then my mother, who feared this love might hurt my schoolwork, forbade me to read novels. So by the time I was sixteen, even rumpled books looked new to me. With something to read, I had a reason not to entertain guests or go gather flowers on the mountain or catch fish in the streams. I was getting closer to "uncle." Whenever I had the need to read or listen to the guitar, he would oblige. "Uncle" and I felt very much at home, at ease with each other, as if we were blood relatives. It was in those days that he fell in love with me. At first, I was surprised and frightened, but later I too fell in love. And then I found out that he had a wife and two children. I was pained by that knowledge, but I couldn't control myself. I needed someone who loved me truly and would not care what others thought.

I asked him to take me home to meet his wife. I would tell her that we both had the right to love whomever we loved. It would then be up to him to choose between us. "How could I be so reckless?" he replied, rejecting my idea. He said to just leave everything to him, not to create a scene. I believed in him, trusted him when he cried about his agonizing obligations or when he spoke of his happiness at being with me. "If in this world there is such a thing as happiness, such a thing as love, then it is you who have taught me its truth. You are my great friend, my great teacher," he said. But he did nothing. Realizing that, I demanded he give me up even in his thoughts. Those were, however, just words. Nothing really happened to cause regret.

When I was in love with him, I never went out with him like this. Anyhow, my faith perished. Now, there was nothing left to believe anymore.

Chau had finished talking. She breathed a deep sigh. Tender feelings came over Sai. A woman so faithful to her love, that was a surprise. To have real love, that was it, there was no need to hide, no need to cover up mistakes of the past, no need to fear anything. It was rare to find a woman who could be that hard on herself. Sai looked at her downcast face and said, "Is it possible I could be one of those men who sets out to steal your love?"

She glanced up. Her eyes peered intently into the veil of mist falling over the chilly lake. From the first time they had met, she had realized deceit was foreign to his nature. That was what she was looking for, someone who did not tell lies or put on airs, someone who loved her deeply and would take good care of her. He said, as if he were the one at fault, "Can I make amends for all the disappointments you've had in love?"

She nodded her head. He continued, "At first, I fell in love with your beauty, your gentle nature, your intelligence. Now I realize that past disappointments have given you an immense depth. I just want to make you understand that I am in love with you, regardless of what faults, if any, you may have." Sai feared that if he did not speak, she would not fully understand him. And why should she? He was talking across an empty space that still set them apart.

Chau looked down, as if lost in thought. Sai remained silent. It was a long while before she spoke, "Tell me some more, my darling."

"You don't really love me, it seems?"

"That's what you want?"

"I will jump into West Lake if you ask me."

"Then jump."

He sprang to his feet to show his determination, but then sat down, close to her. "Enough pain already, I am afraid of mockery."

"You think I am joking?" she said.

"No, that does not cross my mind. But your silence scares me."

"You think that I enjoy coming here so that I can jest with you?"

"You have never said what I long to hear."

"You only like the words?"

"No, but I would love to hear the sound of that sacred word."

"Then, have you asked me in a solemn way?"

"How about now?"

She smiled, nodding her head. Then she smiled, shaking her head. Always a believer in the concrete, he could not trust anything not in his hand. Suppressing a sigh, his face was suddenly downcast.

He sat still, with his head slightly bent toward the windy lake. He heard a sudden soft sound, very quick, near his cheek.

He turned to hold her smiling face and press his cold face against hers, his dry lips over her white teeth. The moment of greatest difficulty had passed. His arms clasped her perfectly round back to his chest. The lake, the trees, the Thang Loi Hotel, its lights shining brilliantly on the other shore, seemed to be set in motion. Nothing could stop the passion of two human beings in their prime. Only when the river bank was deserted, when the stone benches and the places to sit among the tree roots were abandoned, did she ask, "Did you like it?" Naturally, he nodded.

From then on they no longer had to speak cryptically. A new life for both had truly begun. They had to start planning beginning from tonight, the night on West Lake that could never be forgotten.

CHAPTER 8

"Sai, why don't you let me introduce you to a girl?" Huong's offer made the emptiness of the room seem even more oppressive.

After Sai returned from the war, Huong came regularly to see him on those "administrative" days when she had time off. Each morning Huong prepared breakfast for her family, packed her lunch box and left for work. At the office, she sat at her desk busy reading or writing for about an hour, then, announced to her office mate, "If anyone asks, say I've run to the food market for a little while or tell them I've gone to the local branches to get a handle on things."

In the late morning, in offices all across the city, it was common for people to be absent from their desks. Lovers usually scheduled their rendezvous during these times. With parents at work and children in daycare or school, the collective housing projects were as deserted as graveyards. For a few hours, lovers had their privacy in these apartments. Then, they returned to their work and became, once again, respectable members of the community. They were no longer people with illicit partners, tainted by their lascivious behavior. They were respectable citizens with the power to interrogate and criticize. They taught their children to lead moral lives, to have discipline and to be cultivated individuals.

Huong was not this sort of person. True, she had to sneak behind the backs of her husband and officemates to see her former lover. But she had always understood the clear boundary between family and love. She cared for Sai, the way a wife cares for her husband. Sai was the great love of her life. But the caring was strictly spiritual. She already had a family of her own, one she had suffered with and nurtured for ten years. Thirty-four years old, she didn't have the energy to give up what she possessed. She was torn by conflict. She wanted Sai to marry so she could have peace, but she feared another wrong choice would make Sai suffer even more. Still, he had to marry, otherwise her love for him could break up her family. The prospect of family upheaval terrified her.

Afflicted with contradictory desires, Huong very much wanted Sai to get married so that she could have peace, but she feared that if he did, what would happen if her family broke up. These thoughts, though they existed only in her mind, colored her every act and gesture.

With Sai, it was just the opposite. In his days and nights on the battlefield, he dreamed of being "liberated" from family obligations, and hoped that some miracle would give Huong back to him or at least that Huong might bless him with enough of her love that he could say, "We loved each other. Our love was real, so real that it remained unchanged after ten years."

In those days, at the sound of her name, he felt his body warm with happiness. He allowed himself to dream that Huong would always be part of his life, that she would forever be by his side. Still, he did not picture her as a partner.

When he had returned from the South, with his divorce about to take effect, three or four interested parties had sent word about Huong, but by then, too much had happened. Huong was only a sacred memory, an idol that still kindled strong feelings but she was no longer a source of passion, no longer the solution to his needs. Now a completely free man, with the power to select his mate, Sai was free to fall in love with someone like Huong, someone who would be the envy of other men, a surprise to the village, someone in many ways a cut above his former wife. A man's happiness could be increased tenfold by the envy of others.

Still, it took Sai awhile to realize all this. His first day in Hanoi, he had asked Hieu to send for her. Then he insisted on seeing her home and on going out with her again later. Panic-stricken, Huong emphatically refused. "No, no, my darling. You should get married. I will find you someone."

"I don't think I'll marry again," Sai said.

Even though he went out with friends to meet other women, Sai wore a sad face when he saw Huong, making her even more unhappy about his loneliness.

When Sai and Hieu cooked their own meals, she made a point of standing in line for them or getting others to do it for her, so she could buy all the items in the coupon book. When Hieu was out, Huong taught Sai, step by step, how to cook. Tofu, meat, monosodium glutamate, fish sauce. She had to explain how to do everything. With Hieu at home, things were in control; without him, the house and the kitchen became a mess with meals on an irregular schedule. It was misery, due to the absence of a woman's touch.

In the end, Huong had to take care of two places: one, a family that was without joy, but could not be abandoned, the other, a passionate love full of energy that could not be consummated.

"Maybe I should marry someone just to get it over and done with," Sai told Huong.

Her face drooped with sadness.

He continued. "Had you listened to me, had we both started over, things wouldn't be like this."

Huong's eyes started to tear. She hurriedly wiped at her face with a handkerchief and comforted him, "There were times I wished it could be so, but it was not meant to be."

"After I get married, can you still see me?"

"No."

"Then you don't want me to get married!"

"It depends on how the 'other one' will behave."

"We'll be easy with one another, just as we are with other friends." Huong did not reply. He quickly corrected himself. "Of course, our private love is not for others to know."

That was almost the last time they met before Sai's marriage. There was just one more meeting, when she heard of his impending marriage. Unable to restrain herself, she came to see him. Her voice warm with emotion, she asked, "Why do you have to hurry?"

"Because you insisted. Didn't I tell you that I wanted to 'get it over and done with'?"

She smiled cynically and retorted, "I insisted? Or is it that her beauty drives you crazy?"

"You'd be satisfied only if I married someone ugly?"

"What right do I have!"

Sai had a pretext to get angry, an anger necessary at that moment. "I don't understand you at all."

"You still can't understand after twenty years?"

"Don't you remember how many times I discussed this with you?"

"But I've never forbidden you to marry."

"Not forbidden, but you got angry when you heard the news. About a month ago, we talked this over right here, and I've just done what you asked, and yet, now . . . "

"You won't be able to do anything anymore."

"Why not?"

"Because you are no longer yourself."

"Why?"

"Because you will have to make an extra effort just to keep up with her demands. There'll be no time left for other things."

"I won't allow that."

"You will, too."

"Why?"

"Because you don't have the strength to resist."

"What's your basis for saying that?"

"Twenty years of being in love with you and in despair over it. Twenty years of emotional pain."

"I don't know what you mean anymore! Come, tell me what to do now. I'll do whatever makes you happy."

Feeling very much consoled, she said, "It's not that I am selfish, thinking only of my family and children, and nothing of you, it's not even that I'm feeling jealous at your happiness. You know too well why I got married and what kind of life I have had. There were many nights when I held my child in my arms and cried, asking myself why I had to torture myself like this. My husband, I have to say, is a good and kind man. Unfortunately, for some reason, we just don't get along. You probably understand that even better than I do. But it was I who made the decision to marry him, so I have to bear all the sorrows.

"The time you went to B in the South, I found out why you had had the baby. I felt for you, I was angry with you. I felt for myself, was angry with myself. I wished, oh, how much I wished, that you could come North then, at whatever price. We would have been able to get back together because no one understood you more than I, no one loved you more than I. The wishes never came true; I had to draw my sustenance from the children. It's for the sake of the children that one goes on living. I worked very hard to build up that family and to give the children a good education. But there was not one moment when I didn't miss you, when I didn't think of the danger you faced on the battlefield. Love for you was inside of me. I lived on it. Your loved ones – friends and relatives – became my loved ones. And the thought that you would have no one to return to frightened me."

"I saw Tuyet after I had my second child. I urged her not to punish herself and others any more. Frankly, she deserves a lot of sympathy. She cried and said, 'My dear sister, I know that Sai is hurt deeply, but so am I. I love him very much, but he cannot love me back, and I have to live with it. You see, my husband looked at me just once in my whole life and then left me by myself to bring up the baby. For a dozen years, before he went away, I lay awake at night hoping he'd pay some attention to me. You're a woman, you know how it is, a woman in the prime of life, full of energy and desire, lying alone in bed night after night, what agony could be worse? But if I run back home on my own, my parents will chop off my head. *'Live as a human being, die as a ghost of his family. Don't drag your body home. If Sai throws you out, then we will talk.'* I didn't mind it when I was still young, but later there was a time I hoped he would kick me out, strike a few blows against me and boot me out, just to give me an excuse to go home. But he was scared of my parents, of brother Tinh, and later even of his army unit, and so he did not dare toss me out. He just quietly plotted to get away from me, the farther the better. I understand the reasons he joined the army and then went B. I have a child now. I will bring him up myself. He can marry whoever he wishes, I don't care. As long as I take care of my child, no one can turn me out.' "

"You see," Huong continued, "just like Tuyet, I live for my children. Because of the children, I dare not live with the man I love. I only wish, deep in my heart, that you will find someone who is compatible with you, who understands you and who can look after you in my place. To help you make up for those months and years that were lost and to create the right environment for you to get ahead. I believe there are many more good things you can still achieve – and men of your caliber are always in short supply."

In the six months before his wedding, Sai had a chance to stand back and look at himself and consider the feelings of the woman he loved; their depth, he understood, came from endless nights of tears. But he sincerely believed that everything was possible now that he and Chau had fallen in love. Chau was neither dumb nor uneducated. He had not yet discovered any incompatibility between them. On the contrary, there were quite a few occasions when both had to shout "oh" because their thoughts were so similar. Now, he said to

Huong, as if it were a solemn pledge, "Rest easy. I will do my utmost so that you won't be disappointed."

Realizing that things couldn't be changed, that what has been arranged cannot be undone, Huong felt that Sai's pledge indeed meant something. But on Sai's wedding day, she cried the whole night. Cried for whom, for what reason, she didn't know. But that event threw her off for days, hurling her into a state of numbed dejection and despondency. And when the night came, at exactly 7:30, when undoubtedly the strings of firecrackers were exploding in front of the wedding room, she burst out sobbing.

In spite of the disparagement, the dissuasions, of Huong and those close to him, Sai was determined to love Chau. In those days he felt happiness coming over him like a windstorm. Despite occasional moments of annoyance at insignificant things, he felt as if he were swimming in a sea of immense joy, in an intoxication that was almost smothering. Since that first night when they'd declared their intentions on the bank of the West Lake, they had in fact started their married life together. In that moment of ecstasy, Chau had drawn Sai to her breast, "Don't ever leave me," she'd cried. But, even in this moment, that young man from Ha Vi had not been able to refrain from his need for certain results. In that moment he had rudely posed the question "Suppose your mother were sitting there and we were . . . doing this, would it be all right?" Chau hesitated, "If you wished, I would go along," she'd answered. Sai was satisfied. No matter how refined these city types may become, a little vulgarity was never out of place.

Not long after, Chau cried out in fear, "My darling, I might be . . ."

Her worry, in this case, turned out to be the cause of his joy. Sai squeezed her so tightly that she had to struggle to breathe. "Are you really sure?"

She nodded gently. "The day after our first time, I felt anxious in a strange sort of way. And when nothing happened a few days later, I was frightened."

"Good heavens! Why should you be frightened? Don't you want our child?" Chau sat up, pulling his face against her breasts. She embraced him with one hand, patting him rhythmically on the back with the other, as if she were nursing a child, just as Huong had done twenty years ago, to soothe him. As if he'd just recovered what he'd lost for the last twenty years, he obediently reached to her breast. She lowered her head, looked at the other breast, squeezed till it became pointed, and said with tenderness: "You see, it has grown black." He stared up at her with adorning eyes, then with eyes half-closed, he returned to his happy dream.

"Darling!" He did not look up. "Or . . . " Seeing that he did not respond, she hesitated: "Or . . . "

"You're thinking of going to the clinic?"

She nodded silently, without enthusiasm. Sai sprang to his feet, straightening up his clothes.

"If that's what you want, let's part ways right now."

"Are you threatening me?"

"No, I don't make threats, but don't you see that we could be so happy if we had a child?"

"And expose our shame to the whole world?"

"Don't you see that we should get married?"

"Married! And have a baby in three months?"

"Why does it have to be three? Let's say it's about a month early."

"We have to go from the last period I had."

"Then make it two months, more or less."

"Can we have the wedding right now, today?"

"We will have everything ready for a wedding within half a month. Many babies are born in only seven months. But who cares! If they think we have slept with each other before getting married, let them. It doesn't matter in the least."

"For men like you it doesn't matter, but you have to think of a woman like myself."

"God, these days people are so busy standing in line to buy noodles, rice, oil and firewood, no one has the time or the energy to gossip about things like this. If you find anybody who does, just call me, point them out to me. 'Here, he's the culprit!' You think they will dare to accuse me of having a child with my wife?"

Chau burst out laughing, then scolded him, "Stop that, no more idle talk. You always dramatize things. How can you manage to get everything done in half a month?"

"You leave that to me. I will show you a detailed plan early tomorrow morning. Then you'll go with me to complete the necessary formalities. As for the rest, you have nothing to worry about."

She knew that Sai was like a tiger, on most occasions half-asleep, but when the situation called for it, he was fearless. She indeed had nothing to worry about. Sai's experience as a soldier had made him resourceful, unwilling to accept defeat in any circumstances. She was quite relieved. They drew close together, caressing gently, until Chau was seized with a violent stomach cramp. Sai held her body close, asking what she needed. But Chau couldn't speak. "Should I take you home?" Chau nodded, letting him help her onto the bike's back seat. Chau still had the cramp. She could feel its pain increasing, and he was numb with fear. After a long interval, he asked, "How are you feeling? Do you have any medicines at home? Should we stop by the emergency room?" She shook her head. He couldn't tell what this gesture meant: that there were no medicines or that she didn't want to go to the emergency room or that she didn't have an answer to his questions. When they arrived at the gate, he planned to wait until her mother opened the door to let her in, but she waved him away. She might not want her mother to know that she had cramps because of going out with him. With that thought in mind, he rode his bike quickly to the intersection. Then he turned around and waited till the light came on and Chau went inside before he pedaled home like a madman.

Sai woke Hieu up to describe Chau's symptoms. He told him that her condition seemed serious, but he couldn't say what sort of pain she was experiencing. The two then went to consult Hieu's doctor friend.

Sai came to see Chau early the next morning. He had to wait over half an hour for Chau's mother to get up. Only after she'd washed her face, brushed her teeth, and started cooking rice in the kitchen, did he have a chance to say, "Good morning." He then sat down next to Chau. "Do you think anything is wrong? I brought a painkiller, B1, B2, B12, and multivitamins for you. If things do not get better, the doctor, a friend of Hieu, asks you to come in for a checkup." Sai arranged the pills on the bed near Chau's pillow. Chau, who was lying in bed, facing away, picked them up and threw them at him. "Take them away! How heartless can you be!" Shocked by her words and acts, which he would never have thought possible in such an educated woman, from such a good family, Sai grew pale and shook with anger. Stunned for a moment, he walked to the door. Chau abruptly sprang up, grasping his hand.

"Let go of me."

"I apologize."

Speechless for a while, he finally asked, "How can you behave like that to me?"

"I said I was wrong, and I have apologized." Her voice was so endearing he couldn't remain offended. "You don't love me at all."

"I was looking for a doctor all last night. I got the medicine and ran here as fast as I could, waiting for hours. When I saw that you slept well, I went home. It was almost three o'clock in the morning. And now, I am here again. If that's not loving you, I don't know what is!"

"No, that's not it. You don't understand us women at all. Had you comforted me, rallied me with a few kind, loving words, I would have felt that my pain was being shared. But no, you said absolutely nothing; I really felt sorry for myself."

"You didn't say anything when I asked."

"You asked, like a judge interrogating a defendant, and I was in the middle of an excruciating pain. How could anyone respond in a situation like that?"

Sai could make no sense of this. Did she just want a few words to comfort and console? Why any lazy, dishonest man could do that.

"You see, when one is sick and dispirited, who can a woman share her sorrows with other than the one she loves?"

"There's no need to waste time and energy running around like mad. I believe that once we are living together, you'll be able to adjust. With time, you will get used to it."

Sai had no idea of the many things that he would have to get used to. Nothing major he thought, nothing difficult, just a little attention would take care of things. But somehow the incidents ended up seeming petty, annoying and unpleasant. Once, paying her brother a visit, Sai offered a warm greeting, then went to prepare the tea himself. After, he offered cigarettes, holding out the pack with both hands in a very polite manner. Later, when they had left, Chau grumbled at him, "Why do you have to act like that?"

"What? That's how I've always been with people."

"I know. You have a heart of gold. That's why I love you. But here your sincerity is questioned and sneered at."

"Is that so!"

"He is the head of the Bureau of Organization. He is used to showing contempt for those who are not upright and serious. He thinks that they come to flatter, to ask him for special favors."

"But that never crossed my mind."

"True. With your ability, you won't have to beg for his help. But you forget that you are about to marry his younger sister. Observing your behavior, he must have thought that you were up to no good, that you were beside yourself for having made such a good match. He will look down on both of us. You should have been calm and collected, as if to say, 'I love your sister because she loves me, but otherwise I couldn't care less. Today I come to pay you a visit to inform you of our plan, to show our respect. Treat me any way you like. You are the host, I am the guest. I expect a certain courtesy; otherwise I will give you the cold shoulder. When you need my help, we will see.' "

The more Sai listened, the more dumbfounded he became. His face looked as silly as that of a little boy receiving his first lesson at school.

Another time, Hieu and he invited Uncle Ha, his friend the matchmaker, and Chau for dinner. During the course of the meal Chau sat timidly. Repeatedly, Sai had to pick out the choice morsels for her. Later that night, she scolded him. "How odd you are! How many times have I said that you must pay attention. Who wouldn't be happy with a husband as devoted to his wife as you are? But it must fit the occasion. Do you know what you made them think? That you are too attached to your wife, caring only for her and nobody else. It's not good for others to have that thought. It will drive them away. You cannot be happy with just your wife and nobody else. I don't even want to mention those times when you picked out pieces of meat that I had grown sick of and mixed them with my rice so that I could not put them back."

≣ But when he tried not to think about her and to occupy himself with other matters, Sai couldn't be his normal self. Usually, in a crowd, Sai was very versatile. He could talk on and on incessantly or he could sit absolutely still. When he was with friends who were his contemporaries or his seniors, everything was, by mutual agreement, left up to him: he decided whether the gathering would be long or short, whether the discussion would be serious or lighthearted and whether the plans would include food or entertainment.

People appreciated Sai's education and intelligence and especially his devotion to friends. The magnetism of his simple face opened many doors when his friends needed help. Whenever someone ran into a difficult problem, the word went out to "call on Sai" to go "into battle." It was generally understood that if he failed, it would be a waste of time to continue to try and resolve the problem. When Sai fell in love with Chau, his friends all lamented. "We have lost Sai," they said. It was a shame, they added, to see a young man like him being haunted by a girl like that, like a lost soul all the time.

There was an older war correspondent who looked upon Sai as a brother and had written dozens of articles about him. The correspondent was always very serious, and Sai thought him a bit old-fashioned. In a solemn tone, he had chided Sai, "You shouldn't fall in love with that girl. Let me find you someone more your type. Someone fair and honest."

Sai thought that his friend was looking at him as if they were still on the battlefield in the midst of the jungle. His pride hurt, he said, "Thank you. Over thirty or forty people have given me advice on what to do in this matter. You are all ready to bring me someone 'exemplary,' according to your taste. But I can't stand it."

"I guarantee that I will bring you a good-looking and compatible girl."

God forbid, Sai thought. *How could a thirty-four-year-old divorced man find someone fairer than Chau?*

"I only offer you advice to consider," said the war correspondent.

Sai sat silently, he thought about his friend's words before he responded. It was a long time till he felt ready to return to the conversation with the journalist.

He summarized his own situation for himself: Some say Chau is far beyond my reach; others that I can do better. Some say Chau would make an able, resourceful wife; others that she will destroy my life before I know it. But I choose to love and get married for my own sake; I do not love and get married for the sake of others.

Sai knew that twenty years ago, if he'd had the freedom to love whomever he chose, then he wouldn't be so full of hesitation and doubt at this point in his life. A man who was eighteen or twenty could always start over if he made a mistake. Youth meant confidence and the daring to say things freely and recklessly – "I love you" to one, and in the same breath "You are the soul of my soul" to another.

When a girl took these lines to heart, a man didn't have to say anything more. A man didn't need to weigh the significance of every gesture, the meaning of the pitch of every sentence.

Now, however, it was just the opposite. His mistakes would be more significant, and he was always fearful of being judged, being treated with contempt even before he spoke a word or made a gesture. He had to think twice about the things he was going to do, the words he was going to speak. He was frightened of making a mistake, of taking a false step that could not be retraced. So he was always on edge, tense and clumsy.

Finally, Sai responded to the war correspondent's concerns. He spoke with a calm voice. "To be honest with you, our wedding is about to take place."

"I only offer my advice for you to consider," his friend nodded. "The final decision rests, of course, with you."

Sai knew his friend was disappointed, but his friend did not show any sign of displeasure. Indeed, the next day he volunteered to take care of the picture-taking for both of the families and to handle the printing of the invitations and wedding announcements.

Only five days after his decision to marry, the Organizing Committee had its first, and only, meeting. Sai had already assigned tasks to each participant. The meeting would allow Sai to listen to their reports and to review the results to see if any adjustment or changes needed to be made. It was also the day Chau officially started her vacation. When she arrived at Sai's apartment, everybody was already there.

They were all close friends from various departments of the central office as well as from the army, the village and Hanoi. Sai demonstrated his organizing ability. He managed everyone in the confident manner of a boss handling his underlings. Mr. Quang, the External Affairs Officer, has he checked on the date the couple would have to register their marriage? Had Mr. Thu, the housing man, obtained an apartment unit yet? Mr. Hoa, the "General Supply" chief, was responsible for providing cakes, candies, cigarettes, beer and liquor. How many of each item could he obtain? Did Mr. Thanh of the Ministry of Forestry have the bed, the table and the cupboard ready? Did Mr. Dinh, the artist, complete the decoration plan for the auditorium? When it was time to report, each person complained that he had been "ambushed" by surprises. They glanced over at Chau and broke into mischievous smiles. Chau was embarrassed, but at the same time, she appreciated the devotion, resourcefulness and humor of Sai's friends. A dozen people crowded together in Hieu's small room, talking and laughing with relish because the tasks were urgent and troublesome, yet they would be flawlessly dispatched. On the way to inspect their new apartment, Chau chided Sai, albeit happily: "You're asking for favors and yet you spoke as if you were ordering everyone around."

"Old friends, old army buddies, that's how we always do things."

"But you are always so melodramatic, I think it's b-a-d!"

"Men in olden times declared that when a woman said 'hate,' she really meant 'love.' "

"Don't deceive yourself."

"Don't say it too loud. Our baby will break out giggling if he hears it."

She almost burst out laughing, but quickly clenched her teeth as if to hold back an emotion that included a touch of fear and self-pity.

In her look, Sai could sense uncertainty. He inferred that his wife was happy, but at the same time worried about whether the baby would come to term. He was suddenly filled with love. He wanted to say a word of comfort, to express his deep gratitude to the woman who was carrying his child. But he couldn't say it. Perhaps it wasn't the time. He pedaled slowly, with one hand on the handle bar of her bike to pull her along. He looked at her, smiling softly, bashfully. She averted her eyes.

After they had agreed on a date for the wedding, Sai sent a member of the Organizing Committee to deliver a letter to Brother Tinh. "After Tet I will have to take an intensive course to prepare for a trip. Chau's mother is in poor health. Therefore I have proposed and her family has accepted. We will marry on the seventeenth. It's sudden, I know, but I am sure that, as always, you will find a way to take care of everything for me. To be specific, arrange so that we can 'present' ourselves on the ninth of this month. Items needed for the engagement ceremony: one hundred fresh areca nuts, one kilo of Thai Nguyen tea, one kilo of candied lotus seed (you can buy it up here when convenient), one carton of Thu Do cigarettes (in the past Uncle Ha has used his connections to buy them from relations), and one bottle of Lua Moi vodka. Please borrow and hand over to my friend two thousand in cash (one thousand for the bride's family, the other thousand to pay the honorarium commission for the apartment). If you don't have enough, my friend up here will get the rest. After the ceremony, we would like to have a small celebration. Can you take care of that as well? For about thirty people, more or less."

That's all it took, Sai didn't consider how difficult the tasks were or the circumstances of Tinh's family. He simply sent off a few handwritten notes to get what he wanted. It was as if his brother were a warehouse chief, whose only job was to provide, or as if he were an administrative head, whose function was to cater to his superior's desires. There were times when Tinh had felt annoyed at his brother's cavalier requests, but he had never expressed this displeasure to Sai.

Sai took his sweetheart home to the village to introduce her to his relatives. Sai usually came home empty-handed, so Tinh expected nothing from his brother, but this time he was touched by Chau's thoughtfulness and felt happy and proud. After Chau had greeted all the members of the family, she asked Tinh in a low voice, "Dear brother, where is our family's altar?"

"Ah, ah, it's at our elder brother's. . . . What do you need?"

"I would like to offer flowers and incense to our ancestors."

Grasping her meaning, Tinh shouted, "Elder brother, please come. Our sister-in-law would like to offer flowers and incense to our ancestors." The elder brother, who sat next to Hieu, stood up and walked over and stood beside Chau and his brother. Chau solemnly placed five bundles of joss sticks, a bouquet of dried flowers, a dozen fresh areca nuts, a bunch of betel leaves, a bunch of bananas and a dozen oranges on top of the couch.

To clear the air after this moment of solemnity, Mr. Ha spoke, "Do you have an altar at home, my dear niece?"

"No, sir. But during Tet, my mother always lights incense and bows to our ancestors." She gave a pack of Thu Do cigarettes to Tinh. "Would you please offer this to our brothers and uncle for me?" Then she slung her knapsack over her shoulder and walked to the kitchen to greet Tinh's wife, a woman she knew to be very kind hearted and maternal. "My dear sister, I do not have much. Just a little gift for you to give the children."

There were only a few rolls of biscuits, a few boxes of chocolate –

things that Tinh's family already had, but Tinh's wife was nonetheless deeply touched. For the first time, she – a woman who devoted her life to serving her husband's family – was considered important enough to be honored with gifts and then to apportion those gifts among the children. Normally, Tinh distributed items whether those items were purchased supplies or gifts. When he did, Tinh's wife usually felt like an outsider who deserved nothing and who was forgotten when it came to the distributing gifts to the family.

Now, dispensing with formalities, she accepted the presents from Chau. "I'll take them. Let me hand them over to my husband. Will you hold them for me?" she asked Tinh. "Call the children and give them out." She seized Chau's two hands, "Let me tell you something. When you come next time, don't bother with gifts. They cost too much. You are an engineer, but in the city even a toothpick has to be purchased. Try hard to put away something for the baby later. You've got to control the expenses, because Sai will be too open-handed. Men, they just don't know enough about these things. In the future, I'll tell the children to bring you thick soybean sauce every month. For dipping greens and slow-boiled fish. It is much better than fish sauce, and every little bit helps. Our parents have passed away; we live so far apart. You will have a hard time. When you have a baby or feel too burdened, I'll send the children to help you with the laundry, cooking and food shopping. Now, don't mind me at all. You go out there to have some tea and talk with uncle and brothers. Go, soot is already sticking to your hair."

Tinh was in a good mood when Chau visited. He smiled and talked freely. "That's good. Let's go out. Our uncles are waiting, and people from the District Party Committee and offices." He was pleased with the conduct of his future sister-in-law. After the previous week's frantic activity to carry out his brother's requests, he felt relieved. The whole family was having a joyful reunion. His sister-in-law had won everyone's sympathies. Who knew what the future would bring, but outwardly at least, no one could find any fault with her. He was satisfied with the well-made dishes on the three food trays: delicious flavored chicken, crunchy lean meat pie, fried meat roll, dried intestines stir-fried with cauliflower, fresh shrimp, hearts, liver, chicken soup, sea crab, sea shrimp ground into water and mixed with egg yolk to imitate a swallow's nest, with both grainy and glutinous rice. Even a Hanoi feast would not have been better.

When people started drinking tea and coffee, Tinh's wife and a dozen of the little ones closed off the kitchen and noisily ate the leftovers. The elder daughter used her chopsticks to apportion the food among the children. In an instant, they had finished the bowl of vegetable broth she'd poured over the white rice. The children held a piece of meat cake, chicken, pork pie or meat roll between chopsticks, then thrust out their bowls to ask for a scoop of limewater corn cake. Tinh – still smiling broadly – dashed into the kitchen as if to share with everyone today's moment of complete happiness. Surprised to see the children eating corn instead of rice, he uttered a loud "Huh!" The children boisterously asked him to join in. He gestured for them to quiet down. "Why corn, my dear wife?" His wife did not say a word, but quickly approached him and whispered, "With only one ton of rice left, we have to save enough for Tet, and for Sai. If the children have their fill today, there won't be much left. Don't worry about us, go out there and leave us alone."

The eldest daughter also said, "Go out there, Daddy, else Auntie Chau will come in here."

When Sai first arrived back in Ha Vi, he ran about to invite all his aunts and uncles to the house. He didn't want to take Chau round to introduce her to everyone – that would be a tiring, time-consuming task and it also would have put Chau on the spot. But Sai did not need to make the invitations, since the whole neighborhood, invited or not, came over just when the food trays were being served. For days, a rumor had been spreading throughout Ha Vi that Sai was going to marry a beautiful college graduate. So, villagers found their way over to the house to have a look and gossip. At first men and the elders came with their children or grandchildren. Then the women, the aunts came. Finally, brothers and sisters dropped by before they went to work. They brought their betel leaf and lime and offered to share tobacco. And they gossiped. But the largest and noisiest part of the crowd was the children. They formed a throng behind the bamboo screen, and no one bothered to chase them away. All eyes were on Chau whose face was set in a permanent smile as she offered betel leaves and tea to all the guests.

One lanky and dark-skinned boy of about nine or ten showed up. Wearing an army shirt tucked into army pants, he looked like a bundle of straw knotted in the middle. No one knew from what village or family he came from. With him were five other boys, probably used to tending geese or water buffaloes. They stood at the edge of the yard. Finally, the unknown boy insolently pushed himself past everyone and entered the house to stare at Chau. Then, abruptly, he rushed outside, shouting, "Boy, oh boy, the bride is really beautiful." "Quiet, quiet," someone exclaimed after him. All his friends followed.

To soften Chau's embarrassment and to disperse the uninvited guests, Mr. Ha stood up and began to speak in a solemn voice: "After a long period of courtship, Sai and Chau came home today to present themselves to relatives on both sides. They will get married in the near future. Since it is getting dark and vehicles have a way of breaking down on the long road, please allow them to leave for Hanoi so that they can return to their appointed tasks tomorrow." Chau looked up at her uncle with gratitude. She took leave of the people around her and quickly disappeared into the kitchen. Sai and Tinh joined her there.

Tinh's wife spoke, "Hurry up, it's getting dark. Husband dear, they have a knapsack with them, would you show them the food and ask them to take some of it?"

"Yes, yes, bring Chau's sack here to put things in," Tinh chimed in.

Tinh's wife whispered softly, "As for the candied lotus seeds and the cigarettes, please give Uncle Sai money so that he can ask someone to get those for them."

"Good! Good!"

Sai asked his nieces and nephews to get Chau's shawl, jacket and gloves. These were the first words he'd spoke to them since returning to the village. Then he had to hurry away, amid the din of the car engine and the cheers of the village children swarming behind.

☰ Only three people remained, a "supreme general staff" who helped Sai with all the final decisions. Mr. Ha would represent the groom's family in the engagement ceremony and at the wedding; Hieu, chief of the "behind the scenes" organizing committee, would oversee all arrangements, including the celebration party; and Tinh, who would come up with the funds to pay for it all.

Clearly Hieu was the one who would have to put up with the most in this affair. Since Sai went B, Hieu had become a son of the family and Sai's sworn brother. He participated in all family affairs and was always quiet but enthusiastic. In discussions, he expressed his opinion on the proper course of action, but he never insisted on getting his way. Since coming back from the South, Sai had gone to stay with him, turning his tranquil, orderly room into a "slum," disrupting the normal flow of Hieu's days. But Hieu never expressed any displeasure.

Since his courtship with Chau, Sai "ambushed" Hieu many times, waking him up in the middle of the night to go out or forcing him to vacate the apartment in the midst of his sleepy siesta, so the two lovers could talk in private. At such times, Sai would say "you" have to do this, "you" have to do that. Quite often he waited until the last minute, leaving no time for Hieu to prepare or offer advice. Tinh realized that Hieu cared and took responsibility for Sai even more than a brother would. When an event called for "family authority" to deal with the world outside, the role properly belonged to the elder brother. But when important family matters needed resolution, Hieu was always one of the key contributors. That was the reason Hieu had to come home the day before the meeting and could not leave until the day after.

Eventually, all three agreed that preparations for Sai's wedding were complete. Everything had gone smoothly. Tomorrow Tinh would accompany Mr. Ha and Hieu to Hanoi, to "keep watch" until the wedding was over. Sai's nephew, son of the elder brother, and his friend, who was on leave from the army, would be the couriers. Everything appeared in place. The organizers took great pride in having been able to handle the differences between a wedding "in the city" and a wedding "in the village."

Chau's brother, Head of the Department of Party Organization, would represent the bride's family; Ha, Head of the Department of Finance and Accounting, would represent the groom's. The maids-of-honor were expected to be ravishingly beautiful and fashionable; the best men, Sai's two cousins, would be as handsome as travelers who'd just returned from abroad.

The party to welcome the bride would be made up of Sai's friends or his relatives living in Hanoi. Relatives from the village would run errands "behind the scenes." Ha had also made a few other important decisions. He would borrow a Japanese electric generator, brand-new and very quiet, to be placed near the tree in the veranda in case of a blackout. Hieu asked his younger brother, who worked for the Office of Tourism, to get hold of a second, roomier car for the bride-welcoming party, just in case the other broke down. Tinh's uncle on his wife's side was a retired fireworks-maker. He would take direct charge of inspecting, warehousing and shooting off the fireworks.

There was nothing left out of the wedding plan, but Ha felt there was still something missing, something unsettling. And this despite the fact that Chau's presence that afternoon had rounded off the feeling of pride in Mr. Ha's family. Not that the family lacked pride in the first place, since they had never considered themselves second in prestige and dignity to any family in the village – not since the time long ago when one of their ancestors became the District Chief or passed the province exams with the highest honors. In the dark hours when Tong Loi, the hamlet chief, had collaborated with the enemy, causing terror near and far, he had become the first revolutionary of the village, steadfast to the end. Because Ha's family had adhered to a code of personal ethics, social order and family honor, people looked to his family as a model. Now that social relations had taken a modern turn, Ha wanted his family to remain in the front rank. Neither he nor Tinh had expected Sai to make such a good match. The more Ha got to know her, the better Chau looked.

But it was precisely because of this good fortune that Ha was worried. The only way that his nephew could gain a hold upon that girl was through intellectual achievement. It was a moment of great crisis that called for a new system of values, one which the talented could bring forth. Such an accomplishment was not beyond Sai's ability. However, Sai ran the risk of self-destructing in the face of her dazzling qualities. If he failed to hold his own, the two would be mismatched. Sai was already feeling pressured. He had to make an extra effort, for fear of losing everything he ached for. Everybody sensed his apprehension, but no one dared mention it. So after a wide-ranging discussion full of insight and wisdom, the three were withdrawn and the air was heavy and leaden.

Had the judge presiding over the divorce case known the two families in this period, much time would have been saved in the investigation and many tons of paper, used at a time when schoolchildren did not even have paper to do their schoolwork. While the groom's family was thrown into a fever as they made their preparations, the bride's family remained unperturbed, almost indifferent. In fact, the news of the impending wedding didn't cause as much a stir as did the report that fresh tench fish would soon be available in the cooperative store. It was not that Chau's family felt any lack of responsibility for one another. It was that they had heard too many times of Chau's "boyfriends" and of her "impending weddings." Therefore, when she brought Sai home as her suitor and announced the wedding plans, no one objected, no one uttered a word of protest, no one even reacted.

The reason for this lack of reaction was that her mother and two brothers and sister were all furious at her for her eight-year love affair with the electrician. Nobody had kept count of how many boyfriends she'd had during that period, including the three she planned to marry. The family thought highly of all the boyfriends she brought home; she could have had a "wedding arrangement" with any one of them. All were unmarried and, while they may earlier have been involved with other women, all were presently unattached. They were all handsome and well-educated – excellent matches both in form and substance. The family's "urgings" in these cases were all intended to drive her out of the electrician's hands. Even her older brother, the department head of the Party organization, who worried about her like a father and yet treated her equally, as a friend, time and time again had heart-to-heart talks with her to this end. But eventually every one of her suitors turned out to have some blemish, and she ended up back with the electrician. The family knew that she wouldn't listen to advice, so they just said, "Let her be. She has enough brains to make her own decisions."

Chau's brother realized that she was really going to get married only when, on the way to work one afternoon, he stopped by the local office for the marriage registration ceremony. Even so, he didn't want to celebrate prematurely. Except for the vague and slender evidence of an astrologer's estimate that their signs made for a perfect match, it was impossible, he thought, given Chau's temperament, to guarantee that she would "live happily ever after" with the naive veteran.

≣ For years, no one could figure Chau. She was weary of meaningless love affairs. She wanted to put an end to her virtually unrequited love, but she could not find another object for her affections.

The men pursuing her all seemed vacuous and hollow; long on looks and well-versed academically, but beyond the book learning, there was nothing. They were upright, worldly wise, but dispassionate. Or they were close-fisted and stern, with no sense of the sympathy and mutual respect necessary for love. Or they were capable of performing great tasks, but incapable of little things; or they were guileless. There was a time when Chau yearned to marry just to get it over with, but the closer she got to a man, the further she felt from love.

So, in the end, none of the suitors succeeded in winning her away from the electrician. It was he who had taught her how to analyze different types of people in society. He taught her how to deal wisely with the world. Loving him, Chau felt like a little girl: allowed to be self-indulgent, to get angry, to throw tantrums in order to be consoled and pampered, and at the same time permitting herself to be browbeaten into submission. There were times when he wept like a baby at Chau's caustic reproaches. He would kneel at her feet and beg for forgiveness. But whenever she touched on the subject of his career, he would turn as cold as steel, resolutely brushing her aside. He was a lover who was also a friend, an elder brother who taught her the art of living.

And besides, there was a secret that no one knew or even suspected. She had given herself to him. But even while sleeping with him, she had wanted to escape him. For the last ten years, the dozen who pursued Chau were like little children compared to her Toan, the electrician. Chau seethed with anger and rancor inside. She could not forget; she could not do without him; without him, she could not satisfy the deep and passionate yearnings of a woman who had once tasted happiness with a man. For that reason, even when she was going out with other men, she still carried on a secret affair with him at his apartment. She was ready to bear all, to give up all in order to play house with him once she'd realized that the other men couldn't give her what she yearned for. He made many promises and asked her to be patient. That patience had lasted almost ten years, including the panic-stricken time when they had to hire an unknown doctor to "take care" of the result of a careless night. Still she had confidence and waited patiently. The last time, she was the one who refused to let go of him in the moment of passion. The result of that encounter showed up soon thereafter, when it was already ten days past her regular period. She gave him the news. He again proposed that she go to the familiar place to "take care" of it.

"No, you have to do what you have promised. You have to be my husband legally."

"Please calm down. I can't do it yet."

"What are you still afraid of?"

"I am not afraid. But we have to be constantly alert in order to find a solution."

"I have been."

"Then listen to me. For now, we will do just as we've been doing.

"No! You know my temperament. I won't let you go on deceiving me."

"Then what are you going to do?"

"I will make you keep your promise."

"What if I won't?"

"That won't happen."

"Ugh! A man in love will promise the moon."

"What did you say?"

"I said that if he has to, a man will promise to pull the sun down for his sweetheart to play with."

Chau saw double. She made an effort to continue, "I am different. I won't let you run out on me."

"If you threaten me, let me tell you this in all frankness: No one in this world can force me to do something that I am not yet ready for."

"I will force you."

"No. Be serious. That will never happen. Let me take this chance to speak to you seriously and to tell you that at present things cannot be different. If you love me, we will nurture our love forever and ever."

An earth-shattering slap across his face ended the conversation. That slap took place about a week before she had been introduced to Sai. That was the real reason why a woman as experienced in the way of love as Chau was so ready to entrust her whole life to Sai. But her decision wasn't a deceitful one. She was not seeking a cure for a disease by passing it on to another. She had the means and the brains to come up with a perfectly agreeable way out. She was attractive enough to find another partner; dozens of reputable men would have overlooked the last ten years in order to have the privilege of possessing her.

Chau's love for Sai was an inevitable response to the man who, as Sai put it, stole her life. She needed Sai's love and his sincerity. She thought his heat could rekindle her cold and sorrowful heart. Sai had come at the right time. She yearned to blot out all the passionate feelings, all the memories of a bygone past. She truly wanted to have a family, to engage herself fully in the role of wife and mother. For that reason, even if Sai had quite a few faults, even if there was some incompatibility, she decided to love him, to love him with a love that was full of reverence. She hoped for a future in which she would do everything in her power to make a model family. But human nature is filled with contradictions. On the one hand, no one could expect her to forget everything in an instant to be in total harmony with her new love. On the other hand, she wouldn't allow anyone to remind her of that past. The day they registered to marry, they moved into their new apartment. Still, they only stayed together during the day. After 10 P.M., she returned home to avoid gossip.

One morning before the wedding Political Officer Do Manh dropped by to see Sai. Beside himself with excitement, Sai greeted Do Manh, then disappeared behind the cloth screen to look for Chau. She was crying, partly out of rage, partly because of longing for those moments when she had first tasted the pleasures of love. Tears soaked the pillow case. Sai couldn't understand at all. He begged her to wash her face and come out to meet his former commander. Chau adamantly refused to give up her crying. His throat choked with indignation. Embarrassed, he had to say that Chau could not get up because she had the flu. Simmering with resentment, he asked, when the two sat down at noon to go over the invitation list, "Have you invited Toan?"

The question was such a surprise that without thinking, Chau said, "Toan who?"

Sai's face froze at this obvious lie. "You must have forgotten. Let me go invite him personally."

Tears streaming down her cheeks, Chau stood up without saying a word. She gathered her hat and rode home.

Later, because of her stubborn anger, Hieu had to intercede, going by her house to beg her forgiveness. He had Sai make a personal apology before she agreed to be present at the wedding.

The story of that fight became the first item in the court record:

One day before the wedding, there had already been a tense clash between the two parties.

By itself, this was a mundane event. But due to the lack of mutual understanding, Chau threatened to call the wedding off. Thanks to the intervention of friends and family, and because Sai had realized he was at fault and had apologized, the wedding went forward without any problems.

CHAPTER 9

Sai awoke suddenly to find his wife sitting up at the head of the bed, her back pressed against the wall, her hands clasping the pillow, her eyes opened wide and staring at the lamp on the chest of drawers. Sensing her sadness, he wanted to get up, but he abandoned the thought and asked in a muffled voice, "Can't you sleep, darling?" Either she didn't hear or wished not to respond. She remained still. Concerned, Sai sat up straight, "Are you all right?" She appeared startled, and her eyes narrowed. Then she smiled, smoothed out her husband's chaotic hair and placed his hands on her overstretched stomach. Sai gave her stomach a gentle rub, as if afraid too much force might hurt his baby, who, he thought, should be over a month old now. Sai smiled happily at his wife. She pulled up her blouse and pressed his head against her breasts, then bent down as if to hide him away. Sai felt suffocated. He had to shake his head loose to get air. Chau patted him on the head, signaling him to stay put. He obediently complied.

Such were Sai's impressions of the first few weeks of his marriage. And because of them, he was willing to do whatever it took to keep his wife happy. When informed of the date of the review for the upcoming research assistant exam, he asked, "What do you think, darling?"

"It's a good thing for you to get more education, but . . . " Although she was not able to spell out her reservations, Sai understood that in the days ahead his wife would dearly need his care. After she gave birth, he would have to be away, or if not, he would be spending his time studying a foreign language. In his younger days, he would have tried to do both – attend to her needs and prepare for the exam, but he felt less flexible now. It was like the old saying, "The mouth and tongue of an old person stiffens like dried bamboo sticks and becomes difficult to bend and mold." His mind could not concentrate as easily as it used to. To make headway, he would have to ignore his wife and children. But if he were not with her, his mind would not be at peace.

"Why don't I wait for the next exam? There's one after your delivery."

"It's up to you."

"Then we don't really discuss things together!"

"Of course, I always want to be near you. But I don't want that to influence your plan."

"My plan is to do everything to make you happy. Let's decide to wait for the next time." He was rewarded with a look full of affection, a look which he felt opened him to a world of immeasurable happiness, in which he could lose himself for the rest of his life. Later, he would also made the decision to transfer to a department working on trade union issues and motivation campaigns. That way he would have more time to look after his wife.

In the morning, when Chau rose to boil rice, he also rose. Initially, he just sat by ready to be ordered about. He'd pick up the rice server stick or the soup ladle, pass the fish sauce, peel the garlic or hold the MSG bottle, although all of these were in the cupboard nearby, easily within her reach. Later on, he did everything: boiled the greens, cooked the rice, warmed over the meat dish, made omelettes. As time went by, he grew fond of these activities, while his wife's body grew and she grew more easily tired.

"My darling," he got used to saying, "why don't you rest. Just leave it to me." After everything was done and the table was ready, he would wake her. Allowed to sleep without interruption, she felt stronger and more cheerful. But when she first woke, she appeared always slightly listless, a touch weary, as if to give him a reason for all the pampering.

During breakfast, he scooped the rice and portioned the meat into their lunch boxes. He always gave her a larger portion. She would scold him, "Instead of rushing about, why don't you wait until after we finish?"

"If I get this done first, then I can eat at leisure." After the meal, while his wife cleaned herself up, he washed the dishes and pumped the bicycle tires. Asked by his wife to leave the dishes for her, he responded: "Don't waste your time." When she finished dressing, he was also about ready. "Let's leave the rest till later," she said. He refused, for he hated to leave things undone. He pedaled Chau to work, then went to his office. In the afternoon came the same unvarying round of activities – preparing the meal and doing the laundry – and the same thing the following day. He felt that, with his physical strength, no job was too difficult. When he had time to spare, he took the rice ration book and the entire set of food coupons from his wife. At noon, when work was slow, he stood in line or asked others to stand for him. He bought kerosene, rice, noodles, meat, fish, tofu, MSG, fish sauce, sugar and soap. It was work to stand in line, but not as bad as some claimed.

All in all, it seemed like a peaceful, well-regulated sort of existence, a kind of life that many dreamed about: husband, a grade 6 civil servant, wife, an engineer, no children, a fully furnished apartment. They could be proud of their good fortune when so many suffered in poverty.

Tinh was the first one to worry about their future. Three months had passed since the wedding without a word of inquiry from Sai about his relatives in the village. Even at Tet Lunar New Year, when Tinh sent his daughter to bring a chicken and some sticky rice to Sai, he only said, "Please tell your father that I'm just too tied up, I'm not able to return to visit the village." Worried, Tinh set out to find Sai. He stopped by to visit Hieu first and asked him to come along. Hieu complained that Sai was so engrossed in taking care of his family that he rarely came by to visit. Tinh, still assuming the right to take care of his brother, brought two dozen eggs and a few kilos of peanuts for Sai and his wife. On presenting the gifts, Tinh told them to eat well and take good care of their health.

Chau insisted that Sai remain and entertain his elder brother and Hieu. She would take care of the meal. But having become accustomed to the role of cook, Sai could not sit still. He made a pot of tea, and without pouring the tea into the cups, he ran back to the kitchen to turn the rice while his wife fried the fish. He ran back to the upper room to get a pack of cigarettes and pour the tea, which the two guests had not yet had a chance to drink, then ran to the kitchen again to reduce the water in the rice pot and to boil water for the vegetables.

His wife said, "You are strange. I said to just leave everything to me."

He said, "Good Lord, it's family. No need to be so formal."

"No, go." He reluctantly went.

Sai bustled about doing little things, and the entire meal, delicious and simple, was prepared with great skill by his wife. Even so, when he saw his brother off, Tinh said solemnly, "You must take care. If you trouble yourself too much with the little things, you won't be able to accomplish anything." Sai was a bit irritated by this old-fashioned outlook. Nowadays those who thought only of grand accomplishments were naive. Hanoi wasn't like the village, where the husband could just sit and holler. Tinh had no understanding of the ways of relationships in the city. After all, Sai thought, I might be a college graduate, but she is an engineer, of about the same salary and education level. If I want to put on airs, I'd have to go back to the village where a man doesn't have to get involved in the "little things." Sai was almost choked up by his brother's outdated criticism.

Angry, it took a long time before Sai could respond to his brother's criticism. When he did, he said, "We have to work the same number of hours in the office. At home, each has to do his or her part, especially when she is in a little worse shape than I am."

"I mention it only as a general concern for you to think about. Of course, you have to give her a hand. You can't just let her fend for herself."

Sai returned to his apartment. While putting away the dishes that seemed to lie everywhere, he could hear his wife grumbling, "How many times have I told you, but to no avail!"

"What?" Already angry, his tone was curt. His wife was taken back by his reaction.

"When you do something, do it right. Why didn't you set the table on our bed instead of on the straw mat on the floor? It looked so shabby. We were like a bunch of squatters."

What an idea! She thought just like a woman, paid attention only to the small things. He felt relieved. "It was the family. There was no one here for us to worry about."

"If it were only you and your brother, I wouldn't mind. But because I am here, you can't let Tinh sit like that, let alone Hieu. You lived with Hieu for a long time; don't you know how meticulous and sophisticated he is? Eating on the floor, they will think that I am afraid of dirtying our bed."

"Since it's my doing, if they have any objection, they'll blame me. Why should they blame you?"

"It's your doing, but it'll be my fault. People will think that it's the woman who's stingy. Maybe they'll say you are hen-pecked and dare not ask guests to eat on the bed."

"Who cares if people think that I 'obey' my wife? It's my wife I am obeying, not somebody else's. There's nothing to be afraid of." He argued without conviction. He only wanted to get the argument over and done with. "There is no need to be on guard with friends and brothers, especially with one's own family."

But Chau never considered such matters as trifles. On the contrary, they added to her growing doubt about the possibility that by living together they would gradually come to understand each other and bridge the differences in their personalities. She was appalled by Sai's behavior in front of guests: he rolled his trousers up to the thigh; put his unwashed feet up on the chair, sucked rice noisily during meals, dripping with sweat; and, after, picked his teeth as if he were playing some instrument. Sometimes he even tried to open his mouth as wide as possible, twisting his face into contortions, just so his fingers could reach the bits of food stuck between his back teeth. She reminded him about this behavior but he would immediately forget her instructions, and there was no point trying to remind him of every little thing. At times she felt so ashamed that her face turned crimson. Her anger was so great that it became almost a grudge, which she had reluctantly to swallow.

These were matters that no one later would be able to verify, so that they did not become part of the written record at the trial, but such initial and crucial events might have carried even more weight than the scoldings or lashings of a brutish husband.

In fact, Sai did pay attention to her suggestions. He made a number of adjustments, not because he agreed that his behavior was bad, but because he thought it would make his wife happy. Unfortunately, deep down, her criticisms made absolutely no sense to him; they contradicted everything he'd been taught. The sense of proper etiquette that his parents had instilled in him, the necessity for civility and shows of respect, was now considered to be the conduct of a lowly weakling. The exuberant expression of feeling for one's home village, for one's comrades in the army, was now viewed as vulgar. When he met a friend who ten years ago had used his body as a shield to protect Sai, his thigh torn by two bomb fragments, the two merely shook hands. It was indeed a firm handshake, but nothing more than that. It was all right to say something affectionate, but just loud enough for the other to hear. One could not shout out with joy or dance about while embracing the other. That would be considered childish.

Nowadays, in greeting one's closest friend, who came from the village or from ten miles away, one showed one's enthusiasm with a few choice words. Wild behavior – like grabbing each other's hands, pulling at each other or hiding the other's hat or bag – were not condoned. Nowadays, one entertained one's own guests, giving up the expectation that one's fatigued wife would join you. Her presence was considered a frivolous formality! At times, Sai's pride was hurt by the changes he was making; he seemed to be living someone else's life. Whatever was done was not done because of him, for him, or by him. Everything was Chau's, done according to her wishes. Was that how love was supposed to be? But there was no other choice. And so, trying to compensate, he just had to work harder.

Sai tried to make up for his incompatibility with Chau by working hard and being agreeable. But for some reason Chau became more and more withdrawn, happy one moment, sad the next. She appeared angry and irritable for no reason. He complained about this to some of the elderly women in the apartment complex. They said, "You are doing fine, but you must understand what your pregnant wife is going through. A woman with child is always short-tempered; don't you worry about it. After the birth, everything should be fine." They were probably right, Sai thought. Feeling comforted, he was determined to put up with everything, and he felt even more love for his wife.

After the third month, when he took his wife to work on his bicycle, he felt as if he were carrying a bowl brimful with water; a slight sideways movement on his part would be enough to spill it. There were times when he thought of letting his wife sit on the seat so he could walk the bike along, just to be safe.

In reality, Sai's calculations about the fragile period of her pregnancy were months off the mark. Either to please Sai or because she wanted to believe in his calculations, Chau obediently accepted Sai's solemn solicitations even when the dangerous period that required abstinence had passed. Unfortunately, her husband, though not an idiot, was incapable of grasping the meaning of what looked like a simple matter. Meanwhile, the memory of the bitter love that she had wanted to forget was constantly with Chau. In the old days Chau did not have to say a word and yet the electrician had been able to sense her emotional needs. He never gave her something that she didn't like. But now . . . Chau stayed home sick. Sai went to the office for a short time, then returned home. He sat on the edge of the bed, put his hand over her forehead like a doctor checking on the patient and said reassuringly, "In a little while, a friend of mine from Institute 354 will come by to take a look at you. Are you feeling really tired?" Seeing that his wife still closed her eyes without responding, he realized that he had made a mistake, asking the obvious. He stood up to light a cigarette in order to create an opportunity for sitting closer to his wife. He lightly massaged her temples, her shoulders, and then her arms.

Chau was touched by all this. She took his hand and placed it on her stomach. Although his hand was over the shirt, he could feel something moving underneath. He slipped his hand under her shirt. She cupped both her hands over her husband's, her face brightening. Sitting still like that for a time, he asked, "Anything special you want to eat? I will go get it for you."

"Don't. Just sit with me for a while."

"Darling, try to endure everything so that nothing will affect our baby." She nodded her head obediently, a motion so endearing that Sai, like all the suitors before him, fell victim to it.

His friend, the military doctor, came by. After examining Chau, he gave her some medicines, saying that they had nothing to worry about. After taking the medicines, she would be good as new. "You must try to eat, to speed the recovery." Once again, Sai pressed his wife about what food she would like, so that he could buy and prepare it for her. In deference to her husband and following the doctor's advice, even though she didn't really want anything, she said, "Get me a bowl of *pho*, darling." Eagerly he took the set of tin cans to the *pho* stall at the head of the street. On arrival, he realized that he hadn't ask whether she wanted beef or chicken. After a few minutes of indecision, he borrowed a bowl from the owner and bought both. Still not hungry, Chau had to force herself to finish the chicken *pho*. He pleaded with her to try some of the beef. The thought made her shudder. She asked for some water and lay down to rest. The smell of the *pho* filled her with nausea.

Believing his wife liked the food, Sai bought *pho* again for dinner, and again and again for the next two days, it was all chicken *pho*. Sometimes she could eat a little bit, sometimes she couldn't, but he always faithfully bought more. On the third day, after getting the soup, Sai had to leave for the office. Looking at the soup in the tin can, Chau almost threw up. She had to bring it to the kitchen and put it out of sight. But the smell seemed to follow her to the front room.

As Chau tried to suppress a feeling of nausea, tears welled up in her eyes, and she was overcome with self-pity. Nothing could be worse than to find such incomprehension in one's own husband. He was a husband in name only. She was as lonely as ever, bearing all miseries alone, unable to share them even in times of sickness. Sitting by herself for a while, she scraped together a few essential clothes and went to her mother's house.

Arriving home, unaware of what had happened, Sai panicked. When informed by neighbors that his wife felt he did not take good care of her when she was sick, he was indignant. For the next three days, he cooked only twice. He went to the office, then after wandered about aimlessly. He didn't visit his wife's family. Some saw this as yet another fault of Sai's – he was ignoring his sick wife. A man who had abandoned his first wife, what fear would he have of abandoning another?

When Chau's elder sister heard these rumors, she went to the housing collective to investigate. As she began to understand the true situation, she sought out Sai at his office and asked, "In the last few days, why haven't you come by to take her back?"

"I really didn't know what else to do. I already have a bad reputation; one more thing won't make any difference."

"Don't let your pride stand in the way. You know I only say that because I know what kind of a man you are. You have to show some sympathy. She's still young. She likes to be pampered, to be caressed a bit. I understand that, as a soldier, you are not really good at this. But it will take time for her to know you. From now on, try to indulge your wife. She's with child. Her mood is rather unpredictable. We all have to make a special effort. What else can we do?"

"You know, I hold nothing back for the sake of my wife."

"I know. Just trifles. The husband thinks his wife likes *pho*, so for three or four days, he buys her *pho*. The wife is sick of *pho*. She goes hungry, and each gets angry at the other."

"I asked her to tell me what she wanted. She never said a word."

"A young woman never demands to eat this or that. You have to figure it out yourself."

"Well, if that's the case, I give up." Sai stood in silence, unable to think of anything to say. In the evening, Uncle Ha, Hieu and an older woman from the neighborhood went with Sai to Chau's house to attempt a reconciliation. On Chau's side, there were her brothers and sisters and her mother. Everyone spoke and laughed, affectionately chiding the couple for fussing over nothing. The couple then rode home together on Sai's bike. Still, each side kept its guard up. Neither Chau nor Sai spoke a word during the entire trip home.

Fortunately, Do Manh and his nephew, who had a master's degree in agricultural engineering and had just returned from abroad, provided an opportunity to make up. The two had come to visit Sai and had almost decided to leave when the couple returned. Sai did not dare ask his wife to entertain the guests with him. But Chau realized that she could not let her husband receive Do Manh by himself. After making tea, she deferentially sat down and answered all the Political Officer's questions about work, her health and life. Uneasy, Sai almost stood up. Sensing his discomfort, Chau signaled him to remain seated. She said respectfully: "Dear uncle, let me make some coffee for you and your nephew."

"Thank you, but I'm suffering from insomnia these days."

Sai asked, "Could you go get the cakes and candies for my commander?"

Despite the Officer insistence that he wanted nothing, Chau still had to get up to prepare a dish of cakes and candies. She was very unhappy with her husband's behavior. When people he judged to be distinguished came to visit, he was not satisfied with the welcome unless there was something to drink or eat. It was not that Chau was parsimonious, but rather that she thought he should be more discriminating. The biscuits she distributed were hard, and the box of lime candies should only be used to soothe children or entertain run-of-the mill friends, not the Lieutenant General of an army corps, who, according to Sai, was his benefactor and savior. But since Sai had spoken, she could not hesitate. Deeply embarrassed, Chau put the plate of biscuits and candies on the table. Before she could turn away, the Officer said warmly: "My dear girl, sit right here. I have ulcers – this kind of 'medicine' is just what the doctor ordered." Sai quickly raised the biscuits with both hands and offered them to the Officer and his nephew, as if to divide the spoils. Chau was tempted to give him a scolding, to command, "Put it down," but she kept her mouth shut and ate the biscuits along with everybody else.

Later, although she and the Officer were full and could not eat another biscuit, Sai raised the plate to offer more. This time she had to signal him quickly with a look, telling him not to do that. She said softly, "Uncle, please have some tea."

"If you have boiled water, make it lukewarm for me." The Officer continued to speak of his nephew to Sai. He told them to visit each other often. A few years younger than Sai, the nephew was solidly built, with a calmer manner than his host. Nonetheless, the two seemed completely at ease talking to each other.

Meanwhile the Officer spoke privately with Chau. Acting if he understood all the ins and outs of Sai's family life, he took it upon himself to cite Sai's virtues, which would be very valuable in the raising of a family. He did not leave out Sai's not-so-small shortcomings in the new environment where he now found himself. His words were sincere and filled with emotion, just as were those of others who talked about Sai.

Chau was touched. She knew that her daily frustrations were not entirely Sai's fault. He had many lovable qualities, lovable fundamental qualities, as many had observed. But deep down she was really looking for a husband who had the power to command her and that seemed beyond Sai's capabilities. Sometimes when incensed, he might shout or scold, revealing a paternalistic attitude and a lack of the experience that one found in well-educated people. Otherwise, Sai's behavior was mostly characterized by petty pride. He'd sulk like a child, wanting to be coddled and pampered. What Chau needed – strength and reliability that she could trust in a man – Sai did not have. In short, as he was not the sort of man she could be content with, Chau regretted her hasty decision more and more. However, the idea of separation had not yet come up as a possibility either for her or for Sai. Both put their hopes in the birth of the baby. Giving birth changes the psychophysiology of a woman; the child would bring out the generosity and maturity of the parents.

That greatly anticipated day finally arrived. The manner in which Sai prepared for the event – full of feverishness and confusion – relieved her of any worry about the fact that the baby was not Sai's. According to their calculations, the baby was thirty-five days early. Using the wedding day as a measure, the baby was two months and seven days early. That meant absolutely nothing. Sai had no doubt of his wife's faithfulness, despite the vague rumors he'd heard here and there.

After taking his wife by bike to the maternity ward, he came home at ten. From then until daybreak, he didn't sleep. After checking the baby's swaddling clothes, the cover net, baby socks and shoes, he looked over the milk bottle, the food pan, the wooden horse and the mobile. He cleaned everything they had bought or received as wedding presents, then he rearranged them neatly for easy access. The suspense was like the time he was still in the army, waiting for the sound of the alarm.

Screaming with pain, Chau had clung to the bedposts the whole night. Soaked in sweat, she almost wished she could bite off her own tongue to stop the agony. Without the merciless cursing of the women in labor around her – "that damned husband of mine," "that damned dog," "that murderer" – Chau might have believed that no one in the whole world had ever borne pain like hers, that there could be any greater agony on this earth.

At 4:45, she was put on the maternity table. Within an hour, everything was over. She came back to the bedroom, feeling as proud as a hero who had achieved a great victory, having given the world a baby boy weighing 3.2 kilos. Dozing off for about fifteen minutes, she woke up, anxiously waiting for the moment her husband and friends would show up. Then as if in a dream, a man ran in, knelt at the head of the bed, kissed her parched lips, murmuring in her ear – "Thank you, great mother of mine." He arranged a bouquet of carnations, Chau's favorite flowers, in a vase on the armoire at the head of the bed. They both smiled, sharing their happiness in their child.

All around Chau, people crowded into the room, suddenly filled with the sounds of gracious congratulations and noisy laughter. All the other beds were surrounded by cordial attention. Only she lay alone, seemingly without a family, without friends. She had to pretend to be asleep, head turned toward the wall. The room filled with the strong aroma of sticky rice peppered with chicken liver and heart soup, tiny rice, lean meat pie and pork. There was the clamor of rice sticks, bowls and spoons and the sound of affectionate words of endearment. Everything seemed to gnaw at Chau's heart. She felt totally empty, as if floating on air. She almost fainted from hunger. But there was no sign of Sai. Those women who had earlier inveighed against their husbands were now all dutifully consoled. She, who had tried to absorb the labor pains without uttering vile words of denunciation, now found herself abandoned. As if regretting her valiant effort, she felt a sense of injustice and let herself say, "Damn you, stupid pig. Where the hell do you rest your rotten hide at this moment?"

≣ Sai had been standing outside the iron gate since four o'clock in the morning. The entire two-story building was shrouded in silence. There was no way to find out whether his wife had given birth. He wanted to inform her mother and sister, but it was still too dark. He wandered up and down the street waiting for the morning light. When he returned to the maternity ward, it was six o'clock. The nurse on duty was writing on the board: NGUYEN THUY CHAU – a boy – GIANG MINH THUY – 3.2 kilos. He wanted to race through the main gate to look at his son and check on his wife. But it was still closed. Not knowing the way through the back door, he pedaled his bicycle to his mother-in-law's, then to his sister-in-law's, to tell them the good news.

Back at his apartment, with the help of an elderly woman and a couple of children on the block, he prepared chicken, steamed sticky rice and boiled freshly bought rice. He wondered what his wife would want to eat. He jumped on his bicycle to go to the market for eggs, meat pie, pork, rice pie, bananas and oranges. To everything he bought he added shredded dried meat, barbecued ginger, well-roasted pepper and well-grilled salt. He packed these in two plastic baskets, then hung the bunch of bananas off his bike's handlebar. With the bag of oranges slung over his shoulder and a thermos bottle in his left hand, he set out for the hospital.

He arrived at the maternity ward a little after nine. It was Chau's custom when she was still resting at home to skip breakfast and have her main meal at noon, so Sai thought, he was arriving quite early. His arms full, his body draped with food, he joyously entered the room. In the room unintended indiscretions were difficult to avoid. Every visitor had to make a special effort to direct his gaze only at his loved one. Chau was facing the door. Catching sight of her husband grinning broadly, she quickly turned her head away.

Her mother and sister were furious at Sai. They thought that Sai would be with Chau, and so had not arrived till 8 A.M. to find Chau all alone and fainting from hunger. They had to go out and get food, then plead with Chau before she agreed to take a bite. Sai was oblivious to all this. He arrived and called out a warm hello, then arranged everything he brought on the table, asking his in-laws to pick the right foods for his wife. When Chau examined the dishes one by one, they understood the reason for his tardiness. Clearly, Sai had made inquiries and found out what things were supposed to be done for a woman after childbirth. But, O God, why so many different dishes? In haste one was bound to make mistakes. But blaming him for letting his wife starve was unfair. Chau had been unfair. Knowing what Sai was like, she should have told him not to overdo things. But she had said nothing, forcing him to guess. No wonder he sometimes fell short. A peasant who had spent ten years in the army, how could he understand the demands, the personal tastes, of today's women, especially a sophisticated Hanoi woman like Chau?

Sai's sister-in-law had comforted Chau many times and tried to explain what had happened to everyone in the family. In a situation like this, it was wrong to cast blame. They had not spent sufficient time trying to understand each other. To hide his wife's anger from him, his sister-in-law told him to take some dishes home and rest. She would take care of everything. He could come back at three or four o'clock. She also urged her mother to leave. "You take her home," she said to Sai. Alone with her sister, she cleaned up and steamed the utensils. She told Chau what to eat and when to move. At noon, she let her sister go to sleep and went home herself.

Consoled by her elder sister and seeing all the food her husband had brought, Chau's indignation subsided. But the gesture that to her surprise affected her most deeply came from someone else altogether. It happened around one o'clock in the afternoon. Chau was dozing. There seemed to be someone standing at the head of the bed, silently watching her. Chau thought of looking, but didn't want to open her eyes. What was he doing? She considered asking, "Who are you?" but was afraid of waking others in the room, who might think she was dreaming and talking in her sleep. Moreover, aside from the food in the cabinet, there was nothing lying around that could be stolen. Reassured, she lay still, continuing her fitful sleep. The stranger tiptoed away. She turned toward the wall to shut off an obsessive thought that was leading her nowhere.

At two o'clock, everyone in the room was up except Chau, who was still sleeping. Suddenly, a girl outside shouted, "O my God, Sister Chau has a spectacular vase of carnations." Startled from her slumber, Chau looked up. A glance was enough to tell her who the flowers were from. *My God, thirteen petals!* The number thirteen – how many times had Chau wanted to scratch it out, to bury and run away from it? It was exactly nine months and ten days today. *And he dared to come here?*

When Chau had gone upstairs earlier in the day to breast-feed the baby, she had been struck with guilt on seeing the black color of the baby's long and bushy hair. She told herself that before going home, she would have to cut it all off. Now she regretted not having opened her eyes to see him, to tell him one thing, only one thing: "You rascal, I forbid you to show your face here."

"Was it from your husband?"

"Yes."

"He doesn't look the part; a real man of the world, he is."

"Just joking, it was from a friend of mine. It was from her husband."

His visit was the reason why she was cheerful that afternoon. Later, in the evening, when only Sai remained visiting, she tugged at his arm. "Sit close to me here."

"I left you hungry this morning, didn't I?"

"No."

"It is my first time, and I don't really know anything. If you need anything, would you please tell me?"

She nodded her head – again that nod that had attracted so many men. "From now on, if I need anything, I'll tell you. Don't get anything on your own. You'll just waste money. On the other hand, you should take good care of yourself. If you get sick, who will take care of our baby while I'm still weak?"

"I'll do my best to be careful."

≣ His words were like an oath. Listening to his wife's suggestions and exhortations, he felt that there was no truer, no more important advice. Outside, it was under ten degrees, but if his wife had said, "If you jump into the West Lake, I will feel less anxious," he would not have hesitated.

His voice shaking with emotion, he said, "We have our baby now, if I do anything wrong, you must tell me. Please don't get angry with me. That just makes me feel miserable."

With great tenderness, she looked at him and then obediently nodded her head. He was touched by her gesture and believed in it as if it were his own oath. But who would put faith in the promises of a woman in the midst of a turbulent affair.

≋ After the birth of the baby, Tinh called a meeting of the entire family to announce the news and to emphasize everyone's responsibility to respect the traditions of the family. Although their parents had passed away, the family still observed the traditional ways. The young listened to their elders; the family members aided and protected one another. A "delegation" headed by the eldest sister was formed; it included Tinh, the aunt, his mother's sister, the second uncle's daughter-in-law, and four nieces and nephews. At the gathering, the eldest sister appeared apprehensive. She made as if to speak a few times, then gave up. Despite an effort to be cheerful, her face looked sad.

Finally, Tinh's wife said, "I have an idea. I, too, should go see Chau, because none of the sisters-in-law were present at the wedding. In times of celebration, it was all right for me not to show up; but at times like this, if I weren't there, what would people say except the worst about us? One or two of the nieces and nephews should go. But understand this is not a visit for pleasure, but to help out your uncle. If you want to see Hanoi, wait for another time." Tinh's wife stopped and turned to her thirteen-year-old daughter, "As for Hung, you should go see the baby, then stay to help your aunt and uncle by doing the wash, the cooking, food shopping and baby-sitting. You'll have to lose a year at school; you can go back after a year. Your father and I will make sure that you have a good education."

Hung's eyes teared at this news. Her mother went on speaking. "It's your aunt and uncle you are going to stay with, not some stranger you should be scared of."

On the following day, there was a minor change in the membership of the "delegation." The eldest brother decided to take his wife's place on the trip to Hanoi. His wife said, "Let him go because he knows what to say, and I don't!" No one objected. It was cold, but everyone had gathered early in the morning at Tinh's house to go over the list of presents they planned to bring for Sai. Some had a kilo of green peas or a few cans of sticky rice or a hen or peanuts or a bunch of bananas or a dozen eggs. The gifts were expressions from the heart, for Tinh and his wife had already arranged for everything that Sai needed. Well, Tinh thought, as he scanned the supplies in front of him, we'll have less for Lunar New Year celebration. Still, last year, Sai's wedding cost much more than all this, and we made ends meet, so he could do the same this year for his sister-in-law's birth party. There were eight chickens, five of which were Tinh's; eighteen of the twenty-five kilos of the whitest new rice was from him; seven kilos of sticky rice out of the ten; three dozen eggs out of five; four kilos of green peas out of five. It was only out of the two kilos of peanuts, one kilo of jambose powder, and three heads of bananas that they did not contribute a share; but instead had given thirty limes and two kilos of shredded meat. Out of the six bicycles, their two sat in the back along with the food and containers. From the faint voices echoing through the wind, people in the houses along the way to the boat pier could tell that the Tinh family was taking presents to their sister-in-law in Hanoi. Although the village was not permitted to plant rice, except for a few plants of the *loc* type, they could privately cultivate other crops, and it was these sorts of crops that Tinh took to his brother.

Sai's overcrowded apartment, half of which was already screened off as if for a stage play, could not hold all the visitors from the village. The eldest brother and Tinh went to sit and smoke the water pipe in a neighbor's apartment. The aunt sat chewing betel nuts. Tinh's wife and her second uncle's daughter-in-law sat holding the baby and talking with Chau. Sai and his nieces and nephews were busy preparing the meal. Chau asked her husband to prepare the chicken, but Tinh's wife adamantly said no, no to everything. No buying anything, no new rice. Instead, she wanted them to serve state-store rice mixed with a liberal amount of manioc, in order to "save for Sai."

But Sai prepared a meal consisting of a plate of turnip cabbage, a plate of boiled string spinach dipped in garlic and lime-flavored fish sauce, a bowl of pickled mustard greens slow boiled with saltwater fish, and also the dish that Sai had been eating most for the last few days – a plate of frozen-style meat. On the previous morning, Chau had asked Sai to finish off the meat, but he had saved it. It turned out to be just the right dish to offer guests.

Sai and a handful of his nieces and nephews busily went about the cooking, while the visitors from the village were impressed with the quantity and sumptuousness of the feast. Then they hurriedly took their leave.

Months later they were still moved by the memory of that pleasant dinner, of their Aunt Chau, who seemed even more beautiful than they'd remembered her, and of the gentleness and courtesy of the Hanoians. No distinctions were made, there was no lack of respect for the husband's side of the family. Their aunt expressed regret that work and family responsibilities prevented her from paying a visit to the village and asked the elder uncles and sisters to explain this to others and beg their forgiveness on her behalf.

Those with an education certainly were different! Their words were so sweet and agreeable. A few of Chau's remarks were enough to make the aunts and nieces, the mothers and daughters, feel that their efforts had been fruitful. On their return, they spoke and laughed warmly in the mist of a cold, drizzling rain. By the time they arrived home, everyone was as soft and wet as a newborn mouse, but they still glowed with happiness at the respect and reverence they'd received.

Tinh was satisfied with the decision to send his daughter to stay with Chau. He was sure Hung would be able to adjust. Living with her aunt and uncle would open her mind. She would lose a year of school, true, but her world would be enlarged. Even more significant, one of the things that he worried about the most – the wide gap between his wife and Chau – seemed less apparent on this visit. In short, today he was completely satisfied. When he left Chau's house, his daughter said good-bye with reddened eyes. He laughed and said in jest, "If I could stay here with your aunt and uncle, I would certainly do so. To enjoy myself."

Tinh's daughter was a worthy choice among the seven children of Tinh's house. She was intelligent and resourceful. The third of seven children, Hung was smarter than her older siblings. After her family left, she wiped her tears, went to wash her face at the water pump, then returned to clean the dishes, sweep the floor and wash a basin of the baby's diapers and of her aunt's clothes. On her own, she washed the pair of army uniforms that Sai had stuffed into the window slits and left for days until they had started to smell. In the following days, the bottles, plates and pans – whether used or forgotten and covered with mildew and worms – were retrieved, cleaned, sun-dried and neatly put away. The kitchen looked less cluttered and more spacious. She figured out the marketplaces – where to use the ration coupons and where it was easier to stand in line. Soon she could buy everything according to the regulations.

After a week's stay at the maternity ward, Chau returned home. Her sister came by only occasionally. She was very pleased with Sai's niece. And Chau was in full agreement, "She is smart, knowledgeable, sometimes even better than her uncle."

"You don't say, but give him credit; Sai is a resourceful person."

"Resourceful somewhere, but at home, to tell you the truth, I can't find anything to be happy about."

Chau's sister knew to keep quiet. At the time, women never praised their husbands in front of others and, in turn, never praised their friend's husbands, lest they be thought common or promiscuous. Sai's pampering had made Chau somewhat indolent. She realized that there was no servant as dutiful as a husband who was full of energy and committed, body and soul, to his wife and child. Certainly, Sai understood her better than a servant would, and he was easy to order about. She could get angry at him, and, at the same time, be loved and coddled by him. She felt totally free to express her every emotion. In her "kingdom," the presence of parents or sisters and brothers was constraining, and it was even worse to have her husband's niece around. A month after childbirth, Chau looked as sprightly as a young girl. Although she was still on maternity leave without pay, she already felt more energetic than in the days when she was a young girl. After a month of eating chicken stuffed with bulbous aralia, pork leg, green peas, sticky rice and stewed lotus seeds, she surprised everybody by looking even more beautiful than in her "time of glory" when she was considered among the most beautiful women of Hanoi.

While Chau ate well, Sai and his niece ate boiled string spinach, an occasional tench and tofu cakes bought with ration cards. They'd eat the skin off the lean meat that had been "simmered in fish sauce for Auntie." Sometimes Sai would eat a bit of the stewed pork leg intended "for her." During work hours, he had to run around bargaining for choice food to give his wife; at night, he had to feed the baby twice. Once fed, the baby would often pee three times, requiring three changes of diapers to keep him dry. This was not counting the dozens of chores his niece had to do every day, every one of which he had to watch over and correct so that her aunt would not be displeased. Already ten years older than his wife, after a month devoted to his wife's care, Sai's eye sockets grew hollow and his cheek bones became pronounced. His wife looked like a twenty-two-year-old, while he looked about forty-seven or forty-eight. Visitors not acquainted with the family would greet them as "sister" and "uncle." Chau often had to head off such greetings from officemates or old friends who had not yet met Sai by introducing "my husband" or "my darling" before they entered the apartment.

It was during this time that the bond between Chau and her husband finally ruptured. First, it was the cramped and claustrophobic nature of the flat. The baby occupied the single bed, while the other three shared a double bed cluttered with diapers, bottles, thermoses and a basin for dirty clothes, as well as a vessel to hold the baby's urine. It was so crowded that one could not even turn or breathe. Then there were times when the baby had to be fed or made a mess, or when the electricity went out and it was impossible to see one's way. Aware of his wife's frustration, Sai borrowed a folding bed. After everything was done, especially the chores in the kitchen, he opened it up along the side of the room. Underneath were pans, pots, baskets of fish, vegetables, rice. Fortunately the bed fit just between the cupboard on one side and the two bicycles on the other. From the time they got into bed to the time they got up, they made no movement, there was no walking to and fro, all to avoid any noise that would wake the baby. The niece had to suffer the smells of the oil, the fish sauce, mildewed bottles, vinegar, burned lard, all of which almost made her vomit, but she had to suffer in silence so that her aunt would not know.

Then, Chau started to feel that Hung's presence was superfluous. Noticing a few things not done the way she liked, Chau began to scrutinize everything the girl did. "Look at the pan of milk for the baby, dear." Chau showed her husband the pan that had just been used to boil the baby milk. Streaks from the spill were still visible on the side. Sai knew that the niece had been washing the swaddling clothes while boiling the milk and could not get back to the flame in time. "Just leave it to me, as I've told you." Chau showed Sai the yellow stains of the baby's stool. He took the diapers for a second wash. But all his scrubbing could not remove the spots from the white diapers. "O my God, with waste like this, no replacement is possible, you and your niece ruin everything." She lifted up another pan that was blackened on the bottom after having been used to melt sugar. The niece had been preparing fish and had completely forgotten about it.

After incidents like these, Sai took out all his frustrations on the thirteen-year-old girl. "You are dumb like a pig. No matter how many times I explain it to you, you still don't get it! Get one thing done before you start on something else, don't spin around like a top from one thing to another. You've been accustomed to being careless and clumsy at home; now that you're here, you have to learn to work in a disciplined manner." Only by uttering the most scathing words could he relieve his anger and hope to turn her around.

Sometimes Sai's shouting filled Hung with terror, but it was better than her aunt's silence. Seeing something Hung did wrong, Chau said nothing, showed no emotion. Later, her aunt brought up the matter with Sai, reproaching him. Despite her youth, the little girl saw everything. She had great sympathy for her uncle, who suffered Chau's criticism because of her. Night after night, she cried by herself in that smelly kitchen, but still she could not find a way to ask her uncle and aunt to let her go home. Even if they let her leave, how would she make her parents understand?

One day she returned home from the food market through the rear door and overheard her aunt complaining to friends. "I have enough trouble living with that peasant; now I have to put up with his niece, who is an exact replica of him. They both live in total disorder, never troubling themselves with cleanliness. If things go on like this, I'll go mad."

Without a sound, Hung took the basket of greens and meat to the road outside, then, a half-hour later, she returned through the front door. Three days later, on a Sunday, she asked her aunt and uncle to let her go home for a few days to see her mother, brothers and sisters. Sai immediately said no. "Wait till your father comes here."

Chau said, "How odd you are! Our niece misses her mother and sisters. Why do you stand in her way?"

After his wife expressed his opinion, Sai acted as if he had come to the same decision on his own. He asked Hung, "How many days do you want?"

"About two, three days."

"Okay then, after two, three days, you come back again to take care of the baby so your aunt can go to work."

At that moment Chau walked away, waking up the baby for another feeding. She considered the whole matter something between her husband and his niece. But when the girl did not return, she indignantly told everyone that the little brat from her husband's family had tricked her. "Why," she said to everyone, "did she have to resort to such deceitfulness? Why did she have to run away when I can manage quite well without her? Her entire family, young and old, has no manners. No one even bothered to come and offer an explanation. There is no one in his family who shows me any respect. Why should I show them any?"

All the work now fell on Sai's head. Although the difference between day and night no longer seemed clear to him, if we take the morning as his starting point, his routine went something like this. He got up before dawn to boil water. He poured the lukewarm water from the thermos into the earthen pot for filtering, then put the fresh-boiled water in the thermos. The baby's pacifier, the milk bottle and the thermos had to be rinsed with hot water. He warmed the milk and poured it into the bottle, fed the baby at six o'clock and kept the remaining milk in the thermos and took the child to the baby-sitter.

He boiled one pot of rice, using two different grains – one half the state-store variety, mixed with manioc, the other half, new rice. He made two dishes. He filled one saucepan with chicken, lean meat or heart and liver or kidney. He freely spiced this with ginger, *bot nghe* and pepper. It was already more than six months since his son had been born, but he strictly adhered to the custom of two separate menus. Another saucepan was filled with tofu, sea fish, *ca me* or shrimp with *bi lon*. Only the string spinach or boiled *do du* was shared, but with two separate bowls of sauce for dipping.

His wife rose, rinsed her mouth and induced the baby to pee. Sai went to the water pump to wash dozens of diapers, two or three blankets, and a few sweaters and quilted pants all wet as a result of the night supper that had become part of the baby's new routine. "By the way," Chau asked, "could you just throw in the blouse for me, dear." But the blouse came, as always, with the whole outfit – the top, the underwear, the pants and the slip.

Organizing his movements in the most rational way, as soon as he got up, Sai would take two pails to stand in line at the water pump. He'd put a barrel that could hold several bucketfuls of water nearby. While carrying out other tasks, he estimated when his turn at the pump would come so he could rush back in time. After filling the barrel, he would put the pails down for another turn, asking others to move them along for him. Eventually, his water-filling task became a source of pleasure. Hundreds of people, from the oldest to the youngest, recognized "Mr. Sai's pails." They would move the pails along for him, then collect the water, pour it into his barrel and put his pails back in line again. Once they learned that the pails belonged to Sai, even those in a hurry did not have the heart to protest.

Freed from the task of having to worry about collecting water, Sai could concentrate on washing the clothes with soap and then rinsing them at the water pump. No longer having to wait in line, he took less time washing and yet the clothes were cleaner. His wife complimented him, "You do so much better now." Done with the wash, he came home to set the table so his wife could begin her breakfast. Because she ate so slowly, Chau had to start at least ten minutes ahead in order to keep pace with him. While his wife ate, he hung out the wash.

After finishing breakfast, his wife helped him scoop the rice into their tin lunch cans. She would put a few pieces of meat from her portion into her husband's. Then Chau fed the baby while Sai washed the dishes and pumped the tires.

Finally, Sai picked up the baby and the basket of clothes and diapers; his wife carried the milk bottle and another basket full of bottles and cups. They delivered all this to the child's baby sitter, an elderly woman at the other end of the street. Then they left for work. Sai no longer had to ride his wife on the bike. They both pedaled along together – about halfway before going in different directions. On his bike, Sai always had a sackcloth, a hand basket, a set of tin cans and a nylon bag. During his "official work time," he had to complete the shopping with his family's allotment of coupons. After shopping, the items that would not keep had to be boiled, fried or stewed. In the afternoon, his wife picked up the baby while he dropped by the market stall to stand in line for state-store greens or greens from privately owned gardens. While his wife played with the baby, he washed the morning's diapers. After the evening meal, if his wife asked him to take care of the baby so she could clean, he would act like an authority on washing dishes, with few equals. "Why don't you play with the baby, and leave the dishes to me?" He then went into the upper room to pick his teeth and drink tea. But before the chair got warm, he thought of soiled diapers to be washed; the water to be carried and the greens to be cut for tomorrow; the water to be boiled and used to rinse the bottles for the night; the ironing of diapers that had not dried; the milk to be warmed for the evening and morning meals; the diapers to be changed and on and on. Sai stayed up every night until 11 P.M. before retiring under the mosquito net. He slept fitfully for a few hours, waiting for the baby's after-midnight feeding. It was usually at least one thirty or two o'clock in the morning before he officially completed his tasks for the day.

This was the "complete one-day cycle" of a typical day, a day when the food shopping was easy, the baby behaved and nothing broke or spoiled. Most days, however, some hardship, some complication, large or small, made the day longer and more exhausting. There might be bad weather or a traffic jam or a small theft or something else. Of all the hardships, the most upsetting was the constant squabbling and fighting that led to tongue-lashings from his wife.

The days wore on Sai – there had been 300 of them since his wedding and 196 days since the birth of his child. In that time, Sai had lost nearly twelve kilos and had aged more than ten years. He looked haggard and unkempt, like a cyclo driver working the graveyard shift at the train station.

No one among Sai's blood relatives, including his brother Tinh, came by to see him. His friends also felt inhibited. No one had the courage to pay him a visit in the midst of a mountain of diapers and bottles. When Sai needed his friends' help, he came rushing over in disarray, like a thief on the run. For almost a year, he never finished reading a newspaper article, nor did he completely listen to a news broadcast, although he always kept the radio on. And naturally he had no time for watching the neighbor's TV. But no one could say he was a pessimist, a coward, a toad who just jumped on the plate. Those who thought this were ignorant and envious, and whether his superiors or close friends, he would look at them with contempt as he might some animal and would refuse to recognize their faces. These did not realize that it was through his hard work that he was able to take care of everything from the chopsticks to the apartment. It was because of the love he felt for his family that he could do this and do it freely. He and he alone was the man Chau had fallen in love with, he was the one she had pleaded with, "Please, never leave me." Without time to get to explore her nature more deeply because of the trials of child birth and child rearing, which greatly affected a woman's temperament, he had to be accommodating. There were times when he felt he was choking with annoyance, but he had to make do and put in an even greater effort to keep his wife happy, until the time when she got over her mood swings.

Still, he wondered, *When will these days come to an end?* That question preoccupied Sai so much that on the day when he went before the court, his statement was so poetic that the judge had to suppress a smile by pretending to look down at the legal record in front of him. "In the days I lived with her, it was as if I were swimming in a sea of happiness, just like the times I was swimming in the flooded fields of my village. The sea was so immense that no one could tell where it ended, and I could never tell where or when I would become exhausted and drown myself."

CHAPTER 10

"Would you say that again?" Chau asked.

Annoyed, feeling that by yielding to please his wife, he would end up in an inferior position, Sai responded, "I did what you told me to."

"You put in the whole rose?"

"Yes!"

Chau wanted to yell, "What a simpleton!" Had she been able to shout, she wouldn't have had to swallow the anger inside, which, suppressed, seemed to expand more and more. Instead, she said softly, "I asked you to use ten petals. You threw in the whole rose. No wonder we have problems. Watch the baby so I can go get him some medicine." She hurried to the door for fear that in a few seconds she wouldn't be able to hold back the brutal words she was tempted to hurl, like a bowl of dirty water, at the face of this careless, stupid man.

Earlier in the week, Sai had taken the baby out to show him off while talking with acquaintances. Now the baby had a cold. In the morning, Chau had been able to get a white rose, big as a giant cup, and a few wampee fruits to treat the cold. But then she had had to go back to the office to take care of some urgent business, so she told Sai to put a wampee fruit, ten rose petals and a few drops of honey into a cup, steam it in a double boiler, then let the baby drink a few drops at a time. His pride, which made it difficult to receive instructions from his wife, made him behave as if he already knew everything. "I know, I know," he'd said, then he'd thrown all three wampee fruits and the whole rose into the cup. He'd had the baby drink the entire thing and now the child had a bad case of diarrhea. So bad that, though only seven months old, he was fast becoming dehydrated because of it.

Chau's mother and sister had once told her to make sure that the baby didn't get diarrhea because it could easily become a recurring disease, almost impossible to cure.

Tears welled up in Chau's eyes. What fate brought her to this unfortunate pass? There were so many men of good family and experience whom she had not loved. Instead, she chose this coarse peasant, who was ignorant of so many things and yet always afraid that others might consider him incompetent. He was proud of having won on the battlefield, facing up to the Americans, and thought he should be able to survive anywhere, accomplish whatever he wanted. Having finished only one year of college, he was quite satisfied, quite contemptuous of others. He didn't feel the need to listen to anyone or to enlarge his understanding. He picked up a newspaper or a book only to cover his face and snore. From the day of the wedding, Chau had never seen him thinking over anything, studying anything thoroughly. She felt ashamed when people on the block told her that his prospects were being ruined because she forced him to wait on her. Since both had to work, why shouldn't she ask him to help her out if she found him sitting around doing nothing? Besides, he seemed to enjoy doing physical work. Had he devoted all his efforts to some project, some objective, Chau would have been willing to do everything herself; she would have felt proud of her husband. Chau wouldn't have had any second thoughts if she had to put in extra effort to help her husband advance. She couldn't believe the mistake she had made!

When she came back with the medicine, the baby had six or seven more episodes of diarrhea – that made sixteen times in less than half a day. Bewildered, Chau inserted a pill into a lime and put it on a bed of charcoal until the charcoal turned to white ashes. She mixed the ashes with lukewarm water. Mothers had cured their babies using only three pills prepared in this traditional method. And yet after six pills, Chau's child was still sick. People from everywhere in the apartment complex came by to give advice. Some offered a small spoon of iron sulphate or guava buds roasted until yellow and then liquified. Other suggested young wild grass and purslane roasted until yellow. Someone said it was just a matter of avoiding condensed milk, and someone else suggested boiling roasted, burnt rice into a drink. But the more fluids the baby took in, the more he passed out. All the medicines, herbs reputed to be most effective by the most renowned physicians in Hanoi had no effect.

Finally, Chau's mother, sister and nieces came by to prepare the baby for a trip to the hospital. Chau's brother borrowed a car from his department to take his nephew to the emergency room. Amid the confusion, Chau could only see support coming from her side of the family. As for Sai, had it not been for her angrily ordering him about, she would have thought he was nothing more than an indifferent party who had shown no sense of responsibility toward her baby. As far as Chau was concerned, Sai was simply the one who had brought about the disaster in the first place. How could he have let the baby become so sick before getting help?

On the ride to the emergency room, the baby's pulse became very faint, and his blood pressure dropped to a dangerous level. Once in the hospital, the baby stared vacantly, and his lips were so dry that it seemed as if he would happily swallow bowl after bowl of water. But he was not allowed to drink water because his temperature had reached 41.2° C. Another child in the emergency room, also suffering from dehydration, died on a nearby table. Watching that baby being carried away, Chau screamed and passed out and had herself to be taken to the adult emergency room. Seeing her despair, members of Chau's family looked at Sai as if he were a criminal.

≣ Sai was fully aware of his situation. His face haggard and tearful, he felt numb all over. He ran like a marionette here and there following the commands or scoldings of the family. He was glad to be asked to do something, even though he didn't really understand the reasons for doing it.

Drawing on his contacts, Chau's brother sent a car to pick up his friend, the Vice-Director of the best children's hospital in the city. A group of expert doctors and medical students took charge of the case. Despite some objections and uncertainty, the Vice-Director decided to go ahead with a special treatment to bring down the baby's temperature and to stop what had become a series of convulsions.

For twelve days and nights, Sai sat, with his finger keeping the needle attached securely to his child's vein, and watched every drop of water, every drop of blood, falling slowly from the inverted bottle into the catheter. Drop by drop, tens of liters of water and blood poured into his baby; Sai did not allow his vigilance to falter, to let one drop fall faster or slower than prescribed by the nurse.

Even years later, he would not understand how he could stand vigil for those twelve days and nights. And, years later, he would still feel the pain he had felt when the doctors and nurses stuck their needles into the temple, the forehead and ankles of his baby, looking for the right vein. The child looked like a sick kitten. When a nurse couldn't find a vein, the needle was pulled out, drawing a spurt of blood. The nurse's face would cringe. Her fingers, like a bunch of rounded bananas, would keep jabbing the needle into the baby's head. She would break all the veins and still exclaim, "I can't find one." His heart sinking, Sai blurted out "Will you please . . . ," making one suggestion after another.

"If you are afraid your child is being hurt here, why don't you keep him at home and treat him yourself?"

Years later, Sai still shook when he thought of those days. It was so bad that the very word "diarrhea" would startle him as if he had been attacked by surprise. Chau remained unconscious that first night during the baby's crisis. In the days that followed, she sat by her husband's side – next to the water transfusion table. When Sai went out to eat or to relieve himself in the backyard or to smoke the water pipe, she held the needle in his place. At night, he insisted his wife rest and leave the baby to him.

If it hadn't been for his actions in those critical days, he probably never would have mollified his wife's family's anger. Before, he knew, the family and others were taken with him because he was honest – a hardworking and artless man. True, he was clever in some ways, but it was the cleverness of a peasant, not that of a charlatan. People loved him because he was naive and simple, while his wife was shrewd and experienced. But now, he had created another role for himself – that of the stupid man. Toward such an ignoramus, everybody had the right to show disdain. Despite his unquestioning trustfulness toward others, he could sense that attitude in his wife's family.

Chau stayed at the hospital to be with the baby, while Sai took clothes and diapers home. He did the wash daily and returned with food, since Chau couldn't stand the food at the hospital. Still following the regime for a new mother, Sai tried his best to prepare the dishes Chau liked, to atone for his dereliction. Chau was clearly pleased when everyone in her ward commented on how she was so lovingly pampered by her husband. Even so, there was something that held her back. She became more laconic. Only when it was unavoidable did she communicate with Sai, and even then, she treated him just like everybody else. When Sai and Chau first fell in love, Chau's family appeared indifferent to Sai. But Sai didn't mind. He thought as long as Chau loved him, he would be happy. After the wedding, however, when Chau interrogated or criticized him, her family sympathized with him, and he found in them a source of love and support. But now, detecting contempt from "both sides," he felt like a man climbing up a tree and believing that he was within arm's reach of fruit, only to discover that the distance was far greater than he thought and he was too exhausted to climb further. Still, to withdraw was humiliating. It was the first time since he had gotten married that he felt totally alone, totally ineffectual. He was afraid of the coldness of his wife and her family – a coldness that made it impossible for him to find a "foundation" for any marital happiness. The more he tried, the shakier things became.

After the baby came home, Tinh went to visit his nephew. It wouldn't look right if he didn't go, but he knew it would be an uncomfortable visit. When his daughter had run away from Hanoi, he and his wife had tried for a day and a night to persuade her to go back. But Hung just kept silent, as her parents cajoled and threatened. Finally, Tinh had said, "Get your clothes ready, we'll leave tomorrow. Discussion closed."

Knowing that it would be impossible to disobey, his daughter had started to cry. She got down on her knees and put her hands together as if praying. "Daddy, I beseech you. Mommy, I beseech you. Kill me if you wish, but I cannot go back there." Listening to the reasons why his daughter had returned home, Tinh decided to go to Hanoi to talk to Hieu and Sai's friends. None of Sai's friends had seen him in a long time, but stories had spread, so Tinh soon realized that his brother was being treated poorly. Pained, Tinh returned home. He waited for a month until Mr. Ha returned from the South. Then, Tinh presented the case to him and asked him to summon Sai, so the three could hold a meeting.

"What for?" Uncle Ha said.

Tinh was silent, not knowing how to respond to his uncle's indifference.

Uncle Ha went on. "It seems that I can see almost every day the reactions among our friends, the lack of certainty, the restlessness. Yes, sometimes I want to scream in his face, 'Why have you let yourself fall so low?' But he's very satisfied, even openly proud that he has been able to have a family, to own an apartment. He is more than ready to renounce friends who dare to condemn him. What prevents him from renouncing us? You and I will only dredge up that grudge concerning his previous marriage. The best thing is just to leave it be."

So Tinh had followed Ha's advice and not gone to see Sai, even though he had visited Hanoi three times in the last four months. Most painful to Tinh was the fact that all his expectations for the success of his younger brother now lay in ruins. Tinh could no longer dream that his was a great family that took care of all its members. He could no longer claim that his brother had a bride from Hanoi who showed respect and listened to her sister-in-law in the countryside. Now, Tinh regretted the efforts he had made over the last few decades. In response to his wife's entreaties and out of concern for his nephew, he went to visit Sai, but his heart was heavy, and he felt deeply frustrated.

Chau was sitting on the bed when she saw Tinh coming in from the road. She quickly pushed the partition screen forward and pretended to be asleep with the baby. Sai continued to wash vegetables, only raising his head to ask who was there. Recognizing his elder brother's voice, he came out immediately to greet Tinh, who asked, without emotion, "Has the baby recovered?"

"Oh, yes." Turning around, knowing that his wife was still awake, he called out softly, "Chau?" His wife did not answer. "Let her sleep," Tinh said. He knew that nobody could sleep that soundly in the middle of the day, but still he acted as if Chau were asleep while he made small talk with his brother, speaking as if he were talking to a stranger out on the street.

"When did the baby leave the hospital?"

"It was three days ago."

"Mr. Ha is away, and with nobody coming to the village to visit, I hardly had any news. And no word from you. Today, on the occasion of visiting Hanoi to take care of a little business, I ran into some people who told me about the baby. That's how I know." He pressed tobacco into the water pipe, inhaled, drank a cup of tea, and then picked up his bag. "All right, I feel better knowing the baby is okay."

"Please stay to have a bite with me."

"I've already eaten."

"No, you haven't."

"Bicycling along the road, I passed a decent food stand, so I stopped and ate." Sai knew that it was against his brother's habit to eat at a roadside food stand, but since his wife had refused to welcome

Tinh, his visit could not be a joyous occasion. Sai had no choice but to see his brother off quietly. "Please continue what you are doing, no need to show me out."

Sensing his brother's sullenness, Sai was choked with emotion. He ran along beside Tinh for quite a distance before he could ask, "How are things at home, my dear brother?"

"I beg your pardon?"

"Your wife and the children?"

"Phew. Getting sick over and over again, nothing new."

"Oh! Why didn't you tell me earlier so I could get some medicine?"

"Oh no! It's caused by food shortages. When people get sick in the countryside, very few bother to take medicine."

"Would you tell your wife that I will try to come home in a while?"

"You are very busy, Sai. No need to come home."

Sai's face got redder and redder at his brother's sulking manner. Tinh didn't understand how close to death the baby had been and how hard things had been. During the emergency, no one from his side of the family came to help, though earlier they had boasted to Chau's family about how much they loved and supported each other. Hung made up an excuse to go home and then failed to return – without a word of explanation. Sai had to take the blame for this behavior from his side of the family. It wasn't just that Tinh didn't fully appreciate Sai's situation. Whenever he came by to visit, he dropped hints of reproach and displeasure, which made it all the more unbearable for Sai. But what sent a shiver down Sai's spine and brought him to the verge of tears was what Tinh said before riding away.

"I'll probably have to sell this bike to buy rice for the family. Things are very bad now." It was as if he were saying, "Whatever pennies I had, I used them up to pay for your divorce from Tuyet, to help you buy the apartment and to pay for your wedding. Now that my wife and children are starving, you could care less." Sai knew that nothing could be more humiliating for a man like Tinh than to have to extend a hand and beg, even though it was to beg from his own brother. For that man could not escape being censured and treated with disdain, and worse, being indebted for the rest of his life.

Chau had been full of hatred for her husband since the baby's illness, and her brother-in-law's visit didn't change her impressions of a family that she saw as mired in outdated tradition. She avoided Tinh. Still, she could make out his words of indifference, clearly spoken loud enough for her to hear. Then the two brothers went out, probably engaged in some solemn discussion of topics unworthy of a woman's attention. She felt all the more contemptuous toward Sai's family.

When twenty minutes passed and Sai did not return, she got up to set the table. Although they were now sharing the same food, she wanted to create a measure of separation by serving only herself. She put out the vegetables and scooped the meat and fried shrimp into a bowl. When Sai returned, he would have to get his own bowl and chopsticks and serve the leftover vegetables and meat himself. When she'd finished eating, she left the dirty dishes in the pot and went to bed.

Seeing the leftover vegetables in the basket and the unseparated rice, covered with slabs of burned rice, Sai could picture the look on his wife's face even though she lay with her back to him. Whenever his wife was out or too busy to eat, he always made sure the leftover rice was kept warm. He set out her bowl and chopsticks and arranged the food neatly on the tray. Hanoians were capable of a great deal of incivility, he reflected quietly, then smiled bitterly, as he set the table to eat by himself. After he finished, he cleaned the dishes, pots and pans, washed a basket of diapers and rode his bike to work. When the workday was over and the noise around him had died down, he suddenly saw how utterly meaningless everything was, all the hard work and business. He felt oddly dull. This time he did not throw himself into the traffic, did not ride straight home as on all previous evenings.

He slowly dragged the bike to the front gate, not knowing which road to take or where to go. He rode around Hoan Kiem, Thuyen Quang and West Lakes and still had no idea what to do. On every street he passed, there was somebody he knew, but he didn't dare drop in, partly because he was afraid that everyone had their wives, children or business to take care of, partly because he was ashamed that after everyone's hard work organizing the wedding and finding him a place to live, he had never stopped by to visit his friends, except those whom he could rely on for help or medicine. It would be unseemly now to show his face and unburden his sorrow.

After ten o'clock, he still had no place to go, so he reluctantly returned home. He had to call out eleven times before Chau unlocked the door. After performing that unavoidable act, she went back to bed. He turned on the light to take the bike to the kitchen. Turning the light back off, Chau called, as if giving a command, "Let the baby sleep." He looked for the match to light the kerosene lamp and looked over the room. A basket overflowed with diapers. A pot was filled to the brim with dirty dishes. The rice pot was empty. The meat and vegetables were all gone. He understood that his wife had cooked only for herself. He rinsed the rice and prepared the fire. Waiting for the rice to cook, he soaped the diapers. The rice half done, he went to rinse at the water pump. After finishing the meal, he cleaned up the dishes and pots and pans that he and his wife had used. Later that night, he rose to feed the baby and change his diaper as usual.

In the subsequent five days, Sai and his wife continued to cook separately, and Sai performed all the usual chores. During that time, their situation remained a secret even to the people next door. On Sunday, the two daughters of Chau's elder sister dropped by to see the baby. They insisted on doing the food shopping and cooking for the family. So Sai and his wife ate together again, but, for both, the effect of those five days was not a trivial matter.

For different reasons, both had to make an effort. Chau was fearful of the traces that every love affair leaves behind. Although convinced of the validity of her own feelings, scandal frightened her. When she married Sai, the consequences of her illicit affair had been covered up, and she had become, once again, an upright individual. She lectured her nieces on proper behavior and expressed contempt for loose women. Even before the wedding, she knew that she would find life with Sai irritating, but she had decided men were unimportant. She had drawn up a plan for herself: the only thing she needed was the baby.

Being young and still beautiful, however, she soon discovered she did not want to be alone. When the baby started to make a few hesitant steps, she felt more liberated, more powerful than in her younger days. Given her experience and shrewdness, she found herself commanding the attention of dozens of men – some even over the age of fifty. All were willing to forget their wives and children to stand in line for her and then to break their backs transporting rice and manioc to help out "the baby and her mother." Some helped her by acquiring kerosene, fish sauce, sugar and soap or by applying for coupons at year's end or by getting free medicine for the baby. Some even managed to get tickets to the movies. Whatever difficult tasks there were, the "uncles," the "brothers," were ready to help. Chau was resourceful in being able to live with her husband and raise her baby, while maintaining relationships with other men.

The "uncles" and "brothers" had not exhibited any untoward behavior, so Chau stayed with them, for she had grown tired of the routine at home. Why was it that everyone else appeared so poised and friendly, while her husband always looked pitifully unkempt? Sometimes she received invitations and wanted to take her husband along to some event, but, fearing embarrassment, she reluctantly stayed home. She seemed to be two people. In the office and out in the world, she acted with grace and poise. Articulate, sensitive, cheerful: the embodiment of the ideal woman. At home, however, she was sullen, judgmental, reckless and cold.

After many of their quarrels, Sai had to go to the office and sleep on his desk, and if he returned home, she would scold him in language that could not be repeated to others. Whatever her behavior, Sai always seemed to be the party at fault. Everybody thought so, though no one said it. Clearly, he was coarse and unpolished, and therefore totally incapable of pleasing a Hanoi woman who preferred sweetness and endearments. At least, Sai's appearance and manner gave everyone that impression, for in the office and out in the world, he never made concessions, even on trifles. Quiet and cool, resolute but honest, he lived "flat out." The habits he had formed during almost 20 years in the army were in place, and though people came to understand and value his integrity, everyone wished he could learn to be a bit more diplomatic.

At home, however, Sai was feeble-minded and compliant, letting everything pass as long as it pleased his wife. The more he tried to prove that he was manly, the weaker he looked, weaker and lowlier than any woman. The more he wanted to demonstrate his willingness to humor his wife, the more he seemed to be a forlorn, pathetic figure. One day, after maintaining a cool facade at work, he came home at dinner time, only to find the child missing, and he ran out in panic looking for him. He stumbled badly, his sandals slipped, and his big toe nail cut open, rendering his determination comic. In short, considering the balance of power, the more he tried to prove himself, the weaker he became. The more he tried, the greater the gulf between him and his wife became. Some said that Sai had lost his authority from the beginning of the partnership and had become used to it. That kind of talk upset him. He was not in awe of anyone or anything. His concessions weren't the result of fear but of reflection; he judged it prudent to be obliging.

What Sai craved was the kind of existence enjoyed by the families around him. There was one couple – the husband was a level 2 machine operator and the wife was still young – who particularly appealed to him. Sai's salary alone probably equaled their two salaries combined, and yet their life together seemed full of humor and vitality. Every afternoon the husband gave his wife and their child a ride on his bike. He rode with two sackcloths hanging from the handlebar, one holding the child's clothes and the other, food and vegetables. Leaning the bike against the house, the husband walked around with the child in his arms. He seemed to be enjoy himself. Occasionally he played cards with the neighbors. His wife cooked dinner, then went to fetch him home, "I'll take the baby and give him a bath. Let 'the little one' say goodbye to Daddy and go home for a bath." After finishing the bath, mother and child came out to invite the father back for dinner. On their table, there was always a vase with roses or other beautiful flowers.

Sai also admired others in his building. There was the chemical engineer. His wife was a tailor for an import-export company. Whenever her husband had guests, she would go boil the water and make the tea, while insisting, "Please stay and talk with my husband, but you must excuse me. I am in the middle of something."

And there was the Vice-Director, whose wife was a youthful engineer. Together, they had three small children. The Vice-Director often ran into Sai at the water pump. He was a man who managed to do all his chores and still religiously attend soccer games. And finally, there was the "musician" of the tile factory. Every evening he would have someone over and they'd sing until late into the night. His wife took the children to sleep on a bed shrouded in tobacco smoke and then went about making tea until the guests left. Then she rearranged the table and chairs, cleaned up the cigarette butts and threw out the tea dregs. There were times she had to roast peanuts for their visitors, and the heat drenched her with sweat. At other times, she went out looking for food for snacks, so the guests could stay until two or three o'clock in the morning. Some even threw up on the floor, but she didn't complain. The only time she was angry was when the children prevented her husband from working. "Daddy is composing," she would scold, "who asked you to make such a racket?"

Every family in the apartment complex gave Sai something to desire, to yearn for. His wife, however, found every excuse to lower the curtain over her bed. She left the house and didn't return until guests had left. She came back with a disapproving expression on her face, as if to say, "I am dead tired. Next time when you want to entertain guests, just turn us out of the house before asking them in. A place as big as a nostril can't take all this cigarette and water pipe smoke." If he was in the middle of something and had to stop to receive guests, his wife would remind him when they left, "If you are busy with your guests, let me know ahead of time so I can make other arrangements."

In the beginning, Sai would fight back. But after every fight he would end up walking aimlessly in the streets and then sleeping on his office desk. In time, Chau stopped saying anything and he no longer made any loud protests.

Now, every time a friend of his showed up, Sai was shocked. He'd glance furtively at his wife to assess her reaction in order to decide on a course of action. If the visitor had come by to discuss business or if he was just an acquaintance, Sai would stand at the door, as if ready to go somewhere. He'd exchange a few words, until the guest left. If it was a close friend, he'd say, "Please sit down for a minute, let me just get rid of these dirty dishes." Or, "Let me finish rinsing these diapers." Or, "Let me get the rice pot going." Sometimes he would ask his friend to join him at the water pump or in the kitchen, and he'd carry on the conversation while continuing his chores. He even asked his friends for assistance if it helped speed things along. Sai was most worried when visitors from the village came. Luckily no one had come for over a year now.

How had his life become so dark? he sometimes wondered. After all, he was resourceful and patient. He had a superior academic record and was capable of carrying out any assignment. He was not a pushover – not even for a beauty from Hanoi. As a well-educated peasant, unaccustomed to verbalizing his intentions, Sai had taken careful stock of his predicament, examining it from every angle, and decided to live with it. He was already notorious for abandoning his wife once, and he did not want to be branded as a frivolous person. He was head over heels in love with Chau. The die had been cast: he had to find a way to live with his situation. True, it was an uphill race, but he intended to make it to the top. When weary and despondent, he still refused to admit what others pointed out: he and Chau were a pair of shoes that didn't match. He knew full well that his disposition was something he was born with, given to him by heaven as it were. He could not remake himself to be in tune with Chau. He could only try his hardest.

But now, there was nothing left in his life that he could claim as his own. Certainly his honor and respect were gone. Even the "inheritance" stored in his rucksack – the keepsakes from his time in the army – could not find a spot in the house. In the time he lived with Chau, the rucksack was first put on top of the cabinet, then squeezed under the bed, then hung behind the door, then tied to the rafters underneath the roof. One morning, when Chau climbed on a chair to hang the quilted blanket, her head accidently banged against the maligned rucksack's buckle. She immediately took a knife, cut the straps and threw the rucksack on top of the bed. Only when trying to lay his head on a rather bumpy "pillow" that night did Sai realize that it was there. Stunned, he noticed the cut straps and the quilted blanket hanging under the roof. He realized what had happened. He could imagine the look on his wife's face when she flung the rucksack aside.

As Sai looked up at the quilt, something stuck in his throat and he could hardly breathe. Although ready to drop from fatigue, he could not close his eyes. He lay completely still, trying to be perfectly silent. After his wife switched off the light, he sat up to once more touch the items in his beloved rucksack. His fingers touching the things that he had forgotten for the last five years, he grew short of breath, as if again reliving the hardship of days past: the fits of fever, the bombing attacks, the times when one had to urinate into the water bottle and then drink it, that night when Them lay down on the bank of the brook, when he carried that water bottle, that rucksack pressed on his back, and Them as well. It was understandable that Them did not feel any pain, but Sai himself didn't feel anything either, knowing that the friend he was carrying had stopped breathing. This very metal bowl! he thought, touching the cold, smooth metal. Wasn't it just the other night when he had poured out water for Them so he could swallow his dried provisions? Them had cried out loud, "Let me have a little more. Don't be so stingy, brother." Was it only the other night? O Them, Sai thought, I haven't gone to see your mother and brothers in the last few years! I don't have any time. I am not in any condition, not in any frame of mind, to think of you. And now, I don't even have a place, there is no place for me here. This is not my place.

Lying awake the whole night, he looked emaciated, his face hardened. He didn't regret the torment and wrangling of previous nights, for he had come to a decision. He could no longer continue an existence in which he could not be himself, in which what he possessed was seen as fit for the dust heap and what he didn't possess had to be compensated for everyday. Regardless of how hard he tried, he never got enough, never got it right, and was therefore always duly reprimanded. He had not intended to break up a marriage again. But in fact he could no longer adjust, could no longer pretend to "cultivate" a love, a family, which came from a vision conjured up in a moment of passion. He had to find a way. But which way? He did not know, but he was sure there had to be one.

Once he made this decision, Sai became a quiet, somber man. He kept to himself. He controlled his anger so that no one knew when he spent the night in the office. This time, however, when his second child was about to be born, he was not seen escorting his wife as she did her chores or went to work. Chau was somewhat startled by his indifference and tantalizing insinuations. Was that the principal reason for her decision to return to her parents?

≣ On arriving at the roadway, Sai saw a car make a sudden stop in front of a group of children trying to cross to the road. Seeing that his child was among them, Sai grew pale. Dropping his bicycle, he ran across the street to pick up his son. With one arm holding his son, and the other leading the bike along, he arrived home. Chau sat reading a book. Throwing the bike against the wall, Sai ordered his son to stand still against the cabinet. The child refused, glancing at his mother, who happened to look up at him at that moment. "Thuy, turn your head and look over here." The child burst out sobbing and threw himself on his mother's knees. Continuing to read the book she was holding in one hand, she put the other arm around her son. Sai pulled him away, "Go stand against the cabinet, as Daddy said." The child pulled back, screaming, and threw his arms around his mother.

Chau looked up, irritated, "What kind of game are you playing?"

"Do you know what's just happened? Just sit there and read; you wouldn't care whether your son got himself killed or not."

Chau kept on reading. "I don't care what he's done. You can't treat a child like Pol Pot."

"Spoiling the child like you do will get him killed."

"Don't shoot off your wicked mouth. My child, I gave birth to him. I don't need anyone grieving for me."

Sai couldn't believe her. This time, at least, she did not remind him, "If it were not for my brother and sister, you would have poisoned my child with that rose." But he stood still, saying nothing. Had this happened a few months ago, the two would have been in a furious duel by now, and he would be preparing to stomp out of the house. This time, however, he turned away looking for the water pipe. He said softly, "It's up to you. Whatever you say."

The following afternoon, still resentful, Sai saw his wife walking along with one of her "uncles." He decided to intensify the strain between them to see what would give. Understanding that he had no control over his wife, he had lost the selfish instinct of jealousy. He followed the two of them in order to obtain some concrete proof. The story unfolded like this: At 3:15 P.M., he was planning to dash by an office to get a good grip on its situation, then to stand in line for some greens, and finally leave early to pick up his son. Unintentionally, he caught sight of an "uncle" who was carrying rice on his bike while talking and laughing enthusiastically with his wife. He slowed down just enough to still keep them in view while remaining himself unseen. The two entered a cafe on Dien Bien Phu St. He stood behind a bookstore across the street and bought a newspaper to read. After about twenty minutes, they emerged and continued on. When they made a turn on Thanh Nien Street, Sai turned back.

Neither buying greens nor returning to the office, Sai went home and lay down until 4:30, when it was time to pick up his son. He strained every nerve carrying out all the mundane tasks as usual. After giving his child a bath and doing the washing and the cooking, he saw his wife wearily push the bike against the wall as he was scooping rice for his son. It was ten minutes after six. Although Sai had seen "uncle" carry the rice all the way to the alley before transferring it to the "niece's" bike, Chau had the demeanor of a poor soul who had been waiting in line for hours. She seemed to have suffered from having had to lug the rice back home. Everybody in the apartment complex looked at her with concern. How could he let her toil so? Hurrying out to carry the rice bag, Sai gave her a rebuke: "I've told you to leave this to me. You just do too much."

"Oh well! It happens to be on the way. If I leave everything to you, I'll be blamed for making my husband wait on me."

Sai opened the bag, "Oh, it's high-grade rice. You must have stood in line for a long time."

"I stood in line from 4:30 on. When my turn came, they stopped for half an hour to change shifts. It was not until six o'clock that I got the rice, so I had to rush home."

Sai felt a growing pain, but he maintained a cheerful exterior. This act would have been perfect if Chau had not asked, while he was washing dishes, "Do you want to go see a movie tomorrow night?"

"What movie?"

"I don't know yet, some sort of American documentary."

"Sounds great. Who will baby-sit?"

"If we go, we'll take him to grandma's."

"No, why don't you go. I'll stay to baby-sit. Drag him out at night, if something happens . . . "

"You're really odd. We're married, and you ask me to go out alone."

Sai felt as if a chill had run up his spine to the crown of his head. He said slowly, "Ask someone else to keep you company."

"Who?"

Her quick retort made Sai blurt out: " 'Uncle' or some other young man."

"What 'uncle,' what 'young man'?"

"You mean in the whole time you've grown up, you don't know any 'uncle,' any dear young man that you can ask?"

"Listen, listen, don't act jealous, talking like a peasant."

Sai felt his knees weaken, and his heart speed up. He tried to regain his composure. He said, "I am not jealous yet."

"Don't use those bullying tactics against me the way you did so well against those peasant girls."

"How can the 'country' bully the 'city'? What the 'country' says needs to be based on material evidence, not groundless charges. It's just a matter of whether it's time to say it."

"Then say it."

"There is no need to rush. Maybe I don't need to say anything. It's better to let the one who should speak say it on her own." Contrary to his habitual feverishness, Sai took his time in a confident, calm and collected manner. He meant to mention only what happened the afternoon Chau lied to him. Sai meant that when the time was appropriate, he would bring up the matter, then Chau would confess not just one but many aspects of her relationships with other men. He could not continue this kind of life in which he had to give up so much only to receive counterfeits in return.

Listening to him, Chau panicked. Could it be that Sai knew of what had happened between her and Toan? There was reason to think so, for a month ago, Chau had had something to take care of in Mai Dich District. On her return, Toan quietly followed her on his bike. At the Nam gate, he rode past and then turned his bike around to block her path. Momentarily stunned, Chau didn't know how to respond when he confronted her and asked, "Pardon me, please allow me just one question. Is our child in good health?"

Chau looked stern. "I've told you that I forbid you – "

"I know, but sometimes I miss him so much. I wander about all night on the streets."

"Don't use that phony voice with me. I am sick of it."

"I will put up with whatever you say, but – "

"What do you want?" Chau wanted to run away, but he followed so closely that she did not want to make a turn into Hang Bong Street, where her husband or friends might see her. She had to turn into Phan Boi Chau and wonder what Toan would do next.

"You forbid me, but I miss our son so much that I might take a chance and go see him. And if need be, I'll tell your husband that he has no business taking care of my son."

Chau felt the urge to pick up the bicycle and smash it in Toan's face. She spit out whatever gross, vulgar words she could think of. "I say it again, you charlatan. If you continue to follow me around and ruin my life, then one of us will have to die."

Faced with her hatred, Toan rode away on his bike. Chau, oblivious to potholes and traffic, pedaled on furiously, as if trying to escape him. Could it be that Taon had recklessly come there, playing the villain?

Now, as Sai spoke with her, Chau wondered why, in the past few weeks, he had seemed so placid, neither sulky nor querulous. She covered her face with her hands and sobbed loudly. "O my God, what kind of a family is this? Does anyone else punish his wife in the middle of a pregnancy like this? How can I even put up with it?"

"If you can't stand it at home," Sai said, "feel free to go."

"Are you asking me to leave?"

"No, I would not ask you to leave, but I won't stop you if you go."

"Time shows more and more clearly what kind of person you are."

"It's a bit late, but it doesn't mean that there can't be a remedy."

Sai's nose-tweaking manner made Chau both angry and fearful. She decided that she had to leave. She needed both to respond to her husband's cruelty and to find out what Toan was up to. "All right, you've thrown me out. I will leave. My departure will satisfy the mean, selfish nature of a small-town intellectual."

Sai pressed the tobacco into his pipe and gave an ironic smile. "An intellectual? You flatter me. Too bad I'm not yet up to the rank of your cosmopolitan city types."

"Hold your tongue, you ignorant savage."

Had it not been for the people in the apartment complex and the throng of children crowding outside the window, she would have used even harsher words to vent her anger. She left without her son, sensing the neighbors seemed to support Sai who was holding the child. Thuy wailed and howled for his mother. Finally, a neighbor's boy had to pick him up and carry him away, for no one could bear to see the baby witness the breakup of the household, which tore at the heart of the baby. It should not be his misfortune to suffer this kind of agony at such a tender age.

Once Chau was gone, Sai quickly cleaned up the room. Instantly, the apartment looked more spacious, almost vacant, as if its occupants had decided to abandon it forever, never to return. Sai was forty years old; he felt his life was being broken into pieces. He was heading toward an unknown destination, and there was nothing he could do. Chau had not given him a way out.

Sai went to get his son. Seeing his father, Thuy immediately began to cry.

"Daddy, where's Mommy?"
"Mommy went to the office."
"When Mommy comes home?"
"After you take a good nap, Mommy will come home."
"Daddy takes a good nap too."
"Yes."
"Oh, Daddy and Thuy take a good nap so Mommy comes back."
Father and son talked excitedly for a moment before Thuy moaned, "Mommy comes back yet, Daddy?"
"Daddy said after Thuy takes a good nap, remember?"
"Why yesterday Thuy didn't take a nap, but Mommy came home?"
"Oh, yes, yes, because yesterday Mommy didn't have to go to the office."
"What is the office, Daddy?"
"The office is where people do their work."
"What is work?"
"Work is . . . is so people can get paid."
"What is paid?"
"We get paid so we can buy candies."
"Oh, go buy candies, Daddy. You and Thuy go buy candies. Oh, that's fun!" Sai agreed and the child brightened right away. Sai bought Thuy green bean cakes, sesame sweets and peanut bonbons. Whatever Thuy wanted he got. Had Chau been home, this would not have happened, pandemonium would no doubt have erupted. But how else could Sai pacify his son? Back home, with his hand still clutching the candies, Thuy fell asleep on Sai's shoulder. Sai stepped on something on the ground; it was the green pea cake, fallen from his son's outstretched hand.

At midnight, Thuy suddenly began crying loudly. "O Mommy, O Daddy! O Daddy, where's Mommy? Did Mommy come back from the office?"
"Go to sleep, son. Mommy will come back in the morning."
"No, Thuy doesn't sleep any more. Thuy sleep, Mommy comes back."

His son's sobs tore into Sai's heart. Unexpectedly, tears welled up. Why was life so hard? He put his arms around his son, turned on the light and asked what he would like to do. Sai arranged all the toys before him, but Thuy thrust them away. Thuy asked for the green bean cake; Sai gave him a piece of peanut bonbon. Thuy sulked, demanding the green pea cake.

After two hours, using all the weapons at his command – from storytelling and singing to the threat of Mr. Ngoao, "the bogeyman" – Sai got Thuy back to sleep. At dawn, after Sai had slept only briefly, Thuy was already sitting up outside the mosquito net, whining plaintively. Sai rose and pulled his son into his arms. But Thuy insisted on going to his mother. Sai wiped his son's mouth and face, changed his clothes, tightened up the bicycle's rattan rear seat, pumped the tires and rode his son out to have beef *pho.* He also stocked up on green pea cake, bananas, hard boiled eggs and soft rice cake. Whatever pennies he had left in his pocket were spent to keep his son pacified.

From dawn to dusk, the child ate irregularly, following no fixed schedule. During office hours, Thuy attached himself to Sai's female co-workers – the secretaries in the Office of Documents or elsewhere. For lunch and dinner, Sai had only pieces of black powder bread, hard as a brick from sitting in his pocket, which he broke off from time to time. When the day was over, father and son rode around on the bike. Sai took his son everywhere, from the One-Pillar Pagoda, to Lang Bac, Uncle Ho's Tomb, to the stone chair at West Lake. They did not return home until after nine. The apartment looked dark, damp and cold. Sai used the lukewarm water boiled yesterday from the thermos to wash his son and put him to bed. He then boiled water and let it sit before filling the bottle and the thermos. He washed his clothes, drew a few buckets of water and fed the chicken. When everything was done, he sat down to have a smoke. He turned his face up, slowly inhaling the cloud of smoke as if absorbing for the first time a moment of complete freedom, of control in a room that for a long time symbolized nothing but oppression and discomfort. This was one of those few instances where he felt totally at ease, released from any fear of being commanded or criticized.

But when he was truly in control and had plenty of free time, Sai hadn't the faintest idea what to do. He felt dull and empty. For three days, he and Thuy cooked only once, and yet somehow the days were crowded with chores from dawn to dusk. Then after Thuy had gone to bed, Sai sat alone in the dark, wondering what tomorrow would bring. Little Thuy refused to go to the daycare center. Sai had to yield. Father and son wandered about on the street every day. They ate at no fixed schedule and slept at no fixed hour. On the bike, little Thuy sat in the rear, leaning forward like a frog to hold on to his father's back. He moaned constantly, tears wetting his face, because he wanted his mother.

During this time, Sai spent over a hundred piasters, which he borrowed from the office accountant. He had no idea who else he could borrow from until he next got paid.

While he was finding a way to send word to his brother to let his niece come help out, Thuy fell ill. It was the fifth day after his wife had left. Thuy had shown signs of not wanting to eat the day before, but Sai hadn't noticed. As on other days, after arriving at the office, Sai left Thuy with his young co-workers. About noon, the secretary of the Office of Documents brought Thuy to him and said harshly, "My God, look at the way you care for your son. He has a fever, lying alone in the corner of the office, and you don't even know!"

Panic-stricken, Sai grabbed his son. He was hot. Sai took his jacket off to cover Thuy and asked his friends to ride them home. Sai gathered a few pieces of Thuy's clothes and some bottles, cups and spoons, asking his friends to take them to the hospital. The elderly woman next door came, and, after holding the boy for a moment, told him to keep Thuy at home. "His face is red-hot, his eyes are gummy, his ears are frigid, and he has a cough. It must be measles. You should keep him at home, guard him against water, wind, and cold food. Don't go."

Sai listened. Almost everybody in the apartment complex came to give advice on how to take care of Thuy. In the past, they had all been taken by Sai's good nature and now they were especially sympathetic to his situation – "the rooster raising the chick."

Sai sat on the bed, holding Thuy in his arms for the whole day. The doors in the front and in the kitchen were both kept open so that the neighbors could take turns cooking rice or making soup for father and son. With the rice already in stock, Sai only needed to give out the money. As for what dish was good for him and for Thuy, the old woman would decide. At night, she cleaned up. The support and love of the people in the apartment complex helped to calm Sai's fear. The first few days after Chau left, he thought father and son might not be able to survive, but gradually things started falling into place.

Even so, Sai still hoped that Chau would return. Knowing that

Thuy had been ill for two days, Chau still hadn't come back. The very night after leaving the house, she asked for a ride to see Toan. Once confident that Toan would not do anything against her wishes, she moved out happily. No longer afraid that Toan had exposed everything, she could afford to be vindictive. She wanted to hurt both men: the deceitful scoundrel and the jealous, vengeful peasant. Thinking about Thuy, Chau felt nervous. But things might turn out for the best, for she would teach that peasant a lesson on how to temper his jealousy. She had cried out, "O God," when told of her son's illness, but then she had decided to calm down and wait until Sai came by to apologize, as he had done before.

Some people at the apartment complex urged Sai to go apologize. "Enough," they advised, "for the sake of the child. Forgive her, especially since she's with child." Sai didn't say a word. Out of respect for those who tried to help, he simply smiled, saying "yes" and "no" for formality's sake. He made an oath with himself that even if he and his son had to die together in bed, he would not go looking for Chau or apologize to satisfy everyone's exhortations. Throughout his life, he had listened to everyone, complied with everyone's wishes. Now that he recognized what he'd done, it was too late.

On the fourth day of his illness, Thuy's eyes were so covered with hardened mucus that he could not open them. No longer having the strength to cry out loud, he cried softly and continuously, like a sick kitten.

"Grandma, he has such a bad fever."

"He's pustulating. Grandma bought *mui* seeds, today. Grandma will grind them up to make a warm paste to cover him and speed the growth of the pustules. Let me have the child, Sai. Let me hold the 'little puppy' in my arms so your Daddy can take a break." Sai roasted the *mui* seeds for the old woman. After giving the child the treatment, the old woman assured Sai that there was nothing to worry about, so long as Thuy was put on a strict diet.

"Grandma, let me cook extra so you can join us."

"No, don't bother about me. You should take a walk outside, take your time, breathe in the fresh air, have a smoke or two, and then wash up, if you want. As for the meal, let my nieces take care of it. You don't have to trouble yourself."

Sai had the impression that his own mother was here with him. He wondered what he could do later to repay her for her kindness.

While he had stopped to smoke by the food stall, Nghia called out, "Oh, I've heard your son is sick, but you look so carefree!" Until now, Chau had always been Nghia's idol. Since the day of the wedding, Nghia occasionally paid Sai's family a visit. Sometimes the two met at Chau's mother's house, but beyond a bit of friendly chatting, there was nothing serious for them to discuss and thus no reason to keep in contact. Hearing of Thuy's illness, Nghia, who happened to be on assignment in this area, decided to drop by.

Sai thanked her, which made Nghia cry out, "How come you've become so formal these days?"

Sai shrugged, and Nghia called attention to Sai's mistakes: his marrying Chau was like striking gold, and yet he hadn't known how to correct his improper habits or control his jealousy. "Let me tell you, to find someone in Hanoi as honorable as Sister Chau is not easy, my dear brother! Why do you laugh? It's your overly suspicious nature. You're like Tao Thao, that jealous man in the Chinese legend. Remember his nature only brought so much grief and ruin to his family."

"But, unfortunately, I've never been jealous."

"Are you sure?"

"What's the use of jealousy? What man can lock up all his wife's laughter or block out all her glances?"

"What you say seems really refreshing. But your acts totally contradict your words."

Knowing that this young woman was impartial and honest, Sai said, "Nghia, give me an example of my jealousy."

"You're sure?"

"Yes!"

"If you were not jealous, why did you kick your wife out?"

"Chau said that?"

"She didn't say so, but I know."

"Then what you know is very questionable."

"Questionable, you say. Let me tell you something rather delicate, and you can decide how to handle it. Chau is thinking of having an abortion."

Sai suddenly heard a ringing noise in his ears. He stood still, his face ashen. Nghia felt remorseful, "Knowing how you feel, I shouldn't have told you."

As if just coming to, Sai's eyes seemed fixed on something far away in the distance. He asked with an air of indifference and weariness, "Chau told you that?"

"No, but I know. You can't tell this to anyone, including Sister Chau."

"I'll do as you say."

"I think you must take the initiative to stop this. Seeing you two so strained, I worry."

"I will never stop Chau. She can do whatever she wishes."

"God, why you are so cruel?"

The two fell into silence.

Later, entering the apartment and seeing her little nephew lying almost unconscious in an old woman's arms, Nghia wanted to cry out at the selfishness of the two people for whom she ordinarily had so much respect. How could they abandon a sick child like this?

CHAPTER 11

Major General Do Manh was stationed on the outskirts of Hanoi, and he routinely made trips in to the capital. Through Ha he was introduced to Huong while visiting the city. At their first Sunday meeting at Ha's, he told her, "Although I've just met you, I've heard about you for over twenty years, and I've always held you in high regard." Major General Do Manh then entreated her to come with him, Ha and Hieu to visit his nephew, who was secretary of the district where Ha resided. Do Manh had earlier also invited Tinh to dine with them.

After they finished eating, Do Manh sat drinking his tea. Offhandedly, he inquired of Sai and his family. Ha, Hieu and Tinh all replied without enthusiasm. All three spoke of Sai's errors of judgment, of the discouragement everyone felt and of the fact that no one wanted to have anything more to do with him.

Listening, Do Manh smacked his lips and said, "Things have gone pretty far. Sai's made a blunder and will have to suffer the consequences. If we have a good brother, a good sister-in-law, then everything is easy. If not, they have to deal with their problems, and we go about our own business, no harm done. Through his experiences in life, Sai will eventually sort things out for himself. I urge you, though, not to give up on him or to hold it against him. I am sure it's very hard on him."

That was all he had to say on the subject. Everyone then shared candies and tea, and the conversation turned to other affairs. But Sai was the main reason for Do Manh's trip. He knew that both Ha and Tinh had been displeased with Sai for over a year. He came up with the idea of this social gathering to make sure that those close to Sai wouldn't abandon him to his loneliness. That was how he had always done things. He knew that Ha, Tinh and Hieu would take note of the casual hints over tea.

As for Huong, Do Manh appreciated the fine sentiments she had shown toward Sai's family. But Huong she didn't think she could go too far. When Sai had married, she was saddened and tried to stay out of his way. Angry at him, she avoided his friends and family. After a year without any contact, she learned of how Sai often left home and wandered the streets. She went to see Hieu and Uncle Ha, and then to the village to see Tinh. At first, she had no idea of what her purpose in making these visits was, but now she was quietly thankful that Do Manh showed such concern for Sai. She was glad he was trying to draw everyone back to him. She had a vague feeling that, in the process, people would also be drawn closer to her.

On the bike ride home, Huong told Tinh of Sai's desperate circumstances during the last few years. Tinh felt remorse now at his own ill-treatment of his brother. He asked, as if giving out an assignment to a younger sister, "Over in Hanoi, if conditions permit, would you look after him for me?" Huong thought, then said, "Yes," knowing full well that, at present, it would be impossible for her to fulfill her promise. Later there were times after work she would ride her bike past Sai's office, but if he came into view, she'd speed up and turn onto another street. Still, she found a way to watch over Sai. She sewed him a pair of gloves, a fatigue-colored short-sleeve sweater, a purple wool hat and a pair of sea-blue socks. She gave him a Soviet-made razor sent home by her son, then a medicinal tonic, some antibiotics and even money for tobacco. She presented these gifts through Hieu, asking him not to tell anyone from whom they really came.

In doing this, Huong had no intention of winning back Sai's affection. She no longer felt the excitement of the chase, the foolhardiness of a twenty-year-old. But she did feel a great deal of tenderness for Sai. And there was still an element of love in her actions, a love that lived on the memories of time past. Still, she did not allow herself to express or accept her own feelings. There were times, in fact, when she longed to find a way to become close to Chau, to become her elder sister, so that she could urge her to love Sai, to give due respect to Sai's suffering and integrity, and to stop torturing him. But who was she? Could she give an adequate explanation if Chau found out that she had once been the object of his love? There were times she wanted to leave things as they were and let Sai pay for his misdeeds. After all, it was he who, blinded by beauty, had thrown himself at

Chau and then rushed foolishly into marriage as if in anticipation of an imminent death in the family.

Huong became angry with herself. Why should she have to bother her mind with these things? What good would it do? There were times after she had given Hieu presents for Sai when she felt her own actions didn't make any sense. They were empty gestures that smacked of poor judgment. But she didn't have the strength to ask Hieu to withhold her gifts. Now, Huong wondered what Sai's life would be like after Chau had another baby. Was it possible that, with another child, Chau would come to accept Sai, and the family would have some peace and happiness? If Sai *did* find peace and happiness, what would happen to her feelings? Afraid of pursuing this train of thought to the end, Huong slapped her cheeks with both hands and covered her face.

Chau did not have an abortion, as Nghia had feared she would. Had she sent word just to threaten Sai? Or did her family stop her? Or was there another reason? Sai did not care. But he began to have doubts about a wife who used to have a reputation for being steadfast. Someone who spoke of rash deeds might commit them. Knowing that, he kept quiet. Chau, her mother, her sister, her brother's wife and Nghia returned to the apartment after Nghia had described Thuy's sickness to them. Chau flung the bike against the wall and dashed into the room. She almost burst into tears, but seeing the elder woman from next door holding Thuy, she regained her composure, "Grandma, I am deeply indebted to you! O God, who could have known that my baby would get sick while his father was taking care of him!"

"Every child has to go through this stage. His father has been especially strained the last few days. Just cover him up so that the pustules will come out in a uniform way."

Chau stared at her son. He seemed to have shrunk into a small bundle. Her tears poured down on his quilted diaper. In his half conscious state, little Thuy dreamed he was being held in his mother's arms, but then his mother gently placed him down on the bed and headed for the door. He woke and ran after her in a panic, "O Mommy, Mommy, wait for me, wait for me."

"Mommy here, Mommy here." Chau grasped his hands and held

them tight. "Thuy, my son, Mommy's here. Wake up, wake up, my son. Mommy here. Mommy Chau comes back to you here."

Thuy moved his hands, as tiny as a rabbit's ear, to feel for his mother's hands. He arched his palm as if to grasp his mother's fingers to hold her back, so that she couldn't run away. But his hands could not hold her tight enough. Feeling sorry for himself, he was overcome with tears. The teardrops oozed out of the mucus that had hardened into a thin film over his eyes. Chau quickly used a towel to wipe away the tears and the gummy film that was slowly softening. There were spots of pustules, as uniform as millet, in his eyes. His two cracked lips showed signs of coming back to life – or at least of smiling. His mother immediately recognized the auspicious omen; it was a tremendous reward. Chau stooped to put her face against her son's. She said, "My son's very good. Do you love me?" He tried to nod. "Mommy loves you, Thuy is very brave. My son, try hard to bear up so that you will get well. I'll take you to see Grandma." He cheerfully made an attempt to nod his head.

Thuy's "grandma," "uncle," "aunt," "brothers," and "sisters" all squeezed into the apartment complex, leaning over the bed, watching over the happiness of the mother and son. Finally, the old woman from next door ordered the group to disband. After advising Chau on what to have her son avoid, she, too, returned home.

Following the command of Chau's elder sister, Sai made tea for his mother-in-law and the rest of the family, then rode off on the bike to buy vegetables for the meal. Taking pity on Sai and Chau, the thoughtful older sister pulled all the cloths and pots and pans out of the cabinets and cupboards where they had sat untouched for months. In a while the room and kitchen were thoroughly "redecorated." She represented Chau's pride in the well-bred traditions of her family. Sai and his niece, they embodied disorder and slovenliness; how many times he had been caught red-handed, his false pride prevented him from promising reform of old habits. Unable to find joy inside the family, she had been forced to look outside. That was just common sense and easy to understand. Later, after cleaning and cooking, Chau's elder sister took hold of the child, so that "husband and wife" could invite Grandma to join them in the meal. In everything she said, the elder sister made a special effort to say "husband and wife" or "you two." She left them and didn't return home until nine o'clock in the evening. Although somewhat reassured that "the two" had made up, she still took Chau aside to offer advice: "Keep peace in the family to avoid the scorn of the world."

Even without her elder sister's coaching, Chau realized that in the coming days, she had no choice but to behave with good cheer toward Sai.

≣ The next morning, when Thuy's grandmother took her leave, she said to her son-in-law, "Take Grandma home, and on the way, pass by the office of your sweetheart and request more time off from her to look after our son." If Sai had heard this intimate form of address previously, he would have been so excited that he would have immediately followed her instructions. Now, he simply replied, "Yes, all right," then walked away, taking the water pipe into the kitchen so that the smoke would not bother his son. In a few moments he returned, and then, with deliberation, he got on his bike.

Sai's stubborn behavior made Chau chafe, but it also made her more careful and she reacted with discretion. Sai did not pay much attention to her reaction. He had made up his mind about how he was going to behave. Love was the only thing that counted, and he was through being afraid. Still, he lived with all his heart and soul for his wife and child. Whatever he could do, he would do without regret. But when he could not do something, he no longer tried to impress his wife with his capabilities.

When his son recovered and was able to eat and to go out to play, Sai, as if making up for lost time, slept for hours. One day, when his wife woke him to look after Thuy so that she could get her hair done, Sai allowed himself to appreciate the fact that he had been free, for the first time in a long while, to take a long and refreshing rest.

≣ Five days after his son recovered, Chau fell violently ill and had to be taken to the emergency room. At first, it was thought that her pregnancy was in crisis or that she had some sort of stomach or liver trouble, but it turned out that she was ready to go into labor, after only seven and a half months. This was a medical and a financial emergency. Sai and Chau's combined incomes had been used to pay for her first delivery, their son's illness and other expenses. Sai still owed Tinh and his friends money for the apartment, bed and cabinet. Around the time of Thuy's birth, Sai had received help from family and friends; this time he was on his own, and he had not been able to prepare at all. Fortunately, he still had Thuy's diapers and clothes. But it was not easy to make ends meet. He had to ask for an extension on the one hundred piasters that he'd borrowed when his son was sick. The creditors all took pity on him. They gave him an extension, and they each lent him twenty or thirty piasters more. To supplement his salary and the money he'd borrowed, Sai secretly sold off the uniform he had received when leaving the army. Later, he also sold his pair of black shoes and his parachute blanket; the only remaining mementoes from his battlefield days were also sold for over a thousand dong. In quiet desperation, he gathered whatever strength he had left to support his wife and son.

The second child, born after only seven and a half months, had to be kept in an incubator. Chau cried every time she looked at the baby, who was completely covered with a pallid, blackish skin. Some people, with unkind tongues, said the child looked like a singed puppy. Sai comforted his wife, "Regardless, she is our child. It is unfortunate, but with time we will love her just the same, even more."

But she didn't listen. In fact, everyone in Chau's family pointed fingers at Sai. It was his fault the baby was so sick, they said; he'd had the malaria of the Truong Son mountains, and he'd brought chemical poisons home from the jungles to infect Chau's offspring, causing them grief. Sai clenched his teeth in silence before his wife's accusing look. He knew that she saw him as the culprit who had brought evil to her and dishonor to her family.

With the exception of the people in the apartment complex and of Chau's relatives who had come to visit in the hospital, offering a dozen eggs, a can of condensed milk, and some other things, few members from either side of the family showed up to help with Sai's numerous chores: getting the birth certificate, registering for security population control, applying for coupons, standing in line, washing, cooking for his wife, boiling milk for the baby, washing and feeding his son, taking him to and from the daycare center. For the entire day, Sai rode around and around in circles. Some nights even as late as eleven o'clock, he was still riding to the hospital, with his son, half-asleep, tottering on his bicycle's rear seat.

Sai was exhausted. At night, he lay awake with terrible headaches. On the most difficult nights, he was tempted to get up and ride his bike to Chau's family's home. He imagined he'd bang on their door and shout, "If it weren't for those malaria-ridden men, lugging bombs and bullets on the battlefields for all those years, you wouldn't be able to indulge in your extravagant debauchery, grafting yourself onto government agencies so that you can steal and collect your salaries, so you can make connections and cut shady deals and take bribes. TVs, refrigerators and sofas fill your houses, and still you open your mouths, yapping indignantly about the ills, the poverty, the difficult conditions of society."

But if he were to point these things out to them, they would simply smile. "Don't complain now if you've been had because of your stupidity. It doesn't do you any good talking about your distinguished service; people will only laugh at you. Only those who can't make it accuse others of corruption." Chau had once cornered him, "Listen, if you can exchange your bravery for a bundle of string spinach without having to stand in line, you should be happy. Don't be so proud of those empty, high-sounding words. Otherwise one day you'll starve!" So be it. These people are now considered "modern" and "knowledgeable." Weren't they envied and sought after by others? There was nothing else he could say. He had no choice but to ignore his feelings of impotence and become a quiet, reasonable man.

His daughter's outer skin gradually peeled off and exposed another layer as pale as that of other babies. The impression of disease caught from Sai slowly disappeared with the loss of her blackish skin. Not long after his daughter's improvement, Sai went to buy rice, and then to stand in line for sugar. He had taken only one sackcloth with him, but had learned that white manioc was available. He poured the rice in the sack first, made a knot in the middle, then put the white manioc in the upper half of his sackcloth. Rushing off to go stand in line in the department store, Sai hadn't tied the top of his sack securely. On his bike, he placed the half of the sack with rice on the rear seat and let the half with the manioc dangle below. On the ride home, the sack broke open, and the manioc fell out. Sai stopped to collect it – and met Nghia. She uttered a cry on meeting him, then crouched down to give him a hand. When they were done, she took him to a friend's shop so that he could buy sugar without having to stand in line. On the way, she moaned about his hard life. "Seeing you like this, I feel so bad. I have to say, I really care about you," she continued, with sincerity. "I'll tell you something, but you can't say anything to Chau."

"Why not?"

"I have great faith in you, but I have to ask it. Let me ask" – Sai nodded his head to encourage her – "was it because you treated Chau so badly that she went into labor before her due date?"

"Chau said that?"

"No, but I know."

"You have such a talent for finding out these things!"

"That's why I have to ask you."

"Do you believe that I would do such a thing?"

"Of course not. People in my block gossip like crazy. So I told myself that I would find a time to ask you."

"People gossip about it in your block?"

"You can't tell others that I told you."

Sai slightly grimaced as if to push down the anger he felt. He nodded his head to indicate he wouldn't say anything. Years later, Nghia's story became a standard question posed to his close friends and family in the village. Sai, however, maintained total silence, never uttering a word to defend himself. Riding home after saying good-bye to Nghia, his head was spinning out of control like a pinwheel. He fell into a daze, his control of the handlebars slipped, causing the bike to tumble. His head hit the pavement. Whether from sudden pain or an overwhelming feeling of self-pity, his eyes filled with tears. He quickly wiped them away with his sleeve. Fortunately, the street was almost deserted. No one had seen him. Even if they had, where could he turn for sympathy? Who could he complain to, when it was the insults of others that was making him so angry?

As they prepared the baby for leaving the hospital, Chau turned to Sai, "Mother, brother and sister all think that the baby and I should stay with them for a while, so that her aunt can help out. It would ease a lot of our worry. What do you think?"

A while before he might have been enthusiastic. But now he raised a question: "Husband, wife, daughter, each going in a different direction. When you and the baby are still weak, and yet I – "

In expressing an idea that was actually deceiving, intended to disguise a peasant's real feelings, he was able to touch the heart of the sophisticated woman from Hanoi. Chau was touched by what she took to be her husband's concern. With all sincerity, she offered, "Let Grandma and uncles help, so some weight can be lifted from the father's heavy burden."

"But is it the right thing to do?"

"It is absolutely the right thing to do."

"You decide, then. If you think it will be helpful, go stay with Grandma for a few days. The problem is Thuy. If he goes, it will be too much for Grandma, but if he stays, he won't be happy. Why don't I take him to the country for a few days?"

"All right then. But you must watch out for the ponds and puddles in the fields, they scare me."

"You believe that after all this time, I still can't look after our son?"

"You are very absent-minded, what if . . . And make him bathe frequently, or else he'll catch scabies and mange."

Sai was offended. "Enough, let's not talk about it anymore. Let's do it. You go to Grandma's. I'll take our son for some fresh air."

Although eager to escape the cramped and stuffy atmosphere of the apartment, Sai didn't want to trouble anyone in the village, even his brother and sister-in-law. They were still like parents to him, but Sai didn't want to remain a burden forever. Tinh and his wife were having hard times. Besides, Tinh's gestures and words during his last visit had deeply impressed upon Sai how humiliating it was to beg. Sai had told himself then, "As long as I can, by whatever means, I must manage. If I ask others for help and get into debt, I may never be able to repay them. If I can't repay, I will be indebted for the rest of my life and will suffer a bad reputation because of it."

In order not to bother anyone, Sai used coupons to buy ten kilos of rice. He planned to pay for his meals in every house he visited. Since his wife didn't know about the purchase, she asked him to take along a few kilos of rice. Sai's response was brusque, "Carrying wood back to the forest, what for?"

"Take it. The village is falling on hard times."

"Even if they were to starve tomorrow, nobody would take my rice."

It was a fact that hunger had broken out in the village. The most prosperous families could afford only two meals a day: in the morning, a dish of cooked canna, small and still green, and in the afternoon, soup made from kohlrabi, cabbage and sweet potatoes. Some families made do with only one of the two meals, but they divided it into two to have two meals a day. Though scrounging to put food on his own table, Tinh had finally come up with a pair of hens, two dozen eggs and ten kilos of rice to present to the new mother. Pressed by his wife to bring the food to Sai, Tinh had hesitated, for he hadn't been able to come up with a satisfactory reason to explain why he hadn't brought the food sooner. What luck when Sai and his son arrived! Listening to his brother's cursory account of events in Hanoi, Tinh smiled and said, "All right, your sister-in-law and I have prepared everything for Chau. Sai, your nephew will ride up there with the gifts. He has a scooter and will be able to take you back afterward, too."

Sai couldn't understand why Tinh seemed so affectionate with him again, just as in the days before he married Chau. Still not quite certain, he pushed the thought aside: "No need, they have everything they need up there," he said.

"Don't say that!" Tinh insisted. "It's our responsibility; it's not as if our family has nothing left."

"No? When will you next tell me that it's my fault you've hit bottom and your children are neglected?"

The two brothers fell into an uneasy silence. Tinh's wife wiped away the betel on her lips and spoke. As always, her words were simple, but difficult to ignore, "Don't pull back, my dear brother. Your brother and I are not like others who, after helping someone with something the size of a fingernail, still keep talking about the good deed year after year. I've always told your elder brother, we'll do whatever we can do without regret, but in the fever of excitement, he's generous and holds nothing back. Later he will recall old stories, as if he were trying to reclaim a debt. I plead with my husband and with Brother Sai, from now on, if any one of us commits an error, let's talk things over. Some money, a bowl of rice. Whatever is done, let it be done. Never mention it again, like sisters and brothers of other families."

Tinh felt slightly ashamed. Fortunately, at that moment, Thuy ran home to tell his father, "That person, that 'uncle,' said my daddy's name is not Sai, Daddy."

≣ The days back in the countryside turned out completely contrary to Sai's expectations. Everyone welcomed him warmly and showered him with affection – even though he was one of those villagers who hardly ever came home. For over twenty years he had passed by villagers without recognizing them as they stood wrapped up in tattered clothes by the side of the road. Still, the villagers were willing to act like members of his own family. They called out greetings as he passed by.

"How is my auntie's health these days? Why didn't you bring her and the baby along?"

"My goodness! How come it looks as if you've aged so many years? You're like an old man! I can hardly recognize you. I thought maybe you were the old bamboo seller of Bai market."

"You probably don't know who I am. I am Duoc, the first-born daughter of your Auntie Tho, who is the blood sister of our own scholar-grandpa."

"Hey, you look even older than brother Tinh, maybe even as old as Mr. Ha."

"Doing a lot of intellectual work in Hanoi, naturally he has to age."

Everybody invited him over, offering convenient times to get together.

An attractive girl of about seventeen stared at the people crowding around Sai and talking merrily. At last, she tugged at his arm, "You come by my house tonight, won't you, Uncle?"

"Whose daughter are you?"

Everyone burst out laughing. "Good Lord, she is our eldest brother's daughter." She, too, giggled. When Auntie Chau gave birth to Thuy, she had come up to visit for a day. Everybody chuckled with delight at how confused the esteemed uncle was. Sai's son from his marriage to Tuyet was on vacation from the Military's School of Culture. After taking little Thuy along to visit in the neighborhood, Sai let him play with his elder brother. Little Thuy wanted to play with his brother more than follow his father. Sai told his first son, "Stay within one step of your little brother." These words were like a sacred command to him, and the young man never deviated from his father's directive. After taking little Thuy along to visit the families in the neighborhood, Sai let him play with his elder brother. Sai, meanwhile, followed Tinh to visit relatives on his mother's and father's side – families of the old and new cadres – in the local hamlet and beyond. They set out every day, spent about ten or fifteen minutes with each family, and yet after a whole week, they still hadn't covered everyone.

Sai could strike up an warm conversation with anyone he met. Old or young, taciturn or hot-headed, Sai could always forge a friendship. Every family sang his praises:

"Brother Sai is truly delightful. Wherever that fellow goes, he will be cherished."

"The younger brother seems more eloquent, more adroit, than the older one. What a difference education and travel make! He knows everything and can talk about anything."

For the whole week, every family he visited seemed just like his own. His relatives, their friends and even those who didn't know him – they were all sincere and kind-hearted. The people were truly marvelous. It was moving to see how hard they labored.

If one stayed only in the city, seeing and hearing of the rich and famous, the gangsters and the thieves, one would think that the end of socialism was near. Back in the country, the mind was immediately set at ease. There one could find faith in socialism, the feeling that it would make solid advances, despite serious challenges. These peasants, how kind-hearted and hard-working they were! They would do whatever they were told, eat whatever was provided, wear whatever was available, bear whatever was inflicted and perform whatever formidable tasks were assigned.

What had been tried elsewhere had been tried here. This village had had mutual aid teams, low-level cooperatives and high-level cooperatives, from the subhamlet to the hamlet and then to the next level, for the entire commune, from "letting everything be contracted out" to "having five tasks contracted out, three tasks retained by the cooperative." With all these options, why did these most marvelous of all human beings still suffer from the kind of hunger rarely seen elsewhere in the country?

But even the normal eye of a normal person could detect quite a few things. For one thing, for the last twenty years, after the successive turnover of dozens of chairmen and members of the executive committee, the homemade gong, which had been hung, years ago, at the gate of Canton Chief Loi's house, was still used to sound the signal to go weed or to attend the meetings of the six production teams. The gong had never been moved to a central location. It was about half the size of a railway tie. In 1949, it had been brought back by guerrillas after a road-clearing operation, after that it had been moved from place to place until the mutual aid team helped hang it up as a gong. Now it had a hole in the middle, its bottom was cracked, and its top was rusted through in several places. When struck, it made a dull sound: "kack, kack . . . kack kack." Five times a day at regular intervals, the Vice-Director of Production told his son to go strike the gong: to mark the time for work, for breaks, for returning home and for meetings.

As for the work hours, nobody knew who set them. They had remained unchanged since the time when Sai had joined the army, regardless of the season, the crop, or the weather. The gong was struck first at seven. At eight, everybody arrived. In the afternoon, it was struck at two, but people didn't call out to each other to get moving until at least 3:30.

Every afternoon, Sai wandered all over the fields. He couldn't resist laughing at what he saw. Things looked poorly planned: on the elevated area, rice was planted; on the low-lying field, it was manioc or sweet potatoes; and down into the marsh, there were water ducts. Over the immense paddy field, there was not one irrigation canal. Apparently when water *was* needed, people offered to donate chicken and pigs to the district authorities so that they would rent mechanical pumps. Someone told Sai that labor costs alone exceeded the price of all the collected grain. That did not take into account the expenses for pigs, chickens, rice and alcohol, which had to be covered by other means. As for the expanse of alluvial land along the river, it was about ten kilometers long, cutting a swath along one side of the village. In places, the land was almost one kilometer wide. Elsewhere, it was only five hundred meters across. It contained a hodgepodge of everything: margosa trees, casuarina trees and bananas, peanuts and beans, sesame and corn, mountain rice, manioc and sweet potato, edible canna and kudzu, pumpkin and chayote, casaba melon, watermelon, *dua le*, cucumber, kohlrabi, tobacco, scallion and sugarcane. Sai was told that the land was available for lease. People were free to plant their own crops. At the end of the season, their yield would be calibrated in the equivalent units of corn to be paid to the cooperative.

All the things that Sai saw, all the stories that he heard, made him furious. They also created a deep longing in him for change, for some sort of transformation. But with whom could he share his thoughts? Would talk do any good? Surely, many government offices and specialists had come by, had put forth their recommendations, had issued their orders, with the resultant flurry of resolutions and measures. Those who worked and those who stayed home, those who studied abroad and those who went into commerce: all could be seen proudly displaying their bell-bottom trousers, their tightly fitting shirts, their motorbikes, their radios and cassette players. Some weddings had loudspeakers or even wireless microphones to summon the "dear wedding guests" into the modern age. The problem was not a lack of advanced means nor the absence of a modern mentality. But, still, in the last twenty years, life had not changed a bit. It remained claustrophobic, going-around-in-circles, and dirt-poor. Should he, as a son of his village, as a communist, say plainly what was on his mind?

Tien, Secretary of the District Party Committee, got out of the car and was about to enter the office when a call made him turn around. He was stumped for a few seconds, as he looked at the smiling figure walking toward him, "O Brother Sai! When did you arrive? You've aged so much that for a moment I couldn't tell who you were."

Tien's admiration for Sai went back to 1963. Tien, then an eighth-grade student, had heard of Sai's academic exploits when he had visited his uncle during the summer. Later, when he went to the regimental kitchen to get rice, he had tried to find out what Sai looked like. On a subsequent visit, Tien recognized Sai immediately, but because he was with his uncle and because he thought Sai was unlikely to remember him, Tien had pretended that they'd never met. Now, he took Sai into his office, offered him tea and cigarettes, and told Sai about what he had been doing.

He had been in the Soviet Union to study mechanical engineering. On returning, he was appointed to a post in a Fourth Region district. Two years later he joined the Party. He then had been elected to the Standing Committee of the Party Executive Body, and as Chief of the Tractor Station. After that, he was reassigned as Vice-Chairman in charge of agriculture. He returned to the Soviet Union for further study and research. Two years later, he joined the Ministry of Agriculture and then was transferred to the province to be Vice-

Director of the Bureau of Agriculture. In this way and in response to Sai's questions, Tien reviewed his entire resumé.

"And you?" Tien said. "When did you come home? Why didn't you drop by earlier? For almost a month, I've had to stay in the hamlet, and I haven't run across brother Tinh either. Several times I've been to Hanoi, but things were so busy that I couldn't come by to see you at all." Tien offered to have his office prepare a welcome for Sai, but Sai declined, for he planned to return to Hanoi the next afternoon.

"OK, then," Tien said. "Please make your preparations, and I'll take you back. It is fortunate that I came back here to get ready for the trip to Hanoi tomorrow. Otherwise, you would never have been able to find me."

The formalities over, Sai asked Tien, "Do you visit Ha Vi village often?"

"To tell you the truth, during more than two years in this area, I've only gone there about three times."

"How do you find the situation there?"

"A headache. A stretch of the most fertile land in the district, and yet it is also the poorest and most backward. For the last ten years, it has produced nothing of note, only a few tons of pork, four or five hundred chickens, a dozen or so tons of aromatic bananas, a dozen tons of green peas, some peanuts, some soybeans. . . . Ha Vi sees this as quite a lot, but in reality, it's barely enough to provide the 'spices' for the state's celebration parties; nothing of substance whatsoever! The district has to provide the village with assistance every year. We have to give them hundreds of tons of rice and yet hunger is rampant."

"How does Ha Vi compare to other villages in the district?" Sai asked.

"Well, that's how tough it is. Those wealthy bastards who know how to make a lot of money – like Dong Viet, Dai Thuan, Binh Me – their yields always go up, and their fulfillment of governmental obligations is always outstanding. They far exceed the requirements. The standard of living for peasants in their hamlets is one of the highest or close to the highest in the province, but the level of military service is always poor. As for the mobilization of laborers to reinforce the dikes, deepen the river, strengthen the dams, and build the roads, these bastards are the worst in the district. Many times, after Ha Vi has finished the work allotted for the village, it sells its services to other hamlets. In the last few years, those who are responsible for parts of any construction project have always tried to hire out of Ha Vi. To be able to work in the same section as those 'aboriginals' assures everyone peace of mind. Ha Vi ranks number one in the fulfillment of military service quotas, number one in providing project labor. The village participates in every activity, from contributing bamboo trees to the building of a nursing school to attending meetings. In taking exams, filing summary reports, making presentations, Ha Vi always does best. The only problem Ha Vi has is hunger. They probably would be able to survive even if the district decided not to sell them rice. But who could be so heartless? To be frank with you, although I haven't traveled a lot, of all the places I've seen, none can compare to your village in terms of misery and hardship. There are families who never taste rice – except during Tet and when they are ill. They dare not touch the mutual aid rice, because they have to put it away for emergencies."

"What do you think are the underlying causes of all this?"

After a moment of reflection, Tien said, "For the last few years, I've asked myself that same question. Up until now, the Standing Committee has come to no official conclusions. In my opinion, the principal cause must lie with the Party leaders in the village. If there was a person who knew how to organize and take responsibility, things would be different."

"Is it possible that for the last twenty years or so, the village has had no such person?"

"I don't know for sure. Even if someone like that existed, his superiors would have to have faith in him, would have to be willing to delegate responsibility to him and would have to look unflinchingly at the situation of the village. He would have to destroy the old habits, the old customs, in order to find a way of doing things that is more appropriate to the situation. I think that even if there were someone like that, the district might not support him, might actually dislike him, or might not even realize what they had.

"Or maybe there are a hundred other interlocking causes, one cadre waiting for another, one office in fear of another to make the first move, fearful that the proper procedures of the province haven't been followed, the i's dotted and the t's crossed. It's definitely the case that those in the village who are most experienced and knowledgeable have either volunteered to be 'pared down to size,' or, if not, have been forced to be 'cut down to common size.' It's the culture of the district and the province that requires this."

"Is corruption in the administrative board cheating our people of the things they produce?"

"No. That does happen, but it's not the determining factor. If Ha Vi produces ten, and, say, seven are stolen, there are at least three left. In fact, virtually nothing is being produced. If people pilfer and appropriate on top of that, clearly the village suffers. That doesn't mean we look the other way when there's theft. In the last two years I have disbanded two Party cells for offenses. We have security agents, courts and investigative resources. We have laws, regulations and the support of the people, so we have the power to stop corrupt practices. Unfortunately, in places like Ha Vi, there are not enough people to start the process of cleaning up."

"The Secretary of Ha Vi Party Committee seems like a good man. He's sincere and forward-looking, isn't he?"

"He is a good man. But without a 'head,' you can't generate wealth. In the old days, our forefathers said, 'One who relies on his brain is worth a thousand times more than one who relies on brawn.'"

"Let the district invest cadres to 'bootstrap' things."

"We've done that many times. But after the bootstrap, everything keels over as soon as we return to the district. Besides, the district doesn't have just one village to worry about; we can't do Ha Vi's job for it."

Sai had thought his meeting with the Party Secretary would throw light on the heartbreaking situation in Ha Vi. But clearly Tien knew the situation better than he did. The two talked until the Chief Clerk invited them in to dinner in the guest house. Tien realized he still had on blue overalls that were visibly soiled by white streaks of salty sweat. He asked Sai to wait while he poured a few scoops of water overhimself, and without missing a beat, asked: "Do you see any way to solve the riddle of Ha Vi?"

As he sat down to pour tea, Tien's gestures seemed to say, "Let's take the time to exchange our views on this."

Sai chose his words carefully, "Going to school as a boy, then joining the army in my teens, I was a child of the country. Maybe that's no different from all the people of this earth. I don't always understand things all that well. There is just one thing that I always ask myself about my village: why don't we specialize in the growing of some particular plant, one that goes well with our soil and has a high market value?"

Tien sat up suddenly, stretched out both his arms to grasp Sai's hand. "For sure! For sure!" he said. "From the time I first came to the district and passed by Ha Vi, I've hated the crazy patchwork of its fields." Tien released Sai's hand and sat down, looking dejected. "It doesn't make any sense for me to go there and play the role of Chairman. Talk alone doesn't help. People here have told me that they have talked to Ha Vi time and time again. They have even tried being the village's temporary Chairman."

Both were still thinking about the problem when the Chief Clerk passed by the door. As if startled, Tien stood up, "We should go over this some more when we have another chance. It's not just a matter of sentiment. It's our responsibility."

During dinner, Tien had a chance to ask about Chau and the second child. When Sai left, Tien sent two cans of condensed milk, and for Thuy, a box of candies given to him by a friend returning from abroad.

The encounter with Tien, together with the time he spent in the village, aroused mixed feelings in Sai. It aroused tender, warm feelings; and at the same time it aroused angry, troubling thoughts. He couldn't bring them together – the differences could be neither ignored nor accepted.

As he passed by the Bai open market on his bike, Sai heard someone call his name. Though completely out of touch for the last few years, he still recognized Huong's voice. Sai was thrown into confusion. He knew whom the gifts – which Hieu had claimed were from this or that person – were really from. In the past, he'd expressed his appreciation in silence. Knowing that Huong didn't care much for formality or affectation, he still always wished for a chance to say a few words to her. What words he wasn't quite sure, but whatever they were, they would let Huong know that the things that she had sent were of great value, that they had helped him through some very dark times.

Neither of them knew that the other had come back to the village. Huong had been home for two days, but had not yet had a chance to visit brother Tinh. Now Huong went home, with Sai walking the bike after her. Entering a deserted section of the pathway, Sai closed in on her, "Where did you find the money to get me so many things?"

Huong recoiled with indignation, "My dear fellow, be careful please. Does anyone in the family know?"

"How could they? Sometimes you just worry too much."

"We can't just spill everything out like you do and ruin everything."

"How many men would be as careful as I am?"

"Yes, so careful, and see what happens."

Sai was quiet. Huong knew that she had said the wrong thing but made no amends. At her mother's house, she made Sai give her a clear account of how he had fallen into such a bad state.

"Do you know all the things that have happened in my family?"

"Not yet."

"Brother Hieu and Brother Tinh didn't tell you anything?"

"I would never ask them."

In fact, Huong never had asked them, but she still knew what had happened in Sai's family. But she wanted him to tell her in his own words, so that she could discover his feelings toward his wife and gauge his honesty with her. Even more, she wanted to extract from him a "confession" of the mistakes he had made because he hadn't followed her advice earlier. Sai told her the truth about his relationship with his wife. Huong sighed deeply, urging him to overlook everything for the sake of the children, since it was too late for anything else.

Sai agreed, "It must be so, there is no other way."

Huong tried to suppress another sigh.

There were only the two of them in the house; it was time for Sai to leave. Sai seized her hand. She pulled it free, her face scowling, "What a joker you are, this would make a mess of everything. You are really crazy."

Since the day he fell in love with Huong, this was the first time Sai had felt ashamed. Even three years later, when Sai again ran into Huong in the village, the embarrassment was still there. He dared not look straight at Huong, whose face was getting redder and hotter under the soft light of a crescent moon.

CHAPTER 12

For three years, when Nghia and Chau biked past each other on the street, they simply nodded in recognition. Each, preoccupied with her own life, was too busy to stop. On this day, however, as Nghia saw Chau, she gave out a loud yell and almost collided with another rider.

Nghia was a wife and mother now, but the changes hadn't altered her character much. With great enthusiasm, she asked, "Chau, have you heard?"

Chau looked at Nghia blankly. She looked weary and embittered.

"Toan and his wife have gotten a divorce."

Instantly, Chau was furious. "What's that have to do with me?"

Nghia realized her mistake and fell silent. After a pause, she cautiously tried to explain herself, "I thought . . . you . . . "

"You thought I was still swinging on a trapeze trying to catch him?"

The bit of news, which made Chau so angry in front of Nghia, followed her all the way home from the office. Was it possible that he had finally done what he'd promised to do? She remembered what he used to say: "I am ten times more anxious than you are. The situation is very complicated; we have to wait for the right moment. Only then can we be assured of success. If we aren't careful, people will find out about our relationship; things will become much harder to resolve. Let me take care of this! Won't you agree? My darling, you handle everything beautifully, but sometimes you're just a bit impatient. . . ."

He had never sulked, paid any attention to trifles, or quarreled over petty things with her, even when she'd slapped him that one time. By his side she was no more than a wayward child. He listened to her about everything, later sometimes making fun of her words.

Embarrassed and remorseful, she would have to muzzle him and insist, "Say no more, no more. I won't let you continue." Her face suddenly felt hot. She was aggravated at her own thoughts. She tried to chase them away by riding the bicycle home as fast as she could. Seeing her husband returning with the baby from daycare, she realized she'd forgotten to buy the vegetables. "I completely forgot to stop by the market for the vegetables," she confessed. "I guess I was worried that you'd come home and the baby would be restless."

"That's all right. We'll do without vegetables for a day. You play with the baby so I can start the cooking." She had rarely felt as in love with her husband and her children as she did at that moment. He was truly a generous and good-hearted man. It was so disconcerting to have an old love suddenly blaze up. That night, when the children were asleep, Chau climbed into the bed and embraced Sai passionately. "Make me happy, darling." She tightened her hold, as if afraid he might slip away. "Love me always," she asked.

He nodded listlessly.

"Why so reticent these days?"

"I'm tired."

"Are you depressed because of me?"

"No."

"You lie."

Sai was still feeling fretful and sullen. It was time for him to be moved by his wife but . . . The following morning he rose very early and did the cooking before his wife was awake to begin her chores. The fire was already lit, she went ahead and boiled milk for the baby. When Chau rose and began to clean young Thuy's face, Sai took the baby, rinsed her mouth with salt water and then fed her. As he was holding the bottle upside down in her mouth, his wife sprang all the way over from the kitchen door and snatched the bottle away. "What an idiot! Feeding her this junk!" She emptied the milk into the ditch and wailed, "What a disaster! Always doing everything precipitously, falling all over himself. Several years of experience and he still knows absolutely nothing. Feeds the baby a can of milk that has turned completely yellow. Why didn't you ask when you saw the milk like that?"

He sat in silence, unable to say a word. As with the other squabbles, Chau was not the one to humble herself by making the first move toward reconciliation. Thus, as had happened so many times before, the "cold war" was given a new lease on life. The only difference these days was that for the last eight months, since the birth of the second child, when they were fighting, Chau no longer cooked just for herself, and Sai didn't sleep on the desk in his office.

Chau respected Sai's silence, although she was apprehensive about his inexplicable "improvement." Could it be that family and friends had turned him against the life he led with his wife and children? Chau posed the question to herself, but then disregarded it altogether. She remained confident in her ability to "lead him by the nose." She had complete faith in their life and in her control over him. In the following week, each did his or her own chores. Sai cooked, washed clothes, picked up little Thuy at the daycare center, stood in line to buy rice, manioc, kerosene, and other announced rations. Chau fed the baby, bathed the children, bought food coupons, and minded the children. They only talked when it was unavoidable, when little Thuy could not act as messenger.

This tiff lasted over a week; it seemed like time to make up. But before an opportunity arose, Chua met Toan on the street. Chau was on the way to attend a friend's wedding, when Thuy suddenly pulled at the hem of her dress, "Mommy, Uncle Phong, Uncle Phong."

"What 'Uncle Phong'?"

"Uncle Phong who always visits me at the daycare center and gives me candies and stuff." Before Chau had a chance to look, Toan had come closer. Little Thuy jumped up and down on the rear seat, yelling, "Ah! Here comes Uncle Phong, here, here, welcome, welcome, Uncle Phong."

Chau had no idea that the toys and candies her son brought home as gifts from Uncle Phong, supposedly the father of one of his friends, came from Toan. But she didn't insult him and run away as before. She only frowned, "Why are you so daring?"

Toan understood immediately what Chau was chiding him about. He drew close and said in a low voice, "Please forgive me" – he hurried to explain himself – "I miss our son." Seeing Chau glower and turn her head away, he added quickly, "I miss him terribly. I have no one else now but Thuy."

Chau didn't dare look at him, but she could picture the anguished expression on his oval-shaped face and the sadness in his eyes. Yes, it was a pity – both grown-up sons had departed, and he was by himself. Seeing that her bike was no longer going in a straight line, she made an effort to say something final, "I repeat, from now on, I don't want you to see him any more!"

Her words seemed to be like a knife cut on his face; he stooped slightly, closed his eyes and let out an agonized sigh. "All right! I don't dare act contrary to your wishes. Please take this for our son." Then he quickly slipped a sedge bag – a fashionable item among the well-to-do – onto Chau's handle bar. Before Chau had time to react, he said, "Good-bye, you two! Go before someone sees us." He turned his bike around and rode off.

Chau's mind was in turmoil. Little Thuy pulled at her dress again. "Mommy, where is Uncle Phong?"

"He went back to his house."

"Where is his house, Mommy?"

"Mommy doesn't know."

"Why Mommy doesn't know?"

"Mommy does not know him."

"Does Mommy like to play with Uncle Phong?"

"No."

"Why not, Mommy? He loves Thuy a lot."

"Enough, don't say any more. Mommy is very tired."

"Let's go to Uncle Phong's house."

Chau took her son to the wedding. After, she hurried back to her mother's. While Thuy was busily playing with his grandmother, she examined what was in the sedge bag: denim pants, a sweater, wool pants, a child-size wool hat, candies, sugar, milk and a roll of cream-colored fabric. Just two weeks ago, she had mentioned to two co-workers that she had seen a piece of cream-colored "sec" that she wanted but could not afford. How did he find that out? Trembling, Chau put everything back in the bag, as if afraid someone might see her. Taking only the candies, sugar and milk, she left the fabric and clothes with her mother.

Whenever Chau ran into Toan, her homecoming was odd. At first, she flinched slightly, then she felt particularly loving toward her husband and children. She wanted to do everything to demonstrate her generosity, and she wanted to receive some warmth to compensate for the emptiness she was feeling. Today, after bumping into Toan, Chau arrived home to see Sai talking to the "uncle" who had been transporting rice for Chau earlier in the week. Seeing "uncle," Chau was filled with joy. She deeply appreciated his devotion, and, further, given her present feelings, it would be extremely difficult to confront her husband's icy face.

There was another reason for her pleasure. Chau knew Sai suspected her relationships with the "uncles." What she liked about them was their chivalry toward her. They helped in all matters, large and small, and never asked for anything in return. She found them to be high-minded, and, she felt that in her dealings with them that she, too, had been pure in heart and deed. If Sai suspected them, he would be only shadow boxing with himself. So, on arriving home, Chau showered the "uncle" with affection. Later, if Sai displayed any jealousy, she would start a fight. Looking at the clear mismatch between the "uncle" and herself, everyone would see how unreasonable Sai was. His "irrationality" would be useful later if there were any doubts about her relationship with Toan. Nobody would believe in it; they would discount it altogether. Her strategy was working, and she was very pleased.

Today, Sai, too, welcomed the "uncle" with open arms and genuine affection. Chau couldn't understand why the two were so friendly. When the "uncle" turned away for a moment, Sai said laconically, "Whomever you love and esteem, I love and esteem also. Nothing mysterious about it."

Having discovered long ago that his wife was not totally honest in her dealings with him, Sai had decided not to waste his time spying on all her relationships. He would take things as they came. Sai could tell that Chau's "uncle" needed to have many "nieces." During his visit, "uncle" rolled up his trousers and scratched his legs noisily. His face as well as his clothes were ancient. Sai realized that his wife took advantage of this poor man and felt instant sympathy for him. The two became as close as if they were blood relations.

"Uncle, stay for dinner. It's already meal time. You've had enough meals with the old lady. Have dinner with us today."

The uncle was still hemming and hawing when Sai added, "If you're afraid it will be too late, I will take you home afterward."

"No reluctance at all, but . . . "

"Enough, no more 'but's.' Chau, you hold the baby and talk with uncle, I'll cook."

"Let's give the baby to uncle. Let's cook together to save time."

So it took almost two weeks for the tension in the atmosphere, the feelings of sadness and melancholy, to dissipate. After days of hard work and nights of seething resentment, there was a ray of hope for peace. That night, Sai lay down and fell immediately into a deep sleep. Hearing her husband snoring on the nearby bed, Chau felt her loneliness even more keenly. In times of joy as well as of sorrow, there was no one to connect with; she was living with her husband, and yet it was like living with an ill-humored neighbor. The cries of the baby interrupted her thoughts. She got up briskly, switched on the light and changed the baby's diaper. The little girl didn't eat late at night like her brother. Most nights, after being tucked in at eight o'clock, she slept deeply, just like her father. Little Thuy, however, slept fitfully. Even when sound asleep, his face was contorted as if in great pain; there was something about his features that prevented her from looking directly at him save for when it was late at night. She leaned forward, covering his face with her own, then passionately kissed his cheeks and his head of short, stubbly hair. The child was startled awake and cried out loud. She quickly soothed him, "Mommy here, Mommy here." She held him in her arms, sitting perfectly still, thinking, "There is no one but me who can love him and take good care of him until he grows up to take his rightful place."

≣ In love, those who embellish the truth often attract women much more than those who simply speak the truth. A young girl who fell in love with a married man with children, then lived with him of her own free will, could never be deeply in love with an austere young man of the same age as she was.

Toan knew Chau very well. He knew that her hatred and abusive language were signs that she was still in love with him. Leaning on his shoulder or slapping his face were both expressions of her love. Knowing that the peasant veteran could never awaken Chau's deepest emotions, he was not the least bit worried when she got married. Ten years ago, Toan "stole" Chau's love, as she put it. At the time, Toan, even though he no longer loved his wife, had decided to keep his family intact, while maintaining a mistress. No one could serve him better than his wife. She had given him two children, now grown, but she had lost ground in terms of both her youthfulness and her personal appeal. And nothing gratified his longing more than an illicit love affair, especially with Chau, a beauty who had shunned dozens of younger men. There was nothing more captivating than her willingness to be his nonlegal wife, he, a married man with two children. With a sorrowful face, a sorrowful voice, and sorrowful gestures, he had spoken to Chau of his monstrous, evil wife who had ruined his life. Toan had meant to gain Chau's sympathies and to encourage her to believe he was doing all he could to "free" himself to be with her. Had Chau not panicked when pregnant with Thuy, his strategy would have worked; she would not have been so resolute.

Over the last two or three years, other things had ruined Toan's plans for himself. His first-born had gone into the army, and his second-born had left to study abroad. Only he and his wife were left. His wife developed mental problems; she imagined her husband was becoming tired of her and despised her. When leaving the house or even when going to bed, she put on powder and lipstick. Whenever her husband went to work or out to take care of some business, she became suspicious. What a strange sort of woman. She questioned him vigorously when he returned. Ironically, when he had been sleeping with others, she had had complete faith in him; now that he had been ditched by his lovers and wanted to devote himself to his marriage, she didn't trust him. Not a day passed without a quarrel, big or small, not a week passed without a fight. Toan submitted a divorce application – without his wife's signature – to the court. After a year of unsuccessful "reconciliation," a divorce was granted.

Without checking with anyone, Chau thought that Toan had wanted the divorce long ago, but that the time had not been opportune, as he had said. Now she regretted her impatience and selfishness. Probably it wouldn't change anything, but her heart was filled with sympathy for Toan.

"Who is Uncle Phong?" she asked her son.

"Uncle Phong is my friend."

"Who is your friend?"

"My friend is . . . I don't know."

"No, that's wrong. My friend is Long, say it."

"My friend is Long."

"Who is Long?"

"My friend Long is Uncle Phong's son."

"That's it. Very good, do you remember now?"

"Yes, I do."

"Where does Thuy go today?"

"Thuy goes to Mommy's office."

She took her son to the office, and on the way home she had to go along when Thuy insisted on stopping by his friend Long's house. For days the idea had run back and forth in her mind, and before and after arriving at the office, Chau had Thuy memorize important lies. But when she stood in front of Toan's apartment, her whole body was shaking, as if she had a high fever. The room was on the second floor, with its own separate stairway and entrance. Five years ago, when Toan's wife was at work at the fertilizer factory in Van Dien, Chau would stop by here, for an hour or so. Sometimes she even ate lunch and took her noon break here, as if it were her own apartment. Now, standing by an ice cream stand and looking up at it, she panicked. She knew Toan had been alone these months, had felt sorry for him being unable to see his own son. She'd thought of taking her son there several times. She decided not to go in.

"Mommy, why do we stand here?"

"To buy ice cream, but it's too crowded."

"Oh, yes, yes, let's buy ice cream."

Chau asked for assistance to get Thuy an ice cream pop. Before she could walk the bike away, Toan was in front of her, "Where are mother and son going?"

She blushed visibly. "We're going to the office, little Thuy wanted ice cream."

Little Thuy cried out happily, "Uncle Phong, welcome, Uncle Phong!"

Toan extended his hand for the boy to clutch and raised him off the rattan seat. "Let him see me for a little while."

"No, it's impossible," Chau's answers was weak while Toan – one hand walking the bike, the other holding little Thuy – proceeded to the alleyway by his house. Chau stood still, hesitating. Toan had disappeared into the alley, Chau looked to make sure none of her acquaintances was in the vicinity then wheeled the bicycle toward Toan's apartment.

While she was climbing the stairs, Toan was on the way down. "You go up there with Thuy. I'll go get some cigarettes." It was the same house on stilts made of ironwood, as clean as she remembered, except that the cabinet, the ceiling fan, the sewing machine and the box bed made of wood and bamboo was missing. His wife must have taken them. In his twenty-eight-square-meter room, there was a single small table with a few low-cut stools of the sort found in a teashop. The single bed was left unmade, with the old, much-patched mosquito-net still hanging over it. A shelf seemed to hover just above the bed. It contained a quilt blanket and a bundle, probably of clothes. It was very clear that, without a woman's hand, Toan, though normally tidy, was turning the apartment into a rooming house.

Toan brought back two rice cakes and a gigantic piece of pure pork pie for Thuy. He also brought a bunch of aromatic bananas, and a pack of lotus leaves stuffed with green rice flakes – this was a delicacy of which Chau used to be extremely fond. The privacy of the room put Chau at ease. She spoke somewhat more confidently, "What are you buying all that for? Thuy and I are leaving."

Little Thuy objected, "Let me eat the banana and the rice flakes first."

Toan acted as if he did not hear Chau. "Mommy gives Thuy the rice flake for me," he suggested. Thuy immediately put the rice flake pack on Chau's knees. Chau reluctantly let Thuy eat. "Even if you don't feel like eating, for pity's sake, please try a few flakes on my behalf," Toan begged her. Little Thuy also urged his mother on. He scooped a handful of the flakes and pressed his tiny palm against her mouth. Toan looked at her just as she was glancing up. His look seemed to say, "See, my son and I understand each other perfectly." Her face reddening, Chau turned away. At the noon break, Chau took her son back to the office. The child scampered ahead with nimble short steps. Toan said in a low voice, "I can't believe that I'm having such a happy day. I want to thank you, Chau." Chau picked up her hat, and went to the door, as if running. "Let me see you and our son off, is that all right?"

"Don't."

That afternoon, on the way back from work, she ran into Hieu, who invited her to visit. Chau immediately accepted, letting her son play until dusk. On the way home, little Thuy had already memorized the "mantra" that he had been instructed to bellow as soon as he entered the house: "I went to visit Uncle Hieu, Daddy."

Sai had been home since four o'clock. At five, when his wife and son were still out, he had to go pick up the baby at a house nearby. He was simultaneously playing with the baby, cooking, feeding the baby and doing the wash. All the chores were done, but still no sign of his wife and son. Angered by their inexplicable tardiness, he saw little Thuy scurrying in the door. "Daddy," he called. "Mommy and I went to Uncle Hieu's house. Uncle Hieu gave you water pipe tobacco. Here. In mommy's pocket." He was pleased, knowing the cause of their delay.

But even if he hadn't learned that they had been at Uncle Hieu's or if he didn't know where they were, there still probably would not have been anything worth getting upset about, except for the fact that, two days later, he came home late. He'd stayed at work until eight o'clock because he needed to summarize data in preparation for the minister's trip to the South the following morning. Hungry and tired, Sai didn't dare stop for food. For the past two years, he had lived with no idea of how Hanoi beef *pho* tasted, whether it was hard or soft, sweet or tart. When he came home, his wife was busy tucking in the mosquito net. Her face was heavy. He immediately explained why he'd been so late. She silently got into bed. He went to the kitchen, looking for the rice. A pot lay on the floor, the rice already hardened. A plate of vegetables had been left uncovered. He searched for the vegetable broth. A meal without vegetable broth would be like eating rubbish, especially when he was tired and the rice was already dried out. Unable to find it, he reluctantly asked, "Where's the vegetable broth, do you know?"

Chau didn't respond.

"Any broth left, dear?"

"Poured it into the pigsty."

"What's that you said?"

"I thought you were not coming home, so I gave it to the pig."

His face reddened, and the plate of vegetables in his hand nearly slipped from his grip. He put the plate of vegetables down on the cupboard, then leaned the entire weight of his body against it, his two hands clutching the top. Whether from hunger or fatigue or a feeling of profound anguish, he almost lost consciousness, his legs threatened to give way. It was half an hour later before he could walk to the door. Outside, he paced back and forth breathing in the fresh air. He went back into the house, lit the water pipe and smoked, gathering his records and notes, he switched the kitchen light on, put a book under the low stool to raise it up, then sat down to work. About midnight, after he'd finished, he went to the upper room, stood by the mosquito net, and looked at his two children asleep inside. He had the urge to hold them in his arms, but Chau was in the way, and he didn't want to wake them up.

Looking intently at the two innocent children who would soon be separated from at least one of their parents, he thought, "My dear children, please forgive your father. I never wanted to go through another family breakup, but there is no more room to retreat. There is nothing more I can do to bring you joy and keep you happy. If when you grow up and you want to condemn your father, okay, but please don't condemn what your father does tonight. Your father has been guilty for at least five years or even further back than that. Your father has been guilty since the day he was born."

Sai stood completely still – except for a slight tremor in his lips – for hours. He was startled when Chau sat up. She turned on the light and changed the baby's diaper. He sat down on the bed, calm and collected, as if nothing had happened. Chau rose from under the net, took the diapers to the kitchen, threw them into the water basin, urinated and came back to bed. Sai stood up, blocking her way at the door. "I've something I want to discuss with you," he said.

"There is nothing we need to discuss now."

"If you don't want to, at least let me tell you what's on my mind."

"Say whatever you want, but get your butt out of the way so I can get some sleep. I've got to work tomorrow."

"Let me speak first. We cannot live together any more."

"I thought you had something serious to say. What's the big deal? Just hand in your petition."

"I've already written it up. If you can read and sign it . . . "

"Why on earth do I have to read it? Give me the pen."

She took the pen and signed her name next to Sai's at the bottom of a sheet of paper titled "Petition for Divorce." She then threw the pen onto his bed and hurriedly got back into her bed, as if nothing had happened.

In her self-confidence, Chau thought Sai simply wanted to frighten her. She didn't think a divorce would occur unless she was the initiator. When the court sent her the notice, she was caught completely off-guard. Her face bright red, she felt ashamed before the neighbors. But she still put on a smile, as if to say, "I have a crazy husband, wanting to go to court over a trifling matter. What a happy couple we are!" She still didn't believe that anything drastic would come of it. But during the first appearance before the court to enter statements and the three subsequent attempts at reconciliation in the next six months, she understood what was happening. While for the record she still "loved" him, Sai insisted that there was "no more feeling" left between them: there had been "nineteen times when they cooked their meals separately" and "eleven times when one or the other ran away from home in the four years the two lived together." It was only then that she understood Sai had been quietly preparing for at least a year and that the inevitable breakup could no longer be forestalled.

So it was with Chau. Others, even those close to Sai, were surprised by his move. Only when given notice to attend the court session for the divorce did Tinh ride his bike to Hanoi to have a discussion with Ha and Hieu in order to make "a family decision on the matter."

Ha asked him coldly, "What decision do you want to make? He's old enough to decide for himself. Can you take care of him from now until his old age?"

Realizing he had gone out on a limb, Tinh looked crestfallen, like a child being punished. But having taken the trouble to pedal all the way to Hanoi, he didn't want to go home empty-handed, "With the loss of the father, the uncle will take over. Our family, I think, should at least know what the real story is, so we can choose the appropriate response if it becomes the talk of the town."

"What a pity, why not just mind our own business? Why do we have to cater to other people's opinions? Still, why don't you go to Hieu's, and call Sai. Tell him we'll meet at Hieu's at noon today."

That afternoon, Tinh gave a long discourse on family tradition, on the need to achieve unity even on small matters, on the necessity for discussion and deliberation. He talked so long that Ha, Hieu and Sai became impatient. Still, they pretended to listen so as not to embarrass him. After all, what he said came from the heart, but unfortunately it was familiar material to the others. After the noon break of a little over an hour, everyone would have to return to their tasks at work, so Tinh's inopportune words just bounced off everybody's head. Nobody paid attention. Finally, Tinh concluded, "Now, Brother Sai, report the situation to our uncle and brothers so that they can take part. Brother Hieu is like a blood brother to us. Let's discuss this matter carefully. This is the second time we have had to do this."

Sai was worn out by the prolonged discussion. On hearing the words "the second time," he smiled ironically. "Even if it's the tenth time," he said, "that's all right. We can talk more now or we can wait a week for when the court session begins and continue our discussion then."

"All right, you stand by yourself; the brothers here and I myself aren't worth a damn."

"Please, elder brother, don't say that. I'm not an ingrate. Frankly, I'm just nervous when group discussion is allowed to determine the fate of an individual."

"You mean you married her because of the people here?"

"No, it was my decision. What has happened here is entirely my fault. From childhood until maturity, I had to live with a wife I could not love. Because of that, when I was older, I threw myself away, looking for what I missed, for things that were not really me. In the prime of life, I was not allowed to love; when I was allowed to love, I went into it like a child. A man still in kindergarten in matters of love tried to play the role of an experienced, sophisticated man of the world because he dared not admit his ignorance, his inferiority, even to those eighteen-year-old girls who are already well versed in the arts of love and who could teach him a thing or two about life."

"Probably it was everyone else's fault."

"No!" Sai grimaced, as if pulling the words out. "I've said that it was all my fault. It was even my fault when I was a child. In those days, I lacked the courage to live truly. I did not have to live according to the wishes of others. Had I been determined to follow my own will, my father, brother and unit would have gotten rid of me. Later on, I'd have gained some experience, and I'd have been more knowledgeable, less dazzled by the charms of the city. Calmer and more aware, I would have been able to find a more compatible partner and avoid the endless running around, almost always out of breath, of the last few years. Half of my life I had to love what others loved; the other half I tried to love what I lacked. Now that I find out what I really want, this – "

"What wrong choices have we forced upon you?"

"No! I'm not saying anybody forced things on me, but the time has come when nobody can do that even if they tried. I'm a forty-year-old man. If I still don't know who I am or what I should do with my life, I don't deserve to be alive."

Both Ha and Hieu understood that no one could be as fully conscious of his so-called happiness as Sai. For that reason, Sai had to find a way for himself. Otherwise, as he said, he would just be a forty-year-old man who was still befuddled about who he was, a man who was easily excited by this and that. So, leave him alone. Let him make his own decisions, they said to themselves. Whether they were about his divorce or his plan to obtain an official position in the village, there was no need for them to "participate." In deference to Tinh, the two stayed to take part in the discussion. Seeing that the brothers were in disagreement, Ha and Hieu realized they had to maintain the peace. Nonetheless, they also had to bring up an unavoidably difficult subject: the children.

Sai's desire to have custody of little Thuy was a given. The court definitely would give him that. The issue was where Thuy should stay in order to get the best possible care. Everyone said it would be best to avoid a situation where father and son dragged themselves here one day, there the next. After debating back and forth, they decided that the best place for Thuy was with his Aunt Tinh. There, with his cousins, he would miss his mother less. Whenever Sai took assignments in the district, he could take his son to the office. The two brothers would take turns bringing up the boy; it shouldn't be too difficult.

But Sai was not quite happy with this decision. Although it might be tougher to find food and water in Hanoi, at least it was easier to keep Thuy clean in a place where the streets were paved. In the village, without his presence and with his sister-in-law, nieces and nephews being unfamiliar with the boy's nature, he could fall ill, come down with scabies and mange. Besides, Sai still felt it was best to avoid burdening others. In the end, though he, too, wanted to avoid hauling Thuy from place to place, what he wanted most was to be with his son. He could not let him go. In his whole life, Thuy was the only one Sai had left. He could not let him go. He was his consolation, his friend. Whenever he had a runny nose or sneezed, Sai was worried sick. It would be impossible to let him live somewhere else.

While Sai left for the village to arrange for his son's stay and his new responsibilities, Chau went to see Toan. The court notice actually made Chau feel dizzy. There were many afternoons when she didn't cook or wash her children, but took them out, dirty, to have beef *pho*. Often she had to turn away to hide her tears from the children. But little Thuy knew, "What's wrong with your eyes? Why they have so much water?"

"My eyes hurt."

"Do you want me to give them some medicine?"

"All right, finish your food."

"Mommy, where does Daddy go?"

"Daddy already passed away."

"No, not true. Daddy goes back to the village. I will go to the village too, on a boat with the paddles, you know?"

"No, your mother doesn't know. Your mother wants you to hurry up so she can clean things up."

A few days later, she took the children to her mother for a long visit. Then every afternoon on the way back from work, she pedaled from one street to another not returning home until it was pitch dark. Sometimes she rode by Toan's simply because she had nowhere else to go in those empty and vulnerable days.

Every afternoon, Toan came by to watch Chau leave work and start off on her aimless routes about the city. For a month, he rode his bike near her office after work and waited behind a tree at the end of the street. When she emerged and pedaled off, Toan would follow, riding from one street to another, breaking away only when she made a turn into her alley. Finally, one day while watching Chau wandering about, he decided to force a meeting. He sped forward and asked, as if it were a chance encounter, "Oh! Why are you leaving so late today?"

Startled, Chau turned around and replied, as if in a daze, "Too much work. I had to stay late."

"Drop by my place for a little while, will you?"

"What for?"

"If you're not busy, please come up for a chat, nothing special." Then, with sadness, he asked, "Can I ride along with you for a short while?"

"It's up to you, if you have time."

They pedaled quite a distance before Toan said, "I am fully aware of the agony you have been going through in recent months."

"You still take pity on me?"

The pain was once again visible on his oval-shaped face. He was silent. Chau regretted her slip of the tongue.

"I know that you suffer because of me," Toan said. "If you don't forgive me, please allow me to do something to share your burden."

"So you finally realize that you make me suffer?"

"I know that because I loved you too much, I couldn't control myself. But had you been calm and listened to me, things wouldn't have turned out this bad."

"Calm. You stayed calm so as to continue living with your wife, while I stayed calm to become a prostitute."

"Now, although everything has become clear, you still don't believe me. There's nothing I can do but suffer."

"Now that you have been freed, there is no dearth of beautiful young women."

"What kind of man do you think I am?"

"Men! They are all alike."

"All right, whatever kind of man you think I am, it's all right. I only want to tell you one thing. From now on, I have absolutely no attachments. I will be happy to oblige you as a servant, a friend or an elder brother. Allow me to help you and the children in some way; it will be my duty. As for our relationship, whether you want to consider it or not, it's entirely up to you. I dare not make any demands."

"Enough, I am sick of all these words."

She hurriedly pedaled forward as if in panic, as if she wanted to run away. But two days before the court date, she went to stay with Toan for the night. When hearing the final announcement of the court, she had done the one thing that up to then she had been afraid to do.

≣ "We invite Mr. Giang Minh Sai to continue answering questions from the court."

Sai stood up. The court officer took some notes before raising his head and saying solemnly, "If the court grants the divorce between you and Nguyen Thuy Chau, please tell the court your wishes regarding the properties and the children."

"As for properties, I will leave them all to Chau. For the children, since the baby cannot be separated from her mother, I ask to be allowed to raise the older child, Giang Minh Thuy."

"You can sit down now." His voice became louder. "We call on Mrs. Nguyen Thuy Chau." Chau stood up. The judge tapped the pen on the paper as if keeping the beat, "Have you heard Mr. Sai's proposal?"

"Yes, sir, I have."

"What are your wishes regarding the children and the properties?"

"About the properties, I will accept whatever the court decides. As for the children, Giang Minh Thuy is not Mr. Sai's child."

"Do you have evidence?"

"The proof is that between the time we went out with each other until the day the baby was born, there were only seven months and three days."

"You also gave birth to a second infant prematurely."

"Yes, but little Thuy weighed 3.2 kilos and showed no sign of premature birth."

"Have you ever told Mr. Sai this?"

"No."

"Please continue."

"Yes, my wish is that Mr. Sai shouldn't be allowed to raise Giang Minh Thuy."

"But you do agree that he works very hard to raise his children?"

"Your honor, since the child is not his own flesh and blood, and since he only finds that out today, he won't have the strength to love and care for a child who isn't his son."

There were times when Sai had thought about the circumstances of Thuy's conception, but he was completely unprepared for what Chau said. In a daze, he could no longer hear anything Chau said. In his mind, pictures appeared of the countless times his son had wet his diapers, of the months of sitting through the night, holding on to the needle or taking care of his son so his wife could sleep. He heard his son say, "Thuy loves Daddy the most. When Thuy grows up, Thuy will sell ice cream so Daddy can eat as much as Daddy wants." Or: "Why are Daddy's eyes wet? Daddy cries, Thuy very sad." "My child, O my Thuy, if our relatives in the village learn of this, what would they think of you!" He was startled when the judge called out his name. He stood up, like a robot.

"Have you heard what Mrs. Chau said?"

"Yes, sir."

"What is your response?"

"I don't have any opinion."

That afternoon, with whatever pennies he had left, he bought candy for the children. He took them in his arms and kissed them all over. He slung the rucksack containing the mosquito net and a few pieces of clothes over his shoulder and said to them, "Your father goes away on business," and he hurriedly stepped out of the house. Her face cold and acerbic, Chau looked at him as if at an enemy. But when he left, with the two children running after him in tears, she bowed her head on the pillow and sobbed uncontrollably. When the two children returned, each standing by her side weeping and trying to get her attention, the people in the apartment complex gathered in a crowd outside. Through the splits in the shutter, they could see three figures sobbing on the bed, and they were brought almost to tears. They wanted to tell all young men and women, "You can fall head over heels in love with each other and then tear at each other like cats and dogs. That's your privilege. But nobody should be so heartless as to bring little children into this world just to heap the sins of selfishness on innocent bodies."

CONCLUSION

Huong stood in the middle of the room, which she was coming to see for the first time. Her heart was heavy and sad. How could it get so bad? It was part of a two-room house that Ha Vi village had formerly used as a manure depot. All the roof tiles had been stripped when the cooperative expanded to commune level, leaving behind only the range of bare rafters which huddled together like fingers of two bony palms, planted on top of walls defaced with graffiti of human figures and profanity scribbled in coal and half-baked brick.

After three months reviewing the state of the district, Sai returned to Ha Vi as the district head of the People's Inspection Committee. His job was to investigate and settle complaints brought by the villagers. He borrowed the depot from the village and set up house. He made a roof out of rice stalks and sugarcane leaves, then used a nylon tarpaulin to partition the room in two. The right compartment served as his bedroom. In it was a single bed, covered year-round by a mosquito-net. At the far end, he had set a trunk the size of a suitcase and a cupboard. Both were the meticulous handiwork of his elder brother's son. Hidden behind the cupboard and the trunk was the "kitchen." The left compartment had a table with four square-shaped chairs and four cups next to a kettle filled with old boiled water. The water pipe rested its head on a corrugated iron case that was as long as a prayer box. That was where he received guests, where he "welcomed the people." He told his family and others that the set-up was suitable for his line of work, since the things with which he was involved had to be kept in strict confidence. But the real reason he lived as he did was to avoid burdening those close to him.

After six months as the district head of the People's Inspection Committee, Sai was reassigned to be Ha Vi's Chairman of Agriculture. This assignment allowed him time to make frequent visits to

Hanoi to see his children. Whenever he went, Sai brought his children half of his salary as he'd been ordered to do by the court, as well as newly harvested rice or beans, peanuts, cakes, candies, clothes, socks and shoes. If he was too busy, he would have these things sent.

In less than three years, Ha Vi had been completely transformed, as if it had been lifted from some other region and transplanted. From the air, the village would have looked like a slightly slanted capital T. The bar at the top was the dike that had been built up over the years. It was as big as a main dike and lined with clumps of green bamboo trees. Beyond the bamboos were columns of banana plants, thousands of them, whose stalks were bent by the weight of the fruit. Beyond the bananas were peanuts. The whole expanse of the alluvial land was an immense sea of dark green peanut leaves; its length was so great that to see it all one had to go up in a helicopter. Right at the edge of the water, where the silt kept accumulating every year, were beds of sweet potatoes. Except for the three months of the rainy season, those potato patches remained green year round. Down the center line of the capital T was a roadway connecting the tributary dike to the main dike. It was about four kilometers long. It was big enough for two transport trucks to pass each other. If one stood on the tributary dike and looked toward the main dike, one saw an elevated field to the left. The elevated field was planted mostly with a single type of soybean introduced by agronomist Phan Tan and his colleagues. As Sai's acquaintances, they had agreed to help out with the initial planting. The had advised Sai to plant a soybean which had been given the scientific designation "DC 5." DC 5 produced an explosion of seeds and barely any leaves. A mere two crops of DC 5 yielded hundreds of tons of soybeans. On the right side of the roadway were depots, fish ponds, pig and cow farms and twenty-three brick kilns. On the right side of the road, there were ten teams of people who specialized in making tofu.

The land around the dike allowed for a complete cycle of production: soybean was made into tofu, pigs consumed residual soya and sweet potato leaves. Cows ate the peanut leaves and sweet potato stems. Cow dung was used to enrich the fish pond, and the other animal manure was used to fertilize the soil. Those factories, construction sites and offices that bought tofu, peanuts, beef and fish provided Ha Vi with coal, lime, cement, iron and other necessities. Ha Vi residents could now afford three meals a day, and their meals included rice, fish, tofu and meat. The commune had electricity, plus a radio station, a cultural center, a daycare center and a two-story schoolhouse.

When Huong returned each year for her annual visit with her mother, she would stop to see Sai. Though Sai had been elected a member of the district's Standing Committee, he still lived in a two-room dwelling at the entrance to Ha Vi village. But Huong didn't visit him there, for Sai always took her over to Tinh's house to have tea, or met her at the village's administrative offices. As she passed through an improved Ha Vi, she was frequently astonished by the startling new landscape. Though not able to scan the faces of everyone in the village or listen to all of their excited whispers, she knew who was behind the transformation. That knowledge gave her a sense of inward joy mixed with a feeling of heart-rending anguish. She could not believe that Sai would live like that, as if he had wanted to make himself suffer.

Seeing the metamorphosis of Ha Vi, Huong, as well as Tinh, Uncle Ha, Brother Hieu and other close friends, were greatly relieved, for they had been initially concerned that Sai's decision to take up a post in the village had been the desperate act of an unbalanced man.

This day, Sai was giving a report to an observation delegation and to the press. Tien and Huong sat in the back of the audience and chatted. Tien said, "You see that he looks much healthier and younger than just a few years ago. Success certainly makes a big difference."

"The main factor is that he has your support and the support of others," Huong said.

"Before he came back, I never had any objections if anyone in this village wanted to change the way they did things to make themselves wealthy. The main factor is that he knows the soil here inside out, and the character of the people. With that knowledge, and his single-minded focus, how could he fail?"

Huong smiled. "There are things on which one focuses single-mindedly that fail."

Tien laughed, shaking his head in protest. "Though I do not understand him as well as you do, I know that he single-mindedly thought things through and tried to compensate for what he did not have in order to be in step with a wife who was different from him in all respects. I am in total agreement with what he said to the press this morning.

"I hope that the other regions do not draw any lesson from us," Tien continued, quoting Sai. "The methods of operation that I have reported and the propaganda articles in which you at times exaggerate should be treated as suggestive starting points for people everywhere to think about in regards to their own soil, resources, capital, educational levels, and the innermost feelings and aspirations of their countrymen in order to come up with a successful productive approach. You don't want to make a great deal of noise about success in one place, immediately forcing everyone to copy the model exactly, then destroying that to copy another model. You order it to be done, and those who don't, you call troublemakers; order it to be destroyed, and those who refuse, you call reactionaries. Hence from birth to death, the village is never without 'enemies'; and while people starve, the village always 'exceeds,' 'far outstrips,' the yields of the year before. I am frightened by the thought that from now on every village will plant peanuts and soybeans, even on the low-lying fields fit only for the second crop. When it fails, we will be cursed as a pack of liars."

Listening to him, Huong felt proud. She turned to Tien and said, "I think that Sai is fortunate to have you, for he could not have succeeded without your help."

"On the contrary, Sai helped me see things. If he hadn't returned, I might have exhorted the whole district to follow the model of your commune from inside the dike: every village would then have had to plant two rice crops and one crop of potatoes."

"But as a high official, you always see things more clearly."

Tien said mischievously, "The killing thing is that the high officials never want to admit defeat to their underlings. So, there were times when half of the villagers were hungry, and the district still insisted it had met its production goals. When hard-pressed, the district had to go to the province to request mutual aid rice. They blamed the local officials for failing to gauge the true condition in the villages."

After this "unorthodox" conversation with Tien, Huong realized that she couldn't just leave when the press and other officials departed in their cars. Before Sai went to see the officials off, he said to Huong, "Will you wait for me at my house for a little while? My niece is there and will wait with you."

So Huong entered Sai's room for the first time. It was a terrible, bare-looking place. Could Sai really want to live like this? She set to tidying up the place. Tinh's daughter told her the "history" of the dwelling as she folded clothes and swept the floor. Eventually, the girl had to leave, and there was still no sign of Sai. Just as Huong was becoming impatient and the sky was getting dark making it difficult for her to consider returning home alone, Sai appeared.

Sensing her anxiety, he complained, "Why are you so agitated?"

"I'm scared. Would you walk with me part of the way?"

Sai didn't say a word. She knew that he was hurt by her behavior. But what else could she do! The love of a middle-aged man was not going to make her passionate now, and she no longer had the strength to act rashly. There was no light, and the two were in the same room, but Huong stood apart from Sai, just in case a passerby happened to look into the building.

Night had come, and the air seemed to tingle. Huong stepped out into the middle of the yard. She stayed there, waiting for Sai to finish his water pipe, lock the door and walk her home. Then they started on their way. The more relieved Huong felt, the more silent Sai became.

≋ Having walked quite a distance, they had not spoken a word. "Are you mad at me?" Huong finally asked.

"No."

"Then why don't you laugh out loud?"

"You want me to become a clown?" Huong didn't respond, and Sai felt badly for his words, for it was true she had never played with the love between them. "I'm sorry," Sai said.

As they walked on, far from the village, Huong stayed silent. Sai drew closer to her, "Many times I feel so sad, I miss you so terribly, and yet every time we meet, you reward me with a few words, before you run away as if in panic. For me . . . these days . . . "

The two almost stopped; Huong remained silent.

"Are you still mad at me?" Sai asked.

Huong's head turned slightly, and she touched his arm. She shook her head gently. “Look at me for a moment,” she said. When he looked at her, her bright eyes seemed filled with a wonderful light. He wished to make that light part of the beating in his chest.

“Maybe we can come back to each other, my love.”

“It’s not possible.”

Had she not been so gentle, so tender, had she not so softly stroked his hair and buttoned his army shirt, had she angrily said “No” or made a gesture to put an immediate end to his hope, it would have been much more bearable than her ill-defined caress.

“Try to endure,” she said. “At our age, we can no longer afford this sort of danger. It’s getting late, let’s say good-bye. Listen to me, my love. You are already pained by our separation. But should I now tear apart the little stability I have, even though it’s a stability made out of patchwork, should I offer you the patchwork of my life to make up for your loss? To wipe out one mismatch to form another mismatch is to deceive each other, and nothing will come of it. No, I know, my love. It would have been possible in the early days. We must cherish it forever. Now there is no time left for us. Don’t be sad.”

With these words eminently reasonable and deeply felt, Huong made him accept their situation. But when he walked back in the cold, moonlit night, he felt as if gust after gust of wind was blasting through his body. He walked as if in a daze amid the immense space and desolation of everything that surrounded him. Close to the village, he was startled by the sound of earth being scooped into barrels and of wood being hammered. All twenty-three kilns were glowing – red-hot from top to bottom – and at the edge of the village the lights of the tofu-making teams were still on. These were the third shifts that Sai himself had organized. They helped him during sleepless nights. He would get up, go by the furnace, the brick-making area and the tofu-wrapping plant to look around and exchange pleasantries. When the morning light came, he would have a bowl of bean-curd soup, a whiff of liquor, a few peanuts, and feel more energetic. Everyone said he looked much healthier. His health probably returned the day he came back to the land of his youth. For the land might be full of unfinished business, it might be disorderly and disorganized, but it was the land where he belonged, the land of Ha Vi village.

DO SON, 19 September 1984